TO

R.J. MITCHELL

Son 4

Don!

Robert

THE
HAMMER
A DS THOROUGHGOOD THRILLER

Matthew James Publishing Ltd
Unit 46 Goyt Mill
Upper Hibbert Lane
Marple
SK6 7HX

www.matthewjamespublishing.com

ISBN: 978-1-913230-22-7

Typeset in the UK

1

FOR A MOMENT Thoroughgood shut his eyes, and the only sounds that he could hear were the gurgling of the burn and the foliage rustling in a growing breeze.

His back against the cold stone of the dyke, he was soon brought back to their grim reality by Emma tugging on his arm. He opened his eyes to find hers gazing back, brimming with tears.

'The sniper is… McGrain?' she asked, trying to impose some self-control on her quivering voice.

Thoroughgood nodded. 'McGrain or his number two, Spider; it matters not, they're both former French Foreign Legionnaires. I'm sorry, Em, I should never have brought you here, never have got you involved in this… this bloody mess,' he said, shaking his head bitterly.

She smiled half-heartedly. 'Well, what are you going to do to get us out of it?'

Thoroughgood's right hand reached out and stroked the side of her face, wiping away the moisture trails. 'There is no way out of this for me, Em, but there is for you. As you know, I left messages for the Unit and I can only hope they have picked them up and are on the way but… it isn't looking good. I want you to make your way back to the car, and I will go and meet McGrain. He is tooled up with a sniper rifle and obviously a crack shot, so this is it for me… but it may be I will be enough for him.' And with that he eased the keys to his MG into her reluctant fingers.

Then, as Emma's lips began to move, he stilled them with a finger. 'It's the only way, Em. I need you to try and get hold of Detective Constable Dennis Numan and Sergeant Malcolm at the Unit in Pitt Street and whatever reinforcements you can muster, and I need it pronto. Whatever happens, remember that I love you; now please go.'

Not giving Emma time to reply, Thoroughgood got to his feet and vaulted the dyke. He clamped his hands on his head in an act of total compliance, without knowing why he did it: for the hopelessness of his position meant it was an act of utter futility and one that made it hard for him to stifle a laugh of self-derision.

Twenty feet away and closing, McGrain was coming on with the weapon he had wielded with such deadly expertise hoisted over his right shoulder. Next to him, Spider's teeth shone in a grin... bristling with homicidal intent.

'Shit... what's the choice? Head blown off my shoulders or gutted and stuck like a pig,' muttered Thoroughgood to himself.

Yet the young cop held his ground and defiantly met the malicious gaze of the two men who were, one way or another, certain to bring his life to an end.

McGrain's hawk-like features surveyed his prey, and for a moment he let the silence boom out around them.

Then he spoke: 'Well, mon ami, I would hazard a guess that what we have here is Constable Thoroughgood, the annoying itch that has been begging to be scratched... for good. But our young friend appears to be minus what he came for.' McGrain rummaged inside his reefer overcoat and with a flourish produced the blue Sony tape recorder that had been the whole reason behind Thoroughgood's journey to St Serf's.

The young cop made no effort to hide the magnitude of the blow he had just been dealt, but before he could say anything, McGrain continued to taunt him: 'Yes, indeed your journey has been wasted… in this respect, at least. But I thank you from the heart of my bottom for reuniting me with Gregsy and O'Toole!' he laughed, as he slowly began to open the casing and unwound the tape from the micro-cassette.

Then he tossed it to the waiting Spider, who accommodatingly produced his lighter and applied flame.

'How did you know?' asked Thoroughgood, his words barely audible.

McGrain enfiladed him with his brooding gaze. 'Luck!' he spat.

For once it was Spider who was in a more expansive mood. 'As you now know, we like to bury a wee memento or two in our patch of holy ground; it's a nasty old habit that dates back from our time in the Legion when we would commemorate fallen comrades by retaining their keepsakes at their graveside. This place has proven…' – Spider swept his arm in a circling motion – 'mighty useful in burying bodies, evidence, aye, and the odd… token. And when we were committing the innards of… Whit would you call that piece o' shit, Tony?' asked the man-mountain enforcer.

McGrain smiled benignly. '"Colleague" is the term of endearment you are looking for, mon ami! To cut to the chase, when we committed the remnants of that odious bastard Parlane to the ground, I, or rather, mon frère here, noticed that the positioning of one of the dearly beloved interred in our holy ground had been somewhat readjusted and inside his body bag we had a corpse that seemed to have flipped. That, in turn, caused us to examine the turf that covered those no longer with us. So, perhaps we got lucky or perhaps we made our own luck – who knows? – but the revelations on the tape were most… illuminating… and certainly it wouldn't have been useful for someone like you to hear them, never mind produce them in a court of law!'

Thoroughgood's jaw set: words were pointless.

It was not a sentiment McGrain shared and once again his gravelly Glaswegian delivery broke the silence: 'But then, you never had the horror of searching for your key piece of evidence just to find it had been removed; I will retain the memory of the disappointment on the late Gregsy's ruddy chops when he found the cupboard was bare until my dying day! So, what do we have here? Correct me if I'm wrong, but I think that what we are witnessing is an act of extreme self-sacrifice? How very noble. What say you, Spider?'

His confrère barked a laugh and then stretched out a giant paw and pointed beyond the dyke to the screening curtain of trees. 'I'd say that our young copper's friend does'nae realise that an F2 has a range of 800 metres, a muzzle velocity of 820 metres a second, and, finally, Tony, son, I'd ask the daft wee bastard why we would be likely to let his bitch run free and make dae with a single serving of pig?'

The percussion of his heart was beating a tattoo through Thoroughgood's inner being, but he knew that his only chance lay in the words he spoke. Taking a deep breath, he went for it: 'Look, I get my position is hopeless. But I would also make you aware that en route I alerted both an armed response vehicle and our specialist undercover unit, one of which is an old friend of yours, Mr McGrain. Dennis Numan is looking forward to catching up with you real soon…'

A vicious smile fleetingly lit up McGrain's foreboding features and as it did, he levelled the F2 at Thoroughgood. 'If you're attempting to plea bargain, Constable Thoroughgood, then you need to have something to play with.'

He eased the F2 onto his shoulder, expertly sighting up his quandary, training the gun on Emma's distant form.

In an instant, Thoroughgood stepped directly in front of the muzzle. From behind the weapon, a sneer of cruel delight creased McGrain's stony features. 'How very touching. A knight in shining armour prepared to make the ultimate sacrifice to save his damsel in distress.'

Then, McGrain's lips ceased moving and, from along the barrel of the F2, Thoroughgood saw his trigger finger twitch.

The Widowmaker looked up and his stare seared Thoroughgood. 'The girl is of no interest to us: matters have moved on too far for her escape to be of any importance,' he spat, and with that started to lower his weapon, once again cradling the butt in the palm of his hand, while the barrel rested over his shoulder. 'But you, Thoroughgood, well, right now I'd say all you've got is the dead man's hand and that's a case of read 'em and weep. Now keep walking this way and we can arrange for you to be reunited with your friends for all eternity.'

He was right and Thoroughgood knew it. Just what did he have to bargain with?

In silence he trudged forward, hands still on his head. When Thoroughgood drew level with the brute presence of Spider, McGrain's enforcer uncorked a right hook into his midriff that dropped the young cop to his knees, leaving him gasping for breath.

His hands now holding his gut, Thoroughgood looked up to see Spider's malign, almost feral features looming above him. McGrain's lieutenant took a firm grip of Thoroughgood's black mane, then out of the watery sun came a glinting menace as the enforcer swung his janbiya dagger out and levelled it against his prey's neck.

'How does it feel to have six inches of Damascus steel against your throat, copper?' hissed Spider.

Thoroughgood's desperate gaze reached McGrain's hooded stare. So, this was it. McGrain had merely toyed with him to put off the moment and manner of his demise, and now he'd be left with his throat cut, bleeding out on this miserable piece of ground where so many before him had met a similarly grizzly fate.

'We are only here to take care of the loose ends that could damage our pursuit of an end goal of far more importance. Admittedly through no fault of your own, you have come blundering into my business and become a real pain in the arse, but the only way you could have done that was through information. Because someone led you to Gregsy, allowing our blundering peterman to do the rest of the damage. Which means someone from my side of the fence is feeding you, Thoroughgood. Do I need to waste my breath on the next question?'

Oxygen slowly returning to his lungs, despite the curved blade cradling his jugular, Thoroughgood managed a reply: 'Providing the identity of that informant will kill me, McGrain. So, maybe my hand isn't the dead man's… just yet.'

The words had no sooner left his mouth than Spider's grip of his hair tightened viciously and the janbiya's cold steel started to burn into his skin with a dangerous increase in pressure.

'What do you mean, boy?' snapped McGrain, who nonetheless nodded to Spider to loosen the janbiya's lethal press.

'I mean that Detective Inspector O'Toole served you bloody well as your man on the inside of Strathclyde Police until he got careless. I mean that his position is now vacant, and I mean that I can be your joker.'

'This is all bullshit, Tony. I say we ice him and be done with it. What fuckin' use is a straight-out-the-wrapper rookie to us? Lemme put him in the ground and then let's get the hell out of here before the cops finally decide to get their arses in gear,' rapped Spider.

McGrain, for a moment, appeared lost in thought. The near-silence became deafening, punctuated only by the sound of the burn rushing by.

Then, without warning, he took a step forward, reversing the F2 in his grip as he did so, and smashed it off Thoroughgood's head.

As the cop crashed to the turf, McGrain smiled at Spider. 'I think Constable Thoroughgood has just talked himself into playing a key part in administering The Blood Acre's last rites,' he said.

2

CONSCIOUSNESS RETURNED to Thoroughgood in the form of a pounding cranium and the nickel-iron taste of the blood that had seeped from his head wound down the side of his face and into his mouth.

But that was not all that was in his mouth, for Thoroughgood had been bound and gagged while he'd been unconscious.

As his eyes sought to readjust themselves to the fading February daylight filtering through the rotten, cobweb-wreathed windows of what looked like a kitchen, Thoroughgood tried to take in his surroundings and carry out some sort of appraisal.

Where was he?

He thought back to his arrival at St Serf's: the logical answer had to be the old cottage at the north end of the church grounds. The same cottage from which McGrain had demonstrated such lethal accuracy with the F2.

"So where are McGrain and Spider?" asked the voice in his head.

Quite clearly they knew that help in some form would arrive either via Emma's efforts or the messages he had left, but why leave him here and still alive when McGrain had already worked out he had access to an informant whose intel had led him to The Blood Acre?

"It's a trap and I'm live bait," chimed the voice in his head.

So, either the building or he himself must be rigged with some kind of booby trap.

The realisation set his mind clicking through its mental gears. As former members of the Foreign Legion, it was obvious that

McGrain and Spider would have expertise in this field, and their involvement with the Provisional IRA meant that they would almost certainly have access to all manner of explosive devices.

Thoroughgood found himself replaying some of the conversations he had eavesdropped on when he had been back on shift with Davidson and Rentoul. Their recounts from tours of duty on the Emerald Isle had left him amazed at the ingenuity of the Provisionals, and he had learnt to take more than a passing interest in the latest developments in the PIRA's deadly alchemy.

"Christ, take your pick, Gus… it's either you or the building, then," said the voice in his head, and he found himself nervously scanning his body as best he could from the cords that bound him.

But as far as Thoroughgood could see he was clean, and the recognition led to a fleeting moment of relief.

So, it had to be the building; and by using him as the bait the arrival of help would set off an explosion that would blow both him and the contents of The Blood Acre to kingdom come.

It was a conclusion that would take care of all the loose ends that McGrain had spoken of while relieving The Widowmaker of any need to waste time on him.

All of which left Thoroughgood wondering if McGrain had been informed of his arrival by the late O'Toole before he in turn decided to use the opportunity to terminate their relationship with lethal force.

All the pieces had fallen into place perfectly for McGrain and now he and Spider had slipped away.

The realisation caused sweat to stream from Thoroughgood's throbbing brow, for even if he could break free from the bonds that held him, he had no idea what he was looking for or how he could avoid setting it off.

And if he could work out what form the trap would take, it was almost certain to prove futile if he could not communicate the hidden threat to his would-be saviours.

Thoroughgood shut his eyes and desperately wracked his brains for a way out, but before long he'd slipped back into unconsciousness.

Alex Sturgeon was delighted to point her 'wagon' in the direction of Glasgow, even though the B7067, with its nasty bends, tight lanes and poor visibility, was making the return journey to Scottish Ambulance Service Glasgow HQ take longer than it should have done. She shifted her sizeable bulk, trying to find a comfortable position after so long on the road.

With the dying of the light, the concentration required on this torturous twisting road, which was like something Richard Hannay would have been traipsing in the John Buchan classic The 39 Steps, was increasingly draining at the end of a 12-hour shift.

'Aye, it would'nae surprise me to see the bloody hound of the Baskervilles come chargin' round one of these buggering bends,' she muttered.

Across the cabin, the snoring that had been serenading her came to an end with a choking sound as her partner Ruaridh Davidson regained consciousness, with the help of a nasty jolt administered by Alex's wicked jerk of the wagon steering wheel.

'For fuck's sake, Alex, whit did you go and do that for? I was just restin' my eyes for a wee minute,' snapped her number two.

Alex barked a harsh laugh. 'Ya wee scrote, restin' yer eyes was it? You've been shaking the cabin with yer snoring like some demented bear on heat for the last 15 minutes,' she snapped.

One hundred yards away at the side of the road, sat in the now broken-down MG, Emma McCabe's prayers for help appeared answered when she saw the approaching ambulance. She quickly opened the driver-side door and jumped out.

It was time to gamble.

The ambulance's emergency lights were blacked out and the vehicle sirens stilled; added to the fact that she was a lone female out on a country road signalling for help, surely it all meant she had a very good chance of flagging the vehicle down.

What was against her was her dark anorak and the poor visibility of a twisting B road lined by trees. She would come into view with only a few yards to spare after a vicious bend bathed in the shadow caused by the waning of the day's light.

Taking a deep breath, Emma started to wave her arms and shout at the top of her voice: 'Stop!'

Back in the emergency vehicle, an indignant Davidson roused himself from his slumbers and began to rub his eyes furiously; but as sight returned to his bleary orbs, they suddenly saucered wide open. 'Pedestrian at 12 o'clock, Alex. Ram the anchors on, for Chrissakes, doll!' screeched the pint-sized paramedic to his obese gaffer.

But Sturgeon had already spotted the lone female standing outside the stationary white motor, waving her arms like a human windmill. 'Nae bother, wee man,' she replied disdainfully as she clicked down through the gears and brought the Iveco 4x4 to a halt with an assurance that was borne of 15 years at the wheel of an assortment of her beloved wagons.

'Now what the feck have we got here?' snapped Davidson.

Outside, the frantic female brought her arms to her side and wasted no time in running round to the driver's side of the ambulance. She stepped up to Sturgeon's window and produced a Strathclyde Police warrant card as she signalled to the burly paramedic to roll her window down.

'Police Constable McCabe. There has been an incident at St Serf's church, and we have one officer down and another in danger with other loss of life. I need you to get on your radio set and get your control to relay this to Strathclyde Police Force HQ ASAP!'

On the other side of the ambulance door, Emma's plea was met with customary cynicism. 'All right, sister, just slow it down a minute, what kind of incident are we talking about?' asked Sturgeon, eyeing Emma's warrant card with scarcely disguised suspicion.

'I am talking one officer shot dead, one member of the public shot dead, another officer in mortal danger and two armed gunmen in possession of high-velocity, military-grade weapons. Is that good enough for you?' raged Emma, the adrenaline from her escape from The Blood Acre and the charnel-house scenes of O'Toole's and Gregsy's executions still coursing through her veins.

Her frustration mounting as Sturgeon, apparently disinterested, passed her warrant card to Davidson, Emma yanked the Iveco's door open. 'I have provided lawful identity that I am a current serving police officer, now if you don't get me Ambulance HQ on your set right now I will make sure you are facing a charge of obstructing an officer in the execution of her duty – I promise you, sister!' she snapped, her eyes blazing and her words spiralling from forceful demand to undisguised, screaming threat.

Across the cabin, Davidson got the message. He leant back over Sturgeon's bulk and quickly handed Emma her warrant card, while he ripped the radio hand transmitter from its holder and barked a message: 'Charlie Alpha 9 to Ambulance Control. Come in, over.'

After a moment, the clipped tones of a female controller replied: 'Ambulance Control receiving, go ahead Charlie Alpha 9.'

'I'm afraid we have stumbled across a major incident out in Lanarkshire at St Serf's church and we have been flagged down by a police officer requesting urgent help. I am now going to put you on to Police Constable McCabe, who is an eyewitness to these events and who will explain everything. Constable McCabe, will you please update Ambulance Control?' and with that Davidson handed Emma the transmitter.

She described in graphic detail the events of earlier that day and then relayed her needs in terms of police armed response and The Proactive Unit, then handed Davidson back the transmitter.

It was then that the shock set in.

A massive tremor shook her body to the core and Emma suddenly felt like her legs were about to give way; but before they could, she retched violently at the side of the ambulance.

Almost immediately the vehicle door shot open and Sturgeon jumped out, her previously harsh countenance replaced with a look of concern. 'Come on, darlin', I think it's time we got you in the back for a wee check-up. You're displaying classic signs of shock and after what you've been through there's no wonder.'

From her right-hand side a reassuring hand patted Emma on the shoulder. 'Alex is right, come on, sweetheart, we'll get you wrapped in a blanket and I'll pour you a cup of my magic tea and things will soon be a whole lot better. You've done all you can, Emma,' said Rhu Davidson, smiling reassuringly.

By now, Emma was finding it impossible to stop the tears

from rolling down her cheeks, and through her sobs she said: 'God knows I don't think it will be enough.'

Numan and Malcolm had been conducting a surveillance op on a Paisley criminal when they received the call via Force HQ Radio that their assistance was needed at St Serf's.

'Are you thinking what I'm thinking?' asked Detective Sergeant Malcolm as they swung the unmarked Astra van through the streets of Paisley's toughest housing estate.

'What? That St Serf's is The Blood Acre?'

Malcolm nodded his head before adding: 'Exactly, and God knows what we'll find there; but who cares just as long as the boy is still alive.'

'Amen to that, brother,' replied Numan as he continued to gun the Astra.

Malcolm reached up to turn on the passenger-side light, and Numan saw out of the corner of his eye that the DS had unfolded a map and was busy scouring a part that clearly related to St Serf's.

Then he let a long slow whistle escape from between his teeth. 'Interesting. There would appear to be only two ways out of St Serf's on a single B road and only one of those will take you back onto the M8. I don't know about you, Dennis, but my money would be on McGrain and chum looking to get on the motorway real soon.'

Numan groaned. 'Aye, and of course we have Thoroughgood's MG Metro parked at the side of the road while Emma is comforted by the ambulance crew… ah shit, they'll stand out like a sore thumb!' said Numan and reapplied considerable downward pressure to the accelerator.

Malcolm's left hand drummed nervously on the dashboard. 'There's no doubt about it, the potential for disaster is awesome.

Let's hope the armed response vehicle gets on the scene before these dirty mongrels have slipped their leash.'

The duty armed response vehicle surged down the outside lane of the M8, leaving Glasgow behind in the blazing illumination of its flashing lights and screaming sirens.

Sergeant Bobby Marshall held the steering wheel of the SRi 2-litre injection version of the Cavalier Mk2 in a giant hand, while a Benson & Hedges dangled from the side of his mouth.

His number two, John Bowden, sat in the passenger seat, his moustache twitching as he perused the Ordnance Survey map. 'We'll be taking the next junction aff, gaffer, and then we're onto the B7067 and no more than five minutes from Saint Serf's.'

Marshall replied through a breath of smoke that wreathed his side of the vehicle: 'And somewhere between the slip road and the turn-off for St Serf's we have an ambulance vehicle with a young female cop to pick up. This is all looking a bit messy, especially since we don't have any handle on what's playing out on the ground at the locus. Any update on where the fuck the bird in the sky is, Johnny boy?'

'Hotel Mike 40 is refuelling gaffer, so we ain't gonnae be getting any help from above. Pardon the pun, but we're flying into this one in the dark. That said, from the intel taken from the female cop, we have at least one shooter armed with some pretty serious fire-power judging by the mess he's made of the two vics. So, it could be invaluable to catch her on the way by – also, an eyewitness perspective of the layout of the old church grounds would be a real plus.'

Marshall patted his sidearm with a loving hand and winked in the direction of Bowden's Heckler & Koch MP5A2-A. 'You keep your cannon primed, Johnny, son, and your eyes peeled just in case we find ourselves eyeballing the shooter and his wingman through the headlights, and we'll be just fine!'

'I'm sure we will, gaffer. I just hope this one gets put to bed nice and early: I've got hospitality with my mates at Ibrox the morrow and I'm looking for the Gers to take a few off these sheep shaggin' Aberdeen bastards!'

Marshall shook his nut in a fashion that suggested he'd heard it all before. 'I don't give a fuck what happens at the piggery in 24 hours. All that matters is that we shine tonight whatever shit-storm comes our way. 'Cause I want my fuckin' pips before my 30 is in, and no orange bastard is gonnae be screwing that up for me, Johnny bhoy!' laughed Marshall, sarcastically pronouncing the silent 'h' that denoted the nickname for Rangers' arch-rivals Celtic.

With that, the Cavalier crackled with an almost choreographed laughter as the tribalism of Glasgow's football loyalties once more helped reduce the tension simmering just below the surface of the armed response vehicle crew's taut features.

3

SPIDER HAD TAKEN the left turn out of St Serf's and was setting the black Mercedes-Benz 560 SE on course for the M8, his Glock 17 tucked under his right thigh in a move that harked back to his military training.

'Where's the airfield, Tony?' he asked.

McGrain cleared his throat before replying, which was a clear sign the news wasn't good. 'I'm afraid we've gotta bit of work to do to get there, Spider. It's called Forrest Hill and it's on the way to St Andrews, but the main thing is that when we get there, we will have a Cessna waiting for us, fuelled and ready to go, no questions asked.'

'Christ, Tony, we're going cross-country to get there? Nah, I dinnae like it. Surely we could have got something closer?'

'The answer to that is yes, but not one owned by a sympathiser to the cause, mon ami. Now let's just concentrate on getting back on the motorway, because once we are, it's home-run time!' McGrain flashed his number two a reassuring smile.

In the driver's seat, Spider grunted but kept his eyes trained on the road ahead.

'Okay, I know it isn't perfect, but we are out of here, and one way or another everything that lies beneath The Blood Acre will be blown to smithereens and we can get on with what really matters, mon vieil ami!'

Spider turned his head slightly towards his boss. 'Maybes aye, maybes naw, Tony, but I'd be a damn sight happier if you'd put a 7.52 milly in the bitch's heid.'

'Now that's no way to speak about PC Plod's beloved… what was it he called her? Ah, yes, I think the term of endearment was "Em",' smiled McGrain, amused and pleased in equal measure with his power of recall.

'I don't give a flying fuck what the wee bitch was called, I just wished you had pulled the trigger on her: but then, Tony, as we both know, you've always had a soft spot for the ladies. Just remember that poor teller bitch back in Heysham,' sighed Spider, not interested in keeping the note of disapproval from his voice.

'You mean the lovely Miss Partridge! Aye, that one hurt, big man. I think I had started to rekindle something long dead in sweet Cynthia and we could have had some fun, but it was maybe a case of the right woman in the wrong place and most definitely at the wrong time.' McGrain's reverie came to an abrupt halt as he spotted something on the road ahead. 'Get yer eyes back on the road, Spider, 'cause I think we might have the chance to correct that particular mistake tout de suite.'

As he peered back through his window, Spider saw the white shape of an MG Metro parked half up on a verge, while just yards away an ambulance sat with its hazards flashing.

'Nice. It's the same motor that we saw Thoroughgood and his bitch arrive in at St Serf's,' said the enforcer with manic glee.

'It is indeed, which I imagine means that Strathclyde Polis's answer to Cagney or, for that matter, Lacey is probably sat in the back wrapped in a blanket and waiting for the cavalry to arrive. Whatta pity we got here first!' said McGrain and signalled to his wingman to pull the Merc in to the side of the road.

In the back of the ambulance, Emma did indeed sit enveloped in a blanket cradling a mug of Rhu Davidson's 'magic tea'. She turned to the paramedic. 'Do you think you could check with Ambulance HQ if they have an ETA update for the armed response vehicle, please?' she smiled.

Davidson flicked his gaze towards his gaffer and Alex Sturgeon shrugged. 'It's naw a bad shout, Rhu, it's been ten minutes and they shouldn't be too far away now, plus with it almost pitch-black the last thing we want is them landing on top of us.'

Davidson nodded, climbed through to the front of the cabin and whipped the mouthpiece from its holder; but just as he was about to transmit, a rap on the ambulance window gave him the fright of his life.

When he turned to peer out of the window, he found himself looking down the barrel of a gun, and his eyes filled with terror as the door handle engaged and the driver's side portal opened.

Standing just a yard away, training his Glock 17 directly at Davidson's forehead, was a man-mountain, eyes filled with death. 'Sorry, pal, it's nothing personal, like,' said Spider, and pumped two 9x19mm projectiles into the paramedic's head.

In the back of the wagon, Emma and Sturgeon heard the double tap of the killing but before they had time to react, the vehicle's rear doors were ripped open and there, his hawk-like features oozing menace, stood McGrain.

'Well, well, so we meet again… Em!' he said with relish, just as Davidson's body sprawled across the hatch, causing Sturgeon to yelp out in terror.

'Who the fuck are you?' gasped Sturgeon, clearly in shock.

McGrain smiled benignly. 'Well, as far as you're concerned, I'm a messenger,' he said.

For a moment, a look of complete mystification spread across Sturgeon's rosy cheeks. 'Wh-what are you talking about, man?'

The words were barely out her mouth before McGrain put one foot up on the wagon step, trained his Glock towards the paramedic and pumped two 9x19mm Parabellums her way. 'And now you've just got the message, darlin'!' he spat.

As Spider loomed in the cabin hatch, Emma drew into her blanket, almost curling into a ball. At her feet, Sturgeon lay sprawled out and the floor of the ambulance started to run crimson.

'Time to put her out of her misery, Tony, and I'd like the pleasure,' said the enforcer.

But McGrain had jumped into the rear of the vehicle and, taking great care to avoid bloodying his Barker brogues, he stepped over Sturgeon and sat down on the edge of the vehicle bed, just inches away from Emma.

Slowly, McGrain met Emma's trembling gaze and let an uncomfortable silence draw out, before he turned his eyes towards his number two and said: 'No, I think we will need to keep sweet Em around for a while yet, my old friend. You were right earlier, Spider, my mistaken Christian charity in sparing this dear young lady has made us vulnerable, but by the same token, our – what shall I call it? – re-acquaintance will provide me with the opportunity to address that and darling Em to prove her worth. Big man, I need you to strip the Merc of all our stuff, smash it into the dyke at the side of the road and torch it. I will of course make our young friend a little more comfortable in the back here and after a quick change, we will have the ambulance running and ready to go.'

'Are you mad, Tony?'

'Listen to me, son. Every cop car available is going to be heading to St Serf's and there are only two ways out and only one to the motorway. If we don't use our imagination, we will never make it that far, 'cause when the rozzers come chargin' down this

B road they are going to be playing out two scenarios in their minds. Une, they bang into us fleeing the old church, or deux, we are still on the ground at St Serf's. Either way, we are a lot more likely to make it out of the bottleneck in an ambulance clad in the green uniforms of paramedics than in the Merc. Tu comprends, mon ami?'

Spider shrugged in an admission that his gaffer had a fair point. McGrain turned towards Emma. 'What do you think, little Miss Piggy in the middle?' he sneered.

Her blanket wrapped tight around her, Emma couldn't help herself. 'I think you're a pair of fucking madmen,' she said.

Leaning towards her, until his face was only inches away, McGrain whispered: 'We have been called a whole lot worse, my darling Em, believe me!'

4

THE STRATHPOL AREA armed response vehicle had nego-
tiated the turn-off from the M8 to the B7067 and was now
making swift progress down the long and winding Lanarkshire
road. Inside, there was complete silence.

For as always when first on the scene, even the blackest of
cop humour couldn't take all the tension out of a potentially
life-threatening situation, especially when life had indeed already
been confirmed lost.

It was the more junior member of the crew who spoke first.
'Listen, gaffer, I think it's vital we get a quick word with Constable
McCabe on the way past but, well I don't know about you, I'd
worry about taking her with us to the locus…' said Constable
John Bowden.

'You mean from the point of view that she's probably trauma-
tised, from what we've heard, also emotionally attached to the
other young cop and of course would be an unarmed depend-
ant?' asked Sergeant Bobby Marshall, taking a final drag from
his B&H before he dexterously rolled down the window with
his right hand and flicked the butt out with the forefinger and
index finger of his left hand, all while still retaining control of
the Cavalier's steering wheel.

'You read my mind, gaffer,' admitted Bowden.

Marshall turned his weather-beaten features back towards his
junior ranking officer. 'The only problem I have with that is that
we do not have any kind of layout plan for St Serf's and young

Emma has it all up here,' said Marshall, pointing to his bonce. 'Look, Johnny, let's just take it as we find it. We will know soon enough just how shaken up she is and whether Woman Police Constable McCabe is going to be a liability or an asset at the locus. But we also have to watch how we approach all of this, given what we know about the events at The Blood Acre, as I believe they are calling it. Apparently, the name comes from the Good Book, Johnny, and correct me if I'm wrong, son, despite your support of Her Britannic Majesty's Gers, weren't you an altar bhoy in your youth?' quipped Marshall, humour once again proving an irresistible force in these tense moments.

'I was indeed, Bobby, but then I didn't have any choice in that matter and I certainly do when it comes to my football team! It's your call, gaffer…' said Bowden, but as he was just about to finish his sentence his words faded into stunned silence. 'Jesus H. Christ!' he finally exclaimed.

But Marshall had already read the runes and was slamming the anchors on. Smashed halfway into the dyke bordering the oncoming side of the B7067 was a vehicle, or what was left of it: for it had obviously crashed into the wall and was now a raging inferno.

Marshall's eyebrows creased. Behind the vehicle, in darkness, was an ambulance; but before he could articulate his confusion, Johnny Bowden beat him to the verbal punch.

'Wait a minute… oh shit… I think there are bodies in the vehicle, gaffer. Ain't that PC Thoroughgood's motor? It was described as a white MG Metro in the incident intel we received: aye, over there, the other side of the ambulance,' said Bowden, his features tense.

Marshall bolted into action and almost ripped the handle off opening the door, before sprinting over to the burning vehicle.

Drawing to within ten feet of the flame-wreathed motor, he was forced to shield his face against the extreme heat of the fire.

Despite that, Marshall managed to get enough detail from his quick peek into the mobile coffin. 'We are way too late, Johnny, you better get back to the Cavy, shout up the fire service; and we're gonna need Traffic to seal this road off plus major incident support. But I'm sorry to say we are too late to save these poor sods.'

Three yards behind him, Bowden had drawn to a halt on the broken tarmac of the road, and for a moment the young cop could not find words to articulate even a basic reply.

But Marshall had seen it all multiple times before. He turned to his young partner, placing a reassuring hand on his shoulder. 'Look, Johnny, it ain't pretty, and if there was anything I could do I would, but all we can do is secure the locus and make sure this doesn't turn into a full-on disaster, so for the moment, stick your blues and twos on, son,' said the sergeant, referring to the police lights and sirens.

'But what about Constable Thoroughgood at The Blood Acre... sorry, I mean St Serf's?' asked the increasingly ashen-faced Bowden.

'First things first, son. I'm gonna check all's well at the ambulance as that is exactly where we were told it would be and it seems strange there is no sign of the paramedics out here... unless they were too late to do anything about it and are radioing for help just like you are about to. Anyways, get the shout out and I'll go and check with the medics and see what WPC McCabe has to tell us. Once you're finished with Ambulance Service, get your arse over and join me,' concluded Marshall.

Bowden nodded his head in agreement. A moment later, a new noise filled the air as the extreme heat of the burning car started to produce a crackling sound.

Without turning his head, Marshall knew exactly what it was. The two vehicle occupants were now being roasted and body fat was starting to spark. He quickly gripped Bowden's shoulder. 'Look at me, John. Shit happens. We are cops and this goes with the territory. There is nothing we could have done, so what we've got to focus on is making sure that things don't spiral out of control any further and we don't end up with a pile-up with plenty more loss of life. Always remember preserving life is our core function and it's too late for them. Now, you have your orders, son. Lights on, make the call and then RV with me at the ambulance.'

Marshall's 26 years of police experience kicked in and he used a measured stride to take him to the ambulance, his Maglite torch illuminating his path.

He again tried to square why the paramedics were nowhere near the car crash. He shook his head; the only possible explanation he could come up with was the one he'd suggested to Bowden.

But something wasn't right and the still coming from the ambulance, combined with the vehicle being completely in darkness, began to fill him with a sense of foreboding that in turn made the hairs on the back of his neck stand up.

5

INSIDE THE AMBULANCE, McGrain sat in the driver's seat, a study in still life, as he watched the armed response vehicle's arrival at the scene of the crashed Merc in the vehicle's mirror.

He showed no emotion as he surveyed this potentially disastrous development with a keenness that resembled a bird of prey about to dine out.

He observed Marshall being forced back by the ferocious power of the heat that seared from the flame-engulfed motor; saw the way the younger cop halted in shock and horror as the two bodies of Sturgeon and Davidson flambéed with a snap, crackle and pop and then was sent back to the police vehicle by his senior man.

McGrain removed the safety from his Glock 17 and gently attached a silencer.

In the rear of the vehicle, Emma sat, mouth sealed with gaffer tape, hands tied off with cord and restrained to the vehicle wall slats. Spider hunkered down, motionless, just inside the rear doors, his janbiya casually nestled in his lap like a temporarily discarded newspaper.

As Emma stared at the enforcer, she saw that he was examining the green boiler suit he had stripped from the body of Sturgeon and was now wearing. Despite the ill-fit of the uniform, he was smiling disconcertingly, illustrating just how unhinged this man-monster was.

It was a sight that sent a shiver down Emma's spine and, as her shoulders shook like someone had just walked across her grave, the slight tremor of movement caught Spider's soulless orbs.

For a moment, captor and victim held each other's gaze, before the big man lifted the janbiya's Damascus steel to his lips and kissed it, then lowered the blade and pointed it menacingly Emma's way. 'Once this is over…' he growled and flicked her a wink that made it clear how his sentence should have been finished.

From the ambulance cabin, McGrain's grating voice snapped them both back to the here and now. 'Polis coming our way, Spider. I will deal with him but be prepared for the second cop back at the car running to his rescue.'

'Eh, bien, mon ami,' replied Spider with such casualness he could have been ordering a morning coffee.

Marshall was just yards away from the back of the wagon when McGrain started the Iveco's powerful diesel engine and flicked the lights on.

The effect temporarily disconcerted the approaching cop, who was startled by the sudden thrumming of the vehicle engine and the illumination from the pulsing of the ambulance's emergency lighting.

The sound of the driver's door being opened cracked the night and Marshall made his way down the vehicle's right flank, where he saw the back of a green boiler-suited figure begin to climb out of the cabin.

'Thank God for that, we were beginning to get a bit worried that something was up,' said Marshall as the paramedic turned his way and flashed a reassuring smile.

'There is no need to worry, Officer, everything is under control,' McGrain said and offered Marshall his right hand in greeting.

'Mmm, I don't know if I would quite agree with that. Anyway, it's Sergeant Bobby Marshall,' said the police sergeant and clasped

The Widowmaker's paw in greeting; just as McGrain's left hand whipped the Glock up and pumped two Parabellums into the side of the sergeant's cranium from point-blank range.

'Like I said, copper, everything is under control,' repeated McGrain, his face lit by a vicious grin.

His moment of malicious triumph was fleeting though, and he quickly dragged the slumped weight of Marshall's body to the stone dyke and hefted it over.

From the side of the ambulance, a voice called out in the night. 'Everything OK, Sarge? What are the paramedics saying?' asked PC Johnny Bowden.

Behind the young cop there was the sound of the rear ambulance doors springing open and a thud of boots on asphalt confirmed to McGrain that his vieil ami was on the ground.

Bowden did not even have time to turn around, as a muscle-knotted forearm encircled his neck and the glint of Damascus steel caught in the emergency vehicle's flashing lights, before it was expertly slid across his throat.

'What the fuck…' were the last words Johnny Bowden spoke in his unfulfilled life as his inert mass hit the road, a deadweight.

'Bonne nuit, Monsieur le Gendarme,' said Spider.

Looking down the side of the ambulance at his leader, he wiped the crimson from his janbiya on the left thigh of his newly acquired Scottish Ambulance Service boiler suit. 'Foreign Legion deux, polis zero!'

With that, the night air crackled with their laughter, until McGrain held up a finger. 'Okay, we need to split up: you take the ambulance and I will take the polis motor. If memory serves, there is a turn-off into Forestry Commission land just beyond the bend, and we can ditch it down there and be on our way.'

'Done,' replied Spider.

Inside the ambulance, Emma's ears had picked up the events that had just unfolded and left her utterly bereft of hope. As tears cascaded from her blue-green eyes, she knew that her own fate was likely to be similarly grizzly.

Then, two familiar dread faces appeared at the ambulance's opened rear doors and Spider said: 'Ne t'inquiète pas, ma jolie, on va prendre bien soin de toi!'

Seeing her incomprehension, McGrain helpfully provided a translation: 'Which means, darling Em, "Don't worry, my pretty girl, we will take good care of you!"'

But the malicious smiles on their faces suggested that would prove to be anything but the case.

6

'FOR FUCK'S SAKE, of all the bloody nights to shut down a lane on the Kingston Bridge,' cursed DC Dennis Numan, drumming his fingers on the Astra's steering wheel with increasing frustration.

The traffic was nose-to-tail and the night a sea of red. Nothing he could do in an unmarked vehicle was going to get them through this: the sheer volume was too much for a blue light on top of the motor to make a difference. The only option was to follow the crawling vehicular mass.

At his side, DS Malcolm slipped the vehicle radio transmitter back into its holder. 'Calm down, Dennis. As you heard, the armed response vehicle is now on the B7067 and just a matter of minutes from St Serf's; in fact they're probably there by now, and at least the traffic is moving.'

Numan's sideways glance was laced with bite and he barked a curt 'Aye!' But as the endless lines of traffic in front of him started to stretch he added a relieved 'At last!'

Within minutes the two lines of semi-static traffic had picked up speed and soon they were clear of Glasgow's outer bounds and making quick progress along the M8.

In the passenger seat, Malcolm was examining the Smith & Wesson service revolvers he had managed to get authorised for withdrawal from 'K', Kilo, HQ in Paisley city centre.

'Let's hope we don't have to use these,' he muttered.

'With respect, gaffer, if we do, then we're most probably fucked,' said Numan grimly, with a shake of his head.

The slip road to the B7067 seemed to take forever to come into sight and when it did, Numan almost took the turn-off on two wheels. He proceeded to crest every rise and make every bend like it was Silverstone.

DS Malcolm started to turn a shade of green but said nothing; across the van cabin, Numan shot him an enquiring glance, taking a mischievous delight in his gaffer's car sickness.

'Don't worry, gaffer, we'll soon be there,' he said, winking at Malcolm as the DS took a giant swallow and wound down the passenger window to let a rush of cold night air in.

A moment later, Numan started to slow his speed dramatically. 'Well, what have we here?' he asked.

Diagonally across the potholed excuse for a road that was the B7067, the smouldering remains of a vehicle were embedded in the dyke bordering the road.

Fifty yards behind it lay a white MG Metro, but there was no sign of the ambulance.

Both cops vaulted from their vehicle and approached the smoking wreck with caution; inside it, the chargrilled bodies of Davidson and Sturgeon were barely recognisable as human.

Malcolm was first to comment. 'Poor bastards,' he said.

Two feet away, Numan responded: 'Something's naw right, gaffer. This Merc has obviously had some kind of very recent accident with the dyke, so where is the ambulance? Also, we have had nothing from Ambulance Service confirming their vehicle has moved off. On top of that, Emma McCabe was supposed to be waiting for us to provide further intel on the locus at St Serf's. Pure and simple, it's naw adding up, Cormac,' the DC concluded.

Malcolm was already moving off, at a snail's pace, his Maglite turned on and illuminating the roadway between the burnt-out

Merc and the parked MG Metro – looking for what, he did not know.

'You know what this is like, Dennis? It's like returning to where you parked your motor and finding it nicked. You know where you parked it, you know it should be there, but some bastard has made off with it and you just can't understand it. But why?'

Behind him, Numan picked up the verbal baton and began to run with it: 'It also begs the question: "Where the fuck are the armed response crew?" There's no way the ambulance is going to move off before the first polis motor arrives, be it the armed response vehicle or us. WPC McCabe is old enough in service and smart enough to make sure that no paramedic is going to overrule her on that. Also, where are the bleedin' fire service? If they had been called, then we would have been alerted to that by Ambulance Service. Naw, there's something stinkin' here, gaffer, and it ain't our chargrilled friends in the Merc,' concluded Numan in his customary dark fashion.

But Malcolm's attention was firmly elsewhere. 'Over here, Dennis. I think I've got something,' he advised.

Hunkering down at the side of the dyke, Malcolm had found blood – lots of it – and in the vital red fluid, as his Maglite followed the trail, were what looked like drag marks… boot prints in crimson. He began to gently sway his Maglite back towards the position the ambulance had previously filled and as the illumination swung that way it locked on another spotlight.

For Numan also had his torch out. 'Ah shit, gaffer, me too. I've got another pool of blood,' he said and with that strode past Malcolm and reached the dyke, before peering over it and pointing his Maglite into the foliage.

Leaning half over the crumbling old wall, Numan began to yank at the branch of a birch, clearly trying to hold it back; but the branch rebounded in his face. 'Bastard!' cursed the veteran DC.

In a moment, Malcolm arrived at his side and pinned back the offending branch. With both cops' torches illuminating the other side of the dyke, the horrific evidence of their eyes was unavoidable.

'Sweet Christ,' said DS Malcolm.

'Well, that will be the armed response crew then, gaffer,' said Numan.

The two cops stared almost unseeing at the inert, twisted masses of their two colleagues, their Maglites taking in the telltale signs of their demise.

'Aye, Boabby Marshall, naw a bad sort for a Rangers man,' said Numan administering an unsympathetic last rite before homing his Maglite in on the late sergeant. 'It's naw rocket science, gaffer, he's been shot twice to the head and his boy, well, someone's taken a very sharp blade to his throat.'

Beside him, Malcolm took a step back. 'Come on, Dennis, let's leave them in peace. We need to get a broadcast out for the ambulance. I have no doubt that McGrain and his wingman are in it and that they've taken Emma as insurance... and while you're about it, get help to reclaim the bodies,' ended Malcolm, his voice starting to vibrate with emotion.

'Which would make the two bodies in the motor the paramedics,' chipped in Numan.

Malcolm grimly nodded his head. 'Okay, Dennis, we need to get that broadcast out and we need to get to St Serf's as quickly as we can. The bottom line is that if we aren't already too late, you and I are the only hope the boy has of making it out of The Blood Acre alive.'

'If I was a betting man, I would'nae be fancying his chances, gaffer,' replied Numan as they arrived at the Astra.

7

UNCONSCIOUSNESS had embraced Thoroughgood for he knew not how long; and when his eyes opened once again the inside of his mouth felt as dry as the Gobi Desert and the pounding of his head had not gone away.

He had tried with all he had to force his bonds free and failed miserably. Although he didn't know how much time had slipped by, one thing was beyond dispute: no help had arrived.

What was even worse was the fear that if Numan and Malcolm did arrive – or anyone else for that matter – then they would lose their lives in their attempt to free him.

His only hope was to effect his own escape. That way, if he died then nobody else's death need be on his conscience. Outside lay the bodies of Gregsy and O'Toole, and he knew that was a butcher's bill he had to pick up.

What had become of Emma? Had she escaped or had McGrain and Spider hunted her down on their way out?

Then there was Celine… always Celine. Whatever happened he wondered if he would ever be free of the hold that she still, despite his best efforts, had over him. Even as he faced near-certain death, she was the person who dominated his thoughts.

The enveloping sense of despair that started to seep through his dazed being became overwhelming, and as he shut his eyes, his mind began to replay images from his recent past.

He found himself reliving that night he had visited Celine and had it all out with her, the night she finally called it a day; and all to a David Bowie soundtrack.

"Well that night certainly wasn't hunky-dory!" chided the voice in his head, in his overwrought state, making reference to Bowie's 70s album. In these semi-conscious moments, Thoroughgood's thoughts began to take a turn for the bizarre, and in his head rebounded the words from Bowie's epic 'Life on Mars'.

For right there and then he had decided that was the song he wanted played at his funeral.

"Only one problem, son, you'll be too dead to tell anyone," derided the voice in his head.

Again, the hopelessness brought tears seeping from his eyes as he silently started to repeat the lyrics to his favourite part of the song:

'Take a look at the lawman

Beating up the wrong guys

Oh man, wonder if he'll ever know

He's in the bestselling show.

Is there life on Mars?'

And the silver screen inside Thoroughgood's head played an image of his own coffin starting to disappear as the final piano chords faded out in echo; the curtain came down and he went to meet his maker while his mother and his grandfather looked on.

Thoroughgood could not deny that his life had indeed been 'A godawful small affair.'

Then the rage came.

Bowie could have been inside the empty room so loudly did his words and music boom inside Thoroughgood's head. He roared into the gag in defiance, casting his head back and tossing it to and fro like a madman, his eyes swivelling crazily.

But he refused to be beaten and even in his rage he noticed

something on the fractured windowsill of the garden cottage that could at last help him break his bonds.

Wreathed in cobwebs sat a glass jam jar with a crusted paint-brush resting in it. If he could get over there and somehow smash it onto the floorboards then he would have the cutting edge needed to slice through the cord that bound him.

It was a source of hope that allowed Thoroughgood to focus all his attention and in an instant Bowie had left both his head and the room... presumably for Mars.

Slowly, he started to swivel his body one way and then the other as he dragged the cumbersome old chair forward: no easy matter given it was made with heavy-duty, if woodworm-riddled, oak.

When he reached the windowsill, Thoroughgood made a supreme effort to get to his feet and then bent double as he contorted his body to allow his head to come within striking distance of the glass jar.

"Almost there, just another inch," said his inner voice, for once encouraging.

He reached out and flicked his head against the jar. To his delight, he heard it corkscrew off the windowsill and fall to the floorboards. As the report of its smash met his ears, he dropped back into a seated position and observed the damage, praying that it might bring opportunity.

Instantly he spotted it: a shard of wickedly glinting glass about three inches long. Now all he had to do was manoeuvre his body and the chair onto the ground, then somehow locate this fragment with his fingertips without slicing them off.

Thoroughgood tipped himself over and slowly started to back his body into the broken glass, feeling a hundred pinpricks from the jar's tiny smithereens before his scrabbling fingers located what he wanted.

Grasping it carefully, he manipulated the shard until he had what he felt was its sharpest edge wedged against the cord and began to effect a semi-sawing motion, repeating it over and over, again and again, until he felt the first slight slip of the cord as it began to fray.

Five minutes later, under Thoroughgood's relentless pressure, it snapped and, his hands free, he was able to remove the gag at last.

Thoroughgood heaved: disgusting seepage from his mouth had saturated the gag and the effect of spitting it out left him retching for a moment of nauseating agony.

But now he was free and had a fighting chance.

Staring out the window he scanned The Blood Acre for any clues of what might be waiting. With hope springing eternal and a grim resolve permeating his being, Thoroughgood shouted at the top of his voice: 'You're fuckin' right… there is life on Mars!'

8

FREED FROM HIS BONDS, Thoroughgood surveyed the door with suspicion.

If ever there was an obvious place for McGrain to have rigged up an improvised explosive device that would blow him to kingdom come and do the same with the contents of The Blood Acre, then the door handle had to be it.

By rigging it, success would be ensured whether entry came from outside or from Thoroughgood's own successful escape, if he proved smart enough to pull off a Houdini act – as he had indeed just done.

Despite himself, the tingling of his circulation returning allowed the young cop a brief smile of satisfaction.

Thoroughgood decided that caution was the best bet. Turning to the old oak chair, he hefted it and launched it at the window. Unsurprisingly, the ancient glass pane and its rotten woodwork shattered on impact, and moments later Thoroughgood had climbed onto the sink just below it and was eyeing the view through the window.

Handily, outside was a concrete landing that came at the top of a set of cracked steps and using his elbow to smash out a few more nasty shards of glass, Thoroughgood finally swung himself out onto the landing.

From here he had a great view of the grounds of St Serf's and he carried out a quick assessment of where the perfect location for a victim-operated booby trap would lie.

The first thing he had to do was negotiate a route through The

Blood Acre itself, passing the bodies of O'Toole and Gregsy, a pair of permanently motionless sentries.

Beyond, there was the old waving willow tree and the gravedigger's wheelbarrow and hut; then the rickety footbridge that afforded passage to St Serf's original church burial ground, complete with its ancient gravestones and their sinister medieval symbols, which from Thoroughgood's position seemed like the land of milk and honey.

Taking stock, he arrived at the conclusion that any booby trap would have to come at this side of the bridge, for there were surely just two objectives behind its location: one, to blow the contents of The Blood Acre to oblivion and two, to make sure that he or his rescuers were the architects of such an explosion.

"So how have they gone about it?" asked the voice in his head.

Thoroughgood tried to replay everything he had learnt about the IRA and their booby traps from his run-in with Devorgilla, the flame-haired Irish assassin, a year back. Surely a trip-wire device would be just too obvious, while a tilt fuse device was usually used in vehicle booby traps.

So, the favourite had to be a pressure device similar to the one Devorgilla had rigged to such explosive effect in Mojito's office. Which meant if he was going to make it out of The Blood Acre alive, he was going to have to treat it like a minefield, his life in jeopardy with every footfall he made.

Taking a deep breath, he took hold of the rusted wrought-iron handrail and, eyes devouring each step in front of him, began to descend, praying silently that this didn't turn out to be his stairway to heaven… or hell, for that matter.

Seconds later, he was at the bottom of the steps; and now he began to eye the mud-slicked turf that would take him past Gregsy and O'Toole's corpses.

For a moment, Thoroughgood was temporarily distracted by the question he couldn't answer: "Just who had tipped McGrain off that he was on his way to The Blood Acre?"

The only explanation he could come up with was O'Toole and it was clear that in doing so the DI had signed his own death warrant. But what about Gregsy… had he deserved such a brutal end?

Thoroughgood shrugged his shoulders and muttered into the stiffening breeze: 'I guess it comes with the territory.'

His heart hammering, he placed an Adidas Samba trainer down with utmost care, focussing with every ounce of his concentration on each part of the sodden soil in front of him, as he looked to detect signs of any tampering or fresh movement.

As he drew parallel with O'Toole's corpse, he saw that the his Smith & Wesson was lying with its handle half immersed in a puddle.

"Could be useful," said his inner voice and Thoroughgood found himself nodding his head in agreement. Hunkering down, he reached out to take hold of the revolver, lifting the handle gently from the water between his forefinger and his thumb.

Then his breath caught: attached to the handle was a wire.

McGrain had baited him and like the fool he was he'd been taken in; and now certain oblivion awaited.

Thoroughgood stilled his hand, scared to breathe, praying for all he was worth that he had not sent a vibration up the wire that would trigger the blast.

Such was the intensity of his gaze that his eyeballs started to feel like they were burning through their sockets… but the only sound was the carefree babbling of the burn.

Slowly Thoroughgood started to breathe once more as the wheels of his mind began to function again. Really, O'Toole's revolver was the most obvious possible item for McGrain to wire up as an

44

explosive device. It was a vital piece of evidence and sometime very soon after the locus was reached and examined by the authorities the handgun would have to be secured as evidence.

The bottom line was that located as close as it was to The Blood Acre and the bodies of O'Toole and Gregsy, it would provide the perfect victim-operated booby trap.

For a brief second anger flared inside Thoroughgood. 'Aye, so obvious you bleedin fell for it, idiot,' he chastised himself.

But as his temper threatened to unhinge him, Thoroughgood forced himself to stay calm and think logically; for the one thing he knew was that he could not sit in this semi-hunkered position forever without disaster striking.

Somehow, he needed to prop the revolver in the mud without sending a shockwave up the wire that would be enough to trigger the explosive.

"Good luck with that, mate," said the voice inside his head helpfully.

As the seconds drew into minutes, his forearm and wrist started to throb from the tension that was gripping him and coupled with the unnatural position he had assumed, his first problem was going to be how to adopt a more sustainable posture.

Slowly he began to move his body back from his outstretched hand, doing everything he could to keep his paw steady, until he was almost face down in the mud but nevertheless at eye level with the revolver.

This allowed him to sight along the wire, which he saw ran into the gravedigger's hut. 'Of course,' he chided himself. It couldn't have been more obvious if McGrain had posted a signpost outside the old lean-to saying 'Bomb inside'.

'So, what now?' he asked himself.

9

THOROUGHGOOD needed something that he could prop the revolver up with or something that would do the same job as the wire and thus allow him to replace the revolver as he had found it.

He wracked his brains frantically to see if he could come up with anything, doing a mental inventory of what he had on him. Then: jackpot! A credit card lodged in the mud might just be enough to keep the wire stationery while he got the hell out of there.

'Only one problem, mate, how you gonna get it out your inside pocket without moving enough to pull the wire?' he muttered.

Shaking his head, Thoroughgood realised that only a contortionist would manage to pull off such a manoeuvre, especially since his Harrington was zipped right up.

Lying there in the mud with the damp and the cold seeping through his body and his right hand cramping from the tension imposed by its unnatural angle and stillness, Thoroughgood frantically scoured the earth around him for help.

Nothing.

He scanned his wider surroundings. Next to the gravedigger's hut was a pile of chopped wood that had obviously been the result of some husbandry on the surrounding foliage: but what good was that?

Yet as his gaze worked its way back from the old shack, he could trace a trail of fragments of wood and twig, and at last Thoroughgood's eyes locked on a heavenly offering.

There, lying in the mud just over a foot away, was a two-pronged twig resembling the wishing bone from a prime chicken, and its discovery once again caused hope to spring in his mind.

If he could reach it with his left hand then he would be able to prop it under the wire, gently pushing it up to hold the line steady while he deposited the revolver back where it had come from.

"You've got to be having a laugh, son," sneered the voice in his head... but then what was the alternative?

Slowly he began to push his left hand along the soil, slightly adjusting his body to accommodate the change in his position, all the while doing everything he could to stop his right hand from moving enough to trip the wire.

At the apex of his stretch, his left index finger reached and curled round the twig, and for a moment this splintered two-inch piece of broken twig was the centre of Thoroughgood's universe and his hopes of remaining there in one piece.

Gradually his left hand retreated with the twig in it and now his attention turned to his right hand, the revolver it still held and the height that the trip wire would need to be propped up at to avoid the gun's movement triggering the booby trap.

His super-enhanced concentration seemed to have magnified the minutest detail of his environment to extreme levels, so that the burn began to sound like Niagara Falls; but even so, the hammering of his heart pounded above it.

'Here we go,' he muttered. As his left hand reached out with the twig, he felt like a surgeon about to make the first incision. He placed the twig in the mud and made sure it was secure enough to take the weight coming its way. Then he adjusted its position until it was a hair underneath the wire, almost but not quite touching it.

He turned his gaze to his right hand. Once again, the mud could be his saviour. The wire was attached to the Smith & Wesson's barrel and if he used the soil as a receptacle, he could guard against any further movement.

With the fingers of his left hand he deftly began to manipulate the soil until he had enough on either side to support the revolver's handle, keeping the barrel steady and so maintaining the tightness of the wire when he removed his fingers.

This was it.

Uttering a silent prayer to the man above, Thoroughgood slowly placed the revolver handle into the mud, all the time scanning the trigger wire for movement.

Yet, the mud withstood the weight of the S&W. He took a deep breath, saw the slightest bit of give as the twig held the wire; but to his untrained eye the movement, if any, was almost undetectable.

He counted to ten, so paranoid was he that any movement from his body could bring all his handiwork to nothing; but silence continued to reign and with a further deep breath he started to pull back.

Ten yards away, Thoroughgood fell to a knee and cradled his forehead in his right hand, trying to compose himself and get both his breathing and his heart rate back to normal. As he did so, he felt blood on his hands. Touching his forehead, he discovered the cut that had been caused by the butt of McGrain's F2 – he hadn't even noticed it before.

He was so relieved he didn't know whether to laugh or cry.

'Fuck, I could murder a Stella!' he said out loud and slowly he felt his mouth twitch into a smile.

Thoroughgood had been lucky, for he'd made the mistake of failing to see the obvious threat. It had been a case of not seeing the wood for the trees.

He shakily got to his feet and turned to the next priority: what mattered most now was that McGrain and Spider were caught and that he made sure Emma was okay.

With any luck she had summoned help and also alerted the Unit, so it shouldn't be too long before he had company.

His mind started to play out various scenarios as he attempted to work out how McGrain and his vieil ami had made their escape. Hopefully they had been picked up either by the cavalry summoned by Emma or by members of the Unit.

He reached the old rickety footbridge in a trance as once again his senses began to attune to the world around him. He started to feel the chill of the wind and hear the squelch of the mud underneath him, and he gave a sigh.

Thoroughgood knew that the events that had played out here today would be with him for the rest of his life.

Gregsy hadn't been a bad sort, really. When all was said and done the number-one priority in his life had been his 'old ma' and ultimately that loyalty had been what had helped Thoroughgood snare him and bring him here… to his death.

It was a thought that sent a tremor of guilt through him, but then the bottom line was that he had only been doing his job – and all in the service of saving the lives of many more of McGrain and Spider's potential victims.

As he walked onto the bridge, he grasped the splintered hand-rail and turned around, sweeping The Blood Acre one last time. He caught sight again of O'Toole's slumped corpse and his mind started to dissect the dirty cop's role in all of this.

It occurred to him that O'Toole must have been like him once. A hungry young officer who thought that by building an understanding with a similarly ambitious felon, a parallel line on the opposite side of the track, he could ensure his career was upwardly mobile while also using the information he got to serve the ends of justice to spectacular effect.

But these lines had become blurred and now O'Toole, lying 100 yards away, would only be remembered as a corrupt cop.

Thoroughgood shook his head, for in all of that there was a big lesson. Had he not tried to bargain his way out of his desperate encounter with McGrain by offering a similar quid pro quo?

And what about his relationship with Meechan? A gangster on the make and a man he despised. The man who had stolen Celine from him because he had sacrificed her on the altar of his own vaulting ambition. Was he really any better than O'Toole?

It was too much. The continual self-torment that had become his default position was starting to drive him mad and out loud he shouted: 'Enough!' He let his eyes linger one last time on The Blood Acre, turned and continued his unsteady progress over the ancient creaking span that with his every step seemed certain to give way.

It almost defied logic that the wooden bridge still held over the burn. Thoroughgood found himself examining it for clues as to just how old it may have been when his right Samba trod on the second-to-last slat and from behind him the roar of the blast and the white hot sear of the heat it generated scorched his back.

The explosion took hold of his body and he was launched through the air like a rag doll. As time suspended, in his mind's eye he saw his favourite photograph, the one of him and his grandfather holding the Strathclyde Police squash trophy.

Then he landed… a dead weight.

10

'IT'S AN UNFORTUNATE BUSINESS when civilians get caught up in affairs they have no part in,' said McGrain from his seat in the mobile emergency chair three feet from Emma, herself confined to the ambulance bed.

As she watched him, Emma thought she could almost detect a glimmer of humanity inside what she had previously taken for a cold-blooded killer.

McGrain seemed to almost read her mind. 'In French we say dommage. "Pity". Amazingly, it is, my sweet Em, a feeling that is not beyond me. But unfortunately, in my line of work, one I just can't afford,' smiled McGrain, his thin lips cracking his face. He opened his arms in a gesture of helplessness.

Across the cabin he could see the confusion that was engulfing Emma and smiled reassuringly. 'But please take some solace from the fact that there is no better resting place than St Serf's. Did you know that our dear patron saint was known as the apostle of Orkney and that, so legend has it, he slew a dragon with his pastoral staff? Indeed, buried in the soil venerated by his name we have a few of our own bêtes noires committed to their final resting places!'

For once, the derisive laughter failed to materialise. Emma couldn't work out whether he was taunting her or trying to impress her, and it occurred to her that this was a bizarre thought.

Despite herself, Emma couldn't help asking the obvious question: 'What have you done to Gus?'

McGrain feigned surprise: 'Gus? Ah, you mean your beloved Thoroughgood? I'm afraid when it comes to… Gus… every decision has a consequence, and he made a call to pursue something he should have left well alone,' said McGrain. 'So, dear lady, I think you should remember him in your prayers!' And with that he barked a cruel laugh that was chorused from the driver's cabin by Spider.

'Where are we going?' asked Emma, determined not to let the news of Thoroughgood's death sentence break her.

'Nosey aren't we, my sweet chestnut-haired girl?' said McGrain, and in one lithe movement he left the chair and landed on the bed beside Emma.

Then he took her chin between his forefinger and thumb and from an inch away, his eyes lit large, said: 'Really, dear Em, the question you should be asking is what are we going to do with you?'

McGrain's hawklike gaze held Emma's eyes, and she felt a tremor of fear sear through her being.

Again, his face flickered with that disconcerting half-smile that hinted at a depth that should not have been there, before his dark eyes shifted towards the cabin. 'What's our progress, Spider?'

'It won't be long until we're aff the M8 and that is when things will slow up as we're on the country roads; but the traffic will be virtually non-existent in the Kingdom o' Fife at this time of night, I'd say maybe 40 minutes, at most, Tony,' answered the big man in the rumble that passed for his voice.

'There is one issue that concerns me, Spider. This bloody ambulance sticks out like a sore thumb and it won't be long, if they haven't already sent one out, before there is a lookout posted for it. We are taking a gamble on getting onto the back roads before we get made, big man, and as you know, by nature I'm anything but a gambler,' said McGrain, his features poker-straight until he flicked Emma a wink.

Inside, Emma raged. He was toying with her, enjoying the fact he had the power of life and death over her. Her anger threatened to spill over, but just as she was about to open her mouth, Spider beat her to the verbal punch: 'I think we need to ditch it pronto and I think you also have another big decision, patron. What the fuck are we gonna do with The Gentle Touch here?' barked the big man.

McGrain smiled and drew an index finger down Emma's blanket-clad forearm. 'You never cease to surprise me, Spider: I'd never have taken you for a fan of Jill Gascoigne's!' But even as he delivered his one-liner his eyes never left Emma. 'The answer is I haven't decided, old friend. What do you think we should do with you, Em?'

Forcing herself to remain calm, Emma refused to flinch and tried to stop emotion showing on her face. 'I think you have brought me along as an insurance policy, so that if things get too hot you have something to barter with. I don't suppose there was ever any chance that I walk away from this alive, one way or another. But I guarantee you this: whatever has happened to Gus Thoroughgood, his friends will find you and bring you to justice, McGrain,' said Emma, her voice rising as the contempt she felt towards the man sat inches away spilled over.

McGrain appeared to be reading every tremor of emotion on her features as she spoke. Once she'd finished, he brought his index finger from her arm to her face, and with the back of his hand he caressed her cheek. 'Let me make you one guarantee, Em: there is no way your beloved Gus has walked out of The

Blood Acre and if anyone tried to help him make good his escape then, as they say in French, ils ne sont plus de ce monde: no—'

'"No longer of this world." I have my O-level French, McGrain,' she spat.

'I prefer Tony,' he smiled before continuing: 'What do you think this is, Em? Some cheap crime novel where the good guy gets the girl and walks off into the sunset like some latter-day John fucking Wayne?' He paused for a minute, taking in her ashen features.

Then his philosophy lesson continued: 'I'm afraid I don't do happy endings, which is probably where my nom de guerre, The Widowmaker – which you may or may not be familiar with – comes from. You may be aware from the disruption outside the ambulance that help came and was dealt with. Because the big problem the polis have when they come up against the Foreign Legion is that they are essentially amateurs, and we are trained in matters that would give most of your colleagues nightmares.'

'You flatter yourself, McGrain. You will slip up and when you do, you'll be made to pay,' she spat.

'Perhaps! In my world, Em, everyone and everything has a purpose; but equally, at some time they become expendable. And it is then that I have a call to make…' he concluded, letting his words trail off for dramatic effect.

Despite herself, Emma couldn't help asking the rhetorical question: 'Which is?'

McGrain held her gaze and suddenly his mood changed from playful to malevolent. 'The manner in which I part company with them. But I can promise you one thing: I don't do happy endings.' And with that he stood up and slipped through the hatch to the cabin.

From the blackness of the cabin, Spider's voice reverberated through into the rear of the vehicle. 'That's us now onto the A9. I'd say we can relax and smell the roses, Tony, we are almost at the airfield,' he concluded thankfully.

As she stared at the ambulance wall opposite her, with the confirmation that they were almost at their journey's end, the sense of dread Emma had been suppressing started to engulf her.

For she knew that it in turn meant her demise was imminent.

11

THE AMBULANCE took a left turn and sped along a straight single-track road lined with birches that snapped back like a row of limbo dancers in the cool night air.

In the distance stood a 100-foot whitewashed tower surrounded by three functional looking ground-floor buildings and a Portakabin ringed by a quaint picket fence.

Their next turn took them along what was clearly part of the airport runway, something that was confirmed by the half-inflated windsock attached to a post off to the side of the tarmac.

Moments later the abrupt halt of the Iveco jolted Emma; her heart hammered as she tried to wrack her brain for a way out. She desperately scanned the back of the ambulance for anything that might be of use but found herself shaking her head in frustration: because as long as she was restrained to the vehicle bed, what use would it be?

She heard the vehicle's front doors opening and then a conversation in another language. McGrain's gravelly Glaswegian delivery was evident as was a more lilting voice, while the ebb and flow of their words was punctuated by Spider's booming laugh.

'Good to see you, my friend,' said Connall McGrath, the Provisional IRA's number-one fixer, his melodious Irish almost sing-song, and was rewarded with warm smiles from both McGrain and Spider.

'Likewise, Connall – or should I say "The Leprechaun"?' replied McGrain, before a hearty round of handshakes were exchanged between the trio.

'Aye, you've done well, wee man, yer own private airfield out in the middle of nowhere and no one has a bloody clue what you're bringing in and out!' laughed Spider.

A yard away, the small red-haired figure cocked a thoughtful sideways glance at McGrain's lieutenant and from behind his immaculately trimmed red beard he casually remarked: 'Glad to be of assistance, my friend: after all, your little job down in Heysham has made a hell of a difference to the cause, to be sure.'

Then The Leprechaun's green gaze shifted towards McGrain. 'You took a chance coming to Dalado in an ambulance: are you sure that you haven't attracted unwanted attention, Tony?' The concern on McGrath's thoughtful features was obvious.

McGrain smiled reassuringly. 'What do you take me for, Connall? Not a chance. We considered ditching the ambulance and our passenger along the road, but things went so well after a rocky start that there seemed no point in slowing our progress.'

'Passenger? You have a guest?' asked McGrath.

'We do indeed, Connall, we do indeed!'

With that McGrain beckoned to McGrath to follow him around the back of the emergency vehicle and with a theatrical flourish opened the rear doors. 'May I present WPC McCabe!'

As she stared out at her welcoming party, Emma remained silent, for in truth she did not know what else to do.

Outside the vehicle, The Leprechaun signalled to McGrain to join him at the side of the ambulance. 'I don't like this, Tony. You have a decision to make.' He paused. 'We fly in 30 minutes and I have a coffee to finish while I confirm our flight details with our controller. I suggest you have everything boxed off before then,' he snapped, his irritation clear, and stalked off towards the control tower.

Behind McGrain, Spider's voice thundered into life: 'I knew this was gonna cause a problem, Tony. We should have iced her and dumped her body on the way. Now what?' It was as close to a rebellion against McGrain's authority as his loyal lieutenant was likely to come; and McGrain knew his old comrade was right.

Nodding his head in agreement, McGrain drew his Glock and flicked the safety off. 'I'll sort it, now go and get a coffee, and I will join you presently,' he replied and hauled himself into the back of the ambulance before pushing the rear doors closed.

Once again McGrain sat in the chair opposite Emma, but this time he clasped his Glock in his right hand, on top of a stilled knee. Eyeing it nervously, she realised what he had come to do.

'Tell me, Emma, do you love Thoroughgood?' The question took her completely by surprise.

'What?' she asked, incredulous.

McGrain smiled reassuringly. 'We are running short on time here, Emma, and what you say in the next couple of minutes is very important.'

For a minute she hesitated as she tried to comprehend the context of his question, never mind the correct answer. 'I don't know, I guess. After my mother died, well… nothing has been the same.'

He eyed her with that shrewd, assessing gaze and then the half-smile appeared once again, and his harsh features softened with a hint of warmth.

Suddenly McGrain bent down over the bed and started to loosen the restraints binding her feet, before helping her to stand up with the ties that still bound her hands. Without warning he pulled Emma close to him.

Their bodies intertwined and he could hear her heart hammering as she waited for the bullet.

To her amazement, McGrain holstered the Glock and whispered in her ear: 'Come with me, mo stór.'

12

THOROUGHGOOD stared balefully into his pint glass and didn't know whether to laugh or cry.

He was all too well aware how lucky he had been to survive the blast from McGrain's booby trap with only shrapnel wounds, concussion and severe bruising, but that didn't help to improve his mood.

In truth he couldn't remember anything from the post-blast period. He'd ended his recovery in the Glasgow Royal Infirmary as quickly as he possibly could, and now here he was, upstairs in the UB Chip, warming himself at the hearth of its familiar fire.

He was itching to do something, but had to sit around kicking his heels, trying to find something to take his mind off the dire events that had unfolded. A Partick Thistle man, even the prospect of the derailment of Rangers' defence of the Scottish Premier League barely registered a flicker on his radar. Neither did The Telegraph's continuing post-mortem on Mike Tyson's shocking demolition by James 'Buster' Douglas the previous month.

Although his physical wounds were healing nicely and the dirt, bacteria and assorted fragments of clothing, metal and plastic that had enfiladed him had been removed and his wounds managed expertly to help him avoid falling foul to secondary infection, the scars in his mind were another matter.

While he could square the executions of Gregsy and O'Toole, Thoroughgood found that he could not compartmentalise the grizzly fate that had befallen the ambulance crew and the two armed response cops.

And then there was Emma.

What the hell had happened to her?

She had disappeared into thin air and the missing person enquiry that had now been raised had proven as ineffective as the lookouts issued nationally for her.

It just didn't add up, and Thoroughgood couldn't get his head around it.

But the one line of reasoning he found compelling was that McGrain had not killed her.

The Widowmaker had shown a bloody predilection to end any and all life that threatened to derail his plans, which had left a trail of corpses on both sides of the border, and the lack of any sign of Emma was unnerving to Thoroughgood – if she were dead, she'd have shown up by now.

What could McGrain want with her?

As always, he found his mind straying back to matters of the fairer sex in general. Back in the cottage, when all hope had seemed lost and he'd been at his most forlorn, the alluring presence of Celine had once again taunted him.

He had to accept that whenever he was in extremis, she came to the fore; and yet he had told Emma he'd loved her just before she had made good her escape.

It didn't take a fool to work out that wasn't right. God knows Emma had been through enough with the loss of her mother to cancer, and now here he was once more telling her he loved her just like the last time... the only problem was that since then, Celine had happened.

It was too much for Thoroughgood and he swallowed the

remainder of his pint and crashed the glass down on its beer mat with more force than he realised. He was met with a stare of warning from a pony-tailed bartender.

The rebuke sent a hot surge of anger through him and a fiery retort almost left his lips; but the need for more liquid anaesthetic proved too strong and instead he muttered: 'Apologies, amigo. Any chance you can do me another Fürstenberg… pronto?'

Fishing inside his jacket pocket for some cash, Thoroughgood became aware of a presence at his shoulder, and looking up he saw he had been joined by DS Malcolm and DC Numan.

'You fancy getting them in and taking care of young Gus here, Dennis?' Malcolm asked with a look that suggested no answer was needed.

Numan winked. 'Good to see you again, son. Delighted you are up and about. Why don't you take a pew with the gaffer and I'll sort these,' he said, nodding to the window seat Thoroughgood had just come from.

Moments later the three of them sat ensconced around the table, with DS Malcolm quick to set out his agenda after a mouthful of the UB's famed amber delicacy. 'I'm sorry, Gus, we have nothing more on Emma, the lady has well and truly vanished. It's very hard to come up with a logical explanation for it, other than McGrain holding onto her as some kind of insurance policy. Yet he has made good his escape and then some and still we have nothing and, as you know, in the past he has shown no concern about the body count he leaves in his wake. So, my thoughts are she is still very much alive, although doing what I haven't a bloody scooby!'

Across the table, Numan wiped his foam-specked moustache with the back of a hand before chipping in with his tuppence: 'It's a strange one, Gus, and I have to agree with the gaffer. I think if

McGrain had done her we would know about it. But all we can do is make sure the national lookout for her remains in place and if she is to be found then I'm sure we will get to her…' said Numan, but the lack of conviction in his words shown by the way they trailed off made it clear that the veteran DC was far from convinced that would prove the case.

As an awkward silence started to draw out and Thoroughgood's doleful features offered little hope that he had taken any succour from their best efforts, Malcolm cleared his throat and attempted to move swiftly on. 'Look, Gus, give yourself a break. If the cards had fallen another way, then you wouldn't be here right now or perhaps you would be but minus a limb. Whatever you think of McGrain and his henchman, well, they are professionals, and the level of training and expertise they have behind them in the French Foreign Legion is something you or we are not trained to deal with. I get you are worried sick about Emma but remember, if it hadn't been for you offering yourself up as a sacrificial lamb, she wouldn't have made it out of St Serf's in the first place. After that there is no way you can be carrying the can for the way things panned out,' reassured Malcolm.

Across the table, Thoroughgood's features continued to hang heavy and his sea-green gaze showed not even a flicker of interest.

But DS Malcolm, growing frustrated with the lack of a reaction one way or another, would not give up. 'Come on, just look at the mincemeat McGrain and that big bastard of his made of the armed response unit. For crying out loud, Bobby Marshall was as good a sergeant as we have in Strathclyde Police, but all that experience couldn't save him and his boy, and what about these cops that Spider is supposed to have taken care of down in Heysham?'

Numan reached out and grabbed Thoroughgood's wrist as it began lifting his pint back to his mouth. 'Look, Gus, we get it, both of us: you are bearing the guilt for what happened back at The Blood Acre. Now the girl you are close to and have shared a lot with has vanished in circumstances that are quite frankly mind-blowing. But you need to get on with your life, 'cause if you don't that bastard McGrain would have been as well blowing you to smithereens.'

At last Thoroughgood spoke: 'But people, innocent people, have died, Dennis. Died because of me and all for what? McGrain has gone and the evidence that led me to The Blood Acre gone with him and instead what do I have to show for it? Nothing... nothing but death and all of that was because I was so determined to do whatever I could to make DC.'

Across the table, Numan downed the remainder of his pint as if he had been wandering the wilderness for 40 days and nights, such was the hurry he was in to inject some positivity into Thoroughgood.

'Well, you can cut that bullshit out for a start, son, and here's how. Cormac has moved heaven and earth to get you a position with the newly formed Serious and Organised Crime Unit or SOCU,' he said, spelling it out, 'which, incidentally, is pronounced "soak you",' Numan finished, flashing his wolfish grin.

To his right Malcolm held up his three-quarter-empty pint pot and charged it against Numan's freshly emptied glass. 'Aye, and that shouldn't be any problem to a thirsty boy like you, Acting Detective Constable Thoroughgood!' Then they both let out twin peals of laughter.

Opposite the laughing policemen, Thoroughgood felt his spirits lift for almost the first time since he had discharged himself from the Glasgow Royal Infirmary.

Malcolm had been observing the reaction to the news flickering across his ashen features, and he wasted no time in providing the patient with his diagnosis. 'So you still have a pulse, young man?

Clearly, because the letters ADC seemed to have provided the ideal pick-me-up!'

Malcolm got up and produced the official confirmation of his new and vaunted – albeit temporary – status, and as Thoroughgood read the detail and checked for the signature of the Assistant Chief Constable Crime, Neil Jackson, at the foot of the document, he found himself nodding his head in disbelief.

Numan joined Malcolm on his feet and a round of handshakes and congratulations ensued before Thoroughgood was reseated with the help of a hearty pat on the back from the veteran DC.

Despite himself, Thoroughgood couldn't help a smile from creasing his face, and he gave up attempting to stifle the laugh that followed; but before long a frown was once again back in place. 'But what the hell is the Serious and Organised Crime Unit?'

'Earth to Thoroughgood. Come in, over!' quipped Numan in the act of rising and returning to the bar. 'It's our magnificent new moniker, of course – what do you think, boy?' he asked rolling his eyes to the heavens.

'Grandiose!' replied Thoroughgood, immediately wishing he hadn't.

'Not like you to sit on the fence, ADC Thoroughgood,' replied Malcolm, emphasising the Criminal Investigation Department aide's new epithet and being met by an awkward shrug of the shoulders from his subordinate.

But before Thoroughgood could offer a mealy-mouthed explanation, Malcolm held his hand up. 'Just hold it there, Dennis: as the newest member of Soak You, we have every right to expect him to stand his senior colleagues a round before we get down to business. Correct?'

A yard away, Numan dropped onto his stool. 'A refusal to carry out a lawful order from a senior officer of Soak You would provide grounds for instant dismissal. I agree wholeheartedly, Detective Sergeant Malcolm.'

This time all three of them burst into laughter and five minutes later Thoroughgood had rejoined them at the table with three fresh and foaming pints of Fürstenberg.

When he sat down, his eyes were met with some interesting paperwork and to make sure he gave it due scrutiny, Malcolm pushed it alongside his pint. 'Try not to spill any lager on it, Gus. What you have there is a travel warrant for your impending journey to Manchester!'

Thoroughgood picked up the travel warrant and surveyed it as if the clearly printed details of his impending trip to Manchester Piccadilly station were hieroglyphics.

Despite himself, he could not help repeat the word: 'Manchester?'

Shaking his head in exasperated fascination, Numan laughed out low. 'Feck me, that's right, Manchester… ever watched Corrie?' But this time the chorus of laughter was only from two of them.

13

THOROUGHGOOD grasped the travel warrant and examined its every detail.

His orders were clear: he was to meet DC Paddy Greene in the entrance foyer of Glasgow Central Station to catch the 9.40 pm the next morning, while at the other end they would be picked up at Manchester Piccadilly by Greater Manchester CID and taken to City Centre nick, where he would meet and be briefed by a Detective Chief Inspector Ferguson.

Digesting the information, Thoroughgood had questions. 'Who is Paddy Greene and what's the brief?' he asked.

'That's the spirit!' quipped Numan, laughing.

'DS Paddy Greene will be riding shotgun on this one, Gus, as although we have need of a more – how shall I say it? – fresh-faced member of Soak You, we are also still duty-bound to… er… well… ' stuttered Malcolm, gradually coming to a standstill.

Fortunately, Numan had no such qualms and with a wink he fired off a reply with his usual machine-gun delivery: 'What the gaffer is trying to say is you are still way too young in service to make this one on your own so we needed a babysitter!'

Despite himself, Thoroughgood found his facial muscles tightening. 'So, I'm good enough to be appointed ADC but not wise or experienced enough to be trusted on my own?' He paused. 'DS Greene?'

'It's an old mate of mine from the Scottish Crime Squad who has been persuaded to join our ranks and will ultimately be running the shift alongside Cormac's squad when we get up to full strength. Listen, Gus. Paddy's a decent sort: likes a pint of Guinness, is partial to a bit of skirt and as long as you keep him off the subject of the bloody Sellick then I'm sure, you being a Partick Thistle man and all that, you'll get along just dandy,' he chuckled, his speed of speech making the nickname for Celtic football club, 'sellick', sound more like 'slick'.

To his side, Malcolm smiled with relief after being let off the hook. 'Indeed, I couldn't have put it better myself, Dennis. Now let's get down to the brief,' he said, bringing more paperwork from inside his black Strathclyde Police business case, which Thoroughgood noticed was nattily embossed with the force's Semper Vigilo motto and crest.

'I'm confident you're going to like this, Gus! Basically, you're going down to help Greater Manchester arrest one of our villains. Ever heard of Terry "Jaws" Forsyth?' asked the DS, after taking a hefty swig from his pint.

'Can't say I have, gaffer,' was the monotone reply from Thoroughgood.

'Aye, well I'd say you have some homework ahead, boy, 'cause our Terry falls into the bad bastard category… big time,' summed up Numan in suitably erudite fashion.

'Yes, indeed, thanks for that, Dennis! Our Terence has been a busy boy down south: in particular, the Greater Manchester area, where he is intent on supplying heroin by the shitload to the two dominant drugs gangs, which has in turn led to a turf war. So, we need to get our hands on Jaws, big time, and bring him back up the road to face the music – also to get to the bottom of where the fuck his supply is coming from. Because the only thing we know about Forsyth is that, as I alluded to already, he is causing a bidding war with his product, which is starting to get increasingly nasty.'

Once again Numan was quick with a quip: 'In other words, what you're saying, gaffer, is that Jaws is becoming a bloody big fish in a small Mancunian pool!'

Malcolm met his remark with a roll of the eyes, while the newly appointed ADC failed to suppress a grin; but seeing that the DS was getting slightly exasperated, he moved the discussion on pronto. 'What's DCI Ferguson like?' asked Thoroughgood.

'Major league shagger!' drawled out Numan, emphasising the last word in the sentence into three syllables.

The un-PC answer earned him a frustrated but somewhat half-hearted rebuke from DS Malcolm. 'For Pete's sake, Dennis,' he chided.

Across the table Thoroughgood had exploded with laughter and soon the whole table was engulfed in mirth.

Malcolm was first to regain his composure. 'What Dennis is rather colourfully trying to say is that Marty Ferguson is one of our own, that is to say, a Glaswegian cop and a bloody good one—' But before he could complete his glowing eulogy of the DCI, Numan again felt the need to put some metaphorical meat on the bones of his words.

'Good guy who couldn't keep it tucked and unfortunately or not, as the case may be, knocked up a barmaid in Black-pool when he was down south to give evidence at the trial of some prolific travelling Wegy till dippers,' said Numan, stressing 'Wegy', the slang for Glaswegians. When he had finished, Numan applied his pint point to his mouth, making sure he got away a trademark wink over the rim of the glass.

Opposite him, Thoroughgood was all ears. 'So what happened?' he asked, his glance jumping from Malcolm to Numan as he awaited the conclusion of their colourful narrative of the DCI's love life.

'Well… when Fergie's wife found out he'd been a naughty boy and played away from home, she gave him an ultimatum, and to everyone's surprise he decided to take the free transfer option to Manchester and has been living somewhere in Cheshire in bliss with his new squeeze and their son for a good few years now.'

'Jeez!' was all Thoroughgood could come up with.

Malcolm was working his way through the briefing paper-work and returned his gaze to Numan, suddenly businesslike. 'Dennis, it's over to you from here, as it's down to you that we have the intel on this whole escapade.'

Numan rocked back on his seat, folding his arms. But he had completely forgotten that he was on a stool and not a chair, and just as his eyes saucered wide in the recognition of that incon-venient truth, Thoroughgood's right hand shot out and grabbed him. 'Take it easy, Dennis, no need to go off your rocker,' he said with an amused grin.

Regaining his balance and his composure, an unamused Numan moved on as if nothing had happened. 'I'm lucky enough to have a tout who has managed to infiltrate himself into the fringes of Terry fuckwit's circle and it would appear Jaws is now prepared to cut a deal with one of the Manc gangs for exclusive supply and that it ain't likely to go down well with the other side.'

Again, Thoroughgood cut to the chase: 'So what do we know about the two gangs? I'm assuming you've shared intelligence with DCI Ferguson given the briefing paperwork you've got there, Cormac,' he enquired.

This time there was twinkle in Malcolm's eyes as he looked over at his subordinate. 'Well, being a Thistle man, you're gonna love this, Gus! The two gangs are divided down football rivalries: in the blue corner we have The Maine Men and in the red, The Devils, which I'm sure you grasp means—'

This time Thoroughgood finished the DS's sentence for him: 'The Maine Men derive their name from City's ground, Maine Road, and The Devils from United's nickname, The Red Devils. Christ, it's almost as bad as Glasgow!' he sighed with a shake of the head.

'With bells on, Gus ma boy!' chimed Numan, indicating with his hand that it was time the new ADC found his way to the bar.

As Thoroughgood rose from his seat, Numan got another dig in: 'So the big question is who you gonna support... Oldham Athletic?' And as the unamused ADC turned his back and headed to the bar, the sound of their laughter followed him.

14

THE BLACK HACK pulled up outside the imposing twin-arch entrance to Manchester's iconic Midland Hotel. Overhead, a slight ripple of wind ruffled the Union Jack and Cross of St George flying above the magnificent Edwardian baroque entrance.

The first passenger to leave the taxi was, at a push and with the aid of a decent pair of platform shoes, no more than five foot four. His immaculately suited companion followed him onto the carpeted entrance steps; his head was shaved and where his left eye should have been there was a hideous scar running across the socket.

'I'm gaggin' for a drink, Manny; problem is, we won't know if the bastard has turned up early or late until we hit the bar,' said the vertically challenged male, who sported an expensive and luxuriously cut Paul Weller-style hairstyle, his accent heavily Mancunian.

His battle-scarred companion nodded at the pristinely turned out concierge and offered an amiable 'Evening, George!' as the door to the city's most famous hotel was held open for him.

For Manny 'One-Eye' Summerbee was a regular at the iconic venue. When Summerbee had an important deal to clinch or business meet to make, The Midland was his choice of destination and tonight was important… by any standards.

A boy from the toughest part of Moss Side, he had fought, maimed, extorted and, if need be, murdered his way up from the street corner until his crime syndicate, known as The Maine

Men due to their all-consuming loyalty towards Manchester City, dominated the infamous area just under two miles from the city centre.

If it was worth dealing, The Maine Men dealt it; if it could make money, they extorted and intimidated to bleed it. If it threatened their existence or encroached on their territory, they killed it.

One-Eye ruled his kingdom with an iron fist and his lieutenant, Paulie 'The Midget' Gallacher, was at his side whenever he needed to make the big calls – as he did tonight.

Because Summerbee was, he hoped, ready to make a compelling case for exclusive supply of the heroin and coke that was about to flood the city from north of the border.

As they crossed the gleaming marble-tiled foyer floor and entered the lobby bar, Summerbee and Gallacher exchanged nervous glances, before the latter chimed: 'Hey up, Manny, he's here, over there in the corner: black double-breaster and turtleneck. I'd say he's packin' all right.'

Their entrance was indeed being observed by a dark individual in a crisply pressed suit who sat with his legs crossed, his Oxford brogue toecaps almost reflecting their taut features as they approached him.

This seated figure's still presence was given a sinister hint of menace by the dark aviator sunglasses he wore and the thought rippled through Summerbee's mind that the individual didn't want them to see his eyes. That, he guessed, was because, as the first copper to ever jail him had said: 'The eyes are the windows of your soul.'

Next to him he noticed Paulie instinctively fingering the Beretta he kept shoulder-holstered inside his leather jacket, and their new associate's sudden focus showed that he had also observed this almost superstitious movement.

Then the male stood up and beckoned his two visitors to take a seat. 'Gentlemen, it's good to meet you at last. My name is Forsyth. Terry Forsyth,' he said in a Scottish accent that was more east than west coast. He offered his hand first to Summerbee and then to Paulie, then the three sat down together.

'It's some place, Mr Summerbee: do you do a lot of business in The Midland Hotel?' asked Forsyth, making small talk as he tried to dial down the tension in the air.

Summerbee had played the game a thousand times before. The exchange of banal small talk, a drink and then the cut to the chase began: it was almost like a rite of passage. And as a white-shirted waiter hovered, Summerbee's single eye locked on Forsyth. 'There is no better place to do business, Mr Forsyth. The Grand Old Lady, as we call her here in Manchester, has been the place to be since it opened way back in the early 1900s. Winston Churchill always stayed here and was particularly partial to feasting on the oysters and champagne. The story goes that Hitler himself coveted the building and had it earmarked as a potential HQ if the Nazis had managed to invade. Plus, if you're looking for dinner, The French is the place to eat, believe me!'

Across the marble-topped table, Summerbee thought he saw a dark eyebrow arch from behind the cover of Forsyth's shades, but the Scot proved that he'd done his homework. 'I believe it's also the place where Rolls met Royce? Aye, it's a pity the roof-terrace tea room isn't still open-garden: must've been a helluva view back in the day?'

For his part, Gallacher was impatient to bring the history lesson to an end. 'That's sound, Mr Forsyth, but I'm sure you would prefer something a bit stronger than a brew! I'd imagine with you being a proud Scot an' that, you'll be partial to a "wee dram", as you might call it?' he asked with a thin smile.

Forsyth reciprocated with a smile of his own and immediately it became clear where Jaws' alias had come from: his smile was brilliant in its golden glow, so many crowns did it have.

A foot to his left, Summerbee saw the slight twitch in Paulie's lips as this almost ludicrous sight threatened to bring his wing-man's renowned impish humour to the surface, and Summerbee hoped for all he was worth that The Midget would keep a still tongue.

Sadly, he was to be disappointed.

'Well, feck me, cock, that's some set of molars you've got there! Christ, that must have cost a few bob!' he said, struggling to bring his eyebrows back down from the twin peaks they had scaled above his opaque grey eyes.

Suddenly the sun was hidden behind a cloud, and Forsyth's mouth snapped shut and his jaw set.

"Christ, Paulie, just what we didn't need. Will you ever learn to shut your gob?" groaned Summerbee's inner voice, but the horse had already bolted.

To his side, Paulie had realised the error of his ways. 'Na, Mr Forsyth, you got me all wrong, I'm buzzing for yer molars, they're pure quality!' And to underline the admission of his error he held both hands up in supplication.

Summerbee was quick to move things on: 'How about we share that bottle of scotch, Mr Forsyth: I'm sure a wee drink would help settle us all down nicely?'

A short while later three crystal whisky glasses were charged and Summerbee hurriedly applied the toast: 'Here's to possibilities,

Mr Forsyth: for let me assure you that with The Maine Men they are limitless!'

The Scot sipped his whisky and replaced the glass on a white lace coaster, his face poker-straight. He carefully removed his sunglasses and slipped them into his suit pocket. When he spoke, his delivery was deadpan: 'I'm sure the possibilities with your crew are endless. First and foremost, I and those behind me are businessmen. We have other options on the table and it would be – pardon the pun – criminal, for me not to explore all of these options before deciding which is best for my organisation,' he said, then reclaimed his whisky glass and took a sip while he surveyed the two men sat opposite him.

Across the table, Summerbee and Gallacher couldn't help but exchange a furtive glance of concern, but before they could say anything, Forsyth once again took the initiative: 'Let's cut to the chase, gentlemen. What I need is guarantees, the bottom line and a figure.'

Despite himself, Summerbee, his agitation clear, moved forward to the edge of his seat. 'What I can guarantee you, Mr Forsyth, is that we have the best distribution network in Manchester and excellent outlets further south, including London. We have the muscle and firepower to guarantee no interference and we will pay better than competitive rates to make the deal happen.' And with that he leant back in his wicker chair and gave a disconcerting lop-sided smile that was exacerbated by the fact the scar where his left eye had once been almost provided a secondary smirk.

Across the marble tabletop, Forsyth steepled his hands, but his lips remained still as he thought over these assurances. 'But that isn't what I've heard, Mr Summerbee,' said Forsyth, stone-faced.

This time it was Summerbee's jaw that tightened. 'Listen, Mr

Forsyth, I'm chuffed that you've done your homework ahead of our meeting and full credit to you. But The Maine Men are the dominant force in this city. By Christ, even dibble won't come onto our streets without calling out the bleedin' army!' he said, trying to calm things down with a bit of humour, his Mancunian roots showing through in his calling the police 'dibble'.

Apparently unconcerned that he might be pushing buttons that could turn their encounter nasty, Forsyth persisted: 'That being so, why don't you tell me about The Devils? I believe they may also feel they are the dominant force, as you termed it, in Manchester right now.'

'United scum!' spat Gallacher, not interested in hiding his contempt for their rivals.

Forsyth was far from impressed. 'They may indeed be, but before I entrust £20 million worth of gear with any organisation I must quite clearly make sure that everything is watertight with them. Because if I don't make sure of that and it all goes belly up, then I will pay for it, Mr Gallacher.'

Summerbee tried to pour oil on troubled waters. 'Listen, Terry, I can only give you my word that we are good to take this all on,' he said, and once again offered his hand.

But Forsyth remained motionless. 'What I need is not cheap words and warm handshakes, I need a down payment. In this game, hard cash speaks far louder than words, as you know... Manny,' he said, imitating Summerbee's obsequious use of his Christian name.

'What ya sayin, Forsyth?' asked Gallacher in his biting Mancunian brogue, his notorious temper fraying.

'I want a down payment of £1 million in cash within three days or the deal is off.'

'Nah man… no way!' spat Gallacher, while Summerbee took a deep breath.

Across the table, Forsyth finished his whisky and started to rise; but his gaze remained trained on Summerbee as if Gallacher didn't exist. 'These are my terms, you can take them or leave them. But one thing I can promise you: your loss will be someone else's gain.'

Summerbee balled his hands into fists with such intensity that his knuckles shone white. Forsyth thought the Mancunian was going to launch himself on him, but when it came his reply was straight to the point: 'Aye, it would appear you don't get owt for nowt.'

15

PERHAPS IT WAS a high-risk strategy; but as Forsyth glided over The Midland's glistening tiled foyer floor and weighed up the odds, he was confident he'd played his hand perfectly.

Now it was down to Summerbee and his minute sidekick to come up with the one million and prove they really were the correct organisation for him to do business with.

By the time the cold night air assailed him, Forsyth was already focussing his mind on his evening's entertainment. He straightened his black moustache out as he started to look forward to a visit to Canal Street and in particular the Manto Club that was right at the heart of the city's gay village.

In truth he hated what he did but at the same time it allowed him to enjoy himself, living his life enveloped in anonymity, indulging his sexual whims from city to city without ever hanging around long enough to be exposed and risk his status as the main dealmaker for the syndicate.

But just as he emerged into the shadow provided by the giant arches of The Midland's entrance, he felt something hard, something cylindrical, pressed firmly against his back.

'Take another step, mate, and it'll be your last.'

Forsyth found his world turned to darkness as his head was enveloped in a hood, while his handgun was removed from inside his jacket and he was half propelled, half dragged down The Midland's elegant steps and bundled into a vehicle.

All just outside the entrance of Manchester's most prestigious hotel.

Forsyth's hands were expertly bound before he had hit the back seat of his transport. He immediately became aware of a presence to his left and quickly did the maths: he realised that he had at least two 'companions' sharing the journey with him, but where that journey was going to take him and why was beyond him.

To his surprise, the next voice he heard was female. 'So, it's the famous Mr Forsyth. I'm ecstatic to meet you,' said his captress in an accent that undoubtedly had a trace of Mancunian but at the same time hinted at an expensive education.

Forsyth tried to regulate his breathing and played the straight bat. 'Who am I speaking to and why have you seen fit to abduct me?' he snapped.

Again, the female spoke, her voice silky but slightly smoky. 'You do business with the blue half of the city and think the red half won't be interested and you are a very naive man, Mr Forsyth. I believe that is anything but the case. So, we are taking you for a short ride and then we will sit you down and have a nice sociable chat and see where that takes us.'

But Forsyth was not prepared to sit back and enjoy the ride. 'At least do me the courtesy of letting me know who you are,' he snapped.

Her presence closer to him was underlined by the scent, however slight, of her perfume and the realisation was something that left Forsyth feeling singularly disconcerted: for it was the Chanel No. 5 that his mother, a dancer who had appeared on every stage of Glasgow's five major theatres, had loved. 'We are people who happen to think you would be making a big mistake to do business with Summerbee and his vertically challenged flunky; people who think that you would be well advised to hear us out before you risk your life on a deal with the one-eyed blue devil.'

From inside the hood, Forsyth maintained a determined silence; for he did not know what to say. He had only one option: to sit tight and see how the cards fell.

Ten minutes elapsed before a gradual slowing down of the powerful diesel engine hinted that their destination was almost at hand and an unsympathetic application of the handbrake brought the vehicle firmly to a stop.

Then her scent again drifted through the hood and Forsyth started to remember the words his mother had spoken when he'd first asked her as a 10-year-old kid what perfume she was wearing: "Because, Terry, my darling, if it was good enough for Marilyn Monroe, it is good enough for Arlene Forsyth!" And then he replayed the loving cuddle he had received in the warmth of his mother's arms.

But now, that Chanel No. 5 was being worn by a very different female to his mother, and one who was wielding the power of life and death over him.

'Get Goldtooth here out,' snapped this Amazon and again Forsyth thought that the use of the nickname was at odds with an accent that hinted at so much more than some hard-bitten female gangster.

The door to his right cracked open and two powerful hands grabbed him by the shoulders and dragged him out of the seat, keeping him upright when he seemed about to hit the ground.

Again he was propelled, roughshod, around the vehicle, until the palm of a light but firm hand slapped into his chest. 'It's time you saw the light, Mr Forsyth: after all, you are about to enter a place of worship!' sneered the female.

Her words were no sooner spoken than the hood was whipped from his head and Forsyth found himself, despite having only been kept in the dark for around ten minutes, blinking furiously as he tried to regain his sight.

The first thing he saw were the imposing twin towers of a red brick church and the look of confusion that crossed his face as his gaze lowered to meet his hostess's brought a sliver of laughter from her.

She was five foot six, max, had shoulder-length jet-black and a smouldering but cruel beauty that fascinated but also hinted that she was not the sort to take fools lightly.

In short, thought Forsyth, she had 'don't mess' written all over her.

'Welcome to All Souls, Mr Forsyth. I just hope we can save yours before it's too late!' And again she laughed, this time with a harshness that implied that the joke could well be all on Forsyth.

To her right stood a slapheaded enforcer whose muscled torso was barely restrained by his Berghaus. Forsyth noted a tattoo of what looked like a devil holding a fork sprouting up his neck and above the hood and collar of the coat.

So, it was confirmed. They had to be The Devils, the sworn and deadly rivals of The Maine Men, and the taunting words of the female – of whom the voice inside his head asked "Gina Lollobrigida or Audrey Hepburn?" for some reason – came back to taunt him: "You do business with the blue half of the city and think the red half won't be interested and you are a very naive man, Mr Forsyth."

Forsyth gave a rueful nod of his head. The Devils, and the only female in the organisation with this much clout had to be none other than Lisa Crerand.

But Lisa had already turned and was making her way through the arched stone doorway.

Looking beyond his captress, Forsyth saw that the building, which was surely derelict, was in darkness; but as he was shoved through the entrance, enough illumination was, appropriately, provided by candlelight.

His progress was once again brought to a firm halt when a rough hand held him fast. Twenty feet away, he could see that Lisa was deep in conversation with a silver-haired male who remained seated, his back towards Forsyth and the goon who restrained him.

While he waited for whatever they had planned to unfold, Forsyth took in the sights of All Souls and found a sadness starting to envelop him. He was not a religious man, but his family had been Presbyterian and he recognised all the signs that confirmed this once thriving religious edifice was now closed for the purpose it had been built.

A mausoleum to the dying religion of Christianity. The thought always made Forsyth feel guilty.

At last Lisa looked up and signalled to Slaphead to bring him forward.

As he walked along the threadbare red carpet that ran the length of the central aisle, Forsyth's attention was drawn to the walls on either side of the pulpit, which displayed brass memorial panels in tribute to the fallen of two world wars.

His progress stilled once he had just about drawn level with Lisa and the seated man. As Forsyth turned his gaze on him, the resemblance between the two was unmistakeable.

For although the man's silvery fair hair set him around the late 50s mark, everything else about him, from the piercing gaze and strong jaw to the aquiline nose, suggested he was her father.

When his mouth opened, the voice that emerged was even and steady:

> 'They shall grow not old, as we are left grow old:
> Age shall not weary them, nor the years condemn.
> At the going down of the sun and in the morning,
> We will remember them.'

The man brought out his hands from the pockets of a charcoal covert coat and sprang to his feet with an explosion of movement that suggested he was an individual who had long taken pride in physical fitness. He turned to Forsyth, and the power of his blue gaze underlined he was someone who was not to be messed with.

'Sit down, Mr Forsyth: in fact, why don't you grab a pew?' he suggested, extending an open palm and smiling at his own joke.

Forsyth did as he was bid and took a seat on the front pew to the left of the central aisle. Completely at a loss as to what was going to happen, he stayed quiet.

A couple of feet away from him, his host sat down and carefully pulled the knees of his immaculately pressed suit trousers up, before crossing his legs. 'You know, it always fills me with sadness when I come to visit All Souls: sadness at what has befallen this place, sadness at the dying of the religion I was brought up in, sadness for my grandfather...' – he stopped for a moment and pointed to the right-hand brass plate – 'Patrick Crerand: you can see his name in the list of the fallen, there, 11 down, middle row, Lance Corporal Patrick Crerand, 8th South Lancs Regiment. Indeed, the grandfather I never knew, and by Christ he would be turning in his grave if he had seen what had befallen his church.'

At last, Forsyth had confirmation as to who he was dealing with and he took the opportunity to speak: 'So, if I may hazard a guess… Mr Crerand? Why have you brought me here to All Souls?'

'My name is indeed Gordon Crerand and…' – he leaned back and smiled over his shoulder at the dark-haired woman who was now sitting in the pew behind them, her jaw resting on hands clasped on top of the backrest – 'of course you have already enjoyed the pleasure of my daughter Lisa's company!' And with that a thin smile appeared across his angular features: but Forsyth did not miss the wink that passed between father and daughter.

Forsyth's impatience and frustration began to boil over. 'Perhaps in more civilised circumstances I might agree that it was a pleasure: but I can hardly call being dragged off the steps of The Midland Hotel, hands bound, head hooded, and put in fear of my life an enjoyable experience. Was it really necessary, Mr Crerand? Do you have any clue who I represent?'

Crerand slowly turned his gaze from his daughter so that his chiselled features presented directly in front of Forsyth; then he let his blue gaze impale the Scot. 'Was it necessary? Time will tell, Mr Forsyth.'

Crerand got back up from the pew and paced towards the memorial for the fallen. 'Their name liveth for evermore, to the glory of God, and in perpetual memory of the churchmen of this parish and congregation, who gave their lives in The Great War, 1914–18, this tablet and the memorial cross in the churchyard are erected by their fellow churchmen,' he quoted, clearly from memory.

Then he turned around to face Forsyth once again. 'That is the inscription on the memorial cross that stands at the back of

All Souls, the cross my grandmother brought me to most every Sunday afternoon and where she laid a yellow rose for Papa Paddy. She never forgot him, not until the day she died, God bless her.' Crerand gave a deep sigh and such was the emotion on his taut, pale features, Forsyth thought tears were not far away; but Crerand had not finished his eulogy to a lost generation.

'My grandfather's generation now lie forgotten in their graves and their place of worship in ruin, betrayed by the society they gave their lives to preserve. Do you know that in 1960 the church of St Andrew merged with All Souls and that their memorial plaque was relocated here, only to be stolen and sold for scrap? Now the names of their fallen are lost for all eternity,' said Crerand, the contempt in his voice lacing every word with extra bite.

Bemused, Forsyth attempted to placate his host, increasingly disconcerted by this history lesson and requiem to the fallen of All Souls: 'It is disgusting, Mr Crerand, I grant you that… but I'm not quite sure what it has to do with me?'

Again, Crerand's blue gaze burnt through him. 'The point I am making, Mr Forsyth, is that I don't like change, I don't like disrespect. When I come across it, I make those who desecrate what I revere and hold dear… pay,' he said, the vehemence that coursed through the final sentence leaving the Scot in no doubt that this was being directed at him; but he was still confused as to his own part in all this.

'You are a vain man, are you not, Mr Forsyth?' asked Crerand, again taking his guest by surprise at the change of tack in his conversation.

'Excuse me?' asked Forsyth.

Once again Crerand was pacing in front of the woodworm-rotten pulpit. He continued his sermon, arms outspread: 'But the

Lord said to Samuel, "Do not consider his appearance or his height, for I have rejected him. The Lord does not look at the things people look at. People look at the outward appearance, but the Lord looks at the heart," 1 Samuel, Chapter 16, verse 7, Forsyth.'

'What? Are you mad?' snapped Forsyth.

But Crerand's attention had returned to his daughter and he gave her a brief nod and repeated the process to the two Neanderthals at the back of the church.

Then Crerand strode forward and clamped a hand on Forsyth's jaw. 'Open wide, Mr Forsyth,' he said amenably enough, and when Forsyth kept his mouth shut tight, he rammed his two thumbs into his jaw, until finally the Scot's mouth sprang.

'Just as we were told, well, you have spent a fair few quid on these monstrosities. Your vanity is beyond question,' preached Crerand.

Squirming in Crerand's vicelike grip, Forsyth tried to plead for mercy: he had already realised that something wicked was coming his way. But his captor straddled him and rammed his body back against the pew, pinioning him to the seat.

The strands of Crerand's wispy silvery mane dropped loose across his forehead as he struggled to restrain his captive and then a smile of malevolent delight surfed across his face. 'Bring me the pliers and I will be about the Lord's work!' spat Crerand, his ice-blue eyes pulsing and manic.

16

FORSYTH'S FRANTIC struggling was to no avail, as from either side Slaphead and the other previously unseen henchman, a ginger-haired worthy with a thin scar down his right cheek and a tattoo of the devil holding the fork protruding from above his dark Berghaus, materialised.

They pinioned Forsyth to the rear of the pew by his shoulders and forced his thrashing legs to still. Crerand took a step back and momentarily was joined by Lisa. 'Your forceps, doctor,' she said, and as she passed the metal pliers to her father they both shared a laugh.

Forsyth, his mouth now unimpeded, pleaded for mercy: 'For God's sake, Crerand, you are clearly a religious man and yet you would defile this place of religion with an act of barbarity against an innocent man who has come to Manchester on a legitimate business trip. How can that be the Lord's work as you say? Surely we can talk this over, man?'

Crerand smiled sardonically, his countenance taking on a wolf-ish appearance, as the relish that was building inside him started to pulse from his being. 'An innocent man who has come to Manchester on legitimate business? Where do I start, Forsyth? Legitimate business? You are a drug dealer who has come to my city to agree terms to flood Manchester with your poison. Innocent man? You are a deviant and a sodomite are you not…?' And Crerand let his words trail off into silence as he savoured the reaction on his tormented captive's desperate, heaving features.

Forsyth pleaded his innocence: 'I... I... don't know what you mean? Can't we just have a civilised discussion and clear up this misunderstanding. I have agreed nothing with Summerbee, there is still a deal to be made,' he pleaded, but he had badly misjudged his tormentor.

Crerand's eyes turned gimlet. He exploded with rage as he bounded forward and barrelled his way between his two enforcers, before clamping the fingers of his right hand on Forsyth's jaw. 'A deal to be made, a deal that will see me pollute my own streets and poison future generations? What do you take me for, you piece of vermin?'

But Forsyth was in no position to reply. His eyes bulged and strained at their sockets and he started to drool from his open mouth.

Inches away, Crerand had regained his composure and a cold fury emanated from his eyes as he started to quote from the Good Book once again: 'For from within, out of the heart of man, come evil thoughts, sexual immorality, theft, murder, adultery, coveting, wickedness, deceit, sensuality, envy, slander, pride, foolishness. All these evil things come from within, and they defile a person.'

Then to Forsyth's horror the pliers started to descend into his mouth and clamped onto a golden molar in the upper-left section. The Scot felt an agonising dull snap as they clamped onto either side of his golden crown and he made one last desperate bid to break free.

Instead, he found himself held down even more firmly by the two brutes, and Crerand, his blue orbs shining bright, yanked with all his might on the crown. As the golden tooth began to loosen, Crerand could hear the tear in his head as it pulled at the roots of his gum, even above the sounds of his own screams, and then with an almighty snap Crerand staggered back, raising his trophy above him.

Opposite him, blood and tissue spewed from Forsyth's mouth and the two henchmen who had previously pinioned him let him go, their vile features lit large with vicious smiles.

'Loosen his bonds,' commanded Crerand, and Slaphead immediately did so, allowing Forsyth to clamp his fingers to his mouth as he attempted to stem the flow of blood and mucous.

Crerand took a step forward and against the backdrop of the flickering candlelight he produced a white handkerchief. 'This should help,' he said, as if he was offering a friend a dutiful kindness.

Forsyth's whole being was quivering with the shock of what had just happened to him, but he grabbed the hanky and slapped it against his mouth while a few feet away Crerand examined the golden crown before tossing it over to Lisa, who caught it in a transparent polythene bag.

Then he took a step forward to Forsyth and wiped his bloody hands down the sides of his captive's previously immaculate Hugo Boss suit. 'Let me once again quote from the Good Book, Mr Forsyth. Leviticus 24:19–21 reads: "And if a man cause a blemish in his neighbour; as he hath done, so shall it be done to him; breach for breach, eye for eye, tooth for tooth: as he hath caused a blemish in a man, so shall it be done to him again. And he that killeth a beast, he shall restore it: and he that killeth a man, he shall be put to death."'

Slowly Crerand sat back down on the pew, all the time his blue eyes menacing Forsyth. 'Now you go back from where you have come, my Scotch friend, and tell your organisation that there will be none of their vile poison coming to my city... unless I say so, do you understand me?'

Forsyth, still dabbing furiously at the cavity left by the enforced departure of his golden molar, snivelled and gurgled as he tried to remove some of the detritus from his treasured moustache.

Then, at last regaining some composure and controlling his own hyperventilation, he managed to nod his head in the affirmative as he tried to come to terms with this apparent volte-face.

'You see, Forsyth, we know all about you and your "gang",' spat Crerand. 'Indeed, we have been waiting for you and I can tell you this: although I will allow you the freedom to return to your Scotch midden and bring the news of our meeting and my offer to those that pull your strings, let me make you one promise...' Forsyth lowered the hanky and stared with hatred into Crerand's eyes. 'You will be wasting your time doing any deal with Summerbee and his dwarf, for while I may already have removed one eye from his head, I will be returning to smite him once and for all,' said Crerand, gritting his teeth at the impending retribution he had planned for his sworn enemy.

17

THOROUGHGOOD stared over the top of his cards and tried to work out just what was lying behind Paddy Greene's best poker face.

'Come on, Paddy, we have ten minutes before we are due in at Manchester Piccadilly, play your hand and be done, man, it's not as if I've managed to win a sodding sausage off you so far,' snapped an exasperated Thoroughgood.

Across the carriage table, DS Paddy Greene wagged his finger and pointed to the pile of shrapnel on the plastic-topped table to their left. 'Aye, that little lot will certainly take care of a few pints of bitter or whatever the local delicacy is and…' – he paused theatrically to pucker his lips and blow Thoroughgood a kiss – 'it is far likelier to be put to better use in my pocket than yours, pup!'

Opposite him, Thoroughgood narrowed his eyes and said mockingly: 'Jeez, if you don't play it soon, I'll be an old dog… just like you, gaffer!'

'What was it that Uncle Oscar once said about the young?' asked Greene, his words delivered in as patronising a fashion as possible.

'The quote I think you are looking for is that "youth is wasted on the young" and it is indeed attributed to Oscar Wilde. Now will you please play your hand,' pleaded Thoroughgood.

Greene smirked knowingly and shook his head. 'But patience is a virtue, ADC Thoroughgood, and one that you'd do well to remember!' And with that slapped his hand down with a theatrical flourish.

Across the table, Thoroughgood's eyes bulged in astonishment. 'A royal flush! How the hell did you manage that?'

Safe in the knowledge that his hand was unbeatable, Greene was already shepherding the silver into his pockets. 'Aye, it was a pleasure doing business with you, young fella, but a word of warning: I'd brush up on your poker fast, because Marty Ferguson is a card sharp and if I was you I wouldn't be rushing to sit down with him any time soon, 'cause the stakes are sure to be a damn sight higher than shrapnel!'

Before Thoroughgood could think of a suitable answer, the train intercom advised that arrival at Manchester Piccadilly was imminent, and looking out of the window he began to see the station loom large.

Five minutes later they were stood in the main station foyer waiting for the promised rendezvous. While an increasingly impatient Greene checked his Accurist for the second time, Thoroughgood stood watching the madding crowd ebb and flow as the rush hour took hold, his hands inside his Harrington, his rucksack between his feet.

'We were supposed to be getting picked up at 4 pm by one of Fergie's boys? I don't know about you, Thoroughgood, but after that rotten British Rail coffee, I could murder a beer,' moaned Greene, ripping his raincoat off and slinging it over his shoulder.

But they didn't have much longer to wait and on Thoroughgood's right flank a Mancunian voice snapped the ADC from his people watching. 'Hey up, if it isn't Strathclyde Police's answer to Bodie and Doyle! DS Greene and DC Thoroughgood, I presume?' asked the male, his moustache creasing in appreciation at his own quip.

His face was framed by a pair of thick, square glasses and he sported a mustard turtleneck underneath a checked sports jacket that Thoroughgood thought looked like it could have been a charity shop job that had been saved from the 70s.

Struggling to stop his disapproval becoming all too evident, the young ADC was saved by Greene leaning across him and pulling rank with an outstretched paw. 'Indeed it is! DS Paddy Greene and ADC Angus Thoroughgood, we're here to RV with officers of the GMP Flying Squad, which I'm assuming will be yourself?' said Greene, in somewhat inflated fashion.

An amused sparkle flickered through the shrewd green eyes behind the almost milk-bottle-thick NHS glasses. 'Of course you are, luv!' he said, before accepting the DS's outstretched mitt and adding: 'DC Wally Morgan, chuffed to meet ya.' But when Thoroughgood offered his hand, he found that Morgan had already started to turn away. 'Follow me. The DCI is waiting outside in his motor.'

With barely a backward glance, Morgan's Hush Puppies set a furious pace, which Greene soon found himself falling off, while Thoroughgood, his Army & Navy rucksack clamped to his back, remained firmly on his tail.

He had taken an instant dislike to the DC. Admittedly it was early days, but on first appearances Morgan seemed to represent everything the ADC hated about the cynically weary 'seen it all before' CID officer who figured the world owed him a living, and Thoroughgood took great delight in catching Morgan's heel.

'You fuckin' stupid Jock, watch what you're doin' will ya?' rapped Morgan furiously before bursting through the station's swinging glass doors and heading straight for the taxi rank outside, where a commotion seemed to be brewing.

For a silver BMW 5 Series had managed to insert itself right in the middle of the black-hack taxi rank, its driver nowhere to be seen. The outraged cabbies surrounding it were clearly less than impressed by the transgression.

A couple of feet in front of him, Morgan summed up the brewing altercation in eloquent fashion: 'Ah shit, it's all kickin' off!'

Indeed it was. But while the driver's seat and front passenger seat were empty, the rear-passenger nearside door flew open with an almighty snap that ended in it sending two of the angry cabbies sprawling. Out of the back of the Beamer unfolded a red-haired giant with a vicious Glaswegian accent. 'What's wrong with you lot? Did mummy drop a packet of Smarties and they all turned out to be brave pills. This…' said the giant, brandishing a photographic ID card as if it was some biblical artefact with divine powers, 'is a Greater Manchester Police Warrant Card which allows me, DCI Marty Ferguson, to police the streets of this shithole as I see fit – in any way I see fit! – which will help me preserve life and keep the good people of Manchester safe… and you assorted cockroaches are obstructing my divine and unquestionable right to do so.'

As Ferguson stopped to take a breath, the two fallen cabbies started to regain their feet, with the help of their mates, and a circle of braying taxi drivers began to assail the good DCI from all sides with a torrent of profanity delivered in fermented Mancunian.

'Who do you think you are, you mad Scots bastard? You have no right to encroach on our taxi rank!' snapped one bow-legged individual with a perm that was clearly an attempt to take 20 years off his appearance but instead left him looking utterly ridiculous.

'Now, now, my friend, there is no need to be having a strop when an officer of the law is merely doing his job. I am here to collect two notorious felons from their train and merely waiting on my colleague…' Ferguson's words tapered off, the fire and brimstone from his initial rant now evaporating in the face of a renewed surge from the enraged cabbies, as he saw Morgan and his two new colleagues.

Standing next to the cynical DC, Thoroughgood quickly fished out his cuffs and slapped them onto Morgan's wrists, who snapped: 'What the fuck do you think you're doing, mate?'

But a couple of feet to his left flank, Greene, who had arrived just in time to take in the furore, had seen the wink Thoroughgood had sent him, and although he was uncertain of what the ADC was up to, clearly felt playing along was the best idea.

As Morgan's verbal protest started to develop into an attempt to pull his now handcuffed hands free from Thoroughgood's grip, the ADC dragged him forward and started to elbow his way through the outraged cabbies circling DCI Ferguson. 'Please make way. DC Thoroughgood with a prisoner for the custody of DCI Ferguson,' he said.

Greene got in on the act: 'Clear a path, if you don't mind: we have a dangerous felon here who must be taken to the confines of Manchester City Centre nick ASAP. Please, for your own safety, give ground and back off.'

The not-so-subtle subterfuge had the desired effect and the rage that had previously threatened to engulf Ferguson now gave way to a bewildered concern that the cabbies were actually obstructing important police work.

Ferguson wasn't slow to pick up the baton and run with it: 'Thank you, gentlemen, yes, that's it, one more hoodlum off the streets and you gentlemen that bit safer to ply your lawful trade.' He smiled benignly before applying a semi-mocking thumbs-up, as something of his previous unshakeable confidence returned.

By this time, Thoroughgood had manhandled the becalmed Morgan into the backseat of the Beamer, while Ferguson jumped into the driver's seat and Greene the front passenger position.

'Aye, you and your pup saved my bacon, Paddy son!' laughed Ferguson as he rammed the gear stick into first and hit the horn hard.

A smile of smug self-satisfaction enveloped Greene's fleshy features and he replied: 'Just like old times, boss!' The Beamer screeched out of Manchester Piccadilly almost on two wheels, leaving a crowd of previously seething cabbies wondering if they had indeed just witnessed the events of the previous minutes or if it had all been some surreal dream.

18

THOROUGHGOOD observed the reunion of Ferguson and Greene, a meeting of two old comrades, with fascination as the two swapped stories of their time spent in the Scottish Crime Squad back in Glasgow; but his eavesdropping on their trip down memory lane was brought to an abrupt end with a sharp elbow in his side from Morgan.

'Sorry to mither, but do you mind springin' the chuffin' cuffs, young 'un?' asked Morgan, making it clear that he was anything but sorry.

The sharp dunt to his ribs certainly got Thoroughgood's attention, and for a moment he eyeballed Morgan and received an icy green stare in return. 'Show a bit of gratitude, pal, and I might just,' he snapped.

From the front seat, DCI Ferguson's grey gaze was reading the warning signs in the back. 'Boys, boys, I don't expect you two to become instant bessies, but I do expect you to be able to work together. Now…Thoroughgood, isn't it?' he asked.

'ADC Angus Thoroughgood, sir,' replied the young CID aide a little too formally, something he immediately regretted.

'Excellent, I'll call you Gus, a right good Scots name if ever there was one. Be a good chap and let Wally free, we don't want him bleatin' about his lily-white wrists getting chafed red raw now, do we?' replied Ferguson with an informal order.

'Yes sir,' replied Thoroughgood, distinctly aware of how uncertain the verbal ground was.

'Look, son, I saw exactly what you did back there, it was quick thinking, and don't worry, I know Paddy well enough to ken he'd take the credit for being first man on the moon if he could bloody well get away with it! You got me out of a sticky wee situation with that bunch of mongrels. Soddin' taxi drivers think they are a law unto themselves and sometimes – just sometimes, mind – I like to get it right up 'em and… well, they throw a right old strop. So, what I'm sayin', Gus, is gracias amigo. But just forget about the formalities; from here on you may simply refer to me as Boss, comprendy?' And Ferguson's crooked smile lit up his rear-view mirror.

In the back seat, Thoroughgood had already sprung the whinge-ing Morgan free and didn't bother to hide how much he liked what he'd just heard. 'No problem, Boss!' he replied.

'Excellent! Now Paddy, my old chum, as they say in Manc, I'm gagging for it and I would imagine, given the jet lag, so are you?' he winked at Greene.

'That's the understatement of the decade, Marty! Where are you taking us?' asked Greene.

From the back seat, Morgan beat his gaffer to the punch: 'The Lass O'Gowrie, on Charles Street, it's our informal HQ and they are expecting us, Boss.'

'Good man, Wally. I knew there was a reason you were on my team. Now before we get there let me bring you up to speed with a few things you need to know about the local state of affairs, lads,' said Ferguson.

'We're all ears!' replied Greene.

'Okay, you better tighten your seat belt, Paddy my boy. As you are aware from the briefing pack you received, we are known as the Flying Squad, and that's because we have a roving remit, which is whatever I want to make of it – or, more importantly, whatever Mad Myra wants us to turn our hands too,' said Ferguson.

From the back seat, Thoroughgood couldn't help ask the obvious question: 'Who is Mad Myra, Boss?'

'Assistant Chief Constable Crime Michelle Trautmann is the lady in question and once you see her striking blonde baret you will understand where she gets the nickname from!' replied Ferguson with a knowing roll of his eyes before continuing on with his monologue: 'Now I know you're down here to nick this scrote Forsyth, but we are going to need your help on a wee op that is linked to him and his skulduggery, and I'm afraid we are against the clock on it,' concluded Ferguson just as he swung the BMW out of Oxford Road and onto Hulme Street. 'But first things first: a drink! Right now, we are not just going to a boozer, we are going to partake of refreshment in one of the fine city of Manchester's most historic pubs,' he said.

A foot away from him, Greene remained sceptical. 'It's not like you, Marty, a proud Scotsman, to be using an Irish pub, when I'm sure there are plenty of boozers draped in tartan to choose from.'

'Aah, but there's the rub,' said Ferguson, applying the handbrake as he brought the Beamer to an abrupt stop outside an impressive Victorian red-tiled building. 'We may have just arrived in the centre of mickdom but The Lass O'Gowrie is as Scots a boozer as they come! Now follow me, my brave boys!' the Boss said, beckoning proudly before almost vaulting out of the driver's seat.

The pub was, Thoroughgood had to admit, pretty much his perfect idea of what a traditional English city pub should be. All Victorian red and green, emanating comfort and friendliness. To top it off, a bridge ran behind the pub and from beneath it the sound of rushing water could be clearly made out; even if the pungent smell of the river could be as well.

But Ferguson was not a man to be kept waiting and he had now taken up a position on the edge of the pavement while he gazed admiringly at what had perhaps once been a doorway, but now was tiled up to about shoulder height, a history of the pub engraved on it.

'Right, Curly, I suggest you get 'em in and make sure you have the rest of the Squad assembled in the snug at the back while I give our uncouth Scots friends a wee history lesson!' he said, then barked a short sharp laugh as Morgan scuttled off.

'Let me take you back, back to the peak of the Victorian era and the late 1800s. This area is known as Little Ireland, due, of course, to the large numbers of Irish immigrant labourers living, working and dying in the unregulated squalor of industrialised Manchester and its notorious middens. This, my boys, was a place where gut-wrenching poverty, utter filth and hardship beyond belief were tossed into one giant cooking pot. Add a little blood, sweat and tears, a generous sprinkling of exploitation, greed and outright evil and you have a cesspit of human misery as vile as anything anywhere else in Victorian Britain,' said Ferguson with clear feeling.

Opposite him, Thoroughgood and Greene were mesmerised.

'You, my dear Paddy, being proud second-generation Irish, might well expect, and rightly so, that the landlord of this fine establishment would, of course, be one of your brethren, but no... he was chosen from God's people... he was, of course, a Scot!' crowed the Boss.

Utterly absorbed, Thoroughgood couldn't help himself: 'Hence the poem The Lass O'Gowrie by Lady Carolina Nairne. So, he was not only a Scot but a homesick Scot!'

A couple of feet away, Ferguson looked like the wind had been taken out of his sails. 'Well blow me, Dennis Numan was right, you are a clever little sod, ain't you, Thoroughgood! What's the degree again? Medieval mumbo jumbo?'

Despite himself, Thoroughgood's shoulders went back. 'An MA Hons in Scottish, British and European Medieval History from Glasgow University… sir,' he replied, showing his respect a little too late.

Ferguson closed the gap between the two of them quicker than a bolt of lightning and grabbed Thoroughgood by his Harrington, lifting until the ADC was on tiptoes, and even then he still wasn't face-to-face with the DCI. 'Well, a right little clever Dick, ain't you, son! With all that education behind you it would be a shame to waste it, so, if you don't mind, ADC smart-arse Thoroughgood, you will recite The Lass O'Gowrie right here with the feeling that befits a proud Scotsman abroad paying his respects to a forbearer who helped provide relief from the misery of the masses.'

As Ferguson released him from his vice-like grip, the young CID aide looked over to Greene for some kind of help and was met with a shrug of the shoulders.

A yard away, Ferguson made it clear his patience was wearing thin. 'It's make or break time, son. Now get to it or you can get on the first sleeper back to Glasgow,' he rapped.

Thoroughgood cleared his throat. A quiver in his voice, he at last began his recital:

"Twas on a summer's afternoon,
A wee afore the sun gaed down,
A lassie wi' a braw new gown
Cam' ower the hills to Gowrie.
The rosebud wash'd in summer's shower

102

Bloom'd fresh within the sunny bower;
But Kitty was the fairest flower
That e'er was seen in Gowrie.'

It was a stuttering, self-conscious delivery and at the end of the first verse Thoroughgood drew to a stop, hoping that his ordeal was over.

A foot away, the Boss stood unimpressed, his arms folded and the left foot of his tan brogues tapping a furious tattoo on the pavement.

'Are you deaf, son? I said with feeling. I want to hear a 1990 version of Rabbie Burns delivering this, I want tears, I want passion, not some pathetic, stammering, snivelling excuse of a mumble.' The elevation of Ferguson's eyebrows made it clear Thoroughgood had entered the last chance saloon, never mind The Lass O'Gowrie.

Again, Thoroughgood cleared his throat; despite himself, he suddenly felt ashamed that he had somehow let down the legacy that belonged to Lady Carolina's famous work. Nodding his head to Ferguson, he began to crank up the volume and deliver his passion play:

'To see her cousin she cam' there,
And oh! the scene was passin' fair,
For what in Scotland can compare
Wi' the Carse o' Gowrie?
The sun was setting on the Tay,
The blue hills melting into grey;
The mavis and the blackbird's lay
Were sweetly heard in Gowrie.'

The second verse completed, Thoroughgood started to breathe again, almost. He stole a quick look at Ferguson, and to his relief he received a slight inclination of his red side-shed. 'Pass marks, boy, pass marks: but I'd say still room for improvement. What do you think, DS Greene? Has the boy done good or must he do better?'

Greene, his hands shoved deep inside his raincoat, despite the watery sun above, couldn't help a mischievous semi-grin creasing his fleshy folds. 'Oh, I'm firmly in the must-do-better camp, Marty!'

'You may proceed, boy, but the jury remains unconvinced, I can tell you!' quipped Ferguson.

Once again, Thoroughgood, aware that a couple of regulars loitering outside the main door on their way into The Lass were clearly enjoying his ritual humiliation, did his best to discourage their attendance by shooting them his most intimidating cop-stare. It backfired spectacularly.

'Nice one, cock,' said the nearest male, who looked like he'd just arrived from a Blur concert.

Thoroughgood gritted his teeth, but before a hot retort could leave his lips, Ferguson spoke with his best sergeant-major delivery: 'You are spoiling the moment, boy, and if you don't get your finger out your bloody arse I will haul it over that soddin' wall down there and toss you into the Medlock. Now get a bloody move on, will you!'

Thoroughgood took a deep breath, then launched into the third verse:

'O, lang the lassie I had woo'd,
An' truth an' constancy had vow'd,
But cam' nae speed wi' her I lo'ed
Until she saw fair Gowrie.
Yon bonnie bield ayont the shaw,

Sae loun' that there nae blast could blaw,
Wad she no bide in Gowrie?'

The hot surge of temper that had fired through him had done the trick and every word was delivered with feeling as the nerve-wracked orator at last warmed to his task and began to enjoy himself.

But as he completed the third stanza, the creaking of the pub's unoiled front door once again drew Thoroughgood's attention to the boozer. It was clear that the second regular had brought his friends.

And they weren't just regulars: for slap-bang in the middle of the crowd was the footballer's perm of DC Wally Morgan, who took great delight in raising his pint pot in mock salute.

'Go on, our kid, give it laldy!' he shouted, while behind him a voluptuous brunette in a pencil skirt winked at Thoroughgood wolfishly. 'Come on, pet, don't be shy!'

The finishing line was nearly in sight, just one more verse to get through, and if it rubber-stamped his return ticket to Glasgow, Thoroughgood was determined to go out on his shield.

Summoning up all the emotion and feeling he possessed, he cast his mind back to the Burns supper he had attended in his final year at Glasgow Uni and took inspiration from his theatrical delivery of Tam o' Shanter.

Turning to the assembled crowd of cops and regulars he produced a mock bow. 'It will be my pleasure,' he said, unfurling an arm with some flourish and then turning to Ferguson and Greene. To their disbelief, he winked.

A yard away, Ferguson muttered: 'Well blow me senseless!'

Thoroughgood quickly made sure that he had the last verse consigned to memory. Then he pulled a white handkerchief from inside his Harrington and swept it before him. He stood back, hands on hips, addressing the crowd:

'Her faither was baith glad and wae;
Her mither she wad naething say;
The bairnies thocht they wad get play;
If Kitty gaed to Gowrie.'

A predatory wolf whistle from the brunette interrupted Thoroughgood and almost threw his composure completely.

Nevertheless, he was determined to go down fighting and before he could stifle it, his inner voice broke free: 'Feel free to put a Lagavulin behind the bar, darlin'!'

But from behind him, Ferguson's gruff voice brought Thoroughgood back to the here and now with a bang: 'Boy!'

Pirouetting on a six pence in a fashion that Dennis Law would have been proud of, he turned round and began to walk slowly in what could only be described as a semi-mince towards Ferguson and Greene while he completed the final four lines of The Lass O'Gowrie:

'She whiles did smile, she whiles did greet,
The blush and tear were on her cheek;
She naething said, an' hung her head;
But now she's Leddy Gowrie.'

As he drew to a close, Thoroughgood dropped to a knee, in a position halfway between the DCI and Greene and the spellbound boozers; then taking a deep bow he swept the hanky flamboyantly across his brow, dropped his head and shut his eyes, praying for a favourable reaction.

A wave of applause and cheering engulfed him; but just as he was considering an encore, two powerful hands clamped onto his

Harrington, and looking up, Thoroughgood once more found the Boss staring down at him.

'You'll do for me, boy, that was bloody marvellous! Now for Chrissakes come inside and let me buy you a mint Guinness!' And with that Ferguson hauled Thoroughgood to his feet and enveloped him in a giant arm. The duo, Greene lagging in their wake, strode towards The Lass O'Gowrie, the applauding punters parting like the Red Sea.

As they passed the crowd, an earthy voice said: 'Well, you're quite the showman!' and the brunette puckered a pair of ruby-red lips his way.

A foot away, Thoroughgood's face started to turn the same colour.

19

THE LASS O'GOWRIE was Thoroughgood's idea of heaven, all dark wood, warmth and real ale.

Ferguson dragged him through the boozer towards the snug at the rear. Morgan was already in place with two pints of what appeared to be Guinness with a sprig of mint sprouting out of the stout's creamy head.

Ferguson ripped his overcoat off and threw it at the coat stand in the corner, which promptly toppled over under the weight of the garment's embrace. 'Bastard!' snapped the Boss.

He immediately inclined his head Morgan's way to make sure he would right the uprooted stand, then took the two pints his DC was holding with either hand and slammed one into Thoroughgood's midriff, causing the black stuff to slop over and land on the ADC's Sambas.

Ferguson winked malevolently. 'Have a drink of this sheer nectar and I promise you, Gus my boy, you will never want to drink anything else!' Then he daintily pushed the mint sprig to the opposite side of his pint pot and took a deep draft, all the while eyeing Thoroughgood over the rim, waiting for the ADC to do the same.

Realising that once again he had no other choice but to comply with another of Ferguson's bizarre 'cultural' challenges, Thoroughgood shrugged and did as he was bid.

A lager man to his core, preferring Stella Artois or Fürstenberg, he'd never been a big fan of the black stuff, but as he took a mouthful and savoured the Guinness, he had to admit that with the mint sprig it was indeed 'made of more'.

A yard away, Ferguson wiped the cream moustache from the top of his mouth with the back of a massive paw and said: 'Are you getting how the chocolaty notes of the Guinness are complemented by the freshness of the mint? Now, boy, I want you to take another mouthful and have a guess at what the secret ingredient is.'

Thoroughgood found himself nodding his head in an inadvertent admission that it wasn't too bad at all, and he needed no extra persuasion to take a second draft. This time he swirled it around in his mouth and tried to come up with a guess; but it was like finding a needle in a haystack.

A moment later, he had to state the bleeding obvious: 'Sorry, Boss, I don't have a bloody scooby!'

Ferguson raised his eyebrows in mock shock and turning to his audience, he held out his non-Guinness-holding hand in a gesture of despair. 'Okay, son, I'll give you a clue! But I'm disappointed, bloody disappointed to be honest… a degree in medieval history and yet the boy can't tell me what the pope's favourite drink is! Well I'd say that's a waste of an education, young Thoroughgood.'

At the back of his mind, something triggered a distant recollection and the voice in his head piped up with two words. Before he knew it, his mouth had opened: 'Billy Connolly!' said a triumphant Thoroughgood and his face creased in a huge smile.

Ferguson once again feigned outrage. 'Just how much taxpayers' money has been wasted on your education, boy? Now please put us out our misery: what the hell has the Big Yin got to do with mint Guinness, Sherlock bloody Holmes?'

Thoroughgood raised his pint pot in mock salute and sent

a wink Greene's way, only to find the veteran DS had chosen the moment to bolt for the gents. Once again, he began to feel uncomfortable under the scrutiny of the captivated clientele, who were hanging on his every word. He shrugged and proceeded as best he could: 'Haven't you heard the Billy Connolly joke about the two Glaswegians in Rome gasping for a beer?' he asked of his enraptured audience before letting his gaze end on the Boss. Across Ferguson's ruddy features, a flicker of suspicious realisation at where the ADC was going broke out.

Despite that morsel of encouragement, the silence was deafening. Nevertheless, Thoroughgood ploughed on: 'So the first Glaswegian says to the barman: "Hey Jimmy gie us two pints o' heavy."

The barman replies in Italian: "What?"

"Gie us two pints o' heavy, know what I mean?" repeats the Glaswegian.

The barman replies: "We don't sell heavy in Rome."

"Oh what a bloody bore," says the Glaswegian.

"You are welcome to anything you see here, my friend," replies the barman.

"I tell you what. What does the pope drink?" asks the Glaswegian.

"Well he likes a glass of crème de menthe from time to time."

"Gie us two pints o' that, son, and that'll be great!"'

And with that Thoroughgood swept low in an outlandish bow as his assembled audience broke into a mixture of catcalls and applause.

'Bloody smart-arsed graduate!' quipped Ferguson and downed the remainder of his pint in a oner before turning on his heel and making his way towards a blackboard that was situated in the top corner of the snug.

But Thoroughgood's attention was already elsewhere because the brunette in the pencil skirt and white silky blouse was now a clear and present danger. She coyly slinked into position just in front of him, and a sense of panic started to surge through him because her tongue was caressing her top lip in a gesture that could only be described as predatory.

Yet he was saved from her feline threat by a horrific screeching that brought the bawdy flow of conversation, ribald remarks and laughter to an almost immediate stop.

At the other side of the snug, Ferguson had just drawn his fingernails down the backboard. 'Did none of you ever learn anything from Jaws? Never trust a man stood next to a blackboard!' quipped the Boss.

Then, as Morgan appeared at his side with another pint of mint Guinness, Ferguson said: 'Okay, now we have some quiet, let's get down to business, pronto. The reason we are here is that a snout of mine has helped us out, with some information that we must act on ASAP.'

The combination of Ferguson's clawing of the blackboard and the hint of some intel of the very highest quality was enough to make sure that the room remained near-silent.

But Ferguson wasn't taking any chances and he jerked his head towards Morgan, who duly made his way around the back of the assembled and shouted: 'It's coppers only, anyone without a warrant card, bugger off!'

The crowd dispersed, Morgan giving them a malevolent grin as they passed. He slammed the door shut.

A few feet away, Ferguson rolled up his shirt sleeves and loosened his tie until there was almost no point in him wearing it, then, as he scanned every member of his squad and made sure he had them well and truly hooked, he began: 'Yesterday morning, the wooden tops got a call to attend a report of drug dealing round the back of the Chequered Flag boozer in Hulme. Well, for once the blockheads managed not to make a total balls-up of it and lifted the little shit concerned. Amazingly, he had a nice few deals of smack on him and then blow me if they didn't have the good sense to alert my esteemed colleague DC Morgan here that our newfound friend wanted to parley for his troubles.' With a sweep of his hand the Boss invited Morgan to take the floor.

'Thank you, Boss!' replied the DC as he took the opposite side of the blackboard, on which Ferguson was now chalking the details he had just described. 'Turns out Matey has screwed over his own dealer and been cutting his product so he could cream some extra profit. Sadly, one of his clients pegged it in a squat, word gets back to Mr Big further up the tree and Matey decides it's time to do a runner with his stash.'

By this time Ferguson had finished chalking the board and reclaimed centre stage. 'So what the wooden tops got when they lifted Denny Bartlett was a small-time dealer with a big-time heroin supply worth the best part of 50k. All of which, with Denny's previous, equals serious time. Now, of course, if Denny ends up in the pokey, as we like to call it back in Glasgow, his life expectancy will be shorter than a hen's when Mr Fox drops into her coup!'

Ferguson nodded to Morgan to continue as he proceeded to add these details to his blackboard, which he had divided into four square sections.

'So, when me and the Boss get the call to come down and have a nice chat and a cuppa with Denny, we find him all too ready to spill as if we were his oldest mates, and what he said was indeed mint,' smiled Morgan.

Ferguson swallowed another mouthful of his Guinness and then took up the verbal baton: 'We have an armed robbery coming our way somewhere in the city but, unfortunately, despite my legendary powers of persuasion, Denny was unable to tell us where and exactly who the team are behind it. But he is adamant that it's going down on the Wednesday before payday when the banks are loaded with dosh and that, my friends, means it's happening tomorrow.'

Ferguson had his troops exactly where he wanted them, and he couldn't help the grin from spreading across his face: he was clearly loving every minute of this. 'All of which means I want you all reporting to City Centre nick at 0700 hours in the morning, in plain clothes, comprendy?' he demanded.

Those assembled replied, 'Yes, Boss!' and when Ferguson was satisfied, he smiled and waved his hand. 'Class dismissed.'

Across the other side of the snug, Greene and Thoroughgood got to their feet, not quite sure whether they should follow suit or hang fire, and they subsequently ended up hovering in no man's land as the rest of the Flying Squad did as their boss had bid.

'Oh no, Paddy, you and our kid can stay exactly where you are, 'cause I've got work for you: in fact, it's a starring role and after your matinee performance this afternoon that should be right up your street, young Thoroughgood! Now sit,' commanded Ferguson, pointing at a four-seater table that had just been vacated, if the stale fug of cigarette smoke still wreathing it was anything to go by.

Moments later, the Boss, Morgan, Greene and Thorough-good sat around the table, a fresh round of beers newly arrived as Ferguson waited for the petite blonde barmaid who had just delivered them to slink off. 'Hell of a rear view don't you think, gents? Anyway, to business. I wasn't quite truthful with the rank and file and that was for one very good reason…' said Ferguson, eyeing Morgan.

'We think we may have a rat in the Flying Squad,' Morgan said with some relish.

Ferguson smiled wickedly and then added: 'Which is exactly why myself and Paddy managed to use the ruse of our Scots drug dealer abroad to get some hired guns in to help us out. Then we'll catch Jaws and you can head hame to auld Glasgae toon with your big fish well and truly hooked.'

Over the rim of his pint pot, the Boss winked at Greene and then let his glance linger on Thoroughgood, who immediately felt a sinking feeling in the pit of his stomach.

Finishing his draft of the black stuff, Ferguson, as he was wont to do, wiped the cream of the Guinness away with the back of his hand and cut to the chase: 'We are almost certain that the turn will involve a hit on a security van which is lifting a considerable quantity of wedge from a textile factory in the Northern Quarter and you, my dear Thoroughgood, will be in that security van… capiche?'

Across the table, Thoroughgood almost choked on his mint Guinness.

20

THE FIRST SHARDS of daylight had started to splinter the darkness outside the hangar's giant doors. The shadowy figure seated in the glass-windowed office inside the disused aerodrome inhaled a lungful of nicotine and let the smoke billow out.

Summerbee began to rerun every minute detail of the job he had planned meticulously for the past six months in his mind, replayed every detail he had been fed by the bent security guard whose gambling addiction had both brought him to his attention and marked him as someone who could be very useful.

The guard's addiction had made him vulnerable first to one of The Maine Men's foot soldiers, who befriended him in various bookies around Moss Side and then introduced him to Paulie in a local boozer.

Before the guard had known it, his new-found friends, who had proven so understanding and sympathetic when he moaned about his wife's demand for a contribution to buying the kids' school clothes, had even helped sub him to put shoes on their feet, had started to make dark demands for information on his day job.

By then Cyril Smythe knew he was in way too deep and was unlikely to find a way out.

As Summerbee's one-eyed gaze came to rest on him, Smythe inadvertently shivered and began to fidget with the rim of his security hat, his jaws working up and down as he sawed on the chewing gum inside his mouth.

Summerbee continued to watch him but said nothing.

Eventually Smythe couldn't help himself, and for the third time since he had arrived at the deserted old airfield he asked the same question: 'Is there no other way I can pay you back, Mr Summerbee?'

But before One-Eye could answer, the old half-glass office door creaked open and Paulie Gallacher stood in the frame, his body silhouetted by the slowly spreading light of day.

'All right, our kid? It's 7.30 and time we got you going.' But as The Midget's darting eyes jumped from Summerbee to the trembling Smythe and back, he knew that the guard was anything but all right.

Almost imperceptibly, One-Eye inclined his head to his number two. Understanding immediately, The Midget jumped to Smythe's side and grabbed the lapels of his woollen uniform before the guard had time to blink, then hauled him viciously to his feet.

'What's the problem, Cyril? We've looked after you real good, covered all your debts, made sure you've never been short for a pint and a game of dominoes and, most importantly, made sure that old Hilda has always had money for the pot. Wee Frankie and Tess always had their new shoes when they needed them and money for the bleedin' tuck shop. And now you're getting nervous and gonna be lettin' us down?' he demanded, his voice increasing in pitch and volume as he reached the end of his rant.

'I... I... I'm sorry Paulie, I just feel like I'm gonna vomit... I... I dunno if I can go through wi—' But before he could finish, The Midget slashed an open palm off his jaw. The guard staggered back against Summerbee's desk, only just managing to right himself.

As Smythe regained his balance, he found that a Beretta 92 was locked on his forehead. As he looked along the barrel, he saw Gallacher's pit bull features snarling at him. 'You listen to me, ya piece of snivelling shit. You will do everything you're told to do and afterwards you may just live long enough to see yer missus and kids. Fuck it up and none of you will see the end of the day. Do ya fuckin' understand me, Cyril?' he raged.

By this time Smythe's scrawny figure was starting to shake uncontrollably, but from behind him Summerbee reached out a soothing hand and began to massage his right shoulder. 'Look, Cyril, I know this is tough for you, but all we want you to do is the job we agreed. No one gets hurt, your family are taken care off and you have The Maine Men watching your back for the rest of your natural.'

By this time Summerbee had walked round the desk and was standing next to Gallacher. He nodded to The Midget to withdraw the Beretta and whipped out a Silk Cut, lit it, took a drag and handed it to Smythe.

'Have a smoke, Cyril, take a seat, and we will go over things once again and then you'll be sorted and before you know it we'll be done and dusted.' With that Summerbee guided the trembling security guard over to the chair and let him sit down.

A couple of feet away, Gallacher was still bristling with menace and One-Eye turned his palms face down and dropped them in a gesture to calm down. Then he sat back down at the other side of his desk and drained the remainder of his black coffee.

'Okay, Paulie, you start the ball rolling, pal,' he smiled soothingly at his number two.

'First thing, we drops Cyril half a mile away from the Total Security depot and he makes the rest of the way on foot as usual, arriving at 8.30 sharp. Then he crews up with his passenger guard, undergoes the usual briefing and by 9.30 they are coming out the front of the depot in their bullet- and bombproof bleedin' bingo bus. Then it's off on their rounds, collecting the takings from city centre stores… so far so good, mate?' Gallacher asked, doing his best not to let his inner rage resurface.

Seated opposite him, Smythe was devouring his Silk Cut, but managed to take a timeout in order to supply a nod of acknowledgement.

Across the table, Summerbee surveyed their stooge and tried to stay calm, even though at the moment he was struggling to see how they would get Smythe out the door, never mind compos mentis enough to sit behind the wheel of the security van and do his rounds as if it was just another day.

'Okay, so what happens when you and your colleague arrive at the clearing centre, Cyril?' he asked, keeping his voice calm and his manner all business, as if everything was on track.

'I… I… let Mikey log our arrival with security reception and then Mr Gallacher and one of your boys, masked up, scale the wall from the railway line and join me in the cab. I lets 'em in and then drives the van out to the meeting point and we ships out the dough into a waiting motor…' said Smythe, his eyes starting to saucer as his fag became all puffed out.

Summerbee once again took control. 'Your boy is already in position, Paulie, masked, tooled up, ready to go?' he asked.

'Aah, come on, Manny, what do you take me for? He's in position, the motor has already had its false plates fitted – we got them dropped off from a cockney twat who's been helpful with things like that in the past. We'll be looking like just another couple of white van men ready to fuck about like every other clown who drives a Ford Tranny round Manchester of a day,' rapped Gallacher.

The next bit was the part of the briefing that, given Smythe's brittle mental condition, was of concern to Summerbee, and he thought it best to keep going even though he observed the guard, his cigarette finished, was now dining out on his fingernails. 'So, obviously, Cyril, we have to make it look like you were jumped, forced to do your captors' work and then left in an alley for dibble to pick up. Which means you will be bound and gagged and given some lumps for the sake of realism. I'm sorry, but there is no other way,' concluded Summerbee, smiling benignly.

But before the stuttering guard could get any words out, Gallacher yapped: 'Now listen, Cyril, dibble ain't stupid and they will be askin' you questions, but you stick to the Jackanory and you'll be good as gold; and you know how well rewarded that will make you and old Hilda.'

For his part, Cyril initially looked doubtful but eventually managed to mumble: 'I know what I gotta do, Paulie, I knows,' and underlined the point with a shallow nod of his receding, wispy grey side-shed.

Before they could get any further, there was a rap on the office door and a weasel-faced individual popped his head in. 'The motor's ready for the delivery run,' he said. Then he fixed Smythe with a gimlet eye and added: 'Time you came with us, cock!'

Smythe's darting orbs looked over to Summerbee for some kind of reassurance, some way out; instead, the crime lord said simply: 'You know what to do, Cyril: the time for talking is done.' A yard to Smythe's right, The Midget rose and by way of encouragement slipped his right hand half inside his parka, where his gun lay hidden.

Smythe got to his feet like a condemned man, took a deep breath and, flanked fore and aft by Gallacher and his pet weasel, made his way to a blacked-out Land Rover.

21

THOROUGHGOOD had arrived at Total Security HQ early, been kitted out in full-helmeted security guard gear and briefed by a Total Security director, James Wood. Now he sat in what passed for a cafeteria nursing a coffee and waiting to be introduced to his new colleague.

The problem was that although Ferguson had been sure that the info they had was blue chip, they didn't know when or where the hit would happen; however, that would be counter-balanced by the fact the Flying Squad would be tailing the security vehicle as discreetly as possible.

That in itself would not be easy because although the following vehicle needed to be close enough to react, get too close and whoever was going to pull the turn would spot them and the whole thing would be called off – perhaps to be sprung on another occasion when the Squad didn't have the intel to mount a similar operation.

As he drained the remnants of a black coffee that was as rotten as it was cold, Thoroughgood chided himself that these were things that he wasn't paid to worry about. He was soon snapped from his thoughts when the cafeteria door opened and Wood, a corpulent, ruddy-faced Mancunian who called a spade a spade, returned with his new colleague in tow.

'Detective Thoroughgood, please meet Cyril Smythe, who will be your driver for the day,' smiled Wood as Thoroughgood got up and offered his new colleague a hand of welcome.

The surprise on Smythe's pockmarked features was such that Thoroughgood wondered just how much Wood had told him about his new partner, but nevertheless the driver managed an unconvincing 'Pleased to meet you.'

"Christ, this is going to be a right bundle of laughs," thought Thoroughgood, but despite his concerns, the detective flashed a smile he hoped was reassuring. His firm handshake was met with a limp-wristed return that was in keeping with Smythe's whole body language.

"You don't want to be here and you certainly don't want me riding shotgun," thought Thoroughgood.

With the three men now seated, Wood began to drone on about the whys and wherefores of the route, alongside the locations and duties that they would be undertaking. After 15 minutes they were done and Thoroughgood followed Smythe out into the security vehicle.

Taking a deep breath, Thoroughgood resolved to try and make his journey as bearable as possible, and that meant small talk. 'So, Cyril, how long have you been doing this?' he asked, realising it was probably the most unimaginative opening line he could have come up with, but then, what else was he supposed to say?

'Near ten years now, Detective,' replied Smythe, carrying out a series of checks on the vehicle dash before turning the ignition on, which sent a shudder through the cabin as the Ford Transit's two-litre diesel engine fired up.

Across the cabin, it hadn't been lost on Thoroughgood that Smythe had barely looked at him since they had been introduced. As the driver swung the Transit out of the yard, silence engulfed the cabin.

He tried again. 'So, where's our first stop, Cyril? I'd imagine we have quite a few…' he said, trying to keep his question open in order to draw Smythe into some kind of conversation.

'We have a stop at Bank of Manchester, Burton menswear and a textile factory and maybe one other before we head into the sorting centre to deposit the money,' said Smythe, his gaze remaining firmly on the road.

'Doesn't it worry you carrying all that cash in the van? Ever been held up?' asked Thoroughgood, cutting to the chase and firing out the only question he'd wanted to ask since he'd climbed aboard the Transit.

'Aye, about three years back, me and Dave – my regular partner – got done. Funny enough, just outside the Bank of Manchester branch we is heading to this morning. There's no point being a hero for a fiver an hour when you get a gun pointed at your napper,' said Smythe, shrugging, as his helmeted head at last turned towards Thoroughgood. But he swiftly returned his gaze to the road.

The silence stretched out and with nothing to distract him, Thoroughgood found his mind returning to Emma's plight. He'd heard nothing of her since he'd come to Manchester and her disappearance was a constant nagging worry. Inevitably he began to turn all the options over and over in his head, adding a hefty dose of self-blame.

Where the hell was she?

Given his mental torture, the sound of Thoroughgood's police radio crackling into life was a blessing.

'Earth to Thoroughgood. Come in, over,' said Ferguson.

'Receiving, sir,' he replied.

'All well, lad? You settling into your new job okay?' asked Ferguson.

'No problem, sir, we are on our way to Bank of Manchester for the first pick-up with another three maybe four stops before we head to the clearing centre to deposit the funds. Cyril here has been filling me in about his life as a security guard and it's fascinating stuff,' reported Thoroughgood, not sure that he was coming across as particularly sincere.

'Nice one, Cyril!' said Ferguson, the other end of the radio crackling with his harsh laughter, before he continued: 'Anyway, just keep your eyes peeled, son, we are three cars back in a Royal Mail van, so you ain't the only one who has visited Mr Benn and come out in fancy dress!'

Thoroughgood immediately checked his passenger-side window and caught sight of the postal van. A couple of feet away Smythe was doing the same, trying to keep his face from dissolving into worry and concern.

This had turned into his worst nightmare and it was one he could see no escape from.

'Got you, Boss! It's a case of so far so good. Over and out,' said Thoroughgood and brought his transmission to an end; but as he turned his gaze back into the cabin, he noticed Smythe quickly turn away from his own mirror and somewhere in his gut a tremor of concern broke out. It was perfectly normal for the driver to take an interest, but it was the way Smythe had returned to an eyes-front position that somehow wasn't right.

Yet for all that, the morning proceeded with nothing more untoward than an abrupt stop caused by a hobbling granny electing to step off a kerb at the most inopportune moment.

As the road signage began to indicate Salford, Thoroughgood noticed that Smythe's hands and arms seemed to be shaking slightly. 'Are you okay, Cyril?' he asked, pointing at the driver's left hand, which, although it was clamped on the Transit's steering wheel, was clearly trembling.

Smythe looked down and gave his hand a shake before he cleared his throat. 'It's a wee problem, like. On medication for it, never been the same since that bloody hold-up. Doc calls it something fancy, post-trauma… something or other…' he concluded, at a loss.

'You're suffering from post-traumatic stress disorder, Cyril, pure and simple, and no bloody wonder. Christ, you must be bricking it every time you have a stop to make or a motor pulls alongside,' said Thoroughgood and received a shrug from the driver for his efforts.

But at last he'd found something to fill the silence and now the detective warmed to his task with relish. 'Did you know that the term was first coined back in the 70s in the wake of Vietnam? It's better known over here as shell shock, but it was officially recognised as PTSD by the American Psychiatric Association in 1980. Fascinating stuff, really,' concluded Thoroughgood.

At last he seemed to have said something that interested Smythe. 'It's fuckin' killing me, boss,' said Smythe, and then the dam burst: 'Do you know that a guard is getting attacked on average once a day? That shouldn't be a surprise when you consider we – Total Security, that is – are transporting on average £240 mill a year. Back in the 70s it was relatively safe but three years ago in '87 there was 367 attacks on CIT – cash-in-transit – guards and I was one of 'em. So, there's no bloody wonder I'm a bit on edge, like, boss.'

'You're telling me, Cyril! Anyway, where are we heading next?' asked Thoroughgood.

'Bank Clearing Centre in Salford – we are, as you knows, filled to the gunnels. The drill is that on arrival you go and sign us in before we are admitted to the deposit centre, which is in a fully securitised internal yard. But first we're gonna have to get through these lights – bloody roadworks,' snapped Smythe in frustration at a set of temporary lights caused by the resurfacing of a lane.

But across the cabin, Thoroughgood's curiosity was once more getting the better of him. 'So, Cyril, I've gotta ask, you ever been tempted to do a runner? I mean, what've we taken on board this morning? Maybe five or six million? Pull a fast one and have a couple of getaway motors lined up and another driver ready with the engine ticking over and you're gone, and you can stick your fiver an hour up your arse, Mr Wood, thank you very much, sir!'

For the first time since they had met some three hours back, Smythe actually laughed out loud. 'Do a runner with the dough? Where would that get me? Actually, boss, it happened just last year: a guard down in Felixstowe did one with 1.3 mill but after a year on the run and a new life across the pond his cover was blown when his daughter-in-law blabbed and now he's back over here banged up,' he said, doing his best not to let the desperate reality of his own predicament surface in either his words or his demeanour.

The lights had turned green and the Total Security van trundled on, Thoroughgood shaking his head ruefully at his new colleague's plight. 'Aye, it's a bitter irony that you have people being paid peanuts to risk their lives and guard millions of pounds. The system sucks,' he concluded as he checked his mirror and saw that the Royal Mail van carrying Ferguson, Greene and Morgan had failed to make the lights and was still stationary.

As the Transit pulled into the clearing centre's outer yard, Smythe picked up the logbook and handed it to Thoroughgood. 'Okay, boss, if you take this and get a signature and give them a scrawl for their record we can unload,' he said, in a little bit too much of a rush.

The driver was definitely on edge, PTSD or not, and Thoroughgood couldn't help doing a double take. But then he shrugged his shoulders: if Smythe was indeed jumpy and shaky he certainly had good enough reason for it.

'Sure,' replied the cop. He picked up the clipboard and jumped out of the cabin.

Inside the Transit, Smythe's heart began to hammer. He needed the copper to be inside when The Maine Men hit and he found himself mumbling 'Please don't turn round, boss,' as Thoroughgood strode through the yard to the check-in office.

As the cop reached the door, Smythe started to breathe again. He checked the bordering east wall and saw the top of a ladder appear.

A few seconds later, a balaclava-sheathed figure reached the top of its rungs, swung himself over onto the top of the wall and made the six-foot drop like he'd done it a million times before.

As this pint-sized individual started to sprint across the yard towards the Total Security vehicle, a second, similarly disguised but far bigger figure lumbered in his wake.

Fingering the crucifix hanging around his neck, Smythe took a deep breath and sprang his driver's door open, uttering a silent prayer to our lady.

There was no turning back now.

22

THOROUGHGOOD presented the Total Security clipboard log to the reception staff, then scrawled a signature in the bank record confirming vehicle details and arrival time.

'You're new, aren't you?' asked the reception guard, shoving his copy of The Sun underneath the reception counter.

Thoroughgood nodded, trying to avoid conversation. But the guard, a thin-faced individual who carried the air of a jobsworth, was not about to let things go: 'How you finding Cyril? I don't know how he sticks it after that business a couple of years back: I'd have jacked it in. He's off his rocker! A fiver an hour to have a gun put to your head? He'd be better off sweeping the streets.'

Behind an unconvincing smile Thoroughgood may only have been half listening, but the reception guard had a point and it was one that niggled at him. Jobsworth was right: just why would you continue to put your life on the line for a fiver an hour?

Slowly, the wheels in his mind began to turn. The trembling of the hands and arm, the quick furtive glance in the mirror to check on Ferguson's tailing vehicle and the way he had tried to avoid being seen making that check were all... odd.

Little things they may be, but little things that added up to the sound of alarm bells ringing. "Christ. Smythe even admitted he should be out of the job and his nerves are shot. Better safe than sorry, son!" warned the voice in his head and with that Thoroughgood turned around tout de suite and opened the door back into the entry yard.

'Hey pal! You haven't finished the paperwork and you won't be admitted if you don't, I can tell you that for nothing,' Jobsworth snapped at Thoroughgood's retreating back.

Taking the steps two at a time, Thoroughgood reached the bottom, where the evidence of his own eyes confirmed his gut instinct had been right all the time… the problem was he should have listened to it a damn sight earlier.

A hundred yards in front of him, two balaclava-clad figures were sprinting across the front yard. He scanned the direction from which they had come and caught sight of the top of a ladder still sticking up above the perimeter wall.

Thoroughgood drew his Smith & Wesson .38 snubnose and hit the yard running. As he did so, he tried to take in every detail of the drama that was playing out in front of him.

All that mattered was that he got close enough to drop on to a knee, present the .38 and shout a warning. "When do things ever play out the way you want, muppet?" chided the voice in his head.

By this time the first of the two males had reached the Total Security van, but instead of ripping open the driver's door and wrenching out Smythe, Thoroughgood saw that he had run around the vehicle and was jumping into the cabin through the already opened passenger door.

'Inside fuckin' job!' spat Thoroughgood. But he had more pressing concerns: for the second goon was beginning to slow to a halt just before the security vehicle. He had seen Thoroughgood and in his hand was a firearm.

The only cover came in the shape of some parked staff vehicles, the nearest of which was a Nissan Sunny, nowhere near close enough.

Caught in open ground, Thoroughgood hit the deck, presenting the .38 and determined to try and get his shot off first.

Almost simultaneously both weapons fired, and he heard the sound of a bullet ricochet of the tarmacadam to his left while his own shot had clearly been well wide of the mark.

By now the Total Security vehicle's engine had started, and the Transit lumbered round in a semicircle to pick up the gunman on the passenger side; but before it completed the operation, a salvo of lead was emptied in Thoroughgood's direction and the ground around him seemed to erupt in a series of mini-explosions.

Whispering a silent prayer, Thoroughgood waited for the impact of high-velocity lead in his body, breathed again when none came; meanwhile, the Transit completed its pick-up and sped towards the yard entrance.

Thoroughgood leapt up, replacing the .38 with his personal radio. 'ADC Thoroughgood to DCI Ferguson, the Total Security vehicle has been hit in the bank clearing yard. Two figures in balaclavas and… the driver appears to be in on it. One of the males is armed and shots have been fired. Where are you, come in, over?' he rapped breathlessly.

From the other end of the radio a slight crackling was soon replaced with a volley of profanity: 'Hell's teeth, boy! Where is the bloody van now?' demanded Ferguson, before he added: 'You okay, Thoroughgood? Over.'

'I'm fine, Boss, but the van has motored back out the sorting centre yard with the two males and the driver. Best I can do for direction of travel is they're heading away from the city. Over,' concluded the ADC.

'Okay, we will put out a lookout for the vehicle and scramble all available units. Hang fire just now, Thoroughgood, and we'll get someone to you ASAP… Thoroughgood, come in, over. Was that clear? Come in, over,' demanded Ferguson.

Thoroughgood was now sprinting back to the reception office and he bounded up the steps and almost ripped the door of its hinges.

Inside the office, the reception guard was in a state of panic. 'What is happening? Just who the hell do you think you are?' But the answer in the shape of Thoroughgood's warrant card was already rammed in his face.

'ADC Thoroughgood. Is one of these vehicles parked outside yours?' he asked, his breathing heavy.

'Why do you ask? What's going on?' stammered the guard, still scanning Thoroughgood's warrant card suspiciously.

His question was answer enough. Thoroughgood ripped the .38 back out of its holster and gave the guard something else to worry about. 'Give me the fucking keys or you will be on a charge of obstructing an officer in the lawful discharge of his duty… hand 'em over… now!' he ordered, desperately trying to prod the guard into action.

'All right, all right, keep your hair on will you,' said the guard, finally seeming to get the message. He pulled his keys out of his pocket and slapped them on the reception counter.

'Thank you, your cooperation is appreciated,' said Thorough-good and once again he turned back out of the office and sprinted into the yard. Fingering the keys, he saw they were on a Nissan keyring and headed straight for the Sunny. In seconds he was on his way out of the yard, his foot to the floor.

Inside the Total Security vehicle, Gallacher's machine-gun delivery was firing freely: 'What the fuck was that all about, Cyril? A security guard drawing a soddin' Smith & Wesson? Go on, tell me, Cyril, it don't fuckin' add up,' barked The Midget.

'He's a cop, Paulie, I... I... I didn't know anything about it until I arrived this morning... there was just no way to warn you, I'm sorry, Paulie. Honest I am... but what could I do? Dibble have obviously had a tip-off,' stammered Smythe.

Gallacher's rage was volcanic and he smashed a gloved fist off the Transit dash. Then he took a deep breath and forced himself to think. 'Anything showing in the mirror, Frankie?' he asked his outsized goon.

'Fuck all, Paulie,' responded the muscle.

'Ok, we've got no bloody option but to try and ride this out. How long before we make the switch, Cyril?' he asked, trying to keep his voice even.

'Maybe five minutes tops, Paulie,' replied the security guard.

'This is a fuckin' nightmare. We are absolute sittin' ducks, dibble will be broadcasting a lookout all over the shop, but what do we do? Six mill in the back... Jesus.' Then he turned to Smythe. 'You better say your bleedin' prayers we make the switch, Cyril,' he said. Then as he clocked the trembling in Smythe's hands he spat malevolently: "Cause if we don't, neither you or your family will see the end of the day.'

23

THOROUGHGOOD had no idea where he was heading but he applied maximum throttle to the Nissan Sunny and tried to work out the route the Total Security van was most likely to take.

The gang would be desperate to ditch the vehicle, which stuck out like a sore thumb, and knowing he was an undercover cop, they would be all too well aware that a lookout would have been circulated.

But even as his mind was running through the possibilities, his eyes saucered: for about a quarter of a mile ahead, approaching a roundabout, was the security vehicle itself. Its most likely direction of travel was the A road taking it out of the city and avoiding the motorway, which would have left the van a sitting duck.

He immediately reached for his personal radio and broadcast an update to Ferguson and his crew, who were nowhere to be seen. All of which meant the only course of action open to him was to maintain a safe distance and continue to observe and broadcast the direction of travel.

Smiling to himself, Thoroughgood said out loud: 'That'll do nicely, son!'

The road out of Manchester to the disused aerodrome was light in traffic and the Total Security vehicle made good progress. They reached the roundabout that took them onto the escape route without Smythe even having to dab at the Transit's brakes.

Cresting the brow of a slight hill, Smythe seemed to be relaxing. 'Nearly there, Paulie. I'd say the turn-off is about a quarter of a mile at most,' he said.

Gallacher leaned across the shaven-headed goon in the middle and spat: 'I know exactly how far away we are from the aerodrome from here, you twat; now just get us there in one piece and you might make it home to Hilda for a brew after all.'

'S-s-sorry, Paulie, no problem,' stammered Smythe and returned his eyes to the road ahead.

Gallacher, who was perched just inside the cabin's passenger door, nudged Shaven-head in the ribs and as the man-mountain turned towards him, he inclined his head in Smythe's direction and drew his forefinger across his throat.

The goon smiled viciously by way of a reply.

'Ah shite!' exclaimed Smythe suddenly, for as they had started to descend the other side of the hill he'd seen that their lane was blocked by a stationary council truck with its hazard lights flashing.

The rear wheel on the driver's side was ratcheted up and a couple of council workers were busy changing a flat tyre, while one of them, resplendent in a yellow jacket, stood on the opposite side of the road directing traffic in an almost comic-book manner.

'Bloody worky morons!' raged Gallacher as the Total Security van ground to a halt.

Next to him, Shaven-head came out with an unimaginative solution to their problem. 'Skittle the bastard, Cyril!' he spat.

But for once Gallacher decided upon caution. 'No, that's only gonna make things a whole lot worse. Edge the van up to Mr Traffic fuckin' Warden and let's see if we can make him stand aside nice and peaceable, like,' he said.

'Right you are, Paulie,' said Smythe meekly and did as he was bid.

The Transit slowly trundled towards the workman directing the traffic, who, seeing the van was almost upon him, had held a giant paw in the air to order traffic coming from the other side of the broken-down truck to a halt.

As the Total Security vehicle drew level with him, the workman turned to meet it; Smythe slid the driver's window down to reveal the giant's tousled red-hair and the vicious scar that ruined the left side of his face.

A yard away from the worky, Smythe recoiled, almost into himself, at the fiendish visage now confronting him. But from behind him, Gallacher spat in his grating, machine-gun delivery: 'Why don't you get the fuck off the road, cock, and let us through…' But his words receded into silence as the dawning of recognition broke across his feral features: for sprouting out from the worky's neck and just above the yellow collar of his jacket was a tattoo.

A tattoo of a red devil holding a fork.

Gallacher's right hand slipped inside his jacket, his fingers clamping around his Beretta. He viciously ripped the M9 free of his clothing… but he was too slow.

'Well, well, if it ain't the three soddin' amigos!' said Scarface, and as he did so the trigger finger of his right hand, which was wrapped round the handle of his Micro Uzi, curled tight and from the gun's barrel twenty 9x19mm Parabellums started to enfilade the cabin of the Total Security van.

Instinct took over and Gallacher ducked behind his shaven-haired henchman, whose cranium instantly exploded in a gore of tissue, bone and gristle, while the deadly rain continued to puncture bullet holes in the passenger door.

In the driver's seat, Cyril Smythe attempted to roll up into a ball and duck below the window; but by the time he had managed to do so his torso had been punctured by half a dozen high-velocity projectiles.

Seeing he had taken care of two of the three amigos, Scarface released his finger from the Uzi's trigger just as the passenger door flew open at the other side of the van and Gallacher threw himself out of the cabin.

As he hit the tarmac, he rolled over and, Beretta in hand, attempted to regain his feet; but a knee smashed off his jaw and he dropped stunned and semi-conscious onto the roadway, just as a high-powered motorcycle screeched to stop a yard away.

His vision blurred, Gallacher was aware of the Beretta falling from his grip and then there were shadows; but he still heard a female voice say: 'Perfect, it's just as we had planned. Father will be happy! Throw the poison dwarf in the truck and take him to the rendezvous. Yul, get the Total Security van off the road and under cover to our rendezvous.'

As he was dragged to his feet, Gallacher found himself confronted by a helmeted figure, who slipped the smoke-stained visor up. Inside, two dark eyes sparkled with cruel pleasure. 'Vengeance is mine, sayeth the Lord.'

Then the helmet swung down, delivering a crushing blow onto the bridge of Gallacher's snout, which exploded under the impact; and the lights went out for Paulie Gallacher.

Thoroughgood had just crested the hillock when, wide-eyed, he saw the carnage ahead unfolding.

Instinct took over: he levelled the accelerator to the floor, and the Sunny shot out into the oncoming lane, speeding past the two vehicles that were in front of him and had now drawn to a stop.

As his eyes took in every detail of the scene, he saw that the figure whom he presumed was the smaller of the two males he'd seen sprinting across the Bank of Manchester sorting yard was being dragged, clearly unconscious, into what appeared to be a council truck by two hoods, while a motorbike was propped up on its stand to the left of the Total Security vehicle, the rider nowhere to be seen.

Of Smythe there was also no sign, and as the gap between Thoroughgood and the van decreased, he could see that it had been shot up; but all of a sudden the vehicle started up, which meant that there was someone inside.

Suddenly, a dead body was launched out of the van's cabin, and Thoroughgood found the answer to the question of what had happened to Smythe.

But while the vehicle's passenger door was still open, there was a chance he could get to it before it made off.

Closing to within 50 yards of the stricken security vehicle, Thoroughgood slipped his Smith & Wesson .38 snubnose out its holster, placed it underneath his knee and gritted his teeth.

For he did not know what awaited him.

What mattered most, if he was to give himself a chance of catching a ride on the Total Security vehicle, was that he arrived in control of the Sunny. He counted down the gap: 20 yards… 10… 5… he rammed on the anchors and prayed that the Nissan did not skid.

Thankfully, the saloon came to an orderly stop and Thoroughgood threw open the driver's door and bounded out towards the Total Security vehicle, raising the .38 as he did so.

But he was too late.

In his face he found a Micro Uzi held by the motorcyclist, helmet on, smoked visor shut.

'Drop your gun!' commanded the motorcyclist.

Thoroughgood's features splintered with surprise – the voice belonged to a female.

The delay in his obeisance did not go down well. 'Yes, that's right, clever boy,' she said in reaction to his recognition of her sex. 'For the last time, Officer, lose the gun, get your hands on your head and drop to your knees,' she demanded.

Her voice may have been muffled by the closed visor, but from his limited experience with the Mancunians he had met he could tell it was not a local accent.

Then he realised that in between the fumes of diesel and cordite there was something more feminine blowing on the breeze. His would-be executioner was wearing perfume, and Thoroughgood shook his head at just how surreal this situation was.

As he dropped to his knees, the gauntleted hand pushed up the helmet visor. Inside it, the eyes that shone out were transfixing.

'So, what happens next? You execute a cop for trying to do his job?' he asked, trying to engage this femme fatale and buy himself some time.

It was a mistake.

'What job would that be, Scotch? Trying to save the lives of these murdering scumbags? Believe me, the streets of Manchester will be safer with their... departure,' she rapped with feeling.

'What about Cyril? You've just murdered an innocent family man trying to do a hard day's graft to put food on the table for his kids,' snapped Thoroughgood, his own anger, despite the desperation of his situation, surging hot.

'Listen to me, Officer...?' she left the rest of the sentence to hang.

The ADC smiled sarcastically. 'Do you get some twisted enjoyment in knowing the names of your victims?' he spat.

'Of one thing I can assure you: if you don't answer my question you will die anyway,' she said.

He shrugged and, resigned to his fate, replied: 'Thoroughgood... Angus Thoroughgood.' And inside the helmet he thought he saw the slight creases of a smile play around her eyes.

'Then close your eyes, Angus Thoroughgood, and pray for redemption from your maker.' And with that she trained the Uzi on him.

The time for stalling over and any words pointless, Thoroughgood did as he was bid and prepared to meet his fate.

24

THOROUGHGOOD didn't have to wait long for the Uzi to bark into life.

As the air around him hummed and buzzed with the release of a spray of bullets, Thoroughgood gritted his teeth and waited to be ripped apart.

But the salvo of high-velocity lead came to an abrupt end without him being struck, and within seconds he heard the cabin door slamming shut and the Transit's diesel engine thrumming into gear.

Opening his eyes, he saw that the motorcyclist's gaze remained firmly on him through her helmet, and for a moment their eyes met and held.

As the security van sped away, Thoroughgood let out a deep sigh of relief. He looked around him and saw that the target of the femme fatale's shooting gallery had been the Honda CB 250, which now lay on the tarmac, tyres ripped to shreds and fuel tank bleeding out.

Not far away, the corpses of Smythe and a shaven-headed hood lay at strangely contorted angles on the ground.

Thoroughgood went over to the driver's body and hunkered down. The multiple bullet wounds to his torso and upper chest meant that Cyril had never stood a chance.

But while his first emotion was pity, Thoroughgood's brain started to piece together what had just happened. Smythe had clearly been the inside man for the initial robbery, providing all the information the first gang had needed to track the Total Security Transit to the Bank of Manchester; but it appeared that someone had been watching them.

The fact that the truck had been positioned as it had to bring the fleeing security vehicle to a halt and allow the secondary ambush to be sprung was beyond dispute: but who had been the lone survivor of the ambush who had been dragged away by those ambushing the robbers?

However, Thoroughgood got no further in piecing his mental jigsaw together, for the sight of a Royal Mail Freight Rover almost taking off as it crested the hillock a couple of hundred yards back now had his full attention. Moments later, Ferguson brought the mail van to a stop in a position partially concealing the bodies and the locus of the killings from oncoming traffic. Leaving the Rover's hazards flashing, he unfolded from the driver's seat, followed by Greene and Morgan, the latter white as a sheet.

The DCI's eyes were wild as he surveyed the bodies. Ferguson was clearly on the point of a volcanic eruption; however, the sound of Morgan ordering vehicles on the other side of the road to move on while Greene barked out an assistance call for support to help manage the traffic and allow them to secure the locus seemed to bring the Boss back to reality with a jolt.

'Jesus H. Christ! What the hell have you gone and done now, Thoroughgood?' he said, sweeping one of his huge hands through his red mop; but before the ADC could answer, Ferguson held a hand up to still him.

'OK, Paddy and Wally, the two of you make sure this doesn't turn into a spectator sport and keep these bloody ghouls on the other side of the road moving…' But Ferguson's attention was drawn to a Rover Sterling Fastback that was barely moving in the opposite lane. 'Balls and buggery, who the bloody hell is this… Alan bloody Whicker on tour?' he snapped.

For a moustachioed 60-something-year-old had drawn his window down and had one jerseyed sleeve running along the rim of his windowsill, devouring every hellish detail of the body-strewn road through the bottle tops of his prescription glasses.

It was a sight that caused Ferguson's eyes to pop. The Boss came as close to a sprint as was possible running across the road-way and then grabbed a fistful of primrose sweater. 'Can I help you, Mr Whicker? I'm sorry, but we're rather busy right now and if you don't get into second gear and get the bloody hell out of here I will have you for contaminating a major crime scene, obstructing a police investigation and stealing bloody Shergar. Now beat it!' screeched the Boss at a decibel level Thoroughgood didn't think possible from the human voice.

'Whicker' nearly jumped out of his seat such was the fright Ferguson's almost biblical rage had given him and of course stalled his Rover immediately. Bending down until his pulsing green eyes were now level with Whicker's double glazing, Ferguson whispered: 'You have 30 seconds to fire up your jalopy and get the hell over that hill… do you understand me?'

The driver nodded and as Ferguson took a couple of steps back, he blessedly started up the Rover and snaked off in suitably shaky fashion.

Standing hands on hips, Ferguson swept the vehicles behind Whicker with his ferocious gaze, and gradually they all began to speed up.

A moment later he turned back to find Thoroughgood and Greene covering the bodies with some sacking from the back of the mail van. 'Good work, boys. Help on its way, Paddy?'

'Incoming, Marty,' replied Greene, nodding his head to underline the point.

Then Ferguson, seeing Thoroughgood had wandered over to the bullet-riddled motorcycle, and had hunkered down beside it, notebook and pencil in hand, gave a huge sigh of exasperation. 'God in Govan, boy, will you, for crying out loud, step into my bloody office,' he ranted, and opened the mail van door.

The ADC trousered his notebook and did as he was bid at the double.

Ferguson said one word: 'Shoot.'

Thoroughgood spared Ferguson no details in his account of what had happened, with the key piece of detail being that Smythe had opened the passenger door for the two hooded males while he had remained behind the wheel.

His account of the trap that Smythe had driven his co-conspirators into left Ferguson in no doubt that the gang had been infiltrated.

'Call me paranoid but I wonder if the source of information that allowed Cyril and his mates to meet their Waterloo could have been the same one that has infiltrated the Squad?' asked Ferguson, for once anything but certain of the ground he was on.

Thoroughgood shook his head in the negative. 'I don't see how that could be the case: whoever was lying in wait knew where the gang was heading, presumably to transfer the loot and switch motors. They knew the escape route and we didn't have access to that information, so I think you can rule that one out, Boss.'

Ferguson's fingers drummed on the van dash. 'Tell me more about the member of the original gang who was snatched by the ambushers. Did you get any kind of description?'

Thoroughgood shrugged. 'He still had his balaclava on from his neck up and I never got a facial, but the one thing I can say without a doubt is that he was lucky if he was five foot two!'

'Ha!' exclaimed Ferguson and for a moment they both laughed. 'Or to be precise, how about a midget?'

'What do you mean, Boss?' asked Thoroughgood, at a loss.

'I mean that one of the major players in the two gangs that are feuding over every bloody blade of grass left in this metropolis is similarly vertically challenged. His name is Paulie Gallacher and his nom de guerre is, for obvious reasons, The Midget; and I would put the shirt on my back on him being the person you saw dragged out of the Total Security van. Very interesting indeed!' concluded Ferguson.

Warming to his task, Thoroughgood continued with his revelations: 'There is one other thing, Boss…'

A foot away, Ferguson's overly lush eyebrows rose. 'Well don't beat about the bush, boy.'

'The leader of the ambushers was female, I can guarantee you.'

At the other side of the cabin, Ferguson let a long slow whistle escape from between clenched teeth. 'Stone the bleedin' crows!' he said, but before he could resume his interrogation of Thoroughgood, the sound of a ringing phone started to reverberate from an inside pocket of his overcoat.

Ferguson fished out the black, moulded handset with a pinprick aerial at the side and looked at the viewing panel. 'Aah shite, it's Mad Myra!' he groaned.

Opposite him, Thoroughgood was momentarily mystified.

'ACC Crime Michelle Trautmann, aka the boss of bosses. I need to take it. You don't have a spare telephone book I can stick down the back of me trousers, son?' asked Ferguson with a wink.

Then he clicked on the answer panel and, in perfectly polite English with his gravelly Glaswegian accent almost whitewashed, said: 'DCI Ferguson speaking, how can I help, ma'am?'

Sitting just a matter of inches away from him, Thoroughgood was close enough to get hit with some of the verbal broadside from the other end. 'Cut the bullshit, Marty Ferguson, and get your arse to HQ ASAP. I want a full report on this latest fiasco involving your Flying Squad and I want it now!' Then the phone went dead.

Rolling his eyes to the heavens, Ferguson flashed a lukewarm smile. 'I think it's time you met Mad Myra, son,' he said.

'With respect, do I have to, sir?' asked Thoroughgood, but Ferguson had already turned the key in the ignition.

'You are the only witness to a double armed robbery and the murders of two key players in them, so what do you think the answer to that one is, son?' replied Ferguson, deadpan.

This time Thoroughgood had no answer.

25

THE DRIVE to The Devils' destination was less than 10 minutes from Manchester and despite the time of day, the greenbelt area where the disused Victorian hospital was sited meant that when it came to concealing vehicles, transferring cash and the destruction of the Total Security van, Oatway Hospital was the perfect location.

Thankfully for The Devils, the chaos left behind at the scene of the shoot-out had allowed them just enough time to escape while the police were distracted with securing the locus. By the time the vehicle description had been broadcast, they had reached the relative safety of the minor country roads.

Constructed in 1874 by moneys donated from a prominent local Victorian philanthropist, their safe house had been built with bricks made from locally sourced clay and had once been a magnificent and impressive pile that had mainly catered for the elderly and stroke victims.

Since its closure 11 years earlier, it had begun to be reclaimed by mother nature, with vegetation engulfing its walls, while its innards had been stripped and the roofs showed daylight.

By the time the Total Security vehicle had reached the hospital, the truck carrying Gallacher had already deposited its passenger, and now as Lisa Crerand strode through the eerie internal cloisters of the abandoned Victorian edifice, her helmet swinging from her right forearm, she let a smile of satisfaction play at her full lips.

Everything had gone to plan and before the day was out the cash would be divided up and transferred to various parties, where it would be made to work invisibly for The Devils' various business interests and in particular the Reds nightclub, a 21st-birthday gift from her father that was her pride and joy.

But for now her mind was focussed on her impending meeting with The Midget and just what she had planned for him. The one thing she had learnt from her father was that everyone, friend or foe, had a use, and she had plans for Paulie Gallacher, if he played ball.

If he did not, then his screams would soon breathe new life into the silence that engulfed Oatway; and again she smiled at that prospect.

But although she tried to focus on the work that lay ahead and the objectives behind it, she could not help but replay her chance encounter with the young Scottish cop back at the scene of her exquisitely executed ambush.

It had been obvious he had been a cop to her from the minute she set eyes on him. Six feet tall, he carried himself with a certain surety; but then that was what intrigued her about him and had, she admitted to herself, caused her to spare him the Uzi.

For despite the certainty and sense of right, his sea-green gaze was somehow tinged with melancholy and that had intrigued her, for the simple reason that, as the daughter of Manchester's most powerful crime lord, she had begun to class every male of a certain age as either a sycophant or a chancer.

"Enough of this nonsense, Lisa!" she mentally chastised herself and continued her walk through the arches towards the clocktower, where she was determined to make sure The Midget danced to her tune or paid a dear price.

Moments later she descended a broken set of stairs to the basement underneath the old tower and there, gagged and bound, was Gallacher, flanked by two henchmen. One, a brooding bald man-mountain sporting a red devil tattoo, stepped forward: 'The patient is all ready for his treatment, Lisa!' he said, then laughed cruelly.

Lisa smiled and made a cursory check of Gallacher's bonds. Then she looked back at Slaphead. 'You've done a good job, Yul. Now remove the gag from Mr Gallacher's mouth and we will see whether negotiation is possible.'

The scowl on Yul's foreboding features underlined that he was far from happy about that possibility, but the outsized enforcer did as he was bid. Gallacher gagged when the cloth that had stilled his motor-mouth was removed.

'I trust you are finding our big red chair comfortable, Mr Gallacher?' asked Lisa.

The Midget's anger knew no bounds. 'Listen to me, bitch, you are wasting yer time, and mine too, if you think there is anything to talk about. Just do what you're gonna do and get it over,' he spat.

She smiled and something in her eyes told Gallacher that one way or another he was indeed in for a treat. 'All in good time… Paulie… if I may call you that?' she asked with a beguiling smile.

Held tight in the big red chair, Gallacher strained at his bonds to no avail and, eventually realising attempting escape was an exercise in futility, he took a deep breath and spat: 'Say what you gotta say.'

'My reading of your situation is that you badly needed the six million that was in the Total Security van. Badly needed it to maintain your failing pubs, bookies and brothels, continue

147

to grease the palms of the councillors you have bought out and, most of all, to pay for the drugs you hoped Terry Forsyth would supply you with. Which you thought would in turn make you preeminent in Manchester. Correct?' asked Lisa, removing the motorcycle gauntlets from her hand and examining her ruby-red nails.

His eyes pulsing with rage, Gallacher was having none of it. 'I dunno what you're talking about, Crerand,' he said, his jaw clenching.

The words were barely out of his mouth before she strode across the splintered tile floor and viciously backhanded him with one of the leather gauntlets.

Gallacher shook with rage. 'You little bitch, what's your fucking game?' he demanded.

Standing back, she let her dark stare rest on his rabid, spittle-flecked features. 'I would appreciate it, Mr Gallacher, if you didn't insult my intelligence. Do you think our little encounter was a matter of chance? Surely not. We have information coming to us from within your operation that has kept us very well informed about your plans for the Total Security van. Sadly for you, the late Cyril Smythe just couldn't keep his mouth shut… and has paid the ultimate price. It is up to you whether you follow suit… Paul,' she concluded.

'What the fuck are you playing at, you jumped-up little tart?' snapped Gallacher, his temper continuing to get the better of him.

But Lisa was growing tired of his impotent rage. She nodded to Yul to help make Gallacher aware of his grim reality.

The big man wound up a right hand and cracked it off Gallacher's jaw. He slumped forward.

'Bring him round,' ordered Lisa, and her henchman doused Gallacher with part of the contents of a nearby pail of water.

'What the fuck…' spluttered The Midget as he came to, but as he did so Lisa grabbed his throat and pinioned his head back against the chair.

'You will keep a civil tongue in your head, while you still have the ability to do so,' she warned and then took a step back, annoyed that she had let Gallacher get under her skin.

She turned to her henchman. 'I take it we have searched him? Anything to report?'

'Only a Nokia, which is on the table with the rest of his shit,' replied Yul, the dome-headed enforcer who doubled up as Lisa's bodyguard and number two.

'Interesting and possibly useful,' she said thoughtfully before turning back to the tied-up Midget. 'We have a job for you, Paulie, and your acceptance of it is your only hope at leaving here alive.'

At last it seemed that Gallacher was aware at just how perilous his situation was, and his reply was straight to the point: 'Go on.'

'We are willing to let you go free from here and to take one million of the Total Security cash with you—'

'You're takin' the piss,' he snapped, but was stilled by the raising of her hand.

'Indeed, I am not. You will take the money back to your organ grinder, and then you will ensure that you arrange a meet with Forsyth to conclude your deal. At that meeting you will eliminate both Manny Summerbee and our Scottish business acquaintance. You will then be allowed to leave Manchester with the cash to start a new future somewhere else after you have deposited the rest of the money in a safe-deposit box, the

details of which we will supply you. Do you understand me…
Pauuullllie?' she drew his name out sarcastically.

'Are you completely off yer rocker?' asked the incredulous
Gallacher.

Lisa smiled thinly. 'Not at all. I think, given the situation
you are in, I am making you a very good offer; in fact, it is the
only offer on the table and given it is in return for your life
and a fresh start, you would be mad not to take it,' she said.

Three feet away, Gallacher's face went blank and for once
he remained silent.

'So, at last the penny drops! There is one other condition
attached to our very generous proposal…' said Lisa.

The Midget's eyes narrowed, his feral features riven with
suspicion, but again he remained silent.

'You will tell me where the shipment of Škorpions, grenades
and other military-grade equipment you took delivery of last
Friday is, and you will in turn ensure that we are able to claim
it. This information will be seen as an act of good faith and
an indication that we can trust you,' concluded Lisa, placing
Gallacher under the intense scrutiny of her dark-eyed gaze.

But it was too much for Gallacher and his explosion of rage
underlined that all Lisa's groundwork had been to no avail. 'Are
you joking? No way, bitch, no chance.'

'Have it your way, Paulie, but one way or another we will
have that information,' snapped Lisa and then she clicked her
fingers.

Yul had been holding a rough fabric hood and he slipped
it over The Midget's straining head, then hauled down the
back of the red seat until it was parallel with the ground, with
Gallacher now in a prone position.

From above him, The Midget heard her say: 'You will tell us exactly where your hidden arms cache is and you will do it sooner than later, believe me.'

Standing behind Yul, the second, so-far silent goon – the red-haired, scarred giant – handed Lisa a Wedgewood teapot. She held it in her right hand and exchanged a glance with Yul. 'Pull the hood tight!'

Then, Gallacher felt her presence close to him on the other side of the hood, so close he could smell her perfume. 'You are about to undergo a very nasty little experience that I promise you will loosen your tongue, Paulie… after all, no one likes to drown!'

Then she started to douse his hooded face liberally with the contents of the teapot, alternately watering the areas covering Gallacher's mouth and nose with a generous, steady flow of the liquid while Yul counted out loud.

By the time he had reached ten, the hood was soaking, water had started to puddle on its surface and Gallacher was choking violently as sheer panic engulfed him.

For Paulie Gallacher couldn't swim… and now he was drowning.

26

TO GALLACHER'S RELIEF, the torture halted and the hood was pulled back from over his eyes. Standing above him, Lisa smiled viciously. 'Come to your senses yet, Paulie? It's not nice being waterboarded, is it? The fear and terror the experience causes is the ultimate tongue loosener and one perfected by the Japanese in the Second World War, I believe,' she said triumphantly as she patted the lid of the blue Wedgewood teapot.

It was all too much for Gallacher. He spluttered desperately, then, as his eyes locked on the teapot, he managed to recover himself enough to spew vitriol: 'You crazy bitch, what the hell is the teapot all about? I should have expected as much given your father is some Bible-bashing lunatic, 'cause it's clear madness runs in the family.'

But Lisa's patience was running short and she nodded to Yul to pull the hood back down.

'What an odious little man you are. Before I am through here I will make sure I have taught you some manners,' snapped Lisa, and then she began to repeat the waterboarding as if she was tending roses.

Gallacher gagged and choked and strained with all his might to break his bonds, but it was useless and as Yul's count reached 15, Lisa said: 'Oh dear, we have run out of water. Let's see how the patient is.' And with that she signalled to her subordinate to slip the hood off.

Gallacher's eyes were wide and riven with terror and mucous streamed from his still-bloody nose as he gagged violently.

'So, let me tell you what is happening to you, Paulie. The inhalation of water causes a gag reflex and you're experiencing what amounts to drowning as your body assumes that death is imminent. Waterboarding is designed to overcome the will of the individual by causing physical pain and psychological suffering. I would guess, judging by the effect it's having on you, that you are a non-swimmer? Correct? By the way, how are your lungs? Do they burn, Paulie?' And then despite herself she let out a short, almost shrill laugh.

Strapped to the chair, Gallacher was hyperventilating. Lisa stooped and whispered in his ear: 'Is there anything you want to tell me, little man?'

But Gallacher refused to burst. 'Go to hell, bitch!'

'Okay, if that's the way you want it then we will go for third time lucky. But just let me explain what is going to happen to you, as you experience extreme stress and pain both physical and psychological. I guarantee you – because, my dear Paulie, I have done this before – that as your cognitive processes break down, you will start to realise false memories and both your decision making and your ability to remember whether you have shared information will be seriously impaired. So, the bottom line is that pretty soon you will be a pathetic wretch and you won't even know if you have told me where the weapons stash is or not!'

Then she held out the teapot and let the second male refill it.

Gallacher was at the end of his tether, yet he knew by handing out the information she demanded he would be signing the death warrant of his crew and give The Devils weapons that would fatally tilt the balance of power in Manchester's streets.

Forcing his breathing to regulate, he angled his head to Lisa as if he had something he wanted to share. But as she started to bend down, he hawked a mouthful of saliva and spat at her with all the venom he could muster.

It was an act of defiance that was immediately punished by the crack of a right hand off his jaw, and once again Gallacher went limp; but as Yul threatened to make sure The Midget's lights went out for good, Lisa grabbed him with a restraining hand.

'No more, we need this information. It's just too important to pass on. But once we have it…' She drew a silken handkerchief from her leathers and wiped away the phlegm from her cheek, before shrugging her shoulders in a clear indication that then her enforcer could enjoy his wicked way with their captive.

Once again Gallacher was roused by having the contents of the bucket thrown over him and once again Lisa Crerand stood before him, beautiful, beguiling, feline and utterly malevolent.

'Come on, Paulie, is this really worth it? Don't you want to take your seat in the Kippax Stand and bellow Blue Moon? You never know, City may even qualify for Europe again – would you want to miss all that?' she said benignly.

Groggy he may have been, but Gallacher remained defiant. 'How the hell could I ever take me seat in the fuckin' Kippax after I'd sold my brothers out. Just goes to show you know fuck all about football. You're getting nothing out of me, you snotty-nosed tart,' vowed Gallacher.

As Yul began to pull the hood down over his gore-flecked face, The Midget made one final vow: 'I promise you one thing, girl, and that is that One-Eye won't leave my death unavenged. He still owes your father, and your little stroke with the Total Security van, and what you do with me here will be the death of you and your old man.'

But Lisa had had enough. She locked eyes on the crewman, who had remained silent throughout Gallacher's whole ordeal, and drew a finger across her throat.

He needed no second invitation and drawing a flick blade from inside his anorak, he slipped the switch and set four inches of shining steel free.

He made his way towards Gallacher, but Lisa took a step forward and opened the palm of her right hand. 'Oh no, Radoslav, the pleasure will be all mine.'

She ripped the hood off The Midget's head and leant back down. In his ear she began to sing a song, one he knew only too well:

> 'Blue moon
> You saw me standing alone
> Without a dream in my heart
> Without a love of my own
> Blue moon
> You knew just what I was there for…'

'Time you said that prayer, little man,' she whispered and drew the blade across his throat.

Taking a step back, she handed the flick knife to Radoslav and for a moment watched in satisfaction as Gallacher's vitals spilled out from him.

Helpless and almost lifeless, The Midget held her gaze defiantly until his eyes glazed over

Manny Summerbee devoured his lamb shashlik with his usual delight, savouring every mouthful of the meat garnished with onion and grilled vegetables that was a trademark of The Armenian Taverna.

He'd been coming here for the best part of 20 years and loved the fact that since its opening in 1968 the basement restaurant, situated just along from the city's epicentre Albert Square, had barely changed.

Now, in early 1990, it was like a trope of everything that stood for the 1970s. The look was completed by photographs of celebrities lining the walls, the cream of Manchester staring down at clients.

As always, Manny glanced at the image of Georgie Best smiling at him and shook his head. Best had always been just that in Manny's One-Eye: simply the best. If he had a penny for every time he had wished that The Red Devils legend had worn the pale blue of his club he would indeed have been worth a few bob.

Manny leant back in his booth and sighed, wondering at what might have been. He shifted his eyes away from the face of the United legend and took in the outlandish mural that covered most of the restaurant's walls not bedecked with photos. He smiled. The various figures dressed in traditional Armenian clothing made Summerbee feel like he was dining among old friends.

As he finished another mouthful of lambchop topped with a generous portion of mash, he reached for his cell phone and keyed in Paulie Gallacher's number for the umpteenth time. The silence from his number two was not only deafening, it was becoming a real worry.

He had expected Paulie to join him at the taverna and he knew that the opportunity to celebrate the success of any job with his favourite mixed kebab, a mouth-watering house favourite, was something that Summerbee was sure only death would stop Paulie from enjoying.

Yet here he sat like a lemon, alone except for the presence of one of his minders; and Paulie, now 30 minutes late, was incommunicado.

The worry and concern was beginning to turn his stomach to such an extent that Summerbee pushed his plate to the side of the table. He dabbed at his mouth with a white linen napkin, while his mind worked furiously.

It was then that his outsized cell phone rang out, and he breathed a sigh of relief when he saw Paulie's name and number flash up on the screen.

A smile flickered across Summerbee's taut features. He reached for a glass of his favourite wine – Karas, a blend of Syrah, Tannat, Malbec and Petit Verdot – and toasted his sidekick's imminent report of a job done well. 'The Midget!' he whispered.

'Paulie's probably been on the bevvy already!' he joked to his minder and then picked up the phone. 'Okay pal? I didn't think there was anything known to man that could make you late for a Taverna mixed kebab?' he asked, laughing down the line.

But instead of Gallacher's gravelly tones he was met with a refined, almost accentless female voice. 'Sorry to disappoint, Mr Summerbee. Your friend has been a bit tied up, but he will be dropping in anytime now!' said the anonymous caller and hung up.

'What the fuck…' spluttered Summerbee. A crash caught his attention, as the doors to the basement restaurant banged open and across the carpeted floor rolled a blood-spattered body.

Paulie Gallacher had indeed arrived at the taverna, but he would not be enjoying its delights.

'Sweet Christ…' stammered Summerbee, rising from his chair. But his minder had already stooped over The Midget's bruised features and stated the bleeding obvious: 'He's dead, Mr Summerbee.'

Summerbee reached for the Glock inside his black Hugo Boss single-breaster, stepped over the corpse of his friend and climbed the stairs out of the basement restaurant, a man possessed.

But when he strode out into the daylight there was nothing to be seen, just a normal Manchester street scene of people going about their everyday life.

Princess Street, where The Armenia Taverna was situated, was on Albert Square's northern side and Summerbee made a panoramic sweep of the street with his one-eyed gaze, frantically trying to pinpoint anything that might be connected with Gallacher's gruesome fate.

A hundred yards to his right, in the direction of City Hall, the screeching of burning rubber caught his attention and he saw a silver Sherpa van pulling out from the side of the street before tearing off.

'Bastards,' muttered Summerbee, just as his minder shouted a warning: 'Get down, Manny!'

The urgency and desperation in his bodyguard's voice as much as its volume snapped Summerbee out of his futile search for the deliverers of Gallacher's body. He turned towards his minder in time to hear a high-powered motorcycle fire up. As its sleek lines came into focus, he saw that its rider was toting an Uzi, its barrel bursting into flame and lead starting to fly his way.

Standing out on the pavement, Summerbee was hopelessly exposed; but just as his demise seemed certain, the motorcyclist was forced to make a desperate swerve as a Greater Manchester double-decker resplendent in its orange livery pulled out from a bus stop just yards away.

Summerbee threw himself onto the deck and rolled behind the temporary cover afforded by the vehicle as his minder got off two rounds in reply.

Coming back up onto his knee, Summerbee was able to see a slim figure roar off on a red, green and white Ducati 750 F1.

27

FERGUSON'S BROODING silence was so at odds with his usual larger-than-life persona that Thoroughgood found himself filled with a sense of foreboding as they made their way to Greater Manchester Police Force HQ at Chester House.

They would have to endure their date with ACC Crime Michelle Trautmann, but before that, there was one lead that he wanted to get off his chest. 'Gaffer, there is something that I think might give us a wee line of enquiry in this whole mess.'

Across the cabin of the Royal Mail van, one of the Boss's unruly ginger eyebrows shot up and he gave Thoroughgood a piercing stare. 'Sweet Mother Mary, boy, out with it for crying out loud: before I am put up against a wall I generally like to have a final fag!'

Thoroughgood smiled wanly. 'It's the motorbike,' he said matter-of-factly.

'What bloody motorbike?' demanded Ferguson

'The Honda CB250 that was shot up by one of the robbers before they made good their escape. Shot up by the female who wore the motorcycle helmet and who I think was hoping by doing so would manage to send it up in flames, or at least make it useless as a piece of evidence by dousing it in a hail of lead,' concluded Thoroughgood.

Now he had Ferguson's attention. 'My, my, you are a little smart-arse after all, ADC Thoroughgood,' he said in a mocking high-pitched voice that was intended as a piss-take but also admitted genuine interest.

'Well, I thought that if I could find a VIN number – a Vehicle Identification Number – we may be able to trace purchase details to the dealer it was bought from, perhaps get a copy of a logbook, who knows? But in any case, I think the VIN number may provide us with an opportunity to trace its current owner. Just maybe that could lead us to its rider, the Uzi-toting female I had my run-in with,' said Thoroughgood in a rush.

A smile burst out on the DCI's craggy features. 'God in Govan, the bloody VIN number. Sweet Christ! Just get on with it will you, Thoroughgood!' he demanded, his legendary impatience starting to froth.

Thoroughgood nodded. 'Okay, so the VIN number is pretty much always located on the right-hand side of the headstock tube, which is the rod of steel at the front of the bike where the fork clamps bolt through. The VIN is always stamped deep into the frame there.'

'Okay, clever clogs, good, but not nearly good enough…' said Ferguson, making it obvious he wanted more… fast.

'So, on a Honda bike they have a 17-digit frame number. They have been printing frame numbers since '81 on every single bike and with the Honda number pattern, the 10th digit refers to the year. So, if the tenth digit is an eight then it's a bike from 1988,' concluded Thoroughgood, a little too smugly.

'That's all well and good, matey, but it don't amount to jack shit on its own…' said the Boss, although his interest was clearly piqued.

'Bear with me, gaffer,' smiled Thoroughgood before he continued: 'Quite often when people are trying to conceal the VIN they will scratch it out and then re-stamp a fake number and you need to check the paint, digit alignment… anything, really, that doesn't feel or look right. What I noticed was that the six suggesting the

Honda is an '86 bike, was, on closer inspection, an eight, making it in fact two years old.'

'All of which means before we go and see Mad Myra, you will get your arse into Control and run a Police National Computer check on the number and just hopefully we will have ourselves the owner's details or at least a dealer to go on. In fact, there is no hopefully about it: I need – no, must have – something by the time we get to the 11th floor,' said Ferguson, his grim features brokering no protest.

'Yes Boss,' agreed Thoroughgood.

But Ferguson's attention was already elsewhere as looming large was Greater Manchester Police HQ, Chester House, a testimony to 1970s office architecture that was anything but glowing. 'Now before our audience with ACC Trautmann, I need a coffee and a smoke, and by the time I have finished both I will expect you at her office door with chapter and verse on that bloody Honda and whoever owns it now or sold it to the current owner. Capiche?' smiled the Boss.

'No pressure then, Boss!' said Thoroughgood through a thin smile.

As he always did before he entered ACC Trautmann's office, Ferguson knocked and waited, full of foreboding.

As usual, a short delay ensued, as if Trautmann were considering whether to tell her visitor they were not welcome, before her clipped, precise tones replied: 'Come!'

It was an order that always left the sides of Ferguson's mouth curling in a snigger, just like a naughty schoolboy.

Taking a deep breath, the DCI opened the door and entered. 'Good afternoon, ma'am,' he said with due deference to her exalted status as head of crime.

But all that presented was Trautmann's heavily lacquered blonde hair, which rumour had it could emerge from a force 10 without a strand out of place.

The ACC Crime continued to pen a missive to some subordinate before eventually ordering 'Sit,' only to continue her scribbling.

Ferguson did as he was bid but as the seconds drew on and Trautmann failed to look up, his frustration got the better of him. 'Well this is nice,' he muttered and immediately regretted it.

The pause was momentary, but Trautmann's golden fountain pen quivered in mid-air for a second before she continued writing for around 30 seconds more.

'Mind if I smoke?' asked Ferguson, knowing how much Trautmann hated 'that disgusting habit'.

At that she looked up and her piercing blue stare scorched him. 'Your childish attempts to get under my skin are so transparent, DCI Ferguson, that despite your years of practice it never ceases to amaze me that they still haven't climbed above the puerile chatter of a naughty schoolboy,' she said.

'Thank you, ma'am,' replied Ferguson sarcastically. This exchange of catty remarks was the hallmark of their love-to-hate relationship.

'Tell me, DCI Ferguson, just how do you think Operation Reef is going?' asked Trautmann, steepling her immaculately manicured fingers, all the while keeping the DCI under intense scrutiny.

'Well, the flooding of city centre with uniform and doubling of patrols has definitely had a positive impact. Unfortunately—' but before he could finish his sentence Trautmann took over.

'Unfortunately, "the gold-plated information" …' – and she stopped to provide imaginary quotation remarks with the two middle fingers of either hand before continuing – 'that you promised would lead us to the apprehension of the Total Security van robbers in the act did not prove to be quite so precious, did it, DCI Ferguson? To make matters worse, we then got extra value for our money when the first group of robbers were held up by a second. And we further enjoyed the sight of an armed shoot-out in the yard of the Bank of Manchester sorting office in Salford and the cold-blooded execution of two thugs via semi-automatic gunfire in the middle of one of Manchester's busiest arterial roads. On top of which, almost £6 million in used notes exchanged hands between two different groups of villains, as under our supposedly watchful eyes not one but two armed robberies were concluded. So, you did what, DCI Ferguson? Precisely what?' thundered Trautmann, concluding the damming charge sheet.

She punctuated her tirade by leaning forward in her chair so that her rather prominent cleavage, sheathed in a red turtleneck, could not be missed by Ferguson's dancing eyes, sending the DCI's temperature soaring.

It was the opening salvo of what was known within CID as Myra's 'hairdryer' treatment and Ferguson, who had been left slightly frazzled by an opening salvo he had been prepared for, still found himself squirming in his chair.

'Ah yes, I was just coming to that, ma'am, we believe—' but again Ferguson's faltering defence was overrun.

'You believe what, exactly, DCI Ferguson? That there is a World War Two bomber on the moon? Because your idea of good policing is a completely alien concept to me and to the chief constable.' And at that Michelle Trautmann's icy blue gaze melted slightly as her eyes strayed to the picture of Chief Constable James Henderson that occupied pride of place on her desk.

Trautmann was well known to have 'affection' for the chief, or 'God's Own Cop' as he was known in some quarters for his right-wing, almost puritanical leanings.

As she regarded Henderson's lush beard and brooding gaze fondly, Ferguson sought to seize some of the momentum back. 'I know things have not gone well this morning, ma'am, but we have had some excellent results with the plain-clothes officers we have deployed to act as bait for the street robbers, while the Total Security van job was always going to be a bit more tricky...' But the Boss knew he had chosen the wrong word the minute it escaped his mouth and now he was made to pay for it.

Trautmann's attention snapped back from her love-in with the chief's picture and the hairdryer was flicked to max. 'Tricky? Tricky? You have made Greater Manchester Police a complete laughing stock, turned our streets into a shooting gallery and placed countless members of the public at risk. Add to this the fact that you have completely disregarded the first tenet of police work, which is to serve and protect, and just allowed the single biggest armed robbery in this great city's history to be completed not once but twice... and you call it tricky, DCI?' she concluded, her eyes popping and the pitch of her voice shriller by at least two octaves.

Under pressure, Ferguson's right hand always played with the front strands of his unruly red mop and now was no exception. But he was soon able once again to impose restraint on himself and meet her blue gaze head-on.

Checking his watch, the Boss muttered, 'Where are you, Thoroughgood?' to himself.

'What did you say?' snapped Trautmann.

Uttering a silent prayer to the man above, and anyone else who would listen, he tried to stall: 'There is some good news, ma'am:

we now have a lead, or line of enquiry…' And this time Ferguson deliberately left his words hanging, waiting for an interruption that did not come.

Trautmann leaned back in her outsize black leather swivel chair and clamped both hands on its armrests. 'This better be good,' she fired.

It was at that moment that a light knock on the door punctured the simmering tension between them.

Her brilliant blue gaze never leaving Ferguson's craggy features, Trautmann called out: 'Come.' The Boss gritted his teeth to avoid any sign of mirth while he prayed silently that the new arrival was indeed Thoroughgood.

To the DCI's obvious relief, the ADC made his entrance. 'Good afternoon ma'am,' he said, and then nodded to Ferguson, before adding: 'Sir. ADC Thoroughgood, ma'am, with some evidence that I hope may be of use in relation to this morning's robberies.'

Trautmann sat like a Sphinx, surveying the new arrival with something approaching contempt. 'Ah yes, the young aide arrived fresh from Glasgow. My breath is indeed bated, young man,' said the ACC with an almost salacious emphasis on young man.

'Thank you, ma'am,' replied Thoroughgood, taking her reply as the green light to provide the lowdown on the altering of the Honda CB250's VIN plate. When he had concluded the technical breakdown he took a short breath to allow Trautmann to digest his information before continuing.

'So there can be no doubt the VIN was altered to conceal the true identity of the bike and, more importantly, where it was purchased, but I am pleased to say that with the help of the Police National Computer and force GMP HQ staff I now know the Honda's state of origin.'

For the first time in ten minutes what could almost be the trace of a smile flickered across the ACC's stony countenance. 'Go on,' she said.

'The Honda was purchased in 1988, as I mentioned, from Howard Scott Motorcycles on Gorton Road, Hyde. I have made some further initial enquiries on this and it seems that Scott has come to the attention of local uniform for some involvement in a ringing operation, though these suspicions have never been confirmed in the form of any charges brought.'

Trautmann suddenly leant forward in her seat. To the side of Thoroughgood, Ferguson sneaked a sideways glance at the effect her artful manoeuvre had on the young ADC and smiled smugly at what he saw.

Despite himself, Thoroughgood, who had been preparing to proceed in an orderly direction, did a double take.

Trautmann's immaculately plucked eyebrows raised in enjoyment at the effect of her impressive cleavage and she said: 'So in essence what you are saying, ADC Thoroughgood, is that this Howard Scott is under suspicion for exactly the illegal activity that has been carried out on the Honda to conceal its true identity and where it was purchased?'

Thoroughgood cleared his throat. 'Almost exactly so, ma'am, although in the Honda's case I would suggest that its VIN number has not been replaced by another from a stolen bike, just altered. Though really it amounts to the same thing.'

'Good work, ADC Thoroughgood. It's just a pity that this line of enquiry was not discovered by one of our own, DCI Ferguson,' she said, arching a censorious eyebrow the Boss's way.

'Indeed, ma'am, but nevertheless, it is a line of enquiry I am very keen to follow up immediately, while our boys are searching every lock-up, garage, scrappy and derelict building this side of the Pennines to try and locate the van,' said Ferguson in a rush.

Trautmann got to her feet and turned her back on the two detectives, to look out the window of her 11th-floor office. 'What about the Squirrel?' she snapped.

Behind her, Thoroughgood, taken completely by surprise, tried but failed miserably to stifle a laugh, while Ferguson attempted to drown out his mirth by speaking over his young colleague.

'The Twin Squirrel is in the sky, ma'am, and so far has failed to find a single bloody acorn. But with your permission, ma'am, we will be about our business and follow up this most promising lead. If that is all, ma'am?' he asked, hoping to escape.

But Trautmann had heard Thoroughgood's snigger and she turned towards the two detectives, hands on hips, the wan sunlight highlighting her bleached blonde hair and framing her intimidating figure to startling effect. 'I can assure you, ADC Thoroughgood, there is nothing funny about the use of our force helicopter – The Twin Squirrel Aérospatiale, to give it its correct name – and you would do well to remember that.' Then she trained her blue gaze on the Boss. 'As for you, DCI Ferguson, I hope for the sake of your career there is something positive and concrete from our young Scots colleague's work to show very soon and I expect an update on any developments ASAP.'

Then she swept an imperious hand dismissively towards them both: 'Out.'

28

'WELL THAT was an experience!' said Thoroughgood as he buckled himself up in the passenger seat of Ferguson's BMW 5 Series.

The DCI gunned the engine into life and slipped his silver machine into gear, replying: 'When I first got my transfer through as a DS she was a snotty-nosed DC who thought she had all the answers.' He paused. 'Looking back I guess she did.'

'She certainly keeps you guessing, what with that blonde mane lacquered to the point it wouldn't bend in a tornado. One minute it's the hairdryer treatment, as you call it, and then the next minute she is thrusting her... er... well... assets at you as if they are twin canons. Jeez, I didn't know where to look!'

'So I could see, boy, oh I noticed all right! But you underestimate Myra at your peril, for as you may have noticed from the photo on her desk, she has a very special relationship with the chief. Did you know that he has had a song written about him?'

Thoroughgood shrugged and shook his head in the negative.

'It's called "God's Own Cop", by some bunch of bloody hippies called the Happy Mondays. Fucked if I know how it goes, like, but there you go. All you need to know is that the chief has been our beloved head of crime's sponsor – for want of a better word – from day one and that has, in essence, been behind her rise from humble – though it's something you could never call her – DC to ACC Crime,' concluded Ferguson thoughtfully.

But Thoroughgood had to ask a question that had been burning in his head ever since they had left ACC Trautmann's 11th-floor office: 'Sorry, Boss, but where did the Mad Myra nickname come from?'

Ferguson shot him a shocked glance. 'Call yourself a detective, young Thoroughgood, but you still need your Uncle Marty to spoon-feed you. The clue is in those magnificent peroxide-blonde tresses that have had such an impact on you, boy!' he snorted.

Thoroughgood rubbed his chin as he decided whether to go with the hunch that had already germinated in his ample imagination. 'Has it anything to do with Myra Hindley, The Moors Murderer? I suppose at a stretch you could say that there is, just about, a similarity, taking into account the blonde hair.'

Ferguson laughed out loud, aware that Thoroughgood had been none too keen in supplying the correct but distinctly un-PC answer. 'Bravo! You are indeed correct, ADC Thoroughgood! But please don't ever let Myra hear you call her by her nom du guerre or there won't be a big enough phonebook to stuff down the back of your shorts to save you from the thrashing she will administer!'

The image Ferguson had conjured up set both of them off in a chorus of ribald laughter as the BMW continued its smooth progress to Hyde.

Soon, Thoroughgood attempted to move things on: 'I've got a bit more background on Howard Scott, Boss. I don't know how I missed it, but he was done for armed robbery best part of 12 years back and had a stretch in Strangeways as a result. More recently it seems like he has been a good boy and unfortunately nothing that is current or has stuck. As I already mentioned, there is intel fingering him as part of a ringing operation and when you add that to the dodgy number on the Honda's VIN plate, well, two and two definitely makes four, Boss,' he concluded, folding away Scott's previous convictions printout.

'Aye, the benefits of a solid Scottish education are there for all to see in you, son. So the way we will play this is you can take the lead, and if I feel the need to get heavy and apply a little firm persuasion, well, you'll know soon enough, son!' said Ferguson, administering a side-on wink.

They drew up in front of Scott's motorcycle shop, easy to find thanks to a row of chained bikes just outside the front windows.

As they made their way through the gleaming bikes, they passed a youth who was polishing some chrome to a brilliant sheen. Ferguson nodded to Thoroughgood to do the needful.

'Afternoon. ADC Thoroughgood, Greater Manchester Police. Can you tell me where I can find Howard Scott please?' he asked, flashing the white Strathclyde Police warrant card that was distinctly at odds with the description he had just supplied.

The kid, who had a bowl cut that could have seen him pass for a prepubescent version of the Happy Mondays frontman Shaun Ryder at a push, stopped polishing and looked up long enough to check Thoroughgood out, although helpfully he studiously avoided looking at his warrant card.

Then he rose to his feet and made his way to the doorway, where he hung on the frame and shouted: 'Howard, we gotta visit from dibble!'

Moments later a stocky individual sporting a spiked mullet and resplendent in a pair of Levi 501s and a lightly soiled white T-shirt, both way too tight, appeared at the door cradling a mug. 'Thanks, Ronnie, why don't you go and get me a new pack of fags? Take the money from petty cash and have one on me, while I help the officers out with their enquiry.'

The youth called Ronnie nodded curtly and disappeared out the front of the shop. Scott forced an insincere smile. 'So to what do I owe the pleasure of this visit?' he asked.

Thoroughgood handed him the computer printout of the Honda's details but said nothing.

As he devoured the details, Scott took a slurp of his coffee, before he finally answered: 'Why don't you join me in my office, gents, that's where I have all my records. I will need to check them for this one as we're talking nearly four years back.'

'I think you'll find that it is your records from 1988 that you need to check, Mr Scott,' said Thoroughgood, boring his green gaze into Scott's back as they followed him to his office.

The shop owner said nothing.

Scott's office proved to be nothing more than a glass-fronted cubbyhole and his desk, or what you could see of it, was awash with coffee-stained invoices, while at either side of it were two large grey office filing cabinets.

He immediately went to the furthest away cabinet and began to rifle through the fourth drawer.

Thoroughgood and Ferguson stood just inside the office, either side of the doorway, until the DCI finally gave in to his burning desire to move things on at full pelt. 'Why don't you park your arse in that comfy looking chair of yours and let's just cut to the chase and forget about the play-acting,' snapped the Boss.

Scott turned around and despite himself couldn't stop a grimace from slipping across his worn features. But he did as he was bid and flopped into his desk chair.

Ferguson placed both of his massive paws on the desk opposite him and leant down until he was eyeballing the shop owner directly. 'Now, my young colleague is going to tell you exactly what we know. Then you are going to provide the answers we need because if you don't, we will be taking you back to Chester House and booking you for ringing motors, perverting the course of justice, obstructing police enquiries and the theft of bloody Shergar! Now do you understand me, friend Howard?' demanded the Boss.

A couple of feet away, Thoroughgood smiled thinly and got down to business. 'Yesterday a Honda CB250 was involved in a robbery and the subsequent murder of two people, one of whom was the driver of the Total Security van that was the subject of the turn.'

As Thoroughgood paused for breath, Scott folded his arms across his T-shirt. 'And?' he asked helpfully.

'And the Honda was bought from your premises according to the records we have for it through the Police National Computer. But what is really interesting is that the VIN number has been altered in an attempt to make the vehicle appear manufactured in '86 when it was actually manufactured in '88, when you sold it. Would you care to explain how that came to be, Mr Scott?' asked Thoroughgood amicably.

Scott laughed unconvincingly. 'Come on, Detective, how many bikes do you think I've sold in the last few years? As you can see, my filing system isn't the most hi-tech, which don't make me too popular with the accountant, like. But either way, what has the alteration of the VIN number got to do with me?'

Just as Thoroughgood started to open his mouth, he was beaten to the verbal punch by Ferguson's gravelly Glaswegian tones: 'Listen, mush, and listen good. Who do you think you are dealing with here? This is the Flying Squad and unless you want to be permanently grounded then I suggest you start to cough up,' snapped the DCI.

Across the table, the news that it wasn't just run-of-the-mill CID straight off the book that he was dealing with caused Scott to shift uncomfortably in his desk chair.

He fingered the last Silk Cut from a semi-open packet and lit up, but the tremor in his fingers belied the fact that he indeed had something to hide.

Ferguson, his eyes popping, continued to sear the motorbike dealer with his intimidating stare. 'The VIN number was altered, as you well know, because the bike was always going to be used in something a bit naughty. I'd wager that has been the case on more than one occasion before it came to our attention earlier today. Change the VIN and if it isn't examined closely enough then the provenance of the bike is never likely to be known, but fortunately my young colleague here has excellent eyesight and a keen nose for these things.'

Then Ferguson leant across the desk, grabbed the Silk Cut from its residence in the side of Scott's mouth and stuck it in his mug so that the lukewarm coffee doused it with a slight hiss.

'You, my friend, are covering someone's tracks, and we need to know who that is or…' – Ferguson paused and swept his right hand around him – 'I will have this placed turned upside down, every vehicle in the gaff sequestered and subjected to forensic examination, and while your shop is shut you will be relocated to Her Majesty's Pleasure in Strangeways… where I believe you've already enjoyed a stretch. Now do I make myself bloody clear… Howard?'

But surprisingly, the motorbike dealer refused to fold. 'Look, detectives, I'm real sorry but all I can do is check my records and provide you with the sale details, but given you don't seem to be sure if I should be checking 1986 or 1988 then this could take a bit of time. I… I really don't know what more I can do to help you. Sure, I've done time, but that was back in the late 70s. Ever since, I've been straight and trying to make a crust and an honest living…' he said from behind his best poker face.

'Of course you have, matey!' replied Ferguson sarcastically.

There was a pause. Then from behind the DCI, Thoroughgood spoke up: 'I take it the blow-up is from Donington?'

On the wall that housed the office door an impressive print of Scott and a group of friends posing in the pit lane occupied pride of place.

'Yeah, good spot. It was the '89 British 500cc at Donington and a few of us got a pass to visit Ron Haslam in the pits afterwards, I'll never forget it!' said Scott, seemingly relieved to have the conversation changed to something far more palatable.

The picture had Scott and three others flanking British biking legend Haslam and his attention firmly on the pic, Ferguson realised what his young colleague was getting at. 'Who's the bit of fluff, Howard? Well out of your league, ain't she?'

Standing in full leathers was a dark-haired temptress who had a protective, fatherly arm wrapped around her shoulder by an older male while she sat, smiling, astride Haslam's Suzuki as 'Rocket Ron' crouched down next to her.

As three sets of eyes homed in on the picture, Thoroughgood continued the train of thought: 'What if the smouldering brunette in the picture was the Uzi-toting vixen who filled the air with lead at the scene of the Total Security van robbery?'

The Boss was even less subtle. 'Well, Howard, if you aren't going to fill in our young pal with the identities of your chums maybe I can be of assistance. You were keeping some very interesting company at Donington. If I'm not mistaken, the older gent with the snowy white hair is Gordon Crerand, the undisputed boss of The Devils crime cartel. Judging by the similarities I would suggest there is a familial resemblance between him and the young lady in question. Come on, Howard, is that Crerand's daughter?'

There was nowhere for Scott to run and he knew it. Backed into a corner, he shrugged his shoulders. 'Yes, that's Lisa Crerand,' he admitted.

While the motorcycle dealer's eyes remained locked on the giant framed photo that was clearly his pride and joy, Ferguson and Thoroughgood exchanged a knowing glance, and the Boss quickly issued a warning shake of his head to the young ADC.

Ferguson clamped a paternal hand on Scott's shoulder, which caused the bike dealer to almost jump off the ground. 'Must have been some day, Howard! Anyway, I think we've taken up enough of your time. All I would ask is that you check your records for both years in question and make sure that you provide us with the relevant paperwork.'

As Scott recoiled from the DCI's touch, a look of complete surprise surfed his face as the extent of his reprieve sunk in.

Smiling amiably, Ferguson concluded: 'ADC Thoroughgood will be back for the documentation tomorrow, but if you are feeling particularly obliging we would appreciate you drop it in at the Flying Squad office at Stretford nick. That fair enuffski?'

Clearly at a loss at how to react to this sea change in Ferguson's attitude, Scott nodded in the affirmative.

'Excellent! In that case, it's time for a pint, Detective Thoroughgood, because I need to think, and we have a helluva lot to talk about,' said Ferguson, smiling craggily at the clearly disconcerted Scott.

29

LESS THAN AN HOUR later, they sat once again in the snug at The Lass O'Gowrie waiting for DS Greene and DC Morgan to join them.

Ferguson had come up with a hypothesis that had been radioed to the Flying Squad office and now, thirsty as always, he waited for their arrival with a full update.

'Aah, that first mouthful always goes down a treat, boy! Now, before Laurel and Hardy arrive, it's time I filled you in with a bit of background, which will help put some extra colour into the picture that occupies pride of place in friend Howard's office,' said Ferguson. He paused and, like a human hippopotamus, devoured most of his pint in one monstrous mouthful before coming back up for breath.

As he did so, Thoroughgood took the opportunity to make his own contribution: 'Can I say just one thing, Boss... what kind of coincidence is it that the Total Security van is held up by a female motorcyclist on a bike that traces to Scott's and then we see Lisa Crerand in leathers sitting astride Rocket Ron's Suzuki with her father and Scott standing proudly by with grins as big as a couple of proverbial Cheshire Cats?'

'There is no such thing as mere coincidence, boy! What I've discovered over the last 25 years of coppering is that a coincidence generally tends to suggest you are on the right path. Now my betting is that by the time Morgan and Greene get here we will have information that shows Crerand and Scott go back a long way, in fact I'm betting they will prove to be as thick as thieves. The only thing that was bloody well missing back at the one-stop motorbike shop was a red devil tattoo on friend Howard's forearm… but then maybe he has one somewhere more discreet!' concluded the Boss, barking out a laugh.

Sipping at the mint Guinness Ferguson had insisted on buying for him, Thoroughgood replied: 'Perish the thought, Boss! But one thing's for sure: I'll bet good money on Scott getting on the blower to Crerand the minute we got out his shop. I tell you, Boss, I would never forget the mince pies inside the motorcycle helmet back at the robbery locus, just like one of those wall paintings with the watchful eyes that miss nothing. They were… mesmerising… I've no doubt they were those of the girl in the picture.'

'That's all and well, boy, but what we need is good solid evidence. Do you think any of that flimflam will be enough to get us into Mad Myra's good books?'

Facing him, Thoroughgood's grimace was all Ferguson needed for an answer.

'Exactly! What I need after Wally and your gaffer arrive is that we come up with something that she will swallow: a plan of action, and one that actually has a chance of success. But one thing's for sure: this war between Crerand and his Devils and The Maine Men has taken a decided turn for the worse and it's about time I gave you a crash course on it; so take a good draft, buckle up and get another pint in, will you, son, 'cause I'm parched!' said Ferguson, saluting his junior with his empty foam-flecked pint pot.

Moments later, Thoroughgood plonked two fresh pints of the black stuff down and made himself comfortable. 'Looking forward to Jackanory!' he said with a smile.

'Excellent! Okay, so it may not have escaped your attention that Manchester has two football teams, one who play in red and one who play in blue – pale blue to be precise. They are?' asked Ferguson, mockingly stern like a headmaster.

'United and City,' said Thoroughgood, failing to hide either his impatience or slight irritation at this condescension.

'All right, boy, don't get tetchy now, I have been briefed that you are a Harry Wragg, as all three of you Partick Thistle supporters are known, but this is real football we're talking about! Now where was I? Ah yes, so while in Glasgow your tribal lines are semi-religious with Rangers and Celtic, here in Mancland the divisions have extended along football allegiances to the city's two most notorious gangs: the Devils, who take their soubriquet from United's Red Devils nickname, and the followers of City, who are known as The Maine Men from the Maine Road stadium where those in pale blue strut their stuff. So good so far?'

Thoroughgood started to roll his eyes but thought better of it and gave a quick nod in the affirmative.

'Now at the top of The Devils' ranks sits Gordon Crerand, a man of many contradictions.' He paused. 'You've heard the name?' Seeing Thoroughgood nod, he continued: 'A devoted father to his one and only daughter Lisa and to the memory of his late wife Charlotta, and a devout churchman. Yet by the same token a convicted arms robber, a master of extortion and a man desperate to control the drugs trade that flows in and out of our northern powerhouse. He is also absolutely ruthless and very imaginative in the ways he decides to enforce his will and punish those that trespass against him. Capiche?'

'All good, gaffer!' replied Thoroughgood cocking his pint Ferguson's way.

'Now in the other corner we have Messrs "One-Eye" Manny Summerbee and Paulie "The Midget" Gallacher, numbers one and two of The Maine Men and the sworn enemies of The Devils. Yet, about six years back, peace almost broke out between the two gangs until Summerbee tried to cut Crerand's grass when it came to… guess what…?' asked Ferguson suddenly, testing Thoroughgood's state of alertness.

'A woman!' replied Thoroughgood.

'How very perceptive of you, clever clogs. For that piece of stupidity Summerbee was, in Crerand-speak, smitten down and had an eye removed for his troubles, all of which is the stuff of legend among those fine fellows of the Manc underworld. So now, as you are well aware, there is a bitter turf war that has been sparking into life with tit-for-tat acts of violence… until things suddenly took a turn for the worse this morning,' said Ferguson, then paused as he took another mouthful of Guinness.

'Especially if Lisa Crerand has masterminded the hit on The Maine Men!' chipped in the ADC.

'Oh yes, because while losing six mill to The Devils is bad enough, it's also common knowledge that The Maine Men took delivery of a consignment of military-grade firepower last week and were on the verge of agreeing a major drugs deal with our fellow Scot Terry Jaws; but while the former may have put the latter in doubt, make no mistake, Thoroughgood, what that means beyond all doubt is that vengeance shall indeed be on a biblical scale!'

His crash course complete, Thoroughgood, for once, had nothing to say, for the implications were clear: one way or another, Manchester would be painted a particularly crimson shade of red.

But the sound of silence that had engulfed the snug was soon broken by a female Mancunian voice: 'Ay up, Boss!' Shaken from their respective broodings, Ferguson and Thoroughgood looked up to see the brunette in the white blouse and pencil skirt who had given Thoroughgood palpitations near enough the same time, same place, the previous day.

'Wally and DS Greene are just behind me,' she said with a mischievous twinkle.

'And lucky men they both are, Molly!' laughed Ferguson roguishly before he remembered his Ps and Qs and with a clearing of the throat, but failing to tear his eyes away from the new arrival, he added formally: 'ADC Thoroughgood, forgive my manners, let me introduce you to DC Molly Malone, a second-generation Irish émigré, and important member of my squad. What you got for me, Molly?' he asked as he gestured for the DC to sit down.

As she smoothed out the pencil skirt that showed off every one of her contours, DC Molly Malone smiled sweetly at Thoroughgood before turning her head to meet Ferguson's voracious gaze. 'It's not good, sir, I'm afraid. About the same time you were having your interview with ACC Trautmann, Manny Summerbee's lunch at The Armenian Taverna was rudely interrupted: about halfway through his lamb shashlik, Summerbee was joined by his right-hand man Paulie Gallacher. The only problem was that The Midget was about as well done as Manny's dinner and served stone cold on the Taverna's Axminster,' she concluded gravely.

Beside her, Ferguson's right hand shot to his ruffled fringe. 'Sweet Mother Mary!' he said, staring into his pint pot.

It was then that they were joined by Morgan and Greene, and the news wasn't about to become any better for the Boss.

'I'm afraid you're wanted back at Chester House... the news about Paulie Gallacher's demise has reached the 11th floor... and...' Morgan stuttered, before going on: 'Mad Myra is, well...

as mad as a kangaroo on fire, Boss... 'cause there was an encore to The Midget's arrival...' he faltered, clearly trepidatious at the reaction he was about to get from his gaffer.

Ferguson slammed his back against the booth seat and folded his arms. 'Come on then, get it over with, Wally, for Chrissakes,' he hissed.

But it was the burr of Greene's Glaswegian that took up the verbal slack: 'What DC Morgan means to add is that Summerbee didn't take kindly to The Midget being served as his dessert and he spilled out onto the street above looking for his delivery man and was almost iced... almost iced by a motorcyclist unloading an Uzi like it was the end of days!'

As Ferguson digested the news, he looked up at Thoroughgood and shook his head in an admission that this latest information had supplied further confirmation as to exactly what they had both suspected ever since they had seen the blow-up print on Howard Scott's wall.

Then Ferguson looked back at Greene and Morgan. 'And tell me, is Manny still with us?'

'Thanks to the timely intervention of a Greater Manchester double-decker, he lives to fight another day... he and his henchman were in the wind before GMP could get there... and that, I guess, is going to mean a whole lot more bad news for us and The Devils,' said Morgan.

'I'm sorry Marty, but the ACC Crime wants you back pronto,' said Greene, wincing.

Surprisingly, Ferguson jumped to his feet and drained the last dregs of his pint before slamming it onto the table. 'Give my regards to Broadway, chums!' he said and strode out The Lass O'Gowrie as the others looked at each other helplessly.

30

'SO SUMMERBEE survives, and of course that means he will have only one thing on his mind… revenge!' said Gordon Crerand from across the office desk. He looked into his daughter's eyes and once again asked himself why he had allowed her to get involved in the family business.

Crerand couldn't help shaking his head. Lisa's involvement had been something he had been determined to avoid, but which had ultimately been taken out of his hands: for the plain fact was that she had a special aptitude for their line of work.

Looking into her dark, refined features he saw so much of her late mother, so much of what had made him love Charlotta the first time he had seen her, up on Alderley Edge. But now he felt that he had let his wife down by allowing Lisa to become what she had.

For a moment he shut his eyes and listened to the beat coming from the club dance floor; to Crerand, it was like the thrum of jungle drums. It made him feel old.

After a short pause she spoke: 'You know that we had no other option but to act, Dad. If they had secured the takings from the Total Security van then Forsyth would have been in Summerbee's pocket. How long before the consignment of weapons The Maine Men took delivery of would have been supplemented by a secondary delivery? It was one of these moments when our hand was forced; and tell me, Dad, do you regret the fact that Paulie Gallacher is no longer with us?' asked Lisa.

'Of course not. You live by the sword, you die by it. And I have no doubt you are right about the van and the drugs deal. Certainly the money will make us stronger once we have invested it correctly. But first things first: I have ordered that the security on all our venues is doubled up; for the one thing you can guarantee is that Summerbee will not shut that one eye of his until he has secured payback.'

As Crerand finished his monologue, the desk phone rang. Lisa picked it up and then leant back in the large black leather desk chair, so imposing that it was almost like a throne to her.

'Hi Howard, this is a surprise! How can I help?' she asked and, as she did so, she flicked the phone to intercom.

'It's dibble, Lisa, they've been round poking their nose in about the Honda CB 250 and it ain't just normal plod but the bleedin' Flying Squad,' revealed Scott.

His arms folded across his chest, Crerand did not bother to hide his concern: 'All right, Howard, it's Gordy here. I'm in the office with Lisa. Listen, old friend, do you know the names of the coppers who paid you the visit? That might be helpful.'

'It was a DCI Ferguson and a smart-arse young pup called – what was it again? – Thoroughgood or something like that…' said Scott, his words trailing off.

From the other side of the desk, Lisa provided the full name for him: 'ADC Angus Thoroughgood is his name and he's a Scot.'

A few feet away, Crerand shook his head. 'Bloody Scots! We must have half of Glasgow Police joining up in the GMP. That nutter Ferguson is also a Jock, isn't that right, Howard?'

From the other end of the blower Scott, was more than happy to confirm it: 'Nasty big bastard. I thought I was in for a pasting, Gordy. They came in pretty heavy-handed and that DCI accused me of tampering with the VIN number and more or less said he'd shut me up; but then they ended up good as gold and just told me to make sure I sent the relevant documentation in to them ASAP. Strange it was, real strange, like.'

Crerand exchanged a worried look with his daughter as they both tried to fathom exactly what could have been behind the change in tack by the Squad.

'Is there anything else that they got up to that stands out as maybe not quite right to you, Howard? Something that might not have added up? When have dibble ever left empty-handed when they can turn a premises upside down and trash it just for the sake of it?' concluded Lisa.

'Well, there was one thing that was maybe out of the ordinary… they spotted the photo of us all with Ron Haslam at Donington the other year and wanted to know who the girl in the leathers sitting on The Rocket's bike was…' laughed Scott nervously.

For Lisa it didn't take the penny long to drop. 'Thank you, Howard, that's great. Listen, if there are any other developments please keep us posted and we'll do likewise from our end, but just sit tight for now,' she said

Across the red United coffee mug he had been cradling, Gordon Crerand eyed his daughter; for he was only too well aware that there was more to her cutting Scott short than she cared to let on.

For a moment, father held daughter's gaze, and Crerand let a slight silence develop, which he was apt to do when he wanted Lisa to elaborate on something she was anything but keen to divulge.

The slight firming of her sculpted jaw betrayed Lisa's determination to keep schtum, but as she knew, her father could play the waiting game when he wanted something; and at last she let out a sigh.

'Spill, dearest daughter!' said Crerand, a slight tremor of amusement playing at the corners of his thin lips. This was a game that had been evolving between them since he had been handed the challenge of raising his 'temperamental' young daughter when Charlotta had passed.

'Tell me, please, daughter mine, how you came to meet this ADC Thorough… whatever he's called,' he ordered, the gentle tapping of his Barker brogue betraying his slight irritation.

'It was at the security van. He turned up out of nowhere and the silly sod tried to thwart us all on his own until he realised arguing with an Uzi wasn't a smart career move,' she said, telling the truth, but nothing like the whole truth.

Crerand inclined his head slightly. 'What mystifies me is how you managed to get an introduction from him, name, rank and serial number all supplied, while presumably you held the Uzi to his head? I take it your helmet remained over your head and that he has nothing to identify you with?' asked Crerand, the concern in his voice giving it an edge.

Lisa shrugged slightly in the girlish fashion she always reverted to when she was trying to conceal something from her father.

'Yes?' asked Crerand.

'It's nothing, Dad, just that my visor was up… but what does that give him to go on? Two eyes half hidden by the darkness of the helmet, it's hardly enough to put me on a witness line-up,' she said, adding a slightly forced laugh.

'As always, Lisa, you have all the answers; but you also have your mother's eyes and if, my darling, our clever young Scots copper has had a clear sighting of them and spotted the alteration to the bike's VIN number and then seen you in leathers on top of The Rocket's bike… then, my dear girl, we may have a problem,' concluded Crerand sombrely.

'Trust me, Father, there is nothing to worry about on that score. You were right, the real worry is where and when Summerbee will hit and whether we can get any information on his whereabouts that would allow us to finish what you started – and I almost ended – once and for all, before he has the chance to land the equaliser,' Lisa concluded.

'Trust me, every snout, grass and lowlife, as well as our suitably well-greased friends in the right places in the incorruptible GMP, are being encouraged to provide that information. That said, Summerbee is no fool. He has gone to ground to lick his wounds, maybe even mourn the sad demise of his little friend while he too waits for the information that will lead him to our – or, to be more precise, your – door, Lisa. That is why I have added a couple of my old friends from the army to the floor and door security tonight and why they will be shadowing your every move…'

'But Father—' Lisa began to protest but Crerand's raised palm warned her it was futile.

'I am not prepared to argue with you on this, Lisa. That is my call and you will respect it – honour thy father! Now, as you can imagine, I have much to do, but my old friends will make sure you come home to Chipleys safe and sound when Reds is shut up.' He leant over the desk and kissed Lisa on the forehead, smiled warmly, and then, with a wink, left the office – with a thousand things on his mind.

As her father shut the office door softly behind him, Lisa couldn't help herself from rising from her chair and taking a look through the blinds of her fourth-floor office. As she peered into the darkness that almost concealed the Rochdale Canal from the flickering streetlights, her teeth clenched.

Reds was her pride and joy and she was determined that nobody, including one-eyed Manny Summerbee, would destroy it or take it from her.

On the ground floor, the club's cocktail bar, simply called Best's Bar – named after and dedicated to the legendary United star George Best and garlanded by photographs and memorabilia from his playing career – had become a fixture for those that wanted to be seen in the city's happening venues.

There were also two other themed bars, one, The Madchester, dedicated to the rich, vibrant and unique Manchester music scene and the other, Les Femmes, a tribute the heroines of Lisa's youth.

All of which had turned a former yacht-builder's warehouse enveloped in red Accrington brick into the most famous live music venue in the city; and it was an empire that Lisa had created, designed and built all from the rich and fertile imagination her father had so hoped would lead her into a life far away from the world he operated in.

Annoyed at the feeling of being under threat, she snapped the blind shut and glided across the office floor, opening the door and slipping out into the corridor, keen to make her way to the second-tier dance floor and bar where she could enjoy the sounds played by Reds' in-house DJ, Reg Wilson.

But as she slipped into the corridor, she found the hulking presence of a crew-cut brute facing her.

His military bearing and straight-backed stance left her in no doubt that he was one of the ex-forces minders her father had brought in.

'Evening Miss Crerand,' said her new babysitter. She smiled wanly at him and slipped down the corridor, but the heavy footfall behind her confirmed that her father was indeed good on his word.

31

RESPLENDENT in a black cropped vest top and tight black leather trousers that amplified every curve, Lisa perched on her favourite bar stool at the top end of the bar, which allowed her to enjoy a perfect panoramic view of the second floor while she sipped on her habitual Pernod, blackcurrant and lemonade.

The dance floor had been innovatively sectioned off by black and white bollards that could easily have been lifted from the city's streets, while three central iron pylons that ran along the centre of the floor were painted in multicoloured chevrons and helped keep the rigs of pulsing lights firm as they throbbed above the dance floor.

At 10.50 pm the dance floor was only partially full, but already the atmosphere was building. Lisa found it hard to believe that this was the same dance floor where celebrities as exalted as Madonna had performed their newest singles for entranced crowds and even live TV all throughout the 80s.

As she sipped her drink through a straw, she lost herself for a moment in the memories that had made the venue so special to her; but these were soon replaced by other memories of a far more recent time.

She did not regret ending Paulie Gallacher's life, but there was no doubt there would be a tab to pick up for his demise, and although she had not wanted to admit it to her father, he had been right to add the extra muscle to her security team.

Although judging by the look of Radoslav, who occupied a raised position just inside the second-floor door, and the way he was eyeballing the crew-cut ex-squaddie who was only a few feet away, not everyone was happy with the extra hired help.

She tried to focus on more practical matters, like preparing for the club's eighth birthday party, which was due on May 21; but her planning was soon interrupted.

'All right, darlin', you're lookin' real lonely, like, why don't you join me on the dance floor, sweetheart?' asked a male twenty-something-year-old wearing a black Lacoste sweatshirt and trying to look cool by constantly flicking his centre-parted bob cut out of his eyes with a snap of his neck.

The smell of nicotine and booze was almost overpowering and when the strands of his hair parted, she could see that his eyes were glazed, which suggested his favoured poisons were not limited to liquid form.

Having endured similar advances a hundred times before, Lisa smiled sweetly. 'Sorry, but I'm waiting for someone.'

But the punter failed to take the hint and leant over, slipping a grubby paw onto the bare skin of her shoulder and whispering a sweet nothing in her ear – one that was anything but sweet.

Across the bar, Crew Cut had spotted Lisa's uninvited guest and started to stride towards the unsuspecting would-be Lothario, but she beat him to it.

Swaying to her side, she grabbed the wrist of the hand the man had plonked proprietorially on her right shoulder and twisted it round so that her suitor was forced up onto his toes; then she rammed a knee into his back and forced him face-first onto the bar.

'What the fuck…' protested Bob Cut, his face rammed onto the bar.

But Lisa was already flanked on one side by Radoslav and on the other side by Crew Cut; and she smiled at them both in turn before saying: 'I'll let you gents fight over this piece of meat, but make sure he is photographed and made aware he is banned from Reds… for life, Radoslav!'

The big enforcer nodded in agreement. Crew Cut propelled the groaning punter towards the door, Radoslav riding shotgun.

But Lisa's attention was already elsewhere, for from behind her a voice said: 'It's nice to meet you once again, Miss Crerand.'

To her left, sitting on a barstool three feet away, his sea-green gaze locked on her, was the Scottish detective. He smiled her way and extended his hand.

'ADC Thoroughgood. I believe we have already had the pleasure of meeting, albeit in fairly grizzly circumstances… Miss Crerand. I'm delighted to see that Mr Uzi is not with you tonight!' said Thoroughgood as a grin twitched at the corners of his mouth.

He was bold and it unsettled her, as for a moment Lisa struggled to provide the type of smart, quickfire reply that was usually her stock in trade; but despite herself she could not help a slight tremor of amusement lighting up her refined features.

Judging from the way he returned the compliment, she thought that Thoroughgood enjoyed the sight. But as he began to open his mouth, he was surrounded by his friends and straight away Lisa saw that the company he was keeping was of the copper variety.

In between the voluptuous figure of a female in a pencil skirt a size too small and a middle-aged male who looked like he'd just left his golf club bar, their eyes continued to hold.

But the female in the pencil skirt and a white silk blouse that wouldn't have looked out of place on Crystal Carrington in an episode of Dynasty had spotted that Thoroughgood's attention was not on her low-buttoned top and had turned towards Lisa. 'Can I help you, princess?' she asked. Lisa put her in her mid-thirties.

Lisa smiled icily and held out her hand. 'My name is Lisa Crerand, and this is my club. We are always happy to take care of members of Greater Manchester Police,' she said and then turned to her left and clicked her fingers just loud enough for a white T-shirted barman to spring to attention behind the counter.

'Tony, please take care of our friends from GMP and set them up with a round on the house.' Then Lisa turned back to the brunette. 'Enjoy the free drink… honey!' she said and spun on her heel, all the time aware that Thoroughgood's gaze had never left her.

Back at the bar, Thoroughgood took a mouthful of the lager the house had provided and scanned the dance floor, while Morgan made it clear he'd rather be elsewhere: 'Look, there's a seated section at the top end of the floor, but I'd rather we hit Best's. What do you think, Molly?'

But Molly already had other ideas. Thoroughgood felt a tug at his wrist and realised she was dragging him onto the dance floor; the look in her eyes meant that resistance was futile.

For Thoroughgood, the moments that followed were indeed murder on the dance floor, as Molly subjected him to a full monty of gyrating hips, pouting lips and flouncing arms all in time to Electronic's 'Getting Away With It', which he had to admit was quite a feat.

Excusing himself on the last beat of the song, Thoroughgood made his way to the gents, desperately thinking how he could make good his escape without giving offence to DS Paddy Greene, who had still to join them.

When he returned to the bar, to his relief Molly had now dragged Morgan onto the floor and Thoroughgood was delighted to contemplate his pint alone while he waited for Greene to make his entrance.

It was at this point that Thoroughgood noticed a male make his way to the bar. What had drawn the cop's attention to the new arrival was the fact that he had kept a pair of aviator shades on despite the fact that he was in a nightclub. Thoroughgood gave a rueful shake of his head and mouthed the word 'Plonker' to himself. He took another draft of his pint, an unidentified house lager that left him wincing.

Yet soon there was something far more interesting on his radar, as Lisa Crerand had returned to the bar area and, despite himself, Thoroughgood couldn't keep his eyes off her.

She moved with an assured feline grace that was bewitching, and her shoulder-length jet hair was as sleek as every curve of her body. The realisation that his observations were now crossing a line from a professional to personal capacity made Thoroughgood shake his head to clear his mind.

"How can you even look at another woman when Christ knows what has happened to Em?" the voice in his head berated him.

But Thoroughgood's guilt trip was brought to a juddering stop as he was buffeted from first one side and then another, the bar seeming to have become instantly packed.

The lager escaped from his pint glass and washed down over his hand and on to his treasured Adidas Sambas. 'You want to watch where you park your feckin' elbows, mate,' he snapped at the sweat-drenched clown who was the culprit for his soaking.

As he shook the lager off, Thoroughgood's attention was again drawn to the male in the aviators, for he had just turned, and

Thoroughgood could see a rucksack hanging from a shoulder of his Fred Perry bomber jacket.

The voice in his head asked: "So what do you need a rucksack for in a club like this… twat?"

Almost immediately he shrugged the suspicion off as surely the house security would have checked the contents of any bag coming onto the premises.

Thoroughgood also noticed that, despite his aviators, the man couldn't conceal that he was taking a more than passing interest in Lisa Crerand, who was back on her barstool, sipping on her drink almost Sphinx-like, with a grace that was again proving mesmerising to Thoroughgood.

Forcing himself to turn his eyes from her, Thoroughgood returned his attentions to the dance floor, where Molly Malone had now draped her arms around Morgan's shoulders and was grinding her hips into him.

Rolling his eyes to the ceiling, Thoroughgood said a silent prayer that Greene would arrive and allow him to make his excuses and a sharp exit stage left, but as he scanned the doorway there was no sign of the DS and once again Thoroughgood returned his attention to his pint.

Suddenly, a firm hand on his shoulder snapped Thoroughgood's attentions elsewhere.

'There you are, Gus. Jeez, whose idea was it to come here? Surely not Wally Morgan's?' asked Greene.

Thoroughgood smiled and pointed over to the dance floor, where Morgan and Molly seemed to be intent on recreating a scene from Flashdance. 'Molly can be pretty hard to refuse!' he laughed.

Greene shook his head and offered to buy Thoroughgood a pint. In the interests of bar etiquette, the ADC felt unable to refuse. As Greene got them in, Thoroughgood's gaze once again returned to Aviators, who had now taken his rucksack off the bar stool and pushed it against the bottom of the bar.

Then he took a step back and sneaked a quick glance at Lisa Crerand, who remained a study in still life sat just five or six feet away.

"Something ain't right, pal," said the voice in his head and for once he had to agree.

Just then Morgan and Molly Malone arrived at his side. 'Come on, Gus, let's have another spin, that sounds like Joy Division coming on!' she said slightly huskily.

Thoroughgood barely heard her words for he was locked on Aviators, who had now started to make his way from the bar on a route that would take him to the exit and was doing so at a fair rate of knots.

Thoroughgood shrugged off Molly's attentions. 'I'm sorry, DS Malone, but I've got something more important to do,' he snapped. Leaving her smouldering in a semi-volcanic rage, he put himself on an intercept course between the exit and Aviators.

But the man had now seen the cop coming and took a sharp left onto the dance floor, where he was almost instantaneously swallowed up by the gyrating masses.

Getting his hands on Aviators was clearly going to take time and could get messy; but Thoroughgood knew that the contents of the rucksack were of far more immediate importance.

Striding back along the bar towards the rucksack, he knew that if his worst fears were correct then he had only moments, if that long, to avert disaster.

It was then that he saw that he had attracted Lisa Crerand's opaque gaze. She had risen from her seat and was now slinking towards him, which would put them on a collision course almost exactly opposite the rucksack.

"Shit," said the voice in Thoroughgood's head, just as Bernard Sumner's 12-string Eko guitar meandered through the strains of the Joy Division classic 'Love Will Tear Us Apart'.

Above the heavy bass and thrumming beat, Thoroughgood shouted: 'Go back!' But Lisa clearly could not hear him, and a look of complete mystification crossed her refined features.

Acting on instinct, he broke into a sprint and tackled her to the floor, just as the violence of the blast from the bomb that Aviators had left in the rucksack ripped through the bar.

32

AS THEY HIT the ground, the screaming erupted, and everything seemed to turn white.

Slowly, Thoroughgood felt his senses return to him. His eyes flickered open and he realised that they were shrouded in dust.

Underneath him he felt a murmur and just inches away Lisa's dark gaze fixed him and their eyes held.

Just as he opened his mouth to ask if she was okay, she supplied the answer… with a kiss.

Taken completely by surprise, Thoroughgood gave in to the moment and reciprocated… briefly… before he regained his composure and eased himself away from her.

He rose to a knee and slowly checked for any damage to his body. A yard away, Lisa had also risen to her knees and was mouthing something to him, but he could not hear what she was saying: it felt like he was underwater.

She reached over and placed a hand on his right shoulder, gave a tug and presented a vicious splinter of wood that had clearly impaled itself in him… although, adrenaline pumping, he felt nothing.

But his attention was already elsewhere because the effects of the blast were grim, and the bar was now a gaping hole full of smashed wood and broken glass, while the roof above it had also partially collapsed.

But Thoroughgood was already on his feet and making his way towards the spot where Morgan, Greene and Molly had last been. He passed a prone figure who showed no signs of life, while the sobbing of a badly cut female, who was being consoled by a friend, was heart-rending.

As he tried to work out what had had happened to his colleagues, who were nowhere to be seen, Thoroughgood soon realised that the bar had taken the brunt of the blast. While the damage in that section was bad, it was clear that the explosive device must have been of the homemade variety, as the carnage was quite localised, and was clearly designed to take care of just one person: Lisa.

Thoroughgood made his way into the corridor outside, pulled out his personal radio and started to broadcast an urgent request for emergency assistance, just as he spotted Greene and Morgan each taking an arm of a bloodied reveller to help him make his way out from the carnage.

But there was no sign of Molly.

As his broadcast came to an end and he began to turn back to see what help he could offer to the injured, he saw to his relief that Molly had just left the ladies.

'What the hell happened?' she asked in typically direct fashion.

Thoroughgood realised with relief that his hearing appeared to be returning, even if sounds still seemed like they were coming from underwater.

'An improvised explosive device of the homemade kind, I'd say. I see the guys are doing their bit helping the injured,' he answered.

'Thank God for that, I thought they were still in there,' she answered slightly awkwardly. 'We better get in there and see what we can do. I'm assuming you've put out the help shout?'

Thoroughgood nodded in the affirmative and then said: 'There's more, Molly. I got a make on the suspect, cast iron. Around six foot, dark hair, ridiculous aviator sunglasses and wearing a navy Fred Perry bomber jacket.'

The DS was starting to jot down the details after Thoroughgood repeated them, when she saw the wound on his shoulder.

'That looks a nasty one, Gus, and I wouldn't be waiting too long to get it seen to. I'll check in with Wally and DS Greene just in case they can add something of value,' she said, starting to make her way down the corridor, which was being flooded by dazed partiers.

Thoroughgood headed back through the doors, not sure what use he could really be, but determined to do his best whatever that may be.

Inside the bar, Lisa had already taken charge and Crew Cut and Radoslav both had their hands full with injured dancers.

The throbbing of the music had thankfully been stilled and now the only sound inside Reds was the sobbing and groaning of the injured, the shocked and the badly shaken.

As he attempted to make his way through the debris, Thoroughgood saw that Lisa was kneeling over the member of her bar staff who had recently served him.

Thoroughgood couldn't see the barman, but when Lisa felt his presence and looked up, she gave him a shake of the head that made it clear the young man hadn't made it.

'I've broadcast for urgent emergency assistance and the ambulances shouldn't be too far away. Are you okay?' he asked.

Her smile was wan. 'Better than some… thanks to you… Detective Thoroughgood.' Again she held his gaze, for the intensity of the moment that had just passed between them and the fact that he had saved her life had changed everything between them.

Opposite Lisa, Thoroughgood was at a loss for words. The sight of her, now dishevelled, dust-strewn and smeared with what looked like the blood of others, did nothing to distract from the confusion he felt towards her.

'I would like to see you again… Angus… if you would like?' she asked in a way that made it clear she did not often get turned down.

But before he could answer, a familiar voice from behind him filled the airwaves: 'Jesus H. Christ, Thoroughgood, you've got more lives than a cat!' said DCI Marty Ferguson, clamping a hand on his shoulder.

As Thoroughgood turned around, the Boss shook his head. 'Paddy filled me in on the way through: homemade explosive device you think… intended for… well…' the Boss stammered to a halt.

'I am well aware it was intended for me… DCI Ferguson,' said Lisa, adding Howard Scott's description of Ferguson from the motorbike shop to the evidence of her own eyes, before continuing: 'I have a lot to be grateful for, thanks to Detective Thoroughgood. Sadly, the same can't be said for my barman and some of the clubbers you probably passed on the way in.'

'Very true… Miss Crerand. I'm sorry, but I'm duty-bound to ask if you have any idea who might be behind an attempt to take your life… albeit that may indeed be a stupid question,' said the Boss from behind his best poker face.

Even in the milling mess of shocked and injured people, and smashed and fractured debris, the question, although the obvious one, had the effect of bringing a chill to the atmosphere around them.

Meeting Ferguson's enquiring gaze, Lisa got straight to the point: 'I think we both know that your suspect list should start and finish with one name: Emmanuel Summerbee. If I was you, I wouldn't waste too much time in speaking to him.'

Ferguson's unruly eyebrows shot up. 'And just why would that be, Miss Crerand?' he asked.

'Because, DCI Ferguson, I would say Mr Summerbee's life expectancy has just been drastically reduced.'

Ferguson gave a short sharp nod of his head. 'Now Miss Crerand, I appreciate what you have just been through, but I would be very careful about what you have to say to an officer of the law in these… er… turbulent times. For now, however, we have officers on the way who are specialists in dealing with this type of incident and they will want a full statement from you, if you are up to giving one?' asked Ferguson, with an arch of an ample ginger eyebrow.

The stony look on Lisa's face was all the answer he got. Turning to Thoroughgood, Ferguson for the first time noticed the crimson seepage on his shoulder. 'I think you need to get yourself checked over, boy, and then we need you back at the ranch ASAP, as I'm told you might have some useful information to share with us. Meantime, I need a quick word with DS Greene…' he said, but his words soon started to trail off because at the entrance to the dance floor, in full uniformed glory, was ACC Michelle Trautmann.

'Sweet Mother Mary,' said the Boss, whose features had turned a whiter shade of pale, and immediately made off in the direction of the ACC Crime.

Thoroughgood watched the Boss shuttle off before his eyes returned to Lisa. He saw that she was shivering and, without thinking, he unzipped his Harrington and slung it over her shoulders.

'I think the shock may be starting to kick in, Miss Crerand, maybe it's time we got you checked over?' he asked with a reassuring smile.

But she shrugged. 'I need to make sure my staff are okay and that poor Tony is taken care of first. In any case, looking at your shoulder, I'd say you are in more need of medical attention than I am, Detective.'

The removal of his Harrington had indeed caused the wound to throb and Thoroughgood found himself clamping his right hand down on it, turning the sleeve of his white cotton Oxford shirt a bloody crimson. 'I think you might be right there,' he said awkwardly, not wanting to tear himself away from her but reluctantly taking a step back, desperate to avoid saying something that he would regret.

Thoroughgood needn't have worried, as Lisa took control. 'But how will I return your jacket... my hero?' she said coyly.

'That is something I don't think will be a problem for you!' he said, before adding: 'One other thing... Miss Crerand... I love your scent!' Then, enjoying the unsettling effect his last remark had had, he headed for the door.

33

HIS SHOULDER cleaned, stitched and bandaged, Thoroughgood sat in the back of a uniform patrol car taking the fast route back to Flying Squad HQ, Stretford Police Station.

As he watched the rain pattering off the vehicle windows, the thought that he had been blown up twice in one month and still lived to tell the tale, bar a few grazes and cuts, left Thoroughgood thanking his lucky stars.

He once again found himself being drawn back to the events that had unfolded at The Blood Acre. Thoroughgood couldn't help but wonder for the thousandth time what had become of Emma.

How could she just have vanished into thin air? Despite lookouts and a national missing person enquiry, nothing had been turned up. Thoroughgood remained convinced that the police would have found her body if she were dead.

He had no doubt that McGrain had the network and ability to escape British soil if he wanted, but why would he take Emma with him? Her use as an insurance policy was surely limited to domestic situations, not international.

The fact that Interpol were now also on the lookout for her just meant that McGrain was inviting unwanted scrutiny on himself.

It just didn't add up.

Lost in his own world of torment, Thoroughgood thought back to the last time he saw her, perhaps drawn there by a sense of guilt following his moment with Lisa. He may have foolishly declared his love for her, but how did Emma actually feel about him?

Inside his head, his inner voice was having none of it: "Get a grip, man, how does this help?"

As his imagination got set to run away with him, Thoroughgood was brought back to the here and now by the uniform officer in the passenger seat turning towards him and saying: 'That's us here now, ADC Thoroughgood. You'll get the Flying Squad offices on the second floor. Go through the uniformed bar and take the stairs.'

Startled, Thoroughgood nodded his gratitude and got out in the rear yard of a red brick building that could have been a cop shop anywhere in the UK. Moments later, he was ushered through the charge bar area, finding it strange that after over 48 hours working with the Squad, this was to be his first visit to their HQ: at almost 2 am on a Saturday morning.

When he made his way up the stairs to the second floor, the smell of the disinfectant struck him as mighty similar to the cheap stuff used back home in Glasgow. No doubt the Flying Squad's offices would be just as similar.

He wasn't disappointed.

The general office was open-plan, while Ferguson's domain was windowed off at the top end. A table Thoroughgood guessed was for the Boss's number two was parked just outside the DCI's office.

The walls were a cornflower blue and although the blinds that adorned the windows of Ferguson's office were half tilted to closed, the door was open and from it the unmistakeable tones of his Glaswegian accent were bellowing out.

For a second, Thoroughgood hesitated, before lightly rapping on the open door.

'Come,' replied Ferguson in what was clearly meant to be an impersonation of the ACC Crime's high-handed invitation to enter her 11th-floor bureau.

As he walked in, Thoroughgood was met by the sight of Ferguson's tan brogues on his table, while the Boss cradled a glass half full of whisky. Opposite him sat DS Paddy Greene, who raised his glass Thoroughgood's way. Morgan, Molly Malone and two other plain-clothes squad officers leant against the shuttered windows.

'Here we are, the boy blunder has arrived at last! We'd just about given up on you, Thoroughgood: what happened? Couldn't you tear yourself away from Miss Crerand while the rest of us were slogging our guts out trying to trace the suspect?' he fired off in double time.

'I'm sorry, Boss, I was just getting patched up. Did you have any luck with—'

But before he could finish, Ferguson, as was his wont, interrupted: 'Fred bleedin' Perry? The answer is no, we bloody well didn't, although uniform, bless their cotton socks, did recover his discarded jacket floating down the Rochdale Canal.'

Aware that all eyes were trained on him, Thoroughgood shrugged awkwardly.

Without warning, Ferguson's fearsome features softened and he pulled out the top-right-hand drawer of his desk and produced a glass before filling it with a large measure of Bell's. 'Here, drink this, boy. I think you've earned it, and in any case, you're going to need it given your next assignment,' he said, winking wolfishly at Greene, who shifted awkwardly in his seat.

Then he flicked his hand towards the rest of the officers to let them know that their audience was at an end. 'It's been a long and difficult night, but I want you all back in for a 1000 hours muster, Saturday morning or not. You know what we have planned. Class dismissed.'

As the rest of the Squad filed out, Ferguson dragged out a stool from the side of his filing cabinet and pushed it across the floor at Thoroughgood. 'Have a seat, boy,' said the Boss, exchanging a knowing glance with Greene.

It was the DS who got the ball rolling: 'That was good work tonight, Thoroughgood. Unfortunately we still had one fatality, but it would almost certainly have been more if it hadn't been for your sharp eyes and the way you acted on your gut instinct... It's a good thing our impromptu scouting of Reds happened when it did, or—'

Without bothering with any niceties, Ferguson cut across the detective sergeant: 'The bottom line is that without you, Lisa Crerand would no longer be with us and that will, I'm sure, make her father very grateful. But I also noticed, from over my shoulder, that she seemed all too happy to accept your jacket when you so gallantly offered it to her. So, answer me one question, my boy... is there something between you and Miss Lisa?' asked Ferguson benignly.

Unsure what to make of this line of questioning, Thoroughgood played for time and took a sip of his whisky before answering. 'All I did was what I would have done for any young lady who was starting to show signs of shock,' he fudged.

'Yet DS Malone seems to think there me be more than that to it, Gus?' enquired Greene.

Before Thoroughgood could answer, Ferguson cut in: 'Look, boy, what we are... exploring... for want of a better word... is... is if there is an opportunity for something to develop between you and Lisa Crerand that could help us in bringing this turf war between The Devils and Summerbee's team to an end before there is any more loss of innocent life or blood spilt,' he said, uncharacteristically cautiously.

From the look on Thoroughgood's face it was clear that the penny had indeed dropped. 'How can I answer that, Boss?' he shrugged.

Across the other side of the desk, Ferguson swivelled his feet back onto the floor and slammed his whisky glass down. 'Not to put too fine a point on it, boy, but in case you haven't noticed, we are in the middle of a feud that's painting Manchester red and have suffered an armed robbery that has left us with a six-million-pound black hole, while I have ACC Trautmann threatening to drag my balls through the mincer; and you can't answer me a simple bloody question?'

Then he looked over to DS Greene. 'Paddy, talk some sense into the boy, will you?'

Greene nodded and got down to it: 'Look, Gus, I took Lisa Crerand's initial witness statement but I did add the caveat that we may need more detail, so a window has been left open for us – or rather, you – to revisit and perhaps start to ingratiate yourself even more within her affections. But to be honest, I think by saving her life you've made a pretty good start in that regard!' said Greene, smiling reassuringly.

Opposite him, Thoroughgood knew it was time to come clean, and in a rush he said: 'I agree with you, Paddy. She wants to meet up with me, Boss.'

Across the table, the Boss let out a long slow whistle, while Greene gave a surprised shake of his head.

'Now that is music to my ears. Go on…' said Ferguson.

'Well for a start she wants to return my jacket,' volunteered Thoroughgood.

From his chair DS Greene replied: 'The only problem with that, Gus, is how long is that going to take? Do you think Gordon Crerand is going to hang about? As soon as he gets an opportunity, he will have Summerbee iced and make no mistake, he will leave no stone uncovered in that pursuit.'

'Paddy has a point. After all, did not the lady herself say, to quote Miss Lisa, "Mr Summerbee's life expectancy has just been drastically reduced"? So we do not have the luxury of time being on our side before things are escalated again. All of which is why from later this morning my officers will be turning, with the aid of uniform support, all known addresses relating to Manny One-Eye.'

'So how is this going to work, Boss? Because I don't see how you can possibly expect any instant rewards, as was mentioned, in terms of information. Lisa Crerand is clearly no one's fool: she would smell a rat a mile away,' said Thoroughgood, unfolding his hands, at a loss.

Opposite him, Ferguson sat staring into his steepled fingers. Inside his office, the sound of silence rebounded around the corn-flower-blue walls.

It was Thoroughgood who opened up first: 'I may have an idea, Boss, but that depends on one thing.'

Ferguson's red mop lifted. 'Which is?'

'Were you serious about there being a rat in the Squad?' asked Thoroughgood.

For once, Ferguson was pragmatism personified. 'In all seri-ousness, no. It's a ruse to keep those bastards out there on their feet. I want them to think I am watching them all the time, look-ing for slip-ups and trusting no one. I might be hail fellow well met when we are all in class at The Lass O'Gowrie, but there is another side to me. I use that to leave them a bit uneasy. In my experience it has paid rich dividends,' he concluded, before adding: 'Why?'

'Because I'd like to volunteer for the vacancy as your chief rat!'

34

MANNY SUMMERBEE stared into his Bushmills and tried not to drown in his rage.

Below his office, the bar of The Blue Moon was in full karaoke flow and Summerbee hated it.

As the strains of some Friday-night diva murdering Lisa Stansfield's 'This Is The Right Time' reached his ears, Summerbee's single eye rolled to the heavens... again.

Situated on Victory Road, his impressive two-storey pub was a key watering hole on the route to his beloved Manchester City's Maine Road Stadium, and as a teenager and young man it had been his favourite pre-match destination under its previous guise as The Gardeners Arms.

Now he sat cradling a Bushmills, peering through the blinds and into the night as he contemplated the disastrous attempt to take care of Lisa Crerand that would have brought the ultimate revenge on her father... the man who had inflicted the hideous injury on him that would scar and define 'One-Eye' Summerbee for the rest of his life.

These thoughts, despite himself, caused his right index finger to play at the black patch he sometimes wore over his empty eye socket.

He knew that his hated rival loved his daughter more than life itself. Since the death of her mother he had indulged her, and as Crerand had started to lose some of his interest and passion for The Devils' nefarious activities, it had been Lisa who had emerged as the real power behind the throne.

Thus, his reasoning: have her iced and not only would it bring the ultimate revenge, as well as never-ending misery, on Crerand, but without their de facto leader it could have also proved to be a lethal blow his nemesis and his organisation would not recover from.

Instead it had all gone pear-shaped.

A short rap on the door signalled that Summerbee's company had arrived. 'Come in, Pearce,' he said. The door opened and his liegeman walked in.

'I trusted you to make sure that jumped-up bitch was taken care of once and for all and instead you manage to blow up one of her bar staff. What kind of amateur job was that, Scouse?' he demanded, his knuckles going white with the pressure they were exerting on the whisky glass. 'Take these fucking sunglasses off before you speak to me or you'll need to have them surgically removed,' he added.

Jimmy 'Scouse' Pearce did as he was bid without delay. A second-generation Irish Liverpudlian, he had been a foot soldier in The Maine Men's ranks until Paulie Gallacher had taken a shine to him. The Midget had raised him up after he'd dealt particularly brutally with the encroachment of a team of teenage drug dealers on a Maine Men patch and now with the former's demise, opportunity had beckoned.

But he had botched it. Summerbee, fully updated on what had happened at Reds, was out for blood, and Pearce knew his survival depended on him making the strongest case possible for his self-preservation.

'Aaach… I'm sorry Mr Summerbee, but would you believe it, Sweet Mother Mary, the place was crawling with coppers on a night out and one of them made me and clocked the rucksack.

Believe me, boss, it was hard enough to get it in past the house security. The key parts had to be concealed in a milk bottle and an orange-juice carton with the petrol in one, the timer and Semtex in the other, and linked by a wire taped to the bottom of both. It was always going to need Lady Luck to flash her pearlies on us if everything was going to work out,' said Pearce in a hurry.

'Don't bullshit me, Scouse. I gave you this job to show me you could fill the gap caused by Paulie's departure and you failed me…' said Summerbee, staring into Pearce's taut features.

'I had no option but to leave when I did, Mr Summerbee. It was one of the young coppers who made me. He was coming my way fast. I had no option but to flick the switch and set the timer in motion and pray to the man above that Crerand and the nosey bastard copper were fried in the explosion, then get the hell out of there before he got to me. Otherwise there would have been no explosion,' said Pearce, fighting his case for all he was worth.

As Summerbee remained in silent contemplation, Pearce worked to defend himself. 'I only just managed to lose myself on the dance floor when the explosion went off and she was sat like the Queen of fuckin' Sheba just a few feet away from it. We woz that close, Mr Summerbee, that bleedin' close. Then as I was making my way out, I saw that bastardin' copper had got to her and managed to get her out of the way of the direct blast. You gotta believe me, boss, there was nothin' more I could have done, and I can tell you it wasn't easy to scarper.'

But across the table Summerbee had lost interest in the failed assassination attempt, because now it was going to be all about making sure he and The Maine Men were ready for the backlash.

The fingers of his left hand rubbed his stubbled chin as he thought long and hard about how the cards might fall, before he returned his one-eyed gaze to Pearce. 'Okay, I'm prepared to cut you some slack here, Scouse, because as it happens I had someone on the premises who has already provided me with a story very similar to yours. Maybe you are right, maybe Lady Luck just wasn't looking our way when we needed her to be. In any case, I want you to get some sleep and keep the phone on because we need to be on our toes. That prick Crerand will want payback and the coppers will have me in the frame.'

Across the table, Pearce breathed a sigh of relief. 'Thank you, Mr Summerbee.'

But his boss hadn't finished with him. 'Sadly, my dear Scouse, I'm afraid before you get some shut-eye I have another job that need's doing. I need the weapons stash moved from the lock-up. When you get downstairs, Everton and Jamie will be waiting. They know what is required and where it is to be relocated. Make sure it's done, and make sure you and the other two select something fucking heavy-duty from the stock, because we will have bad business to be about very soon and you will need to sleep with your weapon under your pillow. Do you understand me, Scouse? In the coming days you will have every chance to prove to me that Paulie was right about you. But I'm warning you, if you let me down again it will be the last time you will make that mistake.'

Scouse's features remained stone, but he was saved from a further verbal onslaught by the ringing of Summerbee's desk phone. When One-Eye answered, a female voice sprang into life at the other end of the blower, and he struggled to stop a look of surprise creasing his granite features.

Pointing his thumb at the door to send his minion on his way, Summerbee smiled with anticipation. 'Twice in one night, pet!

To what do I owe this unexpected pleasure?' he asked, smiling into the receiver.

From the other end of the blower, a voice that was smoky as a Kentucky bourbon filled the airwaves. 'You need to get out, Manny, the Squad are mounting a joint operation with uniform and they are going to be busting down every door you could be behind. Ferguson wants your balls and thanks to that young Scots copper he has a pretty good description of your bomber. I'll do what I can to throw the scent elsewhere but later today they will have a photofit for Scouse, and when that happens... well, the finger will be firmly pointing your way, Manny.'

Summerbee's gave a deep sigh. 'Jesus, Mol, this is a fucking disaster. But thanks for the warning. Don't worry about me, I'll be in the wind soon enough, but if that fuckwit Ferguson thinks he is going to stop me wiping out The Devils and making sure Crerand and his whelp are silenced once and for all, he has another thing coming.'

But One-Eye's informant was unconvinced. 'We've got two problems, Manny. Ever since that Glasgow copper and his babysitter turned up it's made life real difficult for me to get close enough to Ferguson to find out what's going on. I'm only getting the info last minute and it's making life tough for us to stay one step ahead. You need to do something about that first and then take care of the Crerands. Get rid of Ferguson and his Scots spawn and then things will open up for me: we will have control of the Squad and The Devils will be history.'

'You may just have a point. Maybe I've let Paulie get me looking at this the wrong way. Look, you know where I'm gonna be lying low over the next 48 hours... is there any chance I can see you there, love?' asked Summerbee, his voice, laced with salacious intent, dropping an octave.

'I'll do my best, honey, but I've got a part to play first,' said DS Molly Malone, before adding: 'You need to start thinking about this from another angle, Manny. This war can't go on, otherwise you are going to end up six feet under like Paulie or behind bars for the rest of your natural. We have to play smart. Remember, I have ACC Trautmann's ear and she hates Ferguson as much as I do: it's time we made that count!'

'As always, you're right, love. I've let the business with Paulie cloud my judgement; but trust me, my brain is firmly engaged now and I have something planned for Crerand and his bitch that will end this once and for all,' said Summerbee, his voice pulsing with intent.

At the other end of the line, the confusion was evident. 'What do you mean, Manny? I thought you agreed to do things my way?'

'Believe me, Molly, when the end comes for the Crerands, I will make sure my alibi is pristine and there is no trail back to The Maine Men. It's time we put a contract out on Crerand's head and I have had a name put my way who will do a professional job,' concluded Summerbee with obvious satisfaction.

'Good boy!' replied Malone from down the line and then the phone clicked dead.

35

THOROUGHGOOD made the 15-mile journey out to Cheshire in silence, but his mind was anything but quiet.

The Crerand's mansion was, he had been made aware, situated within what was known as the Golden Triangle: the locale where footballers, millionaires and TV stars had settled in impressive numbers, and one of the most sought-after residential areas outside of London.

Driving through the village, Thoroughgood had to admit it was everything you could want from an affluent, quintessentially English hamlet, and today the cafes were busy with people enjoying the pleasant early spring sunshine that bathed the pavement tables and chairs.

Having barely had four hours' sleep, the combination of the adrenaline that still coursed through his veins, the manic workings of his mind and the throbbing of his shoulder – not to mention the sandpit that passed for a bed in the police accommodation that he and Greene were now sharing – meant that Thoroughgood was tempted to pull over, treat himself to a double espresso and join the basking punters in the late-morning rays.

Instead, he kept the unmarked police Escort on a steady course. He shook his head, willing his distractions away. The truth was, he needed to concentrate: he did not know what awaited him at Chipleys, the Crerands' Grade II listed property situated in an acre of lush and rolling lawn, and he needed his wits about him.

The first thing that concerned him was whether Lisa Crerand would even be in. Yet being honest with himself, he had to admit that the fact he had chosen to make the drive out to the Crerand's home had a lot to do with the fact that he wanted to meet her father.

Although he'd heard snippets of this and that about The Devils' leader, Thoroughgood was very keen to take his measure himself, and the chance to observe father and daughter together and see how the dynamics of their relationship worked was something that had the wheels of the young detective's mind in overdrive.

Out in the countryside, the horizon opening up, he soon saw the sweep of an immaculately striped lawn from the Congleton Road, leading to an impressive courtyard and an imposing residence. However, before he could draw up to the front door, the foreboding presence of seven-foot wrought-iron gates mounted with a surveillance system and flanked with an imposing red brick wall confronted him.

He rolled down the driver's window of the Mark IV Escort, the feeling of inadequacy gnawing at him as he prepared to press the intercom system.

'DC Thoroughgood from Greater Manchester Police, I am here to speak with Miss Crerand concerning the incident at Reds nightclub last night,' he said, conveniently forgetting the 'A' for aide that prefixed his new title, and which he was already feeling undermined his status.

There was a short pause and then a male voice replied: 'Please make your way up to the house, Detective. Your ears must be burning, my daughter and I have been discussing your heroics last night all morning. I will be delighted to meet you in person,' said Gordon Crerand, with a delivery that Thoroughgood noticed was void of all intonation.

As the gates began to whirr open, Thoroughgood slipped the Mark IV into second and enjoyed the crunch of the drive's gravel under its tyres as he made the 800-yard journey up to an archway set below the entrance building.

From the window above the arch, he saw a leonine figure regarding his progress.

As he brought the Escort to a standstill, Thoroughgood saw the large white oak door was open and a medium-height, sandy-haired male strode out across the paving.

Leashed to his right hand, a Rottweiler strained, tugged and lunged in Thoroughgood's direction. Thankfully, they came to a stop a couple of feet away from his vehicle.

Aware that the male was placing him under intense scrutiny and concerned that he would let the Rottweiler go at any second, Thoroughgood got out of his vehicle slowly with his warrant card clasped in his open palm. 'Detective Thoroughgood, from Greater Manchester Police, here to see Miss Crerand,' he said.

The male, who was clad in a sharp grey suit with a white open-necked shirt, eyed the card suspiciously. 'I am sure you are, Detective, but your warrant card says quite cwearwy you are an officer from Strathcwyde Powice…' he said. Then he looked down at the Rottweiler, with whom he seemed to have some kind of telepathic understanding, then continued: 'What do you think, Nobby? Do we bewieve this… Officer?'

Inwardly, Thoroughgood groaned as he waited for the hired hand to make up his mind if he was going to throw him to his dog or not. But before he could do so, a voice interjected: 'It's okay, Uprichard, you can call Nobby off. This is Detective Thoroughgood, the man who came to Lisa's rescue last night. We have been expecting him. Please let him through.'

As he walked past, giving dog and hired help as wide a berth as possible, Thoroughgood couldn't help having a pop at the male now identified as Uprichard: 'For your information, you are correct, it is a Strathclyde Police warrant card, but I am on secondment with Greater Manchester Police.' Thoroughgood smiled insincerely before adding: 'Interesting name... Uprichard,' and flicked a quick wink the suit's way.

'I was onwy doing my job, Detective, pwease accept my apowogies. For your information, my family name is of Welwsh origin,' said Uprichard, taking a step back and dragging the still bridling beast with him.

But as he made his way past, Thoroughgood caught the hired hand's hostile gaze and there was enough presence in his languid stance and stony countenance that suggested Uprichard was someone who should not be taken lightly.

When he arrived at the door, Gordon Crerand held out a hand of welcome. 'It's not something I say often to an officer of the law, but I'm pleased to meet you, Detective, and even more pleased you did what you did last night. My daughter means everything to me.'

Somewhat taken aback by Crerand's candour, Thoroughgood smiled unconvincingly and provided a solid handshake in response. 'I appreciate your kind words, Mr Crerand, but I was only doing my job.'

'I'm glad you did, Detective. Now come on in and join me for a coffee.' And with that Crerand made his way into a huge, white-tiled entrance foyer, which led into an equally impressive open-plan kitchen.

It was like the footballers' pads he had seen when he had on occasion found himself leafing through the pages of Hello! Magazine on a visit to the dentist.

In the middle of the carefully designed kitchen area, a set of luxurious leather high seats were spaced out around a breakfasting surface of immaculate black-marble finish situated in the centre of the otherwise pristine white surround. It was clear that no expense had been spared.

'Please take a pew and let me get you a coffee, Detective. How do you like it?' asked Crerand, as if he was a concerned grandfather.

'Black,' replied Thoroughgood, his gaze straying through the doorway and back out into the entrance foyer.

Crerand had not missed his interest. 'If you're looking for Lisa, she will be with us shortly after she finishes her morning swim. May I ask what has prompted this follow-up call, Detective?' he asked amicably.

Thoroughgood nodded his head in agreement that it was indeed time to get down to business. 'We have a suspect description which we believe relates to the individual who planted the explosive device, and I have a photofit of this individual I am very keen to let Miss Crerand see.'

Crerand handed Thoroughgood his coffee but now his welcoming demeanour had been replaced by a more severe countenance. 'I believe you are on secondment with GMP and perhaps you are not fully aware of the situation in Manchester, Detective Thoroughgood? Helpful as they may be, I do not need a suspect description and a photofit to identify who was behind the attempt on my daughter's life. In this city, there is only one man stupid enough to make that mistake, if not in person, certainly by proxy. His lackey means nothing to me…' he concluded, letting his words trail off into a stony silence.

Thoroughgood saw no point in prevarication: 'You're referring of course to Emmanuel Summerbee, whom I believe you have a not insignificant history with, Mr Crerand?'

Crerand laughed out loud. 'A not insignificant history is indeed one way of putting it. Our paths have crossed, and I have made sure that when that happens, I am the man with the whip hand,' replied Crerand, emphasising the last two words.

'The man who had one of Summerbee's eyes removed and who has just gazumped his crowning glory, the six-million robbery of a Total Security van; and then delivered his right-hand man to him with his throat slit,' said Thoroughgood, unable to quell his mounting anger and realising that he was playing a dangerous game away from home.

As he leaned back against the gleaming kitchen's immaculate marble surface, Crerand's blue stare turned icy. The crime lord took a sip of his morning latte, all the while watching and assessing Thoroughgood.

'If you are here to accuse me of something, then I'm afraid I will need to contact my brief and he will, I promise you, have a field day with your conjecture and guesswork. So, for your own benefit, Detective Thoroughgood, perhaps it is best you stick to the purpose of your visit.'

But before Crerand could finish his sentence, Thoroughgood's attention had strayed elsewhere, for behind her father the lithe form of Lisa Crerand in a luxurious white towelled dressing gown had padded into the kitchen. The detective couldn't keep his eyes off her.

She came to a stop still gently towelling her glistening wet hair, but her brown eyes held Thoroughgood's and as Gordon Crerand turned to greet his daughter, none of that was lost on him.

It was then that Thoroughgood realised that he was able to take in her features in daylight for the first time, neither concealed by a motorbike helmet nor under the artificial nightclub lighting, then blemished by the shock and fear of having almost been blown up.

Her skin somehow had a sheen to it that was both golden and dark, and Thoroughgood wondered if she had Italian heritage. It gave her brown eyes, which he thought may have been flecked with green, a smouldering intensity.

Her nose was slightly long yet beautifully refined and her full lips were once again mesmerising him, as they had done at Reds when they had found themselves in the embrace that ensured that life had triumphed over death for both of them.

'Good morning, Detective, this is a pleasant surprise! To what do we owe this unexpected visit… business or pleasure?' she asked, her words dripping with mischief and a slight impish smile playing at the corners of those lips.

But it was Gordon Crerand who answered: 'Very much business, Lisa. The detective has come with a photofit created from an eyewitness account of the individual he believes was responsible for the bombing. But then we know how reliable eyewitnesses can be!' concluded Crerand dismissively.

At that moment there was very little that could force Thoroughgood to tear his gaze away from Lisa Crerand, but her father had achieved the almost impossible. 'Oh, I have every reason to believe this eyewitness account, Mr Crerand,' he said, imposing a neutral tone on his words with difficulty.

'And why would that be, Detective?' snapped Crerand.

'Because you see, Mr Crerand, I am the witness, and if I had not been, then your daughter would not be standing right next to you.'

36

THOROUGHGOOD saw Crerand's jaw clench, but before he could say anything, Lisa got there first: 'Father, I would also remind you there is another reason that Detective Thoroughgood is here: I have an item of clothing that belongs to him and is soiled with the blood he shed in order to save me. I think it would be wrong, in these circumstances, not to do everything I can to help him with his enquiries. Wouldn't you agree, Father?' she said, the note of reproach in her voice all too clear.

From Crerand's brooding silence it was obvious that this was anything but clear to him, as it was going against the grain of a lifetime's suspicion and loathing towards the police that his civilised veneer could no longer conceal.

It was with reluctance that he finally relented. 'Indeed. Lisa will show you to our lounge and you can make yourself comfortable there while she gets changed. I'm sorry, Detective, I understand you are just doing your job and as I said, I am grateful for your actions. Now if you will excuse me, I have work to do in my office.' And with a curt nod Crerand departed.

As her father strode out of the kitchen, Lisa closed the gap between herself and the cop. She reached out her right hand and ran her fingers lightly down Thoroughgood's forearm. 'Would you like to show me the photofit and suspect description?' she asked with a smile.

From inside the anorak he had borrowed from Stretford Police Office, which was at least one size too big, Thoroughgood brought the paperwork out and slapped it onto the kitchen island, flattening it down until the artist's impression of the male he had seen deposit the rucksack at the bar was staring Lisa in the face.

For a moment there was a slight furrowing of her previously unblemished brow and then she looked back up at Thoroughgood. 'It's hard to say behind the aviators, but there is something familiar about this guy; I just can't pinpoint it. Look, are you in a rush?' she asked.

The question took Thoroughgood by surprise. He shrugged in admission that the perfect opportunity may be beckoning, given this was his only scheduled duty of the day and that whatever she had in mind might help him follow through on his discussion with Ferguson and Greene.

'Apart from getting myself another jacket and some new clothes… nope! Why do you ask… Miss Crerand?' he enquired stiltedly.

'Please, call me Lisa! Because it's a lovely day and I would like to get to know you better… Angus. How would you like to go for a walk? I would love to show you Alderley Edge. It's our most famous natural beauty spot, the views are stunning and on a day like this I can think of nothing better I'd like to do. It would also be nice to do something that would help take my mind from what happened last night… and I'd like to sneak away: I'm going crazy with my father's protectiveness after my close call,' concluded Lisa. Smiling back, Thoroughgood could think of nothing else he'd rather do… for professional or personal reasons.

The short journey to the National Trust carpark on the B5087 was made in Lisa's Jaguar XJS Convertible. The hood back and the sun beating down, it was a scenic and memorable drive.

It was made even more memorable by the hints of her perfume, that scent Thoroughgood ached to identify; and the fragrance that was another piece of the evidence that was damming this lovely creature, who was anything but what she appeared to be.

As they drove through the gleaming Cheshire countryside, Thoroughgood couldn't help himself checking in the passenger-side mirror from time to time.

Old habits died hard and they prompted laughter from Lisa. 'As I'm sure you spotted, Chipleys is surrounded by high-tech CCTV coverage, and if anyone is stupid enough to try and get past that, there is Uprichard and Nobby waiting with a warm welcome!' she said, placing a reassuring hand on his right harm.

It was something he had noticed she was apt to do, and the spontaneity and warmth were at complete odds with what he knew was the other side of Lisa Crerand.

Retreating into silence, Thoroughgood allowed himself to relax a little and began to wonder when and how he would bring that other side up to best advantage.

For the bottom line – despite himself – was that he was here for a reason; the only problem being that other factors were starting to get in the way.

"Get a grip, man!" urged the voice in his head. "What about Emma? Are you going to go galivanting with a new woman – a crime boss's daughter, no less – while she is still suffering who knows what?"

He shook his head to try to clear away these self-recriminations, causing Lisa to glance at him. He caught her eye, and the smile she gave him melted away his worries in an instant.

A few minutes later the Jag pulled into the National Trust car park.

Thoroughgood couldn't help himself: 'I can see that you love fast things on both two and four wheels.'

She smiled sweetly. 'That's clearly why you are a detective! Now come on, if we get going we might even make it back for a late lunch down in the village or we could stop at The Wizard pub. But first there is so much to show you and tell you about Alderley Edge. Did you know that there is an army of knights asleep under its rocks who wait to emerge when Britain faces its direst peril?' she concluded, tilting her head whimsically.

'Fascinating!' replied Thoroughgood and found his answer immediately taken for sarcasm by Lisa, who pulled a face.

Before he could explain, Lisa had taken out the small rucksack she had brought with her, unzipped it and thrown his Harrington at him. 'I thought you'd be happy to be reunited with your favourite bomber jacket… now for crying out loud get rid of your grandfather's anorak at the first bin we come across!' She laughed and flicked the switch for the soft top to close over.

Thoroughgood protested as he got out: 'I'm afraid that would be no way to treat Greater Manchester Police-issue clothing.' But he still tore the anorak off and threw it in the back seat; then, after examining it for damage in an overexaggerated fashion, he pulled his treasured Harrington on, relieved.

Lisa pulled a face in mock disgust, swung the rucksack over her shoulder and set off. As she walked, Thoroughgood once again found himself mesmerised by the tight contours of her figure-hugging jeans.

Within moments she reached a wooden gate leading to a winding track. 'Come on, Angus, are you always such a slowcoach?' she laughed, holding it open for him.

'I've always found that when you're on a magical mystery tour it pays to take your time! So, tell me, where you are taking me… Lisa?' he asked, still uncomfortable about the use of her Christian name.

She placed her hands on top of the wooden gate and playfully leant her chin on them. 'It is indeed a magical mystery tour! Where do I start? I'm sure you will find the Wizard's Well fascinating!' she said sarcastically.

Thoroughgood grimaced, although there was a glint of humour in his eye. 'As a student of medieval history, you'll find that right up my street,' he said, before adding in jest: 'Miss Lisa!' Her laughter, light and sunny like the day itself, rang out.

Forking along the right-hand path they forged their way through trees filtering the golden sunshine. Birdsong filled the air as they criss-crossed the maze of forest paths, exchanging nods and hellos with other walkers. Thoroughgood took a deep breath and let the slight chill of the morning fill his lungs.

The chatter between them was easy and constant, but despite the fact he was so obviously enjoying the moment, Thoroughgood needed more, both professionally… and personally.

'Have you and your father been just the two of you for long?' he asked.

Slightly ahead of him, Lisa turned and shaded her eyes against the golden rays. 'We have – as you say – been just the two of us since I was nine. I'm afraid cancer took my mother and… and there is not a day that I don't ask myself what if she had still been here. Would this all have been different?' she said, her eyes concealed in shadow.

Opposite her, Lisa saw the troubled change in Thoroughgood's features as her words immediately brought guilty memories of Emma back to him.

The concern in her face was obvious. 'Are you okay, Angus?' she asked, reaching out and clasping his arm.

'I'm really sorry about your mother, but your story is very similar to what happened to… to a girl I once knew,' he said, unable to avoid some emotion quivering through his voice.

Her hand slid down his forearm and her fingers interwove with his. 'Do you want to tell me about it?'

The opening up of the wounds that had been inflicted by Emma's unexplained departure still hurt, there was no point denying it, and Thoroughgood couldn't help unburdening himself about her disappearance and his secret concerns over what McGrain had done with her.

Fortunately, Lisa proved a good listener.

As they walked and talked, it struck Thoroughgood the verbal traffic was all one way, and by the time they had reached Castle Rock's breathtaking views, he had just about talked himself out.

They stood for a moment in silence and enjoyed the lush green of the Cheshire Plain. Then Lisa released his hand, which he had almost forgotten she was still holding, and sat down on the crag's slightly overhanging rock, propping up her rucksack against her side.

'Why don't we have a drink? I think you've earned it, Angus!' she said, smilingly teasing him about the monologue he'd just delivered.

Thoroughgood, now feeling decidedly awkward, did as he was bid. 'I'm sorry. I guess a lot has happened to me over the past two years and getting blown up twice in the last month hasn't exactly helped! But you know, I'm glad to be away from Glasgow, I just feel like I have so much baggage there… way too much.'

She pushed a water bottle his way and as Thoroughgood took a greedy drink, Lisa spoke once again: 'I am struggling to keep up with your love life, Angus Thoroughgood. First Emma and then what did you call her… Celina?' she teased.

'Celine!' he replied a little too forcefully, before quickly adding: 'Yeah, Celine is now firmly in the past. But I'm sorry; a gentleman should never monopolise the conversation, and to be quite frank, the last 15 minutes have been more of a confession! What about you, Lisa? A girl like you... well, I'm sure you've... er... not been short of offers,' he ended clumsily.

Lisa glanced at him sideways. 'Will this be taken down and used against me, Officer?' she joked.

'Come on, seriously, it's your turn. Is there... anyone?' he asked.

For a moment her eyes returned to the horizon and then there was silence. He thought she gave the minutest sigh before she answered. 'Yes, there was someone once but... much like you, Angus... I found I couldn't trust them. But I don't want to spoil the morning by talking about that. You said you were a student of history, well, I have a real treat for you... it's time I showed you the Wizard's Well. Come on, we're heading off down the natural rock staircase over there. You'll love this, I promise,' she said, jumping to her feet and offering him her hand.

He took it and as she helped haul him to his feet, their bodies locked together, their lips doing likewise.

Eventually, when the desire of the moment passed, they parted, slightly. 'Wow... that was... very nice!' he said awkwardly.

'Very nice! So, you're a hopeless romantic, then. Do you mind if I call you Gus? Angus, I think, is more for your mother!' laughed Lisa.

'You can call me what you want, Lisa, if you just take me to the Wizard's Well!' replied Thoroughgood, inclining his head to the rock staircase.

His reaction plainly surprised and pleased her, and she grabbed his hand again and led him to the bevelled rock steps. At the end of a dirt path, a massive overhanging rock confronted them and underneath it sat a stone trough filled with water from an ancient spring.

'Can you see it… Detective?' she asked, teasing him once again.

'See what?' replied Thoroughgood.

Lisa made her way over to the overhanging rock and traced her finger over a barely visible inscription and read it aloud: 'Drink of this and take thy fill for the water falls by the Wizard's will.'

Fascinated, Thoroughgood stooped over the outcrop and ran his fingers over the ancient writing. Moving his hand up, he traced the features of a bearded face carved into the rock, the eponymous 'wizard'.

But as usual, scepticism was never far away and the voice inside his head escaped: 'The big question is was this written by some wispy-haired Merlin-esque figure or is it the work of some entrepreneur who saw a cynical way of making a fast buck with some mythical mumbo jumbo? I'm sorry, but—'

Before Thoroughgood could finish his cynical dissection of this cherished tourist spot, he received a playful punch in the stomach for his trouble. 'How dare you! Mythical mumbo jumbo? Not at all, it's time I told you the wizard's tale,' said Lisa in a voice that brokered no argument.

Sitting down on another piece of rock a foot away, Thoroughgood opened his arms. 'Go ahead… I'm all ears!' he said with a smile.

Standing in front of him, Lisa warmed to her task. 'According to the legend, a farmer from Mobberly – that's a local village – was passing by to sell his white mare at the market in the neighbouring town of Macclesfield. As he travelled through Alderley Edge, he met a mysterious old man dressed in white who offered to buy the horse,' said Lisa, pausing to take a drink of water.

'Well, the farmer thought for a while, then decided he'd likely get a better price at the market. So he told the old man no. But the old man predicted that though people would look at the horse there, the farmer would not be able to sell it. Instead, he promised to wait for the farmer's return. Well, the farmer made his way to the market and lo and behold, the horse was admired, but remained unsold!' She paused. 'Still awake?' she asked, secretly pleased to see that Thoroughgood was entirely captivated by her tale.

Despite that, he reverted to sarcasm: 'Fascinated!' But as she raised a school teacherly eyebrow, he pleaded: 'No, please go on, it's really interesting… honest!'

She continued: 'So the farmer headed back home with his horse. And on the way, he again met the old man. He offered to buy the horse once more; but this time the old man struck the nearby rock face with his staff to reveal a secret opening with iron gates. He led the farmer inside, where he saw medieval knights in armour, asleep on the ground. There was a white mare by all but one of them, also asleep.'

'Are we almost there?' asked Thoroughgood and received a playful kick from her red Puma trainers.

Then, stifling a laugh, Lisa continued her tale from the days of yore: 'The old man, who the farmer realised was a wizard, told the farmer that his was the last horse needed for the sleeping army of knights. The knights and horses would rest until the country was in its hour of greatest need. Only then would they wake to fight. To his delight, the farmer was given gold coins in payment for the mare and then was led out of the cave. The iron gates closed and the rocks covered the place… and since that day no one has found the entrance!' she concluded with a theatrical sweep of her hands.

'You are a wasted talent, Lisa Crerand…' but before he could finish, she landed on his lap and once again their lips met in sweet union.

37

RETURNING hand in hand to Castle Rock, this time Lisa led him along a path that ran beneath the crag and gently descended towards a stream, before crossing an ancient footbridge.

As they made their way, Lisa once again reverted to tourist guide: 'You might also be interested to know that back in the 60s the Edge was supposed to be the meeting place of a witch's coven!'

'Jeez, wizards and witches… anything else you want to share with me?' laughed Thoroughgood.

'Yep, our next stop is probably the most famous scenic spot on the Edge: Stormy Point! Now come on, try and keep up!' she chided him, before speeding up into a semi-jog.

They soon reached an outcrop of sandy rock nestled between strips of woodland. 'And voila!' said Lisa, presenting the stunning view with an outstretched hand.

Thoroughgood found himself gasping at the quintessentially English vista that spread out below, a green and yellow patchwork quilt of fields as far as the eye could see. She slipped her arm around his waist. 'Over there are the Pennines. They may be a bit hazy, but they are around eight miles away.'

'This is some place, Lisa,' said Thoroughgood.

'Yes… it is the place my mother met my father back in the early 60s. Without Alderley Edge and Stormy Point I wouldn't be here,' said Lisa. Thoroughgood felt her body tremble next to his and pulled her tight, enveloping her in his arms as for a minute or two they let the idyllic view heal her pain.

After a while, Thoroughgood slipped the water bottle out of her rucksack. After handing it back to Lisa and then slaking his thirst he asked: 'So where next?'

Looking up at him she smiled, though he could see the moisture of her previous emotion was still in her eyes.

'The Devil's Grave, the old copper mines and the quarry where – and I know you will love this – there was once, rumour has it, a murder… Then lunch… on me!' she said, forcing herself to regain her composure and receiving a warm smile.

Despite the name, the Devil's Grave proved an anticlimax: it was no more than a fissure in the sandy rock that led below into a shallow mine. As they made their way towards the quarry, Thoroughgood decided it was at last time to up the ante.

'You know that right now all over Manchester, houses, pubs, safe houses and lock-ups are being turned for Emmanuel Summerbee and the arms cache he took delivery of last week. I would imagine that must be music to your ears, Lisa?' he finished, painfully aware at how awkward and completely out of place his words were in terms of what had gone before.

As they began to reach the edge of the shade provided by the glade currently flanking their route, Lisa turned back. 'What do you want me to say to that? I knew this must come up at some point. You know enough about my father and Summerbee to realise it will only finish when one of them is dead. I wish it was all different but…' She left the rest unsaid in a rare show of uncertainty.

But Thoroughgood could not let it go. 'All what was different, Lisa? That you didn't mastermind the ambush on The Maine Men and the Total Security van they had just captured? You didn't have Paulie Gallacher killed and delivered to Summerbee

231

for his dessert as a way to lure him out and finish him off at the hands of Mr Uzi?'

Her olive-brown gaze held his eyes and the anger sparking in her was clear. She turned to walk away, but his hand shot out and grabbed her left wrist. 'I never forget a person's eyes, Lisa. It was you in the helmet at the robbery. I also make sure I take down every detail of a suspect up here,' he said, pointing to his head before going on: 'So, may I compliment you on the red silk lining of your biker jacket and the smart little belt buckles on either side around the waist. The same one you were wearing in the photo in Howard Scott's office the day you were posing in Ron Haslam's pit stop at the British GP—' But before he could continue any further, her right hand shot out and administered a vicious slap that stopped him in his tracks.

'I realised you knew,' she snapped, her eyes sparkling magnificently with anger. 'So just what the hell is this?'

'This is your way out, Lisa. DCI Ferguson needs this feud ended and once we have Summerbee in custody all the attention will fall on you and your dad. I am assuming you were behind the murder of Paulie Gallacher? After all, it was you that ran the ambush on the Total Security van he was in. Then, eureka, his dead body turns up as Manny One-Eye is enjoying his favourite lunch. Interesting one, that. I read the post-mortem report and although he'd died from having his throat slit, Paulie's lungs were full of water… you are very imaginative, Lisa!' he said.

'My father's QC will rip that to shreds. If that's it then what have I got to worry about?' she replied, forcing the emotion from her voice but unable to regulate her breathing.

'Are you kidding? There is more than enough to put you away, especially with the evidence of the star witness who can put you right at the scene of the crime… but there is a way out of this for you, Lisa. You need to give us back the Total Security van. That's the deal: return the van and the £6 million and, well, maybe what happened to Paulie Gallacher, his henchman and the bent guard can be plea bargained away before we get to court. But you need to make a call on that and you need to make that call now!' said Thoroughgood.

Silence reigned, and Thoroughgood realised he had just confounded the whole raison d'être for him being there. He was supposed to be playing the role of the rat on the inside of the Flying Squad and feeding information the Crerands' way; instead, he had let emotion and feeling cloud his judgement… with disastrous consequences.

Lisa's eyes continued to blaze as she ripped her wrist from his grip. 'So that's why you're really here. You've been sent to ingratiate yourself with me, use what happened at the club when you saved my life to gain my confidence, my trust… and then what? Let me hang myself and my father? Never! I thought there was something different about you, Thoroughgood, but you're just like every man I have ever met in my life – excluding my father – a cheap two-bit user. There is nothing sincere, no depth to you dibble. All that matters to you is getting your collar, earning a nice little pat on the back from that bloody Scots orangutan you call your boss and taking the next step up the ladder.' She paused as she was forced to come up for air.

'That's just not true…' retorted Thoroughgood, knowing that in fact that she was more than partially correct.

But with a toss of her sleek black hair, Lisa was gone and heading off down another one of the myriad of forest paths that criss-crossed the area like veins.

For a moment Thoroughgood stood still, hands on hips. This was it, then, decision time. If he went after her then it would be because inside, he had genuine feelings. Genuine feelings for a woman he knew had been behind three gangland murders, whatever the reasons that caused these killings.

But if he stayed where he was then he was going to be heading back to Ferguson with a whole lot of nothing.

"So, you go after her… then what? You're back to square one," said his inner voice. But Thoroughgood wasn't listening, for he found that his Sambas were already tramping the beaten turf of the path that Lisa had walked down.

Her figure initially remained hidden by a copse of birches and Thoroughgood could feel his heart start to hammer with worry that he had taken the wrong route and lost her. But as he crested a slight rise, he could see she was about 50 feet away.

'Lisa!' he shouted and sprinted down the other side as a lazy breeze rustled through the trees, reminding that, despite the sunshine, spring was not fully sprung.

As he closed the gap, Thoroughgood reached out and touched her arm; but although she stood still, she did not turn around. 'Look, this whole thing is a mess I know, but…' he stammered to a stop, not sure how to proceed without going too far one way or another.

She slowly turned around and he could see the moisture trails down her cheeks. The voice in his head warned: "Come on, mate… waterworks are the oldest trick in the book," but again he wasn't listening.

'But what, Angus Thoroughgood? Who is speaking, the policeman or the human being?' she asked, her refined features hard as stone.

'The latter. Believe me, I am a human being first and a cop second. We can get through this, Lisa, but you're going to have to let me help you. Will you do that?' he asked.

For a moment she remained motionless. Then she closed the ground between them and once again they were one.

She took his hand and led him deep into the grove ahead. 'This is a special place for me, Angus… let's make a memory,' she said as they embraced once more and fell on to the soft carpet of the forest floor.

38

DCI MARTY FERGUSON prowled round his office like a caged tiger, for he knew full well that his tenure as head of the GMP Flying Squad had reached its defining moment.

Over the previous hour he had briefed a mixture of Flying Squad and uniform officers who would be spending the morning turning various key locations in an effort to huckle Manny Summerbee.

Ferguson knew that this was the moment he had to bring Summerbee to justice. There was no doubt he was behind the bombing, but what really worried Ferguson was the military-grade consignment of firepower that was lying somewhere in the city, ready to be unleashed on the Crerands and their Devils, not to mention anyone else who got in the way of Summerbee's vengeance and desire to be top dog in the city.

That threat was what was sending shockwaves of trepidation and fear through the Manchester underworld. It was a fear he could not afford to let ripple through into the consciousness of the general public; and incidents like the security van heist and the bombing in Reds were now making it do just that.

He had gambled and sent Thoroughgood out to the Crerands', almost playing him like a joker in a desperate hope that the boy's suggestion that he became the rat who supplied vital info to The Devils would pay off.

He had divided the rest of his manpower into four teams, with DS Molly Malone in charge of Alpha, DS Greene running Bravo and DC Morgan riding shotgun on Charlie, all accompanied by a Flying Squad colleague in an unmarked vehicle, while uniform were poised in Sherpa vans ready to deploy with battering rams, heavy-duty firepower and dogs. He would remain in reserve with Delta.

For a moment he stood looking at the blackboard that he had removed from The Lass O'Gowrie, now propped up in the far corner of his office with details of each of the locations that were to be hit.

Checking his watch, he saw that the 10 am start time was here. Across the city the turns would be going down right now. He took a deep breath, forcing himself to run through the detail yet again.

But Ferguson was snapped from his thoughts by the opening of his office door. His heart sank when ACC Michelle Trautmann walked in.

'DCI Ferguson, I am surprised to see you still in your office when I would have expected you to be leading your officers from the front. I have made myself more than clear regarding how important the results of the operation this morning are to public safety, confidence in GMP and, as I am sure you are aware, your career,' said the ACC Crime, her piercing eyes taking in the details on Ferguson's blackboard.

Caught completely off guard by Trautmann's appearance, Ferguson was left temporarily speechless and right on cue his right hand reached towards his ruddy mop in a sign of obvious agitation that had the corners of Mad Myra's mouth twitching as she enjoyed his discomfort.

But she had not finished: 'The chief constable himself has asked me to provide an emergency briefing for him this afternoon in order that he might have good news to fill the Sunday newspapers and start to turn the tide on the negativity that is becoming attached to GMP… because of your inability to do your job effectively.'

Composure almost regained, Ferguson smiled obsequiously before launching into his response: 'ACC Trautmann, it's always a pleasure to receive a visit from you. If I'd known you were coming I'd have had tea and biccies ready. You are of course right: this morning's operation is absolutely vital to our hopes of taking control of this turf war once and for all. Each target location is the result of painstaking intelligence work in the field by my officers and their informants. May I take you through each location, ma'am?' he asked, insincerity dancing in his eyes.

The ACC Crime narrowed her eyes until they were gimlets, before finally nodding her head in the affirmative.

'Alpha Team are being led by DS Malone, who has personally uncovered information that the arms cache Summerbee and his Maine Men have taken delivery of is being stored at the rear of a pub in Moss Side: the Pepperhill. I expect the pub is being turned as we now speak,' said Ferguson, smiling mockingly.

'Excellent. DS Malone is a fine officer and I'm delighted to see you are at last giving her the opportunity to spearhead the key part of an operation of this magnitude. Carry on,' she ordered.

'Bravo Team are led by DS Greene, who is on secondment with us, as you are aware, ma'am. He is hitting The Blue Moon boozer, which is Summerbee's HQ and home from home. Charlie Team, led by DC Morgan, are at a flat that we believe he uses as a safe house when he is on the run. As you are aware from my report, I am heading Delta Team, which is remaining here on standby in case of the requirement for backup. I am, ma'am, confident we will get the results we need from this morning's operation.'

Trautmann remained unimpressed. 'I very much hope for your sake, DCI Ferguson, that that is the case. Either way, you will have a full report of the success… or failure… of your activity on my desk by no later than 4 pm so that I may relay it to the chief. Do you understand me?' she sneered contemptuously.

Through gritted teeth Ferguson replied: 'Yes ma'am,' and was rewarded with the sight of Trautmann's back as she about-turned; Mad Myra and her shockproof blonde coif bobbed their way through the Flying Squad office.

Ferguson slammed his door shut and, sitting back down on his swivel seat, composed himself, before picking up his radio and calling for immediate updates from his teams.

But he was cut off in mid-bark by the sound of his desk phone ringing out. For a moment he debated whether to pick it up, but soon decided it must be important and ripped it off its holder. 'DCI Ferguson speaking,' he said, ensuring his voice was a controlled monotone.

At the other end, a familiar Scottish accent rang out: 'Boss, it's Thoroughgood, the arms cache has been moved: it's in a house in Buskin Avenue, number 18 to be precise.'

For a moment there was silence from Ferguson's end as his mind quickly assessed what this information meant. 'Where did this come from, boy? Where are you and, more importantly, who are you with?' fired Ferguson.

From the other end of the phone there was a barely perceptible sigh. 'I'm calling you from Lisa Crerand's mobile phone. We are up on Alderley Edge, and she has provided this information voluntarily and a whole lot more. Lisa has been very helpful, Boss, but you need to hit it quick. We are talking major firepower here… hand grenades and Škorpion sub-machine guns that can fire off 1,000 rounds in a minute. If Summerbee unleashes that kind of firepower on the streets it won't matter who the target is, the collateral damage will be off the Richter scale, Boss.'

Ferguson let out a long slow whistle. 'Holy moly!'

But before he could find anything more eloquent to say, Thoroughgood's voice sprang back into life: 'Listen, Boss, there is one other thing: Summerbee has scanners in operation and he is tuned into anything coming out over police frequencies, so you are going to have to maintain radio silence on this one. But if you've got a team good to go it's now or never.'

Despite himself, Ferguson's suspicions were working on him. 'This is impressive info, boy, but just how has Miss Lisa come by it?' he asked.

Again, there was a silence and then a female voice spoke from the other end of the phone: 'Because, DCI Ferguson, without this type of information my father and I would by lying in one of your morgues by now. We have made it our business to make sure we know what Summerbee has planned before he puts it into action. This is the second change of safe house he has made to the arms cache since he took delivery. I am very fortunate that his inability to behave faithfully to the woman who has shared his bed for the last six years has made him vulnerable.'

Reclining in his swivel chair, Ferguson pulled open his desk's top drawer and lifted out the whisky glass that still had a golden dribble left in it from the previous night. He swallowed it greedily, cleared his throat and replied: 'How very helpful!'

But Lisa had not finished: 'There is more, DCI Ferguson. My source has also told me that you may have a similar vulnerability within your ranks.'

Lisa heard what sounded like a glass being slammed down on a hard surface, but she continued: 'Please don't take this the wrong way, Mr Ferguson, but can I urge you to act immediately on the information regarding the arms cache. If you don't, it will almost certainly be moved and before that happens, for the safety of my father's people, we will have to act.'

As he had been digesting the information flowing down the line, the Boss had adroitly poured himself a generous measure of Bell's; he was mid-mouthful when Lisa delivered her ultimatum, causing him to splutter and spray whisky over his desk.

Wiping his mouth with the back of his hand, he at last replied: 'I thank you very much for sharing all of that information with me, Miss Crerand. It is… most valued, and rest assured, it will be acted upon immediately. Now, can you put the boy back on, please?' Ferguson heard her hand back over to Thoroughgood. 'One question, Gus… do you trust her?'

'One hundred per cent!' was the answer.

'That's good enough for me. Tell Miss Crerand we are on our way to Buskin Avenue right now.' With that, Ferguson slammed the phone down and swallowed the rest of his whisky. The realisation washed over him that his rat-catching would have to wait for now, for when it came to the weapons hoard there was no time to waste. He sprang out of the chair. 'Game fucking on!' he shouted at the top of his voice as he strode through the empty Flying Squad office.

39

RECLINING against one of the superb beech trees that flourished on the Edge, Thoroughgood watched Lisa, who sat nestled in next to him enjoying the tree's shade, put her mobile back in her rucksack.

For a moment there a was silence between them as they enjoyed each other's warmth and replayed the moments of pleasure that had gone before the call to Ferguson.

'You know, I just can't get used to these... mobile phones. Do you think that one day everyone will have one?' asked Thoroughgood in a half-hearted attempt at small talk.

'For a detective, you don't half ask some silly questions!' she replied and received a playful nudge in reply.

'What else have you got in there? A white rabbit?' he joked.

But a shadow had passed over Lisa's face. 'Do you think the DCI will act on my information?'

Thoroughgood nodded. 'Quite frankly I don't think he has any other option. Things are so bad and with ACC Trautmann looking for the slightest excuse to bin him, the Boss needs to come up with something big. So, it was good of you to share that... massive, in fact. Thank you,' he said and leaned across to kiss her.

A little later, Lisa finally replied: 'Hopefully it will save lives, perhaps even stop you having to put your Superman suit back on... though I'd pay money to see that one!' And she laughed that light, sunny laugh that was at complete odds with their discussion and situation, as two people thrown together in the most desperate circumstances.

Yet Thoroughgood had not quite finished with business: 'It's strange that the Boss has been worried about having a rat in the Squad for some time, as far as I can see, even though he tried to dismiss it. So, I don't know what has gone wrong in the past, but whoever is tipping Summerbee off has been doing a pretty good job. Did your informant provide the ID of the rat?' he concluded hopefully.

Lisa shook her head. 'Nope. Summerbee's relationship with Colina is… what you might call under strain, and although she has tried to get it out of him, she's had no joy. As you know, there is only so much you can ask without making things obvious. In fact, when we spoke, the fact that he was relocating the guns to her house was the straw that broke the back for her. You see, Colina has a six-year-old lad who suffers from muscular dystrophy.'

'Geez, what kind of nutter would dump high-grade weapons, explosives and the rest of the shit on a woman with all of that on her plate… but then I guess maybe that's exactly why he has done it. He's hiding them in plain sight… almost,' he concluded.

He looked up as Lisa jumped to her feet. 'Which is exactly what Colina thinks. Anyway, surely that is enough for now. Can we get going again? I want to show you the hermit's cave, his shack and the old quarry where he died in very suspicious circumstances way back in 1933. I would have thought that was right up your street… Officer!' she said mischievously and started to head for the nearest trail.

Soon they found a path, taking them away from the main, increasingly busy thoroughfares and deeper into the forest. It gradually led them up an incline that was flanked by more rustling trees on one side and a steep, bush-strewn drop on the other.

It became clear that Lisa was keen to tell Thoroughgood all about the death of the Alderley Edge hermit, almost as if the conversation that had gone before had never happened.

Despite his impatience to bring matters of real life to a conclusion, the voice in Thoroughgood's head warned him not to repeat his mistake of earlier on, particularly in view of the vital information that Lisa had put Ferguson's way and that would now hopefully see the Boss hitting Colina Amos's house in Buskin Avenue and taking Summerbee's arms delivery into the safety of police hands.

'All right, please put me out of my misery… was the hermit of Alderley Edge pushed or did he jump? For crying out loud, just tell me!' laughed Thoroughgood.

Lisa forced a frown. 'John Evans was his name and he was a cartographer and a brilliant man who also happened to be a friend of my grandfather's. He lived in a wooden hut in the grounds of the church quarry in the first half of the century. John was a civil engineer with the railways, but he retreated to the hut in 1915 a broken man after his true love died on the Titanic,' she revealed, with a sideways glance to make sure she still had Thoroughgood's attention.

'Go on… I'm fascinated… honest!' said Thoroughgood sarcastically and received a playful punch in the ribs for his troubles.

Plainly piqued, Lisa tried a new tack: 'Let me, Officer, take you back to the night of July 21, 1933. After a night's drinking, John returned to his hut with two friends only to find that there were no lights on either of his companions' motorbikes. Forced to stay the night, drinks were poured and one of John's mates, a Walter Whitelegg, became sick complaining of a burning sensation in his chest. As Walter's condition worsened, John called a doctor from the Wizard Temperance Hotel, or, as it is now, just The Wizard – which isn't far away and where we may be going for lunch shortly – but by the time the doc arrived, Walter was dead…' Lisa let her words trail off as she checked to see if she had hooked Thoroughgood.

'Okay, you've got me, something ain't right. So, was Walter poisoned? Forgive me, but can I ask how old Walter Whitelegg was?' he asked, his naturally suspicious mindset coming to the fore.

But Lisa held up her hand and continued to recount the tale of the hermit's demise: 'No obvious cause of death was found and an inquest was opened and John cited as a witness, but when he failed to attend they sent for him only to find him dead.'

'You didn't answer my question… how old was Walter and, for that matter, how old was John?' asked Thoroughgood, his full attention on Lisa.

'Okay! So, Walter was 20 and John 50,' she replied.

'I'm sorry, that's young – I know he was a friend of your grandfather's and a brilliant man. Anyway, my gut feeling is there could have been more to their friendship than just that, if you catch my drift. What did the inquest find?' asked Thoroughgood, fascinated.

'Both men were found to have died from potassium cyanide poisoning. The cyanide had been kept in John's hut for gold analysis in relation to the work he was doing charting the mines all across the Edge and trace amounts were in the drink given to Walter, accidentally poisoning him. And then John went the same way,' concluded Lisa.

Opposite her, Thoroughgood's eyes narrowed. 'Okay, so from what I know, a small dose of cyanide was, back in the day, given to patients with upset stomachs, but bloody hell, I would have thought John would have known the difference between what was a safe dose and what was a lethal one. Maybe Walter self-administered the dosage and was a bit heavy-handed but… I just don't buy it. Something isn't adding up. Then you have to ask why did John

Evans kill himself? Forgive me for stating the bleedin' obvious, but back in the 30s, even the slightest whiff of homosexuality could have finished a man and his reputation, certainly a 50-year-old one like Evans, who liked to hang about with guys less than half his age,' concluded Thoroughgood.

'My grandfather thought the same! Anyway, just over there is what is left of John's Bergli hut.' Seeing the questioning look on Thoroughgood's face, she smiled before elaborating: 'Bergli is a famous Swiss mountain hut, I believe. So, do you fancy having a look? We used to play hide and seek in it when my grandfather brought me and my friends up to the Edge,' said Lisa, already walking over to the ramshackle ruin.

From what Thoroughgood could see, the roof had pretty much disintegrated and what was left just looked like wooden sparring, while the timbers that remained in place on the front wall were rotting. There was no evidence of a door, just the hole in the wall where one had been, and the front window was also without glazing.

'It doesn't look like there is a whole lot left to see. But there's something niggling me about what happened to John Evans: you never mentioned who the second friend was?' said Thoroughgood, unable to leave things alone.

As Lisa's gaze met his, he wasn't sure if she was smiling or grimacing. 'That's because he was my grandfather, Carlo...' she said, letting silence envelop her words.

Joining her on the broken veranda in front of what had been the door, Thoroughgood once again wrapped his arms around Lisa and pulled her close. 'That explains everything. Why you wanted to bring me up here and show me the Wizard's Well, the views, jeez, I can be so slow. So I guess all of this,' he said, unfolding an arm from their embrace before continuing: 'is why we are here. While you're telling

246

me the story of John Evans and showing me around Alderley Edge, you are preserving the memory of the grandfather who brought you up here as a child. You said your mum met your dad here and no doubt that is because of Carlo and the good times he had here…' Then Thoroughgood stumbled awkwardly into silence, as the implications of the hole he was digging for himself hit home.

Lisa's head lifted from his chest and she looked up at him. 'You aren't so slow after all, Detective. Yes, my grandfather was John's friend but… clearly he was straight. They knew each other from the railways and Carlo used to bring his organetto – sorry, that's Italian for an accordion – up here to join in at John's musical parties, but then… well… what happened, happened.'

Thoroughgood tried to accentuate the positive: 'Well I guess I should feel honoured that you brought me up on Alderley Edge, to somewhere so special in your family's history. Christ… no pressure, then – the place your mother met your father!' And he grimaced in mock horror.

But the sparkle in her eye was all the answer he needed as once more their lips met and the passion of their embrace, the surrealness of the moment and all that had gone before made for a giddy cocktail that engulfed Thoroughgood.

As the seconds passed and the intensity of their union grew, Thoroughgood started to draw Lisa inside the hut.

It was only the spontaneity of their semi-stumble through the doorway that saved them.

For a new sound now ripped through the birdsong and rustling of the foliage surrounding John Evans's ruined hut. All around them the rotten wood of the ruin's front wall erupted into a thousand vicious flying splinters as the hut was enfiladed by a withering burst of high-velocity lead.

40

THOROUGHGOOD turned their awkward, passion-fuelled stumble inside into a desperate dive, throwing Lisa to the floor and as they landed pushing her over into the cover of the front wall.

'Are you okay?' he asked.

'Thanks to my bodyguard!' Lisa said breathlessly, but he was already rolling onto one knee as she answered.

'Stay down and please get a call for help out. Look, take this,' he said, flicking a GMP card her way. 'It's DCI Ferguson's mobile. With a bit of luck he'll have it with him… and on, otherwise you will need to call it in to GMP HQ,' he finished, his eyes scanning the treeline but also the drop down into the rocky gulley to their left that he guessed was the old quarry.

'Okay!' replied Lisa, before she added: 'But what about my father? He could be here with help even quicker.'

His gaze never leaving the foliage as he tried to work out the direction of fire, Thoroughgood said: 'That's the last thing we need, believe me. Please just phone Marty Ferguson, he'll sort it.' Lisa took out her mobile and started dialling. 'Christ, if only I'd brought a radio with me… bloody schoolboy error,' he muttered, but that was the least of his troubles.

From out of the treeline stepped a tall figure and movement to his left and right flanks confirmed he wasn't alone, as two other hooded figures moved forward to the edge of the cover.

'Happy days,' said Thoroughgood.

A voice rang out: 'Mornin', lovebirds! It was good of you to spend so much time… getting to know each other. It let us get everything together real nice,' said the male in a feral but slightly high-pitched Scouse accent that was laced with malicious intent. 'Look, copper, we have no argument with you, it's your bitch we've come for. She has an important appointment with Manny Summerbee to keep,' he continued.

Scouse stepped out of the shadows, and Thoroughgood realised he was wearing a pair of aviator sunglasses that were all too familiar. 'Like I said, this quarrel isn't anything to do with you, so maybe you just wanna swerve it and walk away. Okay, you're a copper, like, but that don't mean you have to be a divvy. I'd walk away while I could, like, fella. Our first round was just a warning, but next time, you won't be so lucky.'

Lisa leant over to Thoroughgood and whispered: 'The DCI is sending DS Malone and her team and he's going to ask her to bring uniform backup as well… they should be here in less than 15 minutes.'

Crouching behind the door, Thoroughgood assessed the odds. The Scouser was cradling his sub-machine gun, which was smaller than a Kalashnikov, but not quite an Uzi. One goon was keeping his hands at either side of him. The second had his paws in front of his body, but as he remained slightly further back, they were partially concealed in shade. "Gotta be packin'," said the voice in his head, helpfully concluding the threat assessment.

He felt Lisa's hand on his shoulder. 'It's the guy from the club, the bomber, come back to finish what he started. He's right, Gus, this isn't your fight, please walk away,' she said, emotion starting to crackle through her voice.

Turning her way, for a moment Thoroughgood's mind returned to the last time he'd seen Emma back at The Blood Acre and he forced a smile. 'I've made that mistake once already in my life and I'm not repeating it. Whatever happens here, we will get out of it together.' And he kissed her forehead.

But outside, Scouse was growing impatient and another burst of lead, this time aimed into what was left of the hut's roof, covered them in an avalanche of rotten fragments of wood and other decades-old detritus.

'You're starting to seriously piss me off, soft lad. You've got 30 seconds to get the hell out of there and leave me what I came for... copper!' he spat and signalled to his two minions to start a flanking manoeuvre around the sides of the hut.

It was a move that all but confirmed to Thoroughgood he wouldn't be making it out of the hut in one piece whether he chose to accept the Scouser's offer or not.

But from behind him a new, mechanical noise reached his ears, one he knew well. Thoroughgood turned to find Lisa was standing with what looked like a Browning in full presentation mode; and she'd just flicked the safety off.

Despite himself, the sight shocked Thoroughgood and his eyes saucered. 'What... what the hell is this?' he asked.

But he needn't have, for the evidence of his own eyes was compelling. So, this was the real Lisa: she stood before him in the Weaver stance, left hand supporting the right hand, which had control of the Browning.

Her feet were positioned in the classic boxing stance, with her left foot ahead of the shooting-side right foot, which was angled at around 45 degrees. Most of her weight was on the forward foot, with the knee slightly bent and the rear straight while her upper torso leant forward.

It was straight out of the textbook authored by Los Angeles County Deputy Sheriff Jack Weaver back in the 1950s.

She barked an order: 'Look, I need to buy us time while you get the escape route opened up. Why don't you get through the back and get the window sorted while I give the bastards something to think about?' And without further ado, Lisa took the space by the door and started to parley.

'I'm here, honey,' she shouted from the doorway, her mind racing. The problem with the 'Baby' Browning was that its accuracy at range was very limited. This, coupled with the fact that she only had six rounds to play with, meant Lisa knew that she had to make every shot count.

Her appearance at the door had surprised their would-be killers. 'Well, well, if it ain't the poisoned princess herself. What you got planned with that pea-shooter, soft bird?' asked Scouse, before he barked a harsh laugh.

'Why don't you come and find out, you Scouse muppet; but take a step closer and I promise you'll need a new pair of shades,' she taunted.

'Mouthy bitch, I'm gonna shut you up forever,' snapped Scouse and waved to his wingmen to continue their flanking manoeuvres. It was a rash, kneejerk move, borne from the prick to his macho, old-school gangster pride, and the mistake Lisa had been looking for, because now they had closed to within her maximum range of 25 yards.

From the doorway she took a breath, sighted up each of the three individuals, then unloaded three 6.35mm rounds, sending one in the direction of each of their assailants. The second she had discharged, Lisa turned and sprinted through the hut.

She heard a moan from the ground outside the front of hut: she had drawn first blood.

In the hut's rear bedroom, Thoroughgood, holding what looked like an ancient hammer, had smashed the warped framing of the glassless window out and offered a hand for her as she came through.

'It's a three-foot drop onto soft ground… on you go,' he shouted, the tension in his voice obvious.

She smiled and used his knee as a step; she was up and through the window in one fluid move, and a second later Thoroughgood landed on the ground next to her.

'What next?' he asked.

'We need to get down into the quarry, it's our only hope of buying the time we need to stay alive long enough for help to arrive. I think I've winged one of the animals—' But before Lisa could finish her sentence, the sound of heavy-duty semi-automatic fire ripped through the hut, cutting her off.

If the Scouser was at the hut, then that meant at least one of his men would be about to appear from their flanks.

Lisa grabbed his hand and began to sprint for the screen of trees that flanked the path to the quarry, a mad dash through at least 50 yards of open ground.

The sound of gunfire erupted from the rear bedroom of the hut and the hiss of a single vicious projectile scythed through the air about a foot wide of Thoroughgood's left thigh.

They barrelled on, running for their lives. But with safety in sight, Thoroughgood was flagging.

The damage that he had absorbed back at The Blood Acre and the second blast that had sent him through the air as he had saved Lisa at Reds all conspired against Thoroughgood, who found himself heaving in laboured breaths.

He ripped his hand free from Lisa's. 'Go on, I can't keep up. Make the trees and you can cover me,' he said, trying to give her some reasoning to work with.

She glanced back for a second, then sprinted ahead, just as a second bullet exploded into the turf to his right.

Lisa was almost there; but Thoroughgood realised with horror that she still wouldn't make it before his stalker had unloaded again.

All of which meant that one way or another, he was a dead man.

41

LISA'S HEART HAMMERED as she sprinted as fast as she could for the screen of trees. She prayed that she'd make it there before the air behind her filled once again with the vicious whirr of high-velocity fire.

She was so close she could already scent the early spring ramsons, woodruff and Scots pine that populated the woods of Alderley Edge, smells she associated with playing hide and seek with her grandfather, Carlo; something a million miles from her current predicament.

Suddenly, the air thundered with the automatic gunfire that had been her greatest fear. She dived into the cover of the mixed tree and bush scrub, then quickly rolled over and turned onto her stomach, almost too scared to look back.

Thoroughgood was still on his feet, only 10 feet away, but all around him the ground was erupting and exploding as the rear window of the hut flashed with heavy semi-automatic fire.

'Come on, Gus, you can make it!' Lisa screamed frantically. She sighted her Browning, but knew that their pursuers were way out of range.

Thoroughgood felt the oxygen draining from his lungs and his legs burn just like they had done a thousand times before on the beloved boards of his home squash courts at the Scottish Squash Rackets Club in Maryhill.

He gritted his teeth and heard his old friend Ballistic's words in his head: "Come on, laddy, dig!"

He pushed for all he was worth and dived headfirst into a thick clump of swaying grass, using the momentum to keep rolling just as a clump of turf erupted where he had been only a second before.

He felt a hand tug at his Harrington and relief flooded through him. But as he rolled over onto his back, a terrible stab of pain scored him from his right side. He reached down, fearing the worst.

He smiled, finding the old caving hammer he'd taken from the hut there. He quickly lodged it in his belt, while Lisa began to speak: 'We've got to make our way down to the copper mines, it's our only hope. Are you okay to get going first? If you keep following the way through the pines you'll see a picket fence. Just make your way down the path alongside it and when you get to the bottom you will see the entrance to an old copper mine in the sandstone. It's called the Engine Vein – wait for me there,' she said and leant forward to kiss him.

Thoroughgood hesitated, unsure and uncomfortable about being told what to do by the version of Lisa he could not come to terms with.

She saw his indecision and gave him no option: 'Please… just go!' she said, and without further argument he got going again.

As she heard his footsteps recede behind her, Lisa saw that she had indeed winged one of the Scouser's goons. He was still on his feet, though, so again she was faced with three pursuers coming her way. But now she only had one bullet left for each of them and what was worse, the Scouser had seen her.

'Hiya, darlin'! Where's your boyfriend?' he sneered as he marched forward, his sub-machine gun waist high. He waved it in front of him. 'Nice piece of kit, ain't it! Eight hundred and fifty rounds coming your way, and you know what's even better?

There's plenty more where it came from, and pretty soon they will all be levelled at your father… but then that won't be bothering you, soft bird.' And with that Scouse gritted his teeth and started to unload a withering spray of 9x19mm projectiles Lisa's way.

She threw herself flat against the ground and rolled away from the lethal fire's point of impact, knowing that she had to find a way to play for time and stall her pursuers. A few feet back she found herself some temporary cover behind a large scots pine and thanked her lucky stars that the Edge was predominantly woodland.

She had to engage him, get him talking and hopefully buy the time necessary for DCI Ferguson's officers to make it to the rescue. She'd noticed he was holding a Škorpion vz. 61, almost certainly taken from the arms cache that Summerbee had moved to Buskin Avenue, and decided to use that information to her advantage. 'You're very lucky you managed to get your hands on a Škorpion because by now I reckon the rest of your arms stash will be in the hands of the police,' she shouted.

But the Scouser gave a harsh laugh, and his reply was laced with a vicious relish: 'All right, lads, fan out, it's time for a game of hide and seek in the woods… it's time we found our princess!'

'You moved the cache earlier this morning and you moved it to an address in Buskin Avenue… number 18… isn't that right?' taunted Lisa.

All of a sudden, the snap of footfall on turf and twig stopped. 'What are you on about, bitch?' snapped Scouse.

'I mean that your glorious one-eyed leader has been betrayed and that whatever you had planned with these weapons is up in smoke,' said Lisa, knowing full well that her words would be leading them to her, but needing to buy time.

She was right to worry. The Scouser, his teeth gritted in rage, had had enough of small talk. He silently signalled to his men to wrap around the stand of pines where Lisa's taunting words were coming from.

Taking a peek from around the tree, Lisa saw that her window for escape was almost shut. She hunched down and awkwardly sprinted further into the forest, desperately hoping to avoid catching their attention.

But her need for speed meant that she was no longer able to watch her footwork and she failed to see the rise in the earth caused by a giant tree root. Her trainer caught on the tree vein and she was sent sprawling.

Her attempt to escape from the closing jaws of the trap had not gone unnoticed by Scouse, and her fall was like a homing device signalling her exact whereabouts.

'You be careful, princess, I don't want anything nasty happening to you... well, not yet!' he spat and then directed his two henchman to take either side of the copse where the cracking of twig and branch had come.

'We've got her, boys. Just take it nice and easy, remember she's still packin' that pea-shooter!' warned the Scouser.

From a few yards to her right, Lisa heard one of the hoods reply: 'Man, I got one of these motherfuckin' peas embedded in ma shoulder already, Scouse, and I'm gonna make her pay. I can't wait to get my hands on you, darlin'!' he yelled, sending a shiver down Lisa's spine.

As she leant down against a giant tree trunk, she ran her fingers over her right ankle. It was throbbing and she could already see the telltale signs of blueish swelling beginning to show. There was no way out of this now.

She checked the Browning for the hundredth time, despite knowing that she only had three bullets left, and silently vowed to herself that if this was indeed the end, she'd go down fighting.

42

THE WOUND in Everton Lineker's shoulder throbbed, but the thought of the retribution he was about to take on the Crerand bitch was proving a powerful balm.

A six-foot, second-generation West Indian, recruited from one of the Afro-Caribbean gangs of Moss Side, he had proven himself more than useful with gun, machete or fist.

While he knew that Scouse was the man most likely to fill the vacancy caused by Paulie Gallacher's demise, he hoped that there might be an opportunity for a leg-up in The Maine Men crew for himself.

He prowled through the woodland like a giant wounded panther, the only thing on his mind drawing blood from the female who had the temerity to wing him.

'Man, you'll never live that down back on the estate, Everton!' he muttered to himself; but as his eyes locked in on the tree he knew she was hiding behind, everything else became blotted out by his burning desire to inflict pain.

That was a mistake, for Thoroughgood had positioned himself behind an ancient upended oak trunk, looking for the opportunity to shorten the odds.

Now that moment had arrived.

He had only made it halfway down the gulley leading to the Engine Vein before disgust at his cowardice had meant he couldn't take another step.

Maybe Lisa did know what she was doing, but leaving her to delay the inevitable wasn't something he could swallow.

Instead, he'd decided that with the aid of the ancient caving hammer he'd lifted from the hut he would double back to turn the hunters into the hunted.

Now the voice in his head helpfully provided his instructions: "Distract and attack!"

He'd watched as the Scouser and his minions had spread out, seen Lisa fall, and was all too well aware of what was coming next; but now, armed with his ancient hammer, he was determined to make the difference.

He held a broken piece of branch in his right hand and, smiling to himself, he whistled the three-note warble that was the preferred warning of every petty criminal in Glasgow: one he knew would provide the hulking man with food for thought.

Lineker looked to his right, but Thoroughgood immediately hurled the broken branch to the thug's left-hand flank and watched as he had his attention snapped there by the clatter of the wood on the trunk of another tree.

Then Thoroughgood, hammer in hand, attacked hard and fast.

There was nothing skilful about it: all that mattered was that he hit the target with a blow that provided instant incapacitation.

Five yards ahead, Everton Lineker was paralysed by indecision, not knowing in which direction to train his Glock. Suddenly, he heard the sound of footfall and the rustling and snap of bush and branch coming from behind him. He barely had time to raise his arms.

Thoroughgood, hammer held in both hands, came hurtling through the foliage, his scream primeval, and brought down the caving hammer with all his might on Lineker's head.

The big man desperately tried to deflect the blow, but he didn't have the time to mount any effective defence and the hammer's head smashed home on the side of his cranium with a satisfying crunch of bone.

The enforcer keeled over like he'd just been felled by a punch from Mike Tyson and Thoroughgood was on him like a fiend, shifting the hammer into his left hand and following up his initial blow with two short right-hand hooks that guaranteed Lineker was now out of the game for good.

Then he grabbed his Glock and, taking one last look to confirm the goon was out cold, dived for the cover of the nearest tree

The noise generated by Thoroughgood's attack, particularly his feral scream, meant Scouse was already aware that he was a man down.

'Everton… you okay, lad?' he called, concern clear in his voice.

Thoroughgood was already on his feet and starting to weave his way stealthily through the forest in an arc… stalking the stalkers with increasing relish.

Scouse shouted out again: 'Come on, Lineker, you okay, fella?'

There was no reply and turning back to his other wingman, he frantically waved him on. For at the end of the day all that mattered was that they took out Lisa Crerand. If Everton Lineker was collateral damage then so be it; what he could not afford to do was to return empty-handed to Summerbee.

Lisa had also heard what had befallen the first of her attackers and now her remaining pursuers were within range of her Browning… it was time to make every shot count.

The only problem was that she had no idea which of the two Maine Men Thoroughgood would assail next.

But before she could worry about that, she needed to move further back into the forest. She attempted to stand up, but the pain in her twisted ankle shot right up through her leg and confirmed what she had already guessed: she wasn't going anywhere fast.

'Oh dear, it looks like you're a man down and help has arrived, Mr Scouser!' Lisa taunted, realising her best bet was to try to distract her attackers so that Thoroughgood could strike again.

'Who gives a fuck? It's still gonna be too little too late for you, princess,' spat Scouse and started to advance again, his Škorpion locked into his waist

But Lisa didn't have long to wait for her answer.

As he listened to their exchange, Thoroughgood had continued to use the cover of birch and rowan to skirt them in a semicircle, which took him to within ten yards of the outside shoulder of Scouse's second wingman.

Yet his movements, as stealthy as they were, had not gone unnoticed by all the residents of the forest; for the tree he took cover behind had been hosting a great spotted woodpecker, who had been busy drumming a mating call into the bark.

The startled bird flapped off, the frenzy of black and white plumage catching the attention of the henchman Thoroughgood trailed just as the cop levelled the Glock and pulled the trigger.

The subsequent exchange of fire was all the impetus Scouse needed to know that he had to close the deal fast. He let rip with another burst of lead at the tree he knew Lisa was cowering behind and marched on.

Both Thoroughgood and the hood he faced had missed with their initial rounds, but the cop knew from the hail of automatic fire that had been loosed in Lisa's direction that he must close his own confrontation quickly.

He threw himself to his left to change his firing position and loosed another round; then, to his horror, he heard the click as the Glock hit empty.

Thinking quickly, Thoroughgood called to the thug: 'I'm job, pal, and pretty soon this wood is going to be crawling with cops. Then you've got no chance. Throw down your weapon.'

'That's where your wrong, cock, ain't no dibble gonna be riding to your rescue anytime soon,' spat the goon and blasted off three quick rounds the cop's way.

Thoroughgood hit the deck once again, but he failed to anticipate what came next: for his adversary had followed his volley of lead in and now he threw himself onto the cop.

The force and surprise nature of the attack loosened Thoroughgood's grip on the Glock, and the handgun fell from his hand and shot across the forest floor.

His attacker, a stocky bastard with weasel eyes and flamethrower breath that reeked of last night's kebab, was now trying to bring his own weapon to bear on Thoroughgood's face.

The cop desperately clamped both hands around the goon's wrists and struggled to keep the gun's barrel from training on his cranium, but a burst of searing pain from his old shoulder wound showed that he wouldn't last long.

The manic glee in his attacker's feral eyes confirmed that Thoroughgood was starting to lose the battle. 'I'm gonna turn yer head to pulp, dibble!' Weasel spat as the barrel of his Smith & Wesson edged closer to the cop's head.

It was time to gamble.

Thoroughgood still had the old hammer lodged in his belt: the problem was that to get it he would have to take

263

one hand away from the ongoing life and death grapple with his attacker, something that would tip things lethally in the weasel's favour.

There was only one thing he could do. Without a further thought, Thoroughgood hawked up all the saliva he had left in a dry mouth and spat as hard as he could into his attacker's pulsing eyes.

Temporarily blinded, the downward force in Weasel's arms faltered. Thoroughgood ripped his right hand free, pulled the ancient hammer from his waist and smashed the head home high on an ear.

'Bastard!' screeched the weasel. Semi-blinded and now stunned, he toppled off the cop, who rolled over onto his feet and smashed an Adidas Samba off the side of the thug's head.

A groan was the only retort he got from the inert mass of his assailant.

Thoroughgood quickly reached for the dropped Smith & Wesson, only to find the gun was out of ammo as well. 'Shit,' he spat.

Trying to regain his breath, Thoroughgood turned his attention back toward the old beech that Lisa had been sheltering behind and saw gunfire flashing.

43

DESPITE all the practice she had done on the private range in the basement of Chipleys, faced with a determined attacker advancing while firing, Lisa's nerve was beginning to fail her. She had peered out from behind her cover and it was taking all her courage to train her Baby Browning on Scouse.

Aware that her shooting hand was trembling, she cradled it with her left and tried to steady the Baby Browning.

Lisa's mind raced. What if she wasn't steady enough to be accurate?

Scouse had closed to 20 feet. Saying a silent prayer, Lisa manipulated the safety off with her thumb, pulled the slide back to charge the striker then let her trigger finger pull.

The dull thud of lead striking bark was proof that she had missed. The Scouser moved out from cover and continued to advance, zig-zagging from tree to tree. 'You're mine now, soft bird... all mine.'

Now all that mattered was her ability to use her two remaining bullets. Lisa tried to slow her breathing down and impose calm on herself while the voice in her head asked: "Where the hell is Gus?"

Even when accurate, Lisa knew that the problem with the Baby Browning was its lack of 'knockdown' impact: the ability to drop an assailant with a well-placed shot.

The distance between them now down to 15 feet, she fired again, hoping against hope it'd be enough.

This time her shot was accurate but to her disbelief its impact produced a metallic ringing. The bullet had struck Scouse's Škorpion and ricocheted off harmlessly.

He laughed out loud and, his right hand wrapped around the gun, he held both paws out wide and beckoned for her to fire again. 'What you got there, princess, is a mouse gun, and with all that shakin' going on there's no wonder you couldn't hit a feckin' barn door,' he spat and then charged over the final few feet between them.

Thoroughgood, despite the burning in his legs, was running at full pelt, all the while trying to avoid coming a cropper on the tangled detritus of root, branch and bush on the forest floor. As he slalomed through the trees, trying to close the 30 feet or so between him and Lisa, he knew it was taking a damn sight longer than it would have on a straight, flat route.

In short, he wouldn't get there in time.

He'd heard the whine of the Scouser's taunting words and the shots that had rung out from Lisa's Browning. But those had stopped now and with a sinking feeling he realised she had in all probability loosed her last bullet.

Picking up speed, he crested a slight gulley that dipped gently towards Lisa's beech tree and found himself with a clear sight of the Scouser's back.

In his right hand he rotated his grip on the hammer, for while its head had proven useful, there was also a sharp end honed to a vicious hooked point.

Coming down the dip, Thoroughgood gradually slowed to a stop, making sure Scouse hadn't seen him. He raised the hammer, took aim and sent it flying, watching as the head rotated in the air. Unbidden, the words from Motorhead's 'The Hammer' came to him and Lemmy's gravel-scored voice sang in his head: "Oh, don't try to run, don't try to scream

Believe me, the hammer's gonna smash your dream…"

But as the hammer flew through the air, there was another noise… it was the report of the last bullet from Lisa's Browning.

The Baby Browning's sixth and final 6.35mm projectile thudded home into the Scouser's ribs from 10 feet and he winced as he felt bone shatter and tissue rip… but he remained on his feet. 'That all you got, bi—'

But he failed to finish his sentence: the hook end of Thoroughgood's hammer had ripped into his back, burying itself deep between his shoulder blades.

As the impact of the twin assaults hit home, the Scouser's legs dipped just as Thoroughgood launched himself through the air in a rugby tackle and took his man down hard.

The sound of the air in the Scouser's lungs rushing out was music to Thoroughgood's ears and he followed up with strikes from his right hand.

As Scouse's head snapped back from the last of the three short sharp blows, Thoroughgood spat: 'Who's the soft lad now… Scouser?'

Then with a struggle he got up and walked towards Lisa, observing the moisture trails that ran down her cheeks and enveloping her in his arms.

'Are you okay?' he asked.

'I am now,' she replied and reached up to kiss him.

They made their way in silence, Thoroughgood, himself blown and shaky, half carrying Lisa, who was struggling to put any weight on her injured ankle. Behind them, they left the Scouser and his henchmen to whatever fate befell them.

They passed a string of horrified walkers, whose faces were filled with shock at the hellish vision that was Thoroughgood's bloodied and bruised visage, the crimson-dipped hammer now held in his left hand and the heavily limping Lisa.

As they reached the car park, it was Thoroughgood who spoke first: 'You know this can't go on, Lisa. We need this to end, and the only way that's gonna happen is if the Total Security van and the six million inside it finds its way back to police custody, your dad comes to the table with DCI Ferguson and we reach some kind of deal for you and your dad to turn Queen's evidence.'

Lisa looked over at him. 'I know… I can't take any more of this, it's no longer a life, it's just an existence. As long as Summerbee is at large we will be looking over our shoulders wondering when the next bullet with Crerand written on it will be fired.'

Thoroughgood smiled weakly and shrugged; but although he had said nothing, it was obvious what he was thinking: "You chose this life."

Lisa ignored the negative vibes and carried on: 'Great, so we agree on that. Maybe we can have that meet at the club in Best's tomorrow night, around 7? But there is one thing I can't help wondering about…' she said, leaving the obvious question dangling in the air.

'Where the hell were the cavalry?' asked Thoroughgood for her.

For a moment, Lisa's eyes held his; then, her voice made slightly husky from the shouting back at the forest, she said: 'I dunno, Detective, but what I do know is that I want you to take me home with you.'

Thoroughgood smiled back. 'Is that an order, Miss Crerand?'

44

MANNY SUMMERBEE fingered the scar that ruined one side of his face and ran through the socket where his left eye had once been.

The silence was killing him.

By now Pearce should have returned with news the Crerand bitch was dead and despite the string of angry voice messages he'd left, the Scouser had maintained an infuriating radio silence.

It was a silence that did not bode well.

The text message from Molly confirming dibble had hit the second safe house had been a blow, but thankfully one he had planned for.

It had confirmed Colina Amos's treachery, but this was a betrayal he had been determined to turn to his advantage.

Molly had also gone silent and acutely aware that he could not reach out to the DS again and risk compromising her, he was again forced to wait, here in the Victorian farmhouse set deep in the Lancashire countryside that had been the location for their trysts over the years.

He found himself replaying some of the moments he had had with her and how it had all started, when he had found himself sitting next to an earthy, attractive brunette with a wicked sense of humour in the Kippax Stand.

A chance encounter in which he had regaled her with the tale of the gypsy curse that had allegedly been placed on Maine Road in 1922, when during the ground's construction club officials had supposedly engineered the ejection of a gypsy camp from the ground earmarked for their stadium.

That encounter had led to an understanding, a relationship that was casual but increasingly useful for both of them, and one that usually spent its passion in front of the warmth of the living room's log fire here in this old stone farmhouse out in Rossendale. For this was a safe place.

So, it was just as well that he had taken the extra measure of retaining the key items from the arms stash and brought them here to the farmhouse.

But Summerbee wasn't only waiting on Molly. He was expecting another visitor, one who had every bit as much reason to want to provide a brutal payback for the Crerands.

Outside, the thrumming of a powerful diesel engine alerted Summerbee to the fact that his visitor had arrived. He stooped under the low-hung doorway and into the daylight, lit large by the late-February afternoon sun.

Summerbee extended his hand. 'Good to see you again, Mr Forsyth,' he said before adding from behind a stony smile: 'Why don't you come in and have a coffee? We have a lot to talk about.'

DS Molly Malone flattened the accelerator of her Scirocco to the floor as she sped down the M66's outside lane, wheel gripped tight, replaying the events of the preceding hours in her mind's eye.

What should have been a moment of triumph had been ruined by the fresh information that had sent Ferguson and his team to Buskin Avenue.

The meticulous planning that she and Summerbee had put into having just enough ordnance in the stash at the Pepperhill boozer to merit it being taken seriously, while the bulk of the arms had been relocated during the night to Buskin, was to ensure that she got the glory and the kudos she needed to impress Trautmann and turn the heat up on that floundering Scots idiot, Ferguson, but still leave Manny with the firepower to make his well-laid plans happen.

But it had not worked that way thanks to the late information that Ferguson had received and the source of which he had refused to divulge at the post-op debrief.

In truth, Molly was mad. Angry that Summerbee had still elected to place the majority of the haul at the home of his erstwhile lover Colina Amos despite the fact he had assured her their relationship had arrived at a dead end.

Yet one thing seemed off and kept her rage in check. When she had left Ferguson, ahead of his own departure for Force HQ and his date with ACC Trautmann, the Scot had been less than ebullient about his haul. Indeed, the information he had provided on it had been deliberately sketchy and vague, his mood anything but triumphant.

Ferguson knew that Trautmann was expecting the type of haul that could be laid out on the gleaming conference table on the command floor of HQ, perfect for a string of triumphant, glossy photographs to fill the pages of the Sundays and keep God's Own Cop happy on the Sabbath.

Her eyes watering from the bright lights of the traffic that illuminated the darkness of the February night, it was a thought that both gnawed away at Molly but also provided her with some hope.

When she eventually arrived at the farmhouse, she saw that Manny had company, for a Jeep Cherokee was parked outside the farmhouse door.

It was a development she had not been expecting; but before she could think too much on it, she noticed Manny standing silhouetted in the warm glow of the building's inside lighting.

As she approached him, she tried to read his features to work out what had been going on: but the half-full whisky glass in his right hand provided a powerful clue.

'Ah, Molly… whatever happens, thank God I can always trust you.' He smiled, before continuing: 'As you can see, I have company, and it's very interesting company, all the way from north of the border. But I have one thing I must ask of you, love,' he said, leaning down to kiss her before she could answer.

The urgency of his embrace and his lips had temporarily thrown Molly, but as they parted, she let her eyes ask the question.

'Whatever you see in here, whatever you hear in the next few minutes, let me assure you I have planned for every eventuality and some of that planning I could not share with you for your own sake.' And with that he winked with his right eye. She noticed that tonight he was wearing a black leather patch over his left eye socket, just as he had the first time he had met her.

Inside, Terry Forsyth sat in one of the two ancient but comfortable armchairs that flanked either side of the log fire now in full flame. As Summerbee brought Molly into the room, Forsyth produced his golden smile, which, thanks to an emergency visit to a friendly dentist, was once again back to its brilliant best.

'Molly, please meet Mr Terry Forsyth, someone who has almost as much loathing for the Crerands as we do and who has suffered almost as much at their hands as I have,' said Summerbee, getting the formalities started.

Forsyth rose and presented a tepid handshake, before Summerbee gestured to Molly to take the armchair at the other side of the farmhouse's impressive stone fireplace. He poured her a whisky.

As he handed Molly the drink, Summerbee got down to business: 'Mr Forsyth is here to conclude the deal we had started work on back at The Midland before The Devils decided to get involved. Terry has my complete trust and his help will prove vital in us making sure we bring this to the end we want and on our terms,' he smiled reassuringly before taking a sip of his own whisky.

'But first I need to bring you up to speed with everything that has been going on. You might want to enjoy your nip before I start!' added Summerbee, smiling reassuringly, while his single eye swept from her to Forsyth and back.

'Okay, what you did not know, my darling, and this was for your own good, is that I used the device of the arms stash as a stone to kill more than one bird. The guns, grenades and drugs you recovered at the Pepperhill were far more impressive than anything your DCI got his hands on at Buskin Avenue,' he said, before stopping to let the implications of his words set in.

'What he got there was enough to tickle his fancy, but more importantly, to me, enough to confirm that Colina has, as I had believed, turned police informant. In that respect, it will be interesting to see what dibble will do with her next. There was enough in her back room at Buskin Avenue to ensure she should be doing time, give that Scots idiot enough to get a hard-on, but far from enough to stop myself concluding the business deal that Paulie and I had originally projected with Mr Forsyth,' concluded Summerbee, taking another sip of his Jameson as his single eye surveyed Molly for her reaction.

Enjoying the warmth of the flames on her dark features and the fire of the whisky inside her, Molly was doing the maths. A slow smile started to unfold across her face as it all began to add up.

Reading her reaction, Summerbee said: 'Good girl!' before taking another sip of his whisky and with a nod to Forsyth continuing his monologue: 'I could not risk telling you all of this, my darling, as I think while your performance so far has been good enough at least for a walk-on in Dempsey and Makepeace, even you would have been hard-pressed not to give our blundering buffoon of a DCI a sniff of what he may have found useful. Please don't be insulted by this, Molly,' said Summerbee, smiling reassuringly.

'That would explain a lot: Ferguson provided virtually no detail on what he got at Buskin, all he said was that it was substantial!'

Summerbee exploded: 'Substantial! Well I guess you could call the 500 rounds of ammunition, the silencers and, most important of all, the 22 Ceska SA vz.58 automatic rifles and half-dozen Tokarev TT-33 pistols impressive!' He paused. 'Impressive, that is, if they weren't all decommissioned!' he cackled.

From his armchair Forsyth raised his glass. 'Sláinte!'

'Sure, combined with what you got at the Pepperhill they will look great in the Sundays and maybe they will be enough to keep your ACC Trautmann happy, but they pale into insignificance with what is in the barn and what is now secreted in the false compartment in the bottom of Mr Forsyth's Jeep.'

This time it was Forsyth who gave a short laugh, before he smiled Molly's way. 'The batch of Škorpions you have provided us with are a very much appreciated down payment, Manny,' he said, raising his glass in salute.

'Thank you, sir! But let us return to tying up the loose ends for sweet Molly's sake!' said Summerbee, then threw the DS a teasing glance.

'I'm all ears, Manny!' said Molly, allowing the mounting excitement in her to manifest in a lascivious smile.

'So, what we have here is the treacherous Colina either bang to rights and now rightfully heading for time in HMP Styal, or, if she remains free, she will be fingered as a grass. Either way, she will shortly meet with the end her treachery deserves and an itch that I needed scratched will have been taken care of once and for all.' Summerbee paused for further refreshment, and as he finished his whisky he gave a snort of satisfaction.

'What about the coppers?' asked Forsyth before he remembered his female company. 'Apologies… Molly,' he said awkwardly.

Despite herself, Molly grimaced. 'I'm afraid there is no good news. I was asked to divert with my team to Alderley Edge to provide backup for the rookie cop Thoroughgood, who is on secondment from Strathclyde, and the Crerand female… I'm afraid it isn't good news, Manny,' she said, letting her words trail off.

Summerbee stared into his glass, letting a sigh escape before nodding at her to proceed.

'Everton Lineker is under police observation in a hospital ward with a fractured skull, Jamie Hansen is in police custody after being found unconscious with the side of his head sporting a nasty dent and—'

'Pearce?' asked Summerbee.

'He's dead, killed by a combination of being harpooned by an ancient caving hammer in the back and a shot by a Baby Browning that deflected off a rib and ended up in his heart,' she said, shrugging helplessly.

'Jesus H. Christ!' roared Summerbee, his single eye almost exploding from its socket.

'Naturally, I took care of anything that could be traced back to you, Manny, including the Škorpion I found lying next to a giant beech tree. But I'm afraid there is more. I had a bust-up with Ferguson over the length of time it took me to provide the backup to Alderley Edge and the amount of 999 calls from panicked members of the public who had heard gunfire. As you might expect, it was soon pretty clear he wasn't going to be sharing anything much with me; but what I do know is that he is planning a meeting with the Crerands… soon.'

That final piece of information caused Summerbee's one-eyed gaze to retrain on Molly. 'Out of every cloud comes a silver lining,' he said, and raised his eyebrows in Forsyth's direction.

'So, there is obviously a deal in the offing between Ferguson and The Devils. Most probably they return the Total Security van and the £6 million and agree to behave themselves. That allows him to concentrate all his resources on taking care of us. We must use that meeting as the perfect opportunity to fix this fucking mess once and for all.'

It was Forsyth who, as Summerbee paused for another sip of his whisky, spoke up next: 'As you know from speaking with my Irish friend earlier, we can have our people in Manchester with less than 24 hours' notice. All I need is the time and location of this meeting and any relevant details to plan entry and exit. Provide that and the hit will be administered with the utmost professionalism. Clean, precise and the perfect final solution. So, can you provide us with the time and location of that meeting, DS Malone?'

Her eyes flickered with excitement as she looked Summerbee's way, before she let them stray to Forsyth. 'I will do my very best, Mr Forsyth!' said DS Molly Malone.

45

THE IMPATIENT BLASTING of a horn and gunning of a powerful engine signalled that DCI Marty Ferguson had arrived outside Sedgley House, the imposing Victorian Grade II listed house that doubled as the force's training school.

As Greene and Thoroughgood made their way through the impressive arched entrance hall and emerged from the red brick colonnaded portico, the DS couldn't help but send a sly verbal dig Thoroughgood's way: 'So tell me, just how involved are you with the Crerand girl, Gus?'

Descending the worn steps leading down from the mansion, another blast from Ferguson's horn saved Thoroughgood from having to answer, and he jumped into the back of the BMW breathing a sigh of relief that a difficult moment had passed.

But his reprieve was to prove temporary.

'Well here he is, The Hammer! Christ, please tell me how you managed to use some ancient potholing… mallet… to beat up three gun-toting hoods? Come on, boy – or should I be calling you Clark bloody Kent…?' demanded Ferguson, half turning in his driver's seat, his hands clasped in a natty pair of tan leather driving gloves.

Thoroughgood shrugged, then let a half-grin creep over his features. 'Because it was all I could get my hands on, Boss!' Ferguson and Greene exchanged glances before they both erupted into laughter.

'Anyway, you did well, boy, and I hope old man Crerand was bloody grateful. Now, how are you finding Sedgley House, boys?

Did you know that the real Mad Myra, of the Hindley variety, stayed there back in '87 when she was helping us with the search of Saddleworth Moor for the graves of her and that monster Brady's victims?' he asked, raising his over-ample eyebrows.

In the passenger seat, Greene was left incredulous. 'You're having a laugh, Marty?' replied the DS, while Thoroughgood remained silent in the back of the Beamer.

'Nope, the senior officer in charge decided that she could have the use of his flat while dear Myra assisted in his enquiries. Anyway, speaking of assistance, just what do you think we can expect tonight at Best's, boy?' asked Ferguson, sliding his silver machine into first gear and his eyes across his rear-view mirror.

'I think you will find that the Crerands know they need to do everything they can to come to an accommodation with GMP to help end this, and I very much hope that will include the return of the six mill and the Total Security van,' replied Thoroughgood in splendid monotone.

'Was that the pillow talk at Chipleys last night then, laddie?' asked Ferguson, deliberately emphasising the last word and retaining his scrutiny on Thoroughgood through the rear-view mirror.

Thoroughgood shifted uncomfortably and remained silent.

'You see, young man, I had a watch placed on the Crerands' house just in case of any unwanted visitors, and the officers on the observation point told me that a maroon GMP Escort didn't leave the premises until 0930 hours this morning. So, and I will ask this just one time, is there anything you want to tell me, ADC Thoroughgood?'

From the front passenger seat, DS Greene turned half round and said one word: 'Well?'

The shrug of Thoroughgood's shoulders was enough of an admission of what had gone on the previous night to provide the answer both of his senior officers already knew.

'Jesus H. Christ, I told you to get close to her, agreed with your suggestion of playing the rat, but instead you've become her lover! Bloody hell, Paddy, you were supposed to be his babysitter!' erupted the Boss, but from the rear-view mirror Thoroughgood could see a twinkle of mischief in his eyes.

In the passenger seat, Greene held his hands up in an admission it was a case of 'what could he do?'.

'Still, the inside of Miss Lisa's bedsheets had a silver lining, since you've brought them to the table tonight… I mean her father and Lisa, obviously! Care to elaborate on what we can expect?' asked Ferguson.

'Lisa has had enough, Boss, that's one thing I can confirm. We stayed up most of the night talking about it and she promised me she will do everything she can to make sure her father is ready to cut a deal,' said Thoroughgood.

'But what about old man Crerand… what did he have to say for himself? He must have been grateful for your efforts, to say the very least,' asked Greene.

Thoroughgood nodded. 'There's no doubt about that, gaffer. But they didn't go into any detail on how things may pan out while I was there. Lisa twisted an ankle, so that needed a bit of attention… there was a lot going on and not necessarily what you might like to think,' replied Thoroughgood, unable to stop some reproach from entering into his words.

'Indeed,' said Greene, turning back round to face the front windscreen.

'If you don't mind, Boss, I have a couple of questions for you,' ventured Thoroughgood.

'The floor's all yours, boy,' the DCI replied.

'Where the hell were DS Malone and her team and the rest of the cavalry? And did you get your hands on the Škorpion that Scouse bastard was shooting up everything in sight with?' asked Thoroughgood with a shade too much vehemence.

But from Ferguson's reaction in the mirror, it was clear he did not have the answer to at least one of these two questions. 'I don't know what took her so long, but I do know she got there. I'm afraid I had enough to deal with from what I uncovered at Buskin Avenue, but in so far as the hardware she said nothing to me about any… what did you call it?'

'A Škorpion vz. 61; it's Czech-manufactured; and believe me, when the Scouser fired it, it literally rained brass. The other thing I wanted to confirm was that he was the same guy in the club who left the rucksack bomb, but by the end of our little tussle he was minus his aviators!' said Thoroughgood, trying to tie up all the loose ends from his adventure at Alderley Edge.

In the driver's seat, Ferguson was deep in thought, and it was Greene who spoke first: 'Well, it should be safely bagged up as a production. So, it won't be difficult to examine. That said, I would have thought Molly should have mentioned it to you as an item of interest, because my money would be on it being part of the arms cache—'

But before Greene could finish, the Boss interrupted: 'Don't talk to me about that bloody arms stash…' spat the DCI.

While neither Greene nor Thoroughgood were keen to push him on the raid on Buskin Avenue, Greene eventually took the bull by the horns.

'What happened, Marty?'

'I'll tell you what happened; Summerbee has done me up like a bloody kipper,' said Ferguson, his jaw setting.

'But the haul looked great all spread out nice and shiny on the conference table at Force HQ, the coverage in the Sundays was impressive and it was all high-grade stuff… surely?' asked Greene cautiously.

'Aye, it looked great, but I spoke with DS Molly Malone, whose tout informs us most of it was decommissioned and about as lethal as a pea-shooter… minus the peas. We've not had time to test it all yet, but if what she says is true…' groaned Ferguson.

'Can I ask, does ACC Trautmann or the chief know that, Boss?' enquired Thoroughgood, despite himself.

A lift of Ferguson's bushy eyebrows was all the answer he needed on that score.

'Five hundred rounds of ammo and a haul of Eastern European automatic rifles and pistols with a sprinkling of silencers provided a pretty appetising visual feast when combined with Molly's haul, but the bottom line is there were none of these bloody Škorpions you keep rabbiting on about. Nor were there any of the other state-of-the-art weapons of war we were led by our touts to believe were waiting for us, and it looks like your bloody girlfriend has also had her chain yanked!' said Ferguson with a rueful shake of his head.

'So, if this has all been a set-up, where is the tasty stuff? Also, why would Summerbee hang his bird out to dry? If he has sold us a dummy in terms of what he planted at Buskin, why place the arms there; because let's face it, they are still more than good enough to put the delectable Colina inside,' hypothesised Greene.

From the back of the Beamer, Thoroughgood couldn't help but let an involuntary 'Mmm' slip out.

Once again, Ferguson's eyes locked on his rear-view. 'Having a light-bulb moment, Thoroughgood?' he asked.

'It's just a thought, but… what if Summerbee was using this as a decoy stash not only to fool us but also to set up Colina? What if he suspected her of ratting on him?' he asked, shrugging his shoulders.

'So that would mean he was feeding Colina in order for her to grass to whoever she was whispering to, which, as we know, wasn't the law but Miss Lisa. Interesting. Perhaps Summerbee was clever – but not that clever, because he suspected Colina of being on our payroll and not the Crerands'. But then I guess either way the end result was a home win for him… dirty bastard!' spat Ferguson.

'Talk about smoke and mirrors!' said Greene, with a nod of the head.

'All of which brings us back to what we are about to receive at Best's tonight. For the one thing I do know is that Mad Myra will get to hear about the fact the automatic rifles that filled the pages of the Sundays are decommissioned. Almost certainly that information will come to her before I can have them reactivated and do you know why that is, gents?' asked the Boss.

Both members of the DCI's audience remained silent.

'It's because DS Molly bloody Malone is touting to Mad Myra! I'm beginning to feel like Hitler in his bloody bunker sending his armies jogging out to positions on the Eastern Front only to find that old Uncle Joe and his Red bastards are waiting for them with soddin' bayonets fixed. Christ, almost before I can make a decision in the squad room I swear Mad Myra has caught wind of it up on the 11th floor of Force HQ. It's bloody hilarious that only seems to happen when our man-eating DS is present in the muster… capiche?' concluded Ferguson abruptly.

'All of which begs the question, Boss… does DS Malone know about tonight's meeting?' asked Thoroughgood and received a barked laugh from Ferguson for his trouble.

'Well, that is one that left me in something of a quandary, I can tell you, boy, and let me explain why. Darling Molly has resented me ever since the first day I walked through the Flying Squad door as acting DCI and that was because she had been told… by Mad Myra… she was being made DI and would get the job herself. Unfortunately, our ACC Crime was only a Detective Super at that stage and didn't quite have the clout she has now, and when news of one of Molly's liaisons with her gaffer in the vice squad reached God's Own Cop, the chief himself, well, you can guess what kind of a dim view he took on that. So, it cost dear Mol her promotion but not the move. You can imagine how happy she was when some ginger-haired Jock rocked up on an acting post and then got the rank substantive,' said Ferguson.

'But I thought you and she looked pretty cosy back at The Lass O'Gowrie?' asked Thoroughgood.

'What you obviously still have to learn, dear boy, is that in some cases appearances can be bloody deceptive. Nope, our Mol has the knife out for me and with Mad Myra's finger permanently hovering above the ejector button, I could be sent flying quicker than a villain from James Bond's Aston Martin DB5!' concluded the DCI as he swung his BMW next to the kerb at Reds and applied the handbrake.

'So, I take it Molly is out of the loop and back home dining on a hotpot?' asked Greene with an uneasy laugh.

'Not unless that's a mirage standing outside the front door!' responded the Boss with a wink.

In the back seat, Thoroughgood followed his gaze, while the voice in his own head, with its usual immaculate timing, chirped: "Well at least she didn't bring Mad Myra!"

46

WITH MOST of Reds remaining closed following the bombing, Lisa Crerand had opened Best's Bar especially for the summit meeting with GMP, which she now accepted was vital to both her father's and her own survival.

The bar was a totally crimson affair in homage to the red of Manchester United's famous shirts and each wall sported iconic photographs of the man it had been named after and was dedicated to, the incomparable former United number seven George Best.

As she stood sipping her favoured Pernod, blackcurrant and lemonade, Lisa leaned against the gleaming black marble of the cocktail bar, while behind her stood a huge photograph of Best, flanked by the great United manager Sir Matt Busby and another United legend, Paddy Crerand, holding the European Cup after their historic Wembley victory over Benfica back in 1968.

A few feet away from her, Lisa's father sat in one of the grand red leather, American-style horseshoe booths that were positioned along the circle of the bar's rouge-dipped walls, while the black and white tilling of the ceiling gave the impression that patrons were in fact inside a giant football.

Crerand cradled a whisky glass as he stared up at a massive autographed photograph of the eponymous Northern Irishman standing next to the immortal Pelé, a picture from Best's American sojourn with the Los Angeles Aztecs.

As Lisa surveyed her father, she had to admit she had no idea what was going on in his head. While Gordon Crerand had been genuinely grateful to Thoroughgood for saving her life – on not one but two occasions – the leap of faith needed to get him to turn over the six million in cash taken from their gazumping of The Maine Men's security van heist was another matter.

Crerand, from bitter experience, did not trust GMP, and even getting him to the table tonight had taken all of Lisa's powers of persuasion. Yet her father had admitted he had taken a shine to Thoroughgood, even going so far to say that the young Scottish detective was 'different' to the coppers he had previously dealt with.

All of that had helped bring him to Best's tonight. But beyond that, Gordon Crerand had been non-committal about how far he was going to go to broker a peace deal with GMP.

She knew that it was those failed assassination attempts that Crerand nursed an unquenchable thirst to avenge.

Almost as if he could read her mind, Crerand's grave mien and leonine features turned her way and he smiled: a smile filled with love – unconditional love – for her.

At that precise moment Lisa realised this was the real reason Gordon Crerand was seated at the table waiting for the Flying Squad to arrive.

But his attention was soon snapped from his admiration of his only daughter. The giant figure of Lisa's security guard, Radoslav, walked through the door, under a photograph of Best and Nobby Stiles holding the 1964/65 English Division One trophy.

Radoslav presented himself in front of her and as usual got straight to the point: 'The police is here, Miss Lisa,' he said and stood back.

As he walked towards the entrance door of the bar, Thorough-good couldn't help but notice the replica Manchester United Red Devil crest with its trident.

The way the entrance was shaped actually gave you the feeling you were going down the tunnel and about to take to the field of play, or the Theatre of Dreams, as Old Trafford, United's home, was known.

But Thoroughgood apparently wasn't the only one who had been impressed by the sight of the Red Devil crest, for to his amazement he noticed Ferguson reach up his huge right hand and tap the foot of the devil.

Ferguson caught Thoroughgood's furtive glance and met it with a curt 'Yes?' before striding out of the 'tunnel', the detectives in his wake.

As they arrived in the bar, there was a collective gasp at the sight of a working of a bronzed statue that depicted Best, Dennis Law and Bobby Charlton, the three immortals of a golden era. The statue was surrounded by a pool of water, resplendent with fountains and twinkling from the hundreds of coins thrown in by anxious United supporters.

But it was Lisa's seductive appearance that left Thoroughgood truly speechless.

For tonight's meeting, Lisa had selected a power minidress covered in black sequins. Her jet hair was worn long down to her shoulders and every sequin sparkled and amplified the perfect curvature of her lithe body.

Thoroughgood took a step forward and an awkward smile broke across his face. 'Hello Lisa, how is the ankle?' he asked lamely.

'A lot better thanks to round-the-clock icing,' she said, point-ing to a bandage wrapped around the sprained joint, underneath the shimmer of her stockings. Then, apparently on impulse, she leaned over and kissed him on the cheek.

He blushed.

Behind Thoroughgood, the burr of conversation stilled immediately.

Ferguson cleared his throat. 'Good evening Miss Crerand,' he said and stepped forward offering his hand. 'A bad business up on the Edge; the boy did well by you, however, and I'm delighted to see you and your dad are ready to parley.'

Lisa took his hand and smiled serenely. 'After what has gone on over the last three days, I don't think there is any other choice.'

'Indeed,' said Ferguson before beckoning the other two members of his team forward. 'I believe you have met DS Molly Malone and DS Paddy Greene?' he asked, unfolding a hand to present his colleagues.

Thoroughgood watched Lisa's dark eyes meet Molly Malone's uncompromising gaze, and for a moment both women eyed each other, the temperature around them feeling like it had dropped several degrees. 'Miss Crerand, I'm pleased to meet you again and glad to see you have emerged from your trials almost unscathed,' the DS finally said, letting her eyes stray towards Lisa's ankle.

But there was no handshake of greeting and as things looked like getting awkward, Paddy Greene offered his hand with a quick 'Pleased to meet you Miss Crerand,' filling the uncomfortable gap.

Lisa beckoned them over to the table, where Gordon was eyeing their arrivals with a detached interest that resembled a big cat eyeing its prey. Lisa's heart hammered, for the signs were not good. She knew that the frostiness of the female detective would not have gone unnoticed by her father's all-seeing gaze.

But before Lisa could offer any words of introduction, DCI Ferguson took command of the floor: 'Some place you have here, Mr Crerand, whatta bloody player Besty was! It's one of those great debates I've often found myself engaged in, mostly with Paddy back there: was he better than Jimmy Johnstone? Who knows, eh?' said Ferguson offering his hand.

It was a shrewd opening gambit, and Thoroughgood's breath held as Crerand got to his feet. After a short pause, he pumped Ferguson's offered paw. 'Wee Jinky Johnstone: a number seven who you could probably argue is Celtic's greatest player, much like Besty for United!'

The ice had been broken and a mutual smile that meant bread could indeed be broken swept across both men's previously suspicious features.

But Ferguson had not finished his charm offensive and he turned round to Lisa. 'Can I just ask, out of interest, whose idea Best's was?'

From behind him, Crerand's mellifluous tones provided the answer: 'I'm afraid the idea was down to neither of us, but to my late wife Charlotta. To be frank with you, Mr Ferguson, I didn't think it would work.'

But Ferguson's attention had already been taken by something else, for his eyes had locked on the photo of Best with the European Cup that dominated the bar. 'I'm sorry... but I've got to ask this: are you related to Paddy Crerand?' he asked, pointing to the former United midfield enforcer who flanked Best from above.

'I'm afraid not, but that doesn't stop people asking me that question. If I had a penny for every time I've been asked that... well, you know how the saying goes,' said Crerand.

But his answer had opened a window for the Boss to bring the meeting sharply down to business and he seized it. Turning back to Crerand, he said: 'But you are indeed a very rich man, Mr Crerand, and one who has just benefitted from a six-mill cash injection; and ultimately that's why we are here.' He paused for effect, before adding: 'May we sit?'

Crerand's eyes had immediately narrowed and all the warmth that had previously flowed between them from the banter created by their mutual love of the beautiful game evaporated.

As Ferguson and his colleagues edged into one side of the booth and Lisa joined her dad on the opposite side, with the menacing figure of Radoslav hovering behind them intimidatingly, her gaze met Thoroughgood's and she rolled her eyes.

Thoroughgood knew that the next few words would be vital and clearing his throat he asked: 'If you don't mind, DCI Ferguson, may I speak?' He received a curt nod of affirmation.

'From where I'm sitting, we all want the same thing: the end of this feud with The Maine Men and no more bloodshed on the streets of Manchester. The only way that can happen is if we learn to trust each other and that both parties get something out of this meeting.'

Across the table, Gordon Crerand's face remained a mask. 'You make a valid point, Detective. However, while I know what is in it for GMP, I don't know what's in it for us,' he said, then turned his gaze towards Ferguson. 'Let's cut to the chase, Detective Chief Inspector, what am I getting in return for your obvious requirements?'

Ferguson had positioned himself at the edge of the table so that he could extend his long legs out onto the floor, and while his hands remained shoved deep in the pockets of his covert coat, his eyes were darting orbs full of life. He nodded to DS Paddy Greene. 'Time to bring the paperwork out, Paddy!'

The DS duly fished out a Manilla file from his jacket and slapped it onto the middle of the table.

'The case against you, Mr Crerand, is very compelling, believe me. We have missed nothing and what that means in real terms is that you and your daughter…' – Ferguson paused for theatrical effect and let his eyes slip towards Lisa, where they remained slightly too long, before they returned to Crerand – 'will be doing time in separate establishments for abduction, murder and robbery for the rest of your naturals. Is that what you want for Lisa? What you want for your dotage, a retirement spent behind the bars?' asked Ferguson forcefully.

Crerand's right hand shot out and gripped the folder. He lifted it, apparently weighing it up, then tossed it back onto the gleaming lacquered surface and watched with a dismissive smile as the file skited across the table and span to a stop in front of Ferguson.

'Anything that's in there is circumstantial and my brief will have a field day with it,' he spat contemptuously.

It was then that a female voice spoke up: 'With respect, DCI Ferguson,' said DS Molly Malone, jumping to her feet and slamming her hands down on the table, 'why are we even wasting time talking to these people. It's time they were taken into custody!' she demanded.

Ferguson's teeth clenched and his jaw set. With a supreme effort of self-control, he said: 'You will be mindful that I am the officer in charge of this investigation and that I am also the ranking officer here. Now sit down, DS Malone. I suggest you still your tongue.'

For a moment Ferguson and Malone eyed each other. Thoroughgood and the rest of the company watched in fascination as finally the pent-up animosity boiled over.

Across the table, a smile of twisted amusement played at Crerand's thin lips while Lisa's wide-eyed gaze met Thoroughgood's.

For a moment it appeared Malone was going to defy the Boss, but Paddy Greene placed a placatory hand on her wrist. 'Come on, Mol, we've come here to talk,' he said and nodded his head to suggest she sit back down.

It was then that Thoroughgood decided to gamble: 'If you don't mind me saying so, Mr Crerand, Lisa has already had two attempts on her life and doing things your way you still hasn't managed to… neutralise… Summerbee. I think you've got to ask yourself how long you can go on living your lives like this and how long you can stay lucky.'

He had paraphrased Lisa's concerns and the frosty glance she gave him underlined that she knew exactly what he was doing.

Crerand's eyes switched from the young detective to Ferguson as he considered his words, but Thoroughgood had not finished: 'Give us what we want and you will have round-the-clock protection until we bring Summerbee and his arms haul to book. When that is done, I am sure that for your cooperation the DCI will be able to cut a deal that will allow you and your daughter to enjoy the rest of your lives in peace and quiet.'

Ferguson quickly pressed on: 'The boy is right, Mr Crerand. Surely to God, all any of us wants is to live our lives in peace. You must know that we turned a string of addresses for Summerbee and his arms hoard and got precisely what he wanted us to get: a big fat zero. That means he is still out there and still has the firepower to bring about a very nasty end for you and your daughter. Christ, man, is that what you really want? For what? To save your own pride… is it really worth more than your daughter?'

Despite himself, Crerand's eyes twitched in the direction of Lisa and for a moment, suspended in time, they held each other's gaze.

The temptation too much, Thoroughgood delivered the coup de grâce: 'Ask yourself this, Mr Crerand… is this never-ending blood feud what Charlotta would have wanted for your daughter… or you? Surely as a father that's the only question that matters…'

47

CRERAND'S GAZE returned to the Boss. 'DCI Ferguson, you will excuse my daughter and I while we have private word.' Then he inclined his head towards the bronzed figurines of Best, Law and Charlton. He edged out of the booth, taking his whisky glass with him, and made his way past the bar's sparkling tiled floor.

As she stood up, Lisa offered Thoroughgood a weak smile and followed in her father's wake, the detective's eyes remaining locked on her as she walked away.

As the Crerands took up a position at the other side of the fountain, their words were literally drowned out; but the sound of Molly Malone's voice soon fractured the silence around the table.

'This is a joke… DCI Ferguson. How can you let a gangster like Crerand dictate terms to us? I can't sit here any longer while you let the authority of GMP be further undermined. I will make sure—' But as she got to her feet, Ferguson finished the sentence for her.

'ACC Trautmann hears all about this?' he spat as a malevolent grin spread across his ruddy features. 'Oh yes, sweet Molly, I know all about your touting to Mad Myra. It is you that has been undermining me at every step and turn by making sure news of what the Flying Squad is doing gets to the 11th floor before I've even finished briefing the bloody troops,' raged the Boss as he too got to his feet. Then he swept a giant hand in front of him. 'So, go on, DS Malone, run along and tell the headmistress all about it why don't you?'

As Molly Malone swept by him, she sneered contemptuously: 'Oh you can be sure I will, DCI Ferguson. I will also make sure that the ACC Crime knows the weapons you allowed the chief to parade on the Force HQ conference table for the papers were all decommissioned… I am sure she will find that most interesting. I held it back and came here thinking you might have some plan. But you are working with these… people, and Trautmann will know.'

It was the straw that broke the camel's back. 'You grassing bitch!' Ferguson snarled and lunged menacingly towards the DS, but Thoroughgood and Greene almost simultaneously jumped in between the DCI and his tormentor before he could reach her.

'Come on, Boss, calm down,' soothed Greene.

But Molly Malone had not finished. 'You're done, Ferguson. You're going to be sacked in the morning, I promise you,' she taunted, before turning on her heels and stalking off through the doorway of Best's.

Shaking with rage, Ferguson's right hand toyed with his red mop. He turned his eyes to the ceiling and groaned 'Jesus H. Christ!' before stalking over to the bar

Thoroughgood quickly glanced to the fountain, where Lisa and Gordon Crerand had just watched the fireworks, clearly shocked. It was the disbelief on their faces that brought the realisation to Thoroughgood that this may be a now-or-never moment that could avert disaster all round.

He jumped into action. Seeing Ferguson still stood at the bar, his palms flattened on its marble surface and his head hanging as he tried to regain his composure, Thoroughgood nudged Greene. 'Can you take care of the Boss, I need to speak to the Crerands,' he said, adding a reassuring nod.

Greene, who was clearly as shocked as his DCI, raised his eyebrows in agreement and watched for a moment as Thoroughgood headed back to the fountain, before he clamped a reassuring hand on Ferguson's shoulders.

'Two pints of lager, pal,' said Greene to the wide-eyed and watching barman.

As Thoroughgood arrived at the fountain, Lisa was first to react. 'What the hell was that all about?' she asked.

'Forgive me for saying so, but the world you operate in isn't the only one that's riven by feuding and treachery... but that means that time isn't on your side,' he said, not entirely sure his opening gambit had been fit for purpose.

The narrowing of Gordon Crerand's eyes suggested it was not. 'What do you mean, lad?' he asked, his voice laced with added edge.

'I'm afraid that DCI Ferguson has been undermined by his DS. She has the ear of the ACC Crime, Michelle Trautmann, and she – for want of a better phrase – isn't the Boss's best friend. It turns out that most of the haul of semi-automatics at Buskin Avenue were decommissioned, something the Boss neglected to pass on to the ACC or the chief constable, but information that DS Malone will make sure the ACC has in around 20 minutes I'd imagine,' he said in a hurried delivery that underlined the urgency of the situation.

'Judas,' muttered Crerand.

'Why would she do that?' asked Lisa.

Thoroughgood's eyes shifted from Gordon Crerand to his daughter before he continued: 'Because she covets his position, because she has been feeding Trautmann with information all along the way, which has meant the ACC has had her legs under the table of every briefing the Boss holds. It means that now Malone reckons she has finally got the information that will bury the DCI, and if that happens, I can guarantee one thing…' said Thoroughgood, letting his words trail off.

Crerand's eyes locked on the young detective and just as Lisa had been about to speak, her father clamped a hand on her wrist: 'Which is?'

'There will be no deal left on the table. Trautmann will come for you and while Manny Summerbee remains in the wind you will find yourselves in custody and any hope you have of cutting a deal will be gone. I'm sorry, there is no point in sugar-coating it: this is it. If you want a deal and a way out of this, you need to cut it with the Boss right now and make sure that the Total Security van and the cash turn up outside the doors of GMP HQ tonight. Nothing less will save him; and if he goes down, then I promise you, you will follow, Mr Crerand. You and Lisa, banged up in separate prisons for how long? It's just as I said, Mr Crerand, there is no way that is the life that your wife would have wanted for you both. And it can all be avoided.'

Crerand's right hand left Lisa's wrist and rubbed his stubbled chin. All the while his eyes remained locked on Thoroughgood.

It was the hint of indecision that offered the young detective the encouragement he had been looking for. 'It's up to you, Mr Crerand, but if you let the Boss walk out of here then a good man and a bloody decent cop, who you could clearly work with in the future, will be finished, just like you and Lisa, and there will be nothing anyone can do to stop that happening,' concluded Thoroughgood breathlessly while his eyes once again met Lisa's.

'Can you give Dad and I a minute, Gus?' she asked. Thoroughgood nodded and beat the retreat.

He had done his best, seized the moment and played his hand. Yet however compelling his case, he found it impossible to work out which way Gordon Crerand would go.

All he could hope now was that Lisa's influence would help her father see sense. As he walked towards Ferguson and Greene, it was clear from the sombre looks etched on their faces that they also feared the worst.

Ferguson took a long draught of his lager as he watched Thoroughgood's approach across the gleaming floor. 'Well, boy… have you got more good news for me?' he asked.

Thoroughgood shrugged. 'I just made the Crerands aware that if you go down then they will follow. But I'm not sure that Gordon Crerand can get past his own pride and see the wood for the trees. I did my best, Boss.'

'And that, my dear boy, is all I can ask of you. Now let me buy you a pint while we wait for the ship to go down. At least you and the paddywhack here can escape back up the road when this is done. As for me, I dunno what fate Mad Myra will have planned for me. Maybe I'll end up busted back to uniform, but I'd say that's the best I can hope for. Once she finds out these semi-automatics were decommissioned I wouldn't put it past her to have me put on a charge… the bitch would take my pension off me if she thought it was possible,' said Ferguson before he finished the remains of his lager.

As he slipped a tenner the barman's way and pushed the fresh pints in the direction of Greene and Thoroughgood, Ferguson continued the post-mortem: 'In short, dear boy, I'm fucked, and if that's the case we might as well drink to my impending end. Twenty-seven years of police service, man and boy, north and south of the border, finished all thanks to the treachery of a woman. Christ, now I know how Adam must have felt in the Garden of bloody Eden!' he said, allowing himself a rueful smile before taking another mouthful of his lager.

Opposite him, Paddy Greene opened his left hand in a gesture that underlined he was lost for words, while Thoroughgood also sought solace in silence.

But they were snapped from their tormented deliberations by the voice of another female and Thoroughgood felt a light hand on his arm. 'My dad is waiting, if you want to join us, gentlemen,' she said. As she turned round, the smile on her face meant, for Thoroughgood at least, that hope once again sprung eternal.

48

AS THEY APPROACHED the booth for a second time, Crerand had an outsize Nokia pressed to his ear. Looking up, he waved them into the lush red leather seating opposite him while Lisa nestled at his left-hand side.

Crerand's phone conversation continued as they took their seats. 'How soon?' he asked.

Doing his best to strain his ears without making it obvious, Thoroughgood thought he heard a voice saying 'one hour'.

'No fuck-ups, Yul, I mean it. You take every precaution, understood?' concluded Crerand and then he cut the call and pocketed the Nokia inside his suit jacket.

For a moment an awkward silence reigned; then Crerand grasped his daughter's hand and took a breath, before lifting his eyes to meet the gazes of the three cops in front of him.

'I am prepared to cut a deal, DCI Ferguson, and you have the lad here to thank for that,' he said gravely, before sending a nod of recognition in Thoroughgood's direction. 'He is right, sometimes you can't see what is right in front of your nose and need someone else with a fresh pair of eyes to point that out. I could not live with myself if anything happened to Lisa, and now I owe it to my late wife and to the daughter who means the world to me to take what you offer me in return for the cash. But I must be clear on what I expect in return, DCI Ferguson,' he said, meeting and holding the Boss's eyes.

'Pardon my French, Miss, but thank fuck for that!' said Ferguson, his relief all too obvious, before he regathered himself. 'From the phone conversation I couldn't help catching, I am guessing that you have perhaps arranged for the delivery of the van and the cash. If that delivery is to this premises and it will allow me to drive it into Force HQ, then feel free to name your conditions, Mr Crerand,' said Ferguson, the steel returning to his eyes.

'There are three things I need, DCI. I want Lisa kept safe until this is finished and Summerbee is banged up, I want your word you will do everything you can to make that happen as soon as possible and I want a Queen's evidence deal agreed with my QC which will make both myself and my daughter bulletproof… literally,' said Crerand, his eyes slightly narrowing, but remaining locked on Ferguson.

'I would expect nothing less, but first we must be absolutely sure that if you are granted immunity what you are prepared to offer will satisfy the Attorney General and also make it impossible for Mad Myra – sorry, ACC Trautmann – to throw me and you both under a bus,' said Ferguson, offering a smile that was reciprocated by Crerand and Lisa.

The Boss continued: 'What we need to show is this: in the interests of justice, it is of more value to have the suspected persons – and by that I mean you and, let's be clear, Mr Crerand, your daughter as well – as a witness for the Crown rather than a defendant. Secondly, that in the interests of public safety and security, the obtaining of info about the extent and nature of criminal activities is of greater importance than the possible conviction of these individuals, namely you and Lisa. Finally, that it's highly unlikely that any information could be obtained without an offer of immunity. Do you understand me, both of you?'

This time it was Lisa who answered: 'DCI Ferguson, we completely understand you... believe me. You will have our full cooperation, you will have anything that will allow us to live our lives without a target on our backs. Now perhaps we might celebrate this agreement properly,' she said, before standing up and adding: 'Gus, would you mind helping me?' She smiled beguilingly Thoroughgood's way.

'An excellent idea!' agreed the Boss and he also stood up and offered his hand across the table towards Crerand.

A short pause ensued as Crerand appeared to size Ferguson up, but slowly he got to his feet and pumped the big man's hand before repeating the process with Greene and Thoroughgood.

Then Thoroughgood followed Lisa's shimmering, sequinned figure to the bar, where a bottle of Bollinger '88 had already been uncorked by the barman and was chilling in an ice bucket.

The voice in Thoroughgood's head helped provide the summing up: "One they made earlier? Cute, Gus, pal, the bloody deal was never in doubt!"

Yet as Lisa filled two glasses and handed them on to him, Thoroughgood couldn't help a smile breaking out across his face.

'For the Bolly, 1988 was a bumper year! Let's have a toast, Angus,' she said and then raised her glass. 'To the rest of my life, Angus Thoroughgood, and to a life I want you in.' Then as his eyes widened in surprise at her words, she clinked his glass and sipped the Bollinger, all the while her gaze holding his.

For a minute Thoroughgood had to admit it was like all his troubles had been packed up in an old kitbag, just like his grandfather used to say, and they were the only two people in the room.

As they arrived back at the table, they found Ferguson and Gordon Crerand deep in conversation as the horse-trading began.

'There is one other thing I need from you – or, rather, my colleague DS Greene and his boy need – before they head back up the road to Glasgow, Mr Crerand.'

As Ferguson paused slightly, Lisa's sultry gaze located Thoroughgood's green eyes. The news of his departure back home had sent a shockwave of real concern across her sultry features. He silently mouthed: 'It's okay,' and backed his words up with a warm smile; yet it was clear she was less than reassured.

But Ferguson's gravelly Glaswegian had sprung back into life: 'I need you to help us catch a troublesome individual from north of the border, who I believe has been looking for a trade deal in Manchester. DS Greene, if you will?'

'ADC Thoroughgood and I were despatched to Manchester to bring a person of some interest back with us. I believe you know Terry Forsyth and were approached by him to do some business in terms of cutting a… deal?' asked Greene and received a short nod of the head in the affirmative from Crerand. 'We need him bagged and tagged and on the sleeper back to Glasgow with us. Can you help supply the bait for our trap? It shouldn't be too difficult to lure him to a table somewhere.'

Crerand grimaced slightly. 'Perhaps not as easy as you may think, DS Greene. You're right we have met Mr Forsyth and yes, he did try to cut a deal with us, but he left minus one of his hideous golden teeth: the wages of sin. I'm not sure how easy it will be to bring him back to the table after that. Believe me, if there is any way I could help on this I would, but we reckon that Terry Forsyth and Manny One-Eye are now… bedfellows… for want of a better phrase.'

Thoroughgood jumped in: 'Any help you can give us here is vital, Mr Crerand. If we go back up the road empty-handed, it will be a disaster for us.'

'Rest assured, Detective; my father and I will talk this over and see what we can come up with. It may be that Forsyth could be tempted for another parley; after all, he knows we have the funds to pay what he wants, or at least we did until tonight!' said Lisa, before a spontaneous smile slid across her mouth.

As the true meaning behind her words registered with the company, laughter surfed around the table like a rolling breaker. Reassured she had not put her foot in it, Lisa carefully placed the Bollinger on the table, and Thoroughgood, feeling like a waiter and receiving a mocking lift of Ferguson's bushy eyebrows for his trouble, did the needful with the glasses.

Then as the company got to their feet, it was Crerand who raised the toast: 'As you may have guessed, gentlemen, I'm not the sort to get carried away, but the good Lord works in mysterious ways, he giveth and he taketh away… and now I give you to new beginnings!' he said with a laugh.

The toast greedily drunk, everyone sat back down. Crerand continued: 'I think you now know that both my daughter and myself are genuine about peace breaking out between us and yourselves, DCI. You have shown yourself to be a football man, a man after my own heart, so as further proof of that I'd like to offer you an invite, along with the lad here and DS Greene, to be my guests for hospitality next Saturday at United. The timing could not be better, DCI Ferguson, for the visitors are City. What do you say, can we seal this new beginning and perhaps cement our future collaboration with a day out at the Theatre of Dreams?'

Ferguson, who had been stretching back across the rear of the booth, almost rebounded back over the table with hand outstretched, such was his delight at Crerand's offer. 'Oh yes you bloody can!' the Boss laughed and once again the crime lord and the DCI shook hands.

But as both men regained their composure, Crerand had a further question: 'You asked me if I was related to Paddy Crerand earlier, DCI. Well now I have a question for you: are you related to our manager, Alex Ferguson?'

For a moment, the DCI's craggy features were riven with shock and exaggerated disappointment. 'You didn't know? He's my younger brother!' said the Boss and once again the table was drowned in laughter.

The sound of Crerand's mobile going off inside his jacket brought a quick silence to proceedings.

Crerand pulled out the phone and answered with a curt 'Yes?' Then his eyes shot towards the bar's impressive entrance, where a moment later his henchman Yul, flanked by two suits, walked into the bar each carrying two army kitbags.

Crerand stood up. 'The money – all six million of it – has arrived, DCI Ferguson. I will give you the address of the industrial estate where you will find the Total Security van, but I'm afraid it's burnt out. Forgive me, but that is a precaution regarding its possible evidential use that I am sure you can permit me to have taken. But your money is here, and the serial numbers will confirm it belonged to the Bank of Manchester.'

Ferguson smiled. He nodded to Greene to make his way over to the kitbags and verify that was the case. 'Like you said, Mr Crerand, you will permit me this obvious precaution. After all, I can't have the conference table at Force HQ groaning under the wrong dosh!' he quipped, referring to the decommissioned semi-automatics that he had in essence conned Trautmann and the chief constable to parade as genuine.

He needn't have worried, for from across the floor Greene flashed a thumbs-up.

'Excellent!' said the Boss and as he stood up, he met Crerand's gaze. 'You have my word that we will do everything we can to bring Manny One-Eye to book ASAP. In the morning I will send ADC Thoroughgood with details on how we propose to protect your daughter until we have Summerbee. Here is my card, you can call me on the mobile listed at any time, but I will personally keep you posted on developments at our end. If you can do the same regarding Terry Forsyth, should any info reach your ears, it would be appreciated.'

Crerand stood up and after an initial nod he fished out a card and pushed it across the table to Ferguson. 'Oh I think we can bait a trap up that will hook Terry Jaws for you, and you can rest assured we will be doing everything we can to locate Summerbee. In the meantime, DCI Ferguson, can I say that I look forward to you joining me at Old Trafford next Saturday.'

Ferguson smiled and as he offered his hand for a third time he quipped: 'As the greatest manager of them all, Bill Shankly – another Scot, incidentally – once said, "Some people think football is a matter of life and death. It is much more serious than that!"' And again their laughter erupted.

49

DS MOLLY MALONE drew her car to a stop at the back of a deserted B&Q car park and punched in the mobile number of ACC Trautmann. There was to be no going back: this was the moment she had waited for and now she was going to take it.

Molly, with barely disguised glee, gave the ACC the full details of Ferguson's ruse with the decommissioned semi-automatics and as Trautmann digested the true extent of his treachery, her end of the mobile went silent.

Yet the ACC Crime's disconcertingly deep voice soon sprang back to life with a thirst for vengeance flowing through it: 'This information will finally allow me to destroy that bastard Ferguson once and for all, and for that I can't thank you enough, Molly. When the chief hears of this, and the fact he has been made a complete fool of, there will be no hiding place for Detective Chief Inspector Martin Ferguson. His career will be finished and when our Discipline Department has finished with him I think there is every chance the big Scots bastard will find himself in the dock. I will have the guns removed from the evidence compound when it reopens in the morning, and by the time I finish with him Ferguson will be pleading with me to let him jump out of my 11th-floor window!'

The clear delight that her information had caused the ACC brought a warm glow of satisfaction sweeping over Molly; but she was still holding her breath because she had played her hand and now she prayed for her reward.

She tried to keep her mounting sense of anticipation from working its way into her voice. 'I am only too glad to be of service, ma'am. I have always been loyal to you personally and as you know, just like yourself, I have always had reservations concerning the DCI. But I must be honest, I had never expected him capable of this type of duplicity. I am also very concerned as to what may have transpired around the table with Crerand and his daughter tonight: the DCI has shown himself now, beyond doubt, to be a man who cannot be trusted to serve the ends of justice if they conflict with his own private needs.'

'I received your message advising me of this meeting and I am delighted you were asked along. I must admit, I was surprised that Ferguson decided you should join him. But tell me, Molly, just what happened tonight at Reds?' asked Trautmann, her desire to be given the full rundown almost palpable.

'The DCI has offered the Crerands what amounts to immunity from prosecution and around-the-clock protection for the return of the six-million security van heist cash. I'm afraid when I heard and saw the way he was allowing a hoodlum like Gordon Crerand to dictate terms, I could stand it no longer and left,' said the DS as the rage that had spilt over in Reds once again added bite and tempo to her words.

'There is no shame in that, DS Malone! The DCI seems to be acting under the illusion that he is God and has some kind of divine power to make decisions that are way above his pay grade. I thank you for that update, all of which will be vital in helping me serve up the DCI his just desserts. Can I ask one thing of you, Molly, and I think I know the answer: would you be prepared to recount these details to both the chief and myself tomorrow, in Ferguson's presence if need be?'

'It would be my pleasure, ma'am,' said Malone as the edges of her mouth curled in a vicious smile.

'Bravo my dear Molly! That is why immediately after I have presented the irrefutable evidence of Ferguson's treachery to the chief – with your help – I will be recommending that you are made Acting Detective Inspector in charge of the Flying Squad, under my direct supervision, with immediate effect,' Trautmann said, then took a short pause and cleared her throat.

This was beyond Molly's wildest dreams. 'All I can say is a huge thanks, ma'am. I promise you that I will continue to serve you to the best of my ability, loyally and honestly, as always.'

'I would expect nothing less, ADI Malone! But there is one other thing I must ask, Molly: is there any news of Emmanuel Summerbee? If, together, we are going to clear the streets of Manchester of this scum and bring an end to this vile feud then both sides must be under lock and key. Where is the man? He can't just have disappeared into thin air,' said Trautmann.

The wheels of Malone's mind went into overdrive as she sought a suitable way to stall. 'The information that we had in relation to Summerbee being holed up with the arms haul at the home of his former lover Colina Amos, was, I believe, provided by ADC Thoroughgood, the young Scots copper on secondment with us, via Lisa Crerand, so there is no surprise that it proved faulty. However, I am currently pursuing a lead that I hope will provide fruit in that respect, ma'am. As always, I will keep you posted on developments in this respect as soon as I have them. But can I suggest, ma'am, with your permission, that the first thing we do when I am made up is that I have your permission to personally take both Gordon and Lisa Crerand into custody and have them charged with the murder of Paulie Gallacher, the

Total Security van driver and a third as yet unidentified male, as well as the robbery of the six million in cash from the original heist?' asked Molly, expertly steering Trautmann away from the ACC's interest in her lover and laying the groundwork for what she'd do with her imminent promotion.

'I would expect no less, ADI Malone, and that response is exactly why I am promoting you. For too long your light has been hidden under a bushel and now is your time to shine. We will speak in the morning, Molly, be ready for my call!' And with that the other end of the line went dead.

Molly burrowed back into the Scirocco's driver's seat and gently nibbled on her cell phone's aerial as she played out all the scenarios that were unfolding: for the promise of her imminent promotion had upped the ante and now her mind began to formulate a new plan.

Smiling triumphantly, she punched in Manny Summerbee's number.

'Hello, love; what happened, I thought you were calling earlier?' asked Summerbee from the other end and was quickly brought up to speed with the developments of the preceding hour.

'Christ, I wish you had given me some notice, Mol, but tell me, do you think they are still likely to all be on the premises?' asked Summerbee, biting on the tantalising bait that Molly had dangled in front of him.

At her end of the mobile, a smile slipped across Molly's dark features. 'I left them less than 15 minutes ago and at that point the wheeling and dealing had just begun. I'd say there was plenty more to come before they get to a position both parties are comfortable with,' said Molly, luring Summerbee in further.

'For crying out loud, Mol, why didn't you tell me about this meeting? Christ, all the ducks have been lined up in one row and with a bit of notice they could all have been knocked down together…' he groaned in frustration.

'Honey, because I only got the message it was happening right before it started. I dunno, but I got the feeling I wasn't going to be invited originally and maybe Ferguson changed his mind and asked me at the last minute to try and keep me on side. But the one thing I do know is that they are almost certainly all still on the premises, and if I know Ferguson, he will be demanding the six million is handed over there and then before he shakes hands on any deal that will allow the Crerands to turn Queen's evidence,' concluded Molly.

From the other end of the phone came another groan. 'Damn! If only you'd given me more notice…' And then his end went silent and Molly could almost hear the wheels of his mind clicking into overdrive. She prayed he'd take the bait and play the role she needed of him.

An incoming call warning flashed up on her cell phone. 'I'm sorry, Manny, I've got to go, I have another call and I think it could be ACC Trautmann. I will call you tomorrow after everything is done and dusted and Ferguson has been given his medicine… and then maybe we can celebrate out at the farmhouse,' she said, letting her voice drop a seductive octave.

'I will look forward to that, my love,' said Summerbee and heard the other end of the phone click dead.

Molly checked her mobile's screen and saw that her new caller was in fact DC Wally Morgan. Surprised, she accepted his call.

'Hi Mol, hope you don't mind but thought I'd bell you and see how the meeting went? I take it if you're picking up it's over.

The big question is how did it go?' asked the veteran DC.

While Molly had always viewed Morgan as being in Ferguson's camp, she knew that in the new beginning that ACC Trautmann was about to hand her, she would need the experienced DC on her side. If she provided him with his long sought-after promotion to DS and a position as her right-hand man, she was confident that any loyalty he did have towards the grandstanding Scot would be quickly forgotten.

But she needed to choose her words carefully and make the most of this unsought opportunity. 'Hi Wally, I'm afraid the straight answer is I don't truthfully know. I'm sorry, Wally, but I just couldn't stomach the Crerands dictating the terms of the peace. I said what I had to say and I left. I guess by this time that jumped-up little tart Lisa Crerand has probably popped a bottle of Pomagne and they are all toasting the deal they were haggling over. To be honest, Wally, I couldn't take any more, but Ferguson was seriously pissed at me; I thought at one stage he was about to lay hands on me… it was scary, I've never seen him like that… he was… well, like unhinged…' sobbed Molly breathlessly, leaving Morgan to draw his own conclusions.

'Christ Mol, that's bad, real bad. Do you want me to speak to the Boss and try and smooth things over? All right, he has a temper on him, but he ain't the worst and there's always a way out of these things,' offered Morgan.

If Molly was going to play her hand, the moment had just arrived, and now she took the chance: 'I don't think so, Wally. I'm afraid I've told ACC Trautmann about the decommissioned firearms. It's all over for Ferguson, he's finished—'

'Aah, shit Moll—' interjected Morgan, but before he could continue with his negative reaction, Molly took control again.

'Look, Wally, things are about to change big time and these changes will be very good news for you, my old friend…' she said again, drawing up just short of spelling out what the changes were.

'What do you mean?' asked a captivated Morgan.

'I mean that by close of play tomorrow, DCI Ferguson's treachery will be exposed and he will be replaced as officer in charge of the Flying Squad by a new Acting Detective Inspector answering directly to ACC Trautmann and that new ADI will need an experienced and trustworthy DS at her side. I want that person to be you, Wally…'

'Holy schmoly!' were the only two words Morgan could come up with as a reply.

50

'IT'S A FUNNY OLD THING, Gordon – if you don't mind me calling you by your Christian name – that all the great managers are Scots,' said Ferguson in exaggerated fashion, with a whimsical smile spreading across his ruddy chops and holding out a giant hand.

'I don't know about that, DCI Ferguson,' protested Crerand.

The minutiae of their deal hammered out, the conversation had now shifted to what really mattered: a debate on the greatest football manager of them all, and Ferguson, the success of their agreement having restored his composure and his braggadocio, was confident he held all the aces.

'Call me Marty! Now, let's look at the evidence,' said the Boss and flicked up his pinky. 'First up I give you Jock Stein, the first British manager to win the European Cup, all with a team of homegrown Scots from inside a 50-mile radius of Glasgow, and also claim nine domestic Scottish league titles in a row and among every other domestic trophy.'

Then he flicked up a second finger. 'Let's fast forward to 1968 and the small matter of one of your former managers and unquestionably the greatest gaffer to grace Old Trafford, Sir Matt Busby, the architect of your 1968 European Cup triumph at Wembley, plus all these English Division One titles and cups galore.' Ferguson took a momentary pause and flashed a triumphant smile.

'Then of course we have Mr Liverpool himself, an ex-miner from Lanarkshire called Bill Shankly who brought your great rivals all the way from the Second Division to domestic triumph with First

Division titles and European glory with the UEFA Cup and started the boot-room dynasty. The evidence is overwhelming, the greatest manager the game has ever seen was any one of three Scots!'

Crerand smiled Thoroughgood's way, and the young detective couldn't help raise a dissenting voice: 'I'm sorry, Boss, but you've forgotten someone... and he certainly wasn't a Scot... Sir Brian of Clough – well, he should have been knighted in my opinion. Old Big 'Ead took Nottingham Forest from the bottom of Division Two to successive European Cups and the First Division title, which he also won with another provincial side at Derby,' interjected Thoroughgood.

Ferguson gritted his teeth in mock anger. 'Boy, you do know how to spoil a party!'

'You also missed out Don Revie at Leeds, DCI Ferguson,' said Crerand.

'Aye, he did make a European Cup final, Mr Crerand, but suffered a munchin' from Bayern back in '75,' said Paddy Greene and as the debate began to rage afresh, Lisa signalled to Thoroughgood to leave the booth and head out onto the balcony.

Lisa made a quick detour behind the bar while Thoroughgood strode out onto the balcony. He was greeted by the cool night air, the calm only disturbed by an occasional siren wailing out somewhere in the city and the rustle of the door's white drapes.

Suddenly, two giant speakers perched above the sliding glass French doors began to pipe out music, just as Lisa appeared carrying two freshly filled champagne flutes. Offering one, she smiled and said: 'It was time we made our breakout!' She laughed, but received a look of mystification from Thoroughgood.

'Come on, Gus, what are we listening too?' she asked.

'Aah, Swing Out Sister, "Breakout"! Forgive me, my head was elsewhere. It might surprise you to know I bought It's Better To Travel from West End Records in Dumbarton Road, Glasgow when it came out back in '87. Loved it... it was... well... just different!'

'Fitting praise indeed, Detective Thoroughgood, but did you know they are a Manchester group? It's one of my great regrets that so far I haven't been able to get them to play at Reds, but you never know,' she said. She moved to lean on the railing by his side, then continued: 'It's quite a view, Manchester by night, a twilight world!'

He grinned. 'Swing Out Sister again. I'll not be caught out twice!' he said.

Lisa slipped her left arm around his waist and whispered seductively: 'So, can I take you home with me tonight, Detective?'

Turning to look down at her, Thoroughgood smiled. 'Did you need to ask?' he said, and once again they gave in to the moment.

But their passion was soon interrupted by the clearing of a throat from just inside the French doors. 'Erm... I'm... well, sorry to interrupt, but we will be on our way, Miss Lisa,' said DCI Ferguson, flicking Thoroughgood a knowing wink.

As they turned towards the Boss, Thoroughgood realised his right arm was still enveloping Lisa's shoulders and removed it awkwardly. 'Oh yes, I'm glad to see that chivalry is not dead, boy!' chirped Ferguson knowingly before continuing: 'Look, I've radioed up Wally Morgan to pick us up. Paddy and I will take the kitbags down with a little help from your friend Kojak,' he smiled towards Lisa before turning his gaze back to Thoroughgood. 'Then it's back to Stretford nick with it for safekeeping, but I'd imagine you might have other business to attend to tonight, like making sure Miss Lisa gets home safe, so I will see you at HQ at 12 noon tomorrow,' concluded Ferguson and with a final smile he turned on his heels and was off.

Smiling up at Thoroughgood, Lisa said: 'Maybe we should finish what we started.' And once again their lips met.

With a groan, DCI Ferguson placed the kitbag he had been carrying down on the pavement just outside the entrance to Reds. Paddy Greene did likewise and breathed a sigh of relief. 'Bloody hell, I had no idea wads of cash were so heavy, Boss, I'm crackered!' he laughed.

Joining them, Gordon Crerand, Yul and another one of Crerand's henchmen brought the remaining kitbags filled with the cash from the heist.

Turning to Crerand, Ferguson smiled for a moment, before his features swiftly became serious. 'I realise, Mr Crerand, this is quite a leap of faith for you, but you will find my word is good: we have a deal and I gave you my hand on it. I can promise you I am not a man to break my word. As you can imagine, I have a few loose ends to tie up, but I will be back in touch within 24 hours with how we propose to make this all work. I'd just be a whole lot happier if we could lay our hands on that bastard Summerbee. I have half the force looking for him, yet he seems to be one step ahead of us all the time; but by the law of averages he will trip up or someone will grass him up.'

'I just hope that will be sooner than later, DCI Ferguson,' replied Crerand.

From behind the giant frame of the Detective Chief Inspector a diesel engine began to thrum. 'Excellent, that'll be Wally, right on time with our lift. Okay, Paddy, let's get these bags ready for the van,' he said, smiling at the DS. But as he did so, the look of shock flashing across Crerand's normally stony features set alarm bells ringing in Ferguson's head. Seconds later, gunshots rang out and the night was filled with the hiss and whistle of bullets.

'Hit the deck, Boss!' shouted Paddy Greene, the brick walls surrounding the front entrance starting to chip and shatter under the fusillade coming their way.

From the other end of Whitworth Street, a black-windowed Land Rover Turbo Diesel was surging down the road and behind its wheel was Manny Summerbee.

His single eye pulsed with a burning desire for vengeance; and if the only way he could get it was to take it himself, then this was the moment he would extract ultimate payback from the Crerands and wipe the slate clean once and for all.

But he had not come empty-handed and from the passenger side and the rear windows of his Range Rover, three of his henchmen unloaded lethal fire from their Škorpion vz. 61s.

To Manny One-Eye's delight, he saw that his timing could not have been better. He had caught Ferguson and Crerand bringing out kitbags that he rightly guessed were full of used notes: used notes from the Total Security van heist. Used notes that belonged to him.

A smile of cruel anticipation fractured his face and the explosion of sub-machine gunfire lit his grim features up and flickered light across the black leather patch covering his empty eye socket.

It was like a scene from a ten-pin bowling alley, except the skittles were of a human variety and now they were sprawled and rolling across the pavement outside the Reds nightclub. All Summerbee and his Maine Men had to do was rock up and take what belonged to him.

'Piece of fuckin' cake! This one's for you, Paulie!' spat Summerbee.

51

ON THE BALCONY, alerted by the eruption of gunfire, Thoroughgood and Lisa looked down in wide-eyed horror at the carnage on the street below, then sprang into action.

Thoroughgood instantly unholstered his nickel-plated S&W .38 snubnose.

The Black Land Rover had mounted the pavement and was clearly set on mowing down Lisa's father and his minders, as well as Ferguson and Greene; but such was the impact of the hail of lead that was being unleashed from the vehicle, it was impossible to tell who was still alive on the ground outside the entrance of Reds.

The mayhem below was made surreal by the fact that some of the semi-automatic gunfire had enfiladed one of the kitbags carrying the heist money, and now banknotes were starting to fill the air.

But the voice in Thoroughgood's head was already taking charge: "Breathing, mate, nice and calm, sight up!"

He cradled the snubnose double-handed in a Weaver stance and tried to impose stillness on his fingers, while he prepared to deliver his fire single-action, as he had been taught to do on all targets at 25 yards and beyond.

For the only way this could be stopped was if the driver was taken out.

On the ground, Ferguson had thrown himself against the inside of the doorway. As he tried to get onto a knee and fumbled for his revolver, he saw that Paddy Greene had been hit and was bleeding heavily from a gut wound.

Just beyond him, Gordon Crerand was being half dragged, half thrown into the entranceway by Yul, but one of his other lieutenants lay bleeding from multiple wounds on the paving six feet away.

The roar of the Land Rover became louder again as it approached, and Ferguson presented his Smith & Wesson and tried to return fire into the hail of lead that was continuing to be poured their way.

Behind him, Gordon Crerand spat: 'It's Summerbee! We need to get the hell out of here, Ferguson, forget the cash.'

But the Boss ignored him and shouted across the paving to DS Greene: 'Paddy, are you okay, pal?' Then he continued to return fire as best he could from behind the entrance's flanking wall: for there was no way he was leaving Paddy Greene to his fate.

'For fuck's sake, why don't you shoot?' screamed Lisa up on the balcony, but a foot away Thoroughgood remained motionless, his eyes trained down the Smith & Wesson.

He had to take into account the downward trajectory of his shot, as that was the only way he had of gaining any accuracy; but there were two problems with that.

The first was whether anyone was likely to still be alive by the time he could make an accurate shot.

The second was if could he hold his nerve.

Summerbee's features were now close enough that he could make out a vicious smile creasing his features. He pulled the snubnose's hammer back, took a breath and on the exhale pulled the trigger.

'Here we go, time to finish this!' growled Summerbee as he slipped the Land Rover down through its gears and prepared to bring the vehicle to a stop. But as he slowed, a shot exploded through the vehicle windscreen and shards of glass filled the cabin.

'Fucker!' he spat and gritted his teeth, fighting to right the car, which had jerked up against the club's outside brick wall with the shot. The night was filled with the sound of screeching metal and flying sparks, but with some effort Summerbee managed to get the Land Rover back on course... just as a second .38 special projectile exploded through the remainder of his windscreen.

This time the shot was true, and the bullet buried itself in Summerbee's remaining eye.

On the balcony, Thoroughgood watched in near disbelief as he saw One-Eye's head violently snapped back by the impact of his bullet. Immediately Summerbee lost control of the vehicle, and the Land Rover started to leave the paving and flip.

Thoroughgood and Lisa stared as it began its somersault. In the doorway, Ferguson and Yul had just managed to drag Paddy Greene back into the cover of the entrance as the flying vehicle sent the kitbags stuffed full of notes off the pavement, then skidded roof-down along the paving.

'Stay here,' Thoroughgood said to Lisa, then sprinted back through the bar. He charged down the stairs and burst out of the entrance, where Yul was attempting to staunch the flow of Paddy Greene's gunshot wound with the help of a bit of his own shirt he had torn off, and Ferguson was broadcasting an urgent assistance call.

The Boss looked up Thoroughgood's way. 'Check on the scum inside the Range Rover, we don't want round two. I will be with you ASAP,' Ferguson said breathlessly, before adding: 'Oh and good shooting, boy…' Then he administered a trademark wink.

Thoroughgood walked along the pavement cradling the snub-nose just in case… but he needn't have bothered.

By the time he got to the vehicle, which had come to rest upside down against what remained of a street light, he saw that one of Summerbee's goons had been thrown clear and lay in a broken, inert mass on the roadway. The other backseat shooter lay mangled between the two front seats, while the hood in the front passenger seat was impaled halfway through the front windscreen on shards of glass.

But it was the sight of Summerbee sprawled over the steering wheel that really interested Thoroughgood.

Bending down until he was at eye level with One-Eye's corpse, Thoroughgood took a handful of his hair and pulled the dead crime lord back, examining his handiwork. He stared at the corpse for a moment.

'Fuck you, One-Eye!' he spat, and then let One-Eye's head fall free back against the steering wheel.

He heard screeching tyres behind him and turned around, bringing his gun up. But he reholstered his S&W as he saw that Wally Morgan had arrived and was leaping out of his car.

'What the fuck happened here?' asked the veteran DC.

As he hunkered down to take a look inside the wrecked Land Rover and confirm with his own eyes that Summerbee was indeed dead, Ferguson said: 'I'll tell you what happened, Wally, someone has tipped off One-Eye that we were meeting the Crerands here tonight.' Then slowly Ferguson got up and he placed a hand on each of Morgan's shoulders and let a slow, vicious smile develop across his craggy features.

'Now, there were only two other people that knew we were meeting up with the Crerands. One of them was you. The other was DS Molly Malone, who wanted me to jail the Crerands, never mind do a bloody deal with them…' said the Boss, letting his words and all that they implied hang in the air.

From behind his glasses, Morgan's eyes widened. He was between a rock and a hard place and he knew it, for the truth was all too obvious.

She had set this whole thing up so that there wouldn't even be a need for Ferguson to be hauled up in front of Trautmann and the chief, and so no need to air any dirty laundry – laundry that would be particularly filthy if she were in bed with Summerbee, as it appeared.

Shaking his head, Wally Morgan knew self-preservation was all that mattered. 'Gaffer… I… I… think there is something you should know,' he said and promptly spilled his guts.

52

ACC MICHELLE TRAUTMANN sat bolt upright at one end of the gleaming conference table on Floor 11 of GMP HQ Chester House and concluded her damming indictment of DCI Ferguson.

Chief Constable Sir James Henderson sat patiently at the other end, taking the odd sip from a Royal Doulton coffee cup and occasionally letting his glance slip from the ACC Crime to DS Molly Malone, who sat in the middle between them.

Malone's evidence, in what was in effect an unofficial disciplinary court, had been delivered with damming but dispassionate accuracy. Initially detailing Ferguson's ruse with the decommissioned semi-automatic machine guns, which the chief had been allowed to parade to the media as the real and deadly McCoy, she then recounted his 'collusion' with the Crerands, in which Malone made sure she left serious question marks hanging over the DCI's professionalism and integrity and the way he had botched the primary tenets of Operation Reef and bungled the two turns on the addresses raided for Summerbee and his arms cache.

It had not been an easy performance for her. For somewhere inside Molly Malone there was a shred of conscience, and by feeding Summerbee the information that Ferguson and Crerand were meeting at Reds she had known full well that her long-term consort would attempt to grab the bull by both horns – and that that would place him at risk.

But now he was gone and, as she knew when she had fed One-Eye his titbit, the silver lining was that any recriminations that might have found their way back to her relationship with him were gone with him.

The great disappointment for Molly was that Ferguson and the Crerands had survived; yet she had no doubt that by the close of this unofficial hearing, her route to the position she had always craved would be removed of its main obstacle and Ferguson's career left in tatters. Then, the means would have justified the end.

Molly was bulletproof and ready for any accusations that Ferguson was likely to make when he arrived, which would be any minute now.

As Trautmann's clipped tones drew to a halt, Molly, resplendent in a crisp white blouse and charcoal two-piece woollen business suit, looked up and smiled benignly at the chief.

Henderson took another sip from his coffee cup and replaced the drinking vessel precisely in its saucer. His left leg, crossed over his right, swung slightly and he pinched the razor-sharp crease that crested his knee.

Slowly, his dark eyes met Trautmann's gaze and from behind his immaculately barbered beard his deep, bass voice boomed into life: 'It is a damming picture you both paint of DCI Ferguson and his... method of policing,' he said in his deliberate delivery, then continued: 'Certainly his omission of information regarding key items of evidence in the shape of the Ceska automatic rifles and the half-dozen Tokarev pistols, some of which we have before us on the table, is something that is wholly unacceptable, and I very much look forward to his explanation. But before the DCI joins us, I would caution you both, ladies, that he is a brave man who has put his life on the line time and again for GMP and indeed one who has just witnessed a treasured colleague suffer a life-threatening wound in the line of duty,' he said, before he once again caught Trautmann's eyes.

'DCI Ferguson has, lest you forget, also just reclaimed the six million in cash from the armed robbery of the security van and I believe is ready to provide us with details of the agreement he has reached with the Crerands to help us put all of this… mess… to bed,' continued Sir James, before he concluded: 'You would both do well to remember that.' And with that he allowed his intense dark gaze to sweep both women in a warning that he had far from made his mind up on what course of action he would take.

Despite herself, Molly threw a sideways glance towards Trautmann, for this was not what she had expected; but the ACC Crime only had eyes for Sir James.

'I am not disputing DCI Ferguson's bravery, sir. But surely the evidence we have before us, as well as DS Malone's account of his meeting with the Crerands and the fact that our streets were allowed to run crimson, is proof that with his honesty compromised – to say the least – and his policing methods ineffective. We have reached a point where he must be replaced as the officer in charge of the Flying Squad. With respect, sir, I can think of no one better to assume that position than DS Malone and to help lead the Squad into a new more efficient, cohesive and accountable era more in line with modern policing principles. Of course, under my guidance,' concluded Trautmann, trying to seize the moment and underline that the case against Ferguson was overwhelming.

Sir James inclined his head almost imperceptibly. 'You have had your say, ladies, and now it is time we heard DCI Ferguson out.' And with that he flicked the intercom panel at his right-hand side and instructed reception to show Ferguson in.

Outside the conference room, DCI Marty Ferguson sat staring at the portrait of Her Majesty the Queen that dominated the wall opposite. 'Need someone to take the Buck House bins out, ma'am?' he quipped.

But his humour was fleeting, as Ferguson's mind replayed the events of the previous evening and he sought to arrange them in an order that would allow him to present a watertight case for his defence.

Paddy Greene was in Manchester Royal Infirmary Intensive Care, but to Ferguson's great relief he'd been assured by the hospital that his old mate would pull through. He'd arranged a visit for later that evening; but first he had to get through the ordeal that awaited him.

Sir James's chief of staff, a dour-faced superintendent by the name of Johnson, whose lips seemed set in a permanent sneer, got up from his desk and stepped in front of him: 'Sir James is ready to see you, DCI Ferguson. Please follow me.' With that, Johnson turned on his immaculately gleamed Oxford brogues and marched down the corridor.

A moment later, he stopped. Before he opened the door, he turned to Ferguson. 'Enjoy!' he said smugly, before clutching the handle, pulling the door open and introducing Ferguson formally.

The Boss walked in.

He was greeted with the sight of a long conference table and Sir James sitting at the far end, staring dourly at him. On the right-hand side, a few feet away from Ferguson, was the back of ACC Michelle Trautmann; but it was the presence of a smiling Molly Malone halfway up the table to Trautmann's left that shocked him.

In the middle was a pile of guns.

Gritting his teeth, he tried not to let the DS's contemptuous smile break his self-control. He met the chief's stare and did due obeisance: 'Sir, you wished to see me?'

For a moment Sir James held his gaze. Then he gestured to the empty chair opposite Malone. 'Please take a seat, DCI Ferguson. We have a lot to talk about, and I for one am very interested to hear what you have to say.'

Taking a deep breath, Ferguson sat down and prepared to do what he was bid. 'It will be my pleasure, sir, ma'am and… DS Malone,' he replied, letting a clear hint of surprise intonate his pronunciation of Molly's name, while he also let his gaze hold Molly's, fire meeting ice, for extra emphasis.

Then Ferguson cleared his throat. 'Where do I start? Perhaps last night would be the best place. As you know, sir…' – he paused to look Sir James's way before continuing – 'from the full briefing report I had delivered to your office at close of play last night…' And he allowed his words to trail off, his eyes slipping first to Trautmann and then Malone.

The news that the chief had already been presented with Ferguson's version of the previous night's events before they had spun theirs was clearly a surprise.

Ferguson smiled obsequiously at them. 'We have recovered the full quantity of the moneys seized in the initial heist, bar a flutter of notes here and there caused by Summerbee's uninvited visit last night, and also the burnt-out husk of the Total Security van from which it was taken. All of that is directly down to the agreement I reached with Gordon and Lisa Crerand,' he said.

Ferguson halted and inclining his head to a jug of water and the glass alongside it, he asked: 'May I, sir?'

After nodded permission was given and refreshment taken, Ferguson continued: 'The Crerands have also been most helpful in supplying details of a Scottish crim by the name of Terry Forsyth, who has been attempting to cut a deal with both the… late… Emmanuel Summerbee and, interestingly enough, also the Crerands' Red Devils organisation – all to flood Manchester with drugs. I believe their continued help on this going forward will allow us to make his arrest, stop this happening and possibly help us retrieve what may amount to a six-figure drugs haul. The Crerands – as you might expect in return for immunity from prosecution in terms of the Attorney General's guidelines on this – have also agreed to help us with the other details of the feud that has now ended with Summerbee's… untimely demise. In conclusion, I can safely say that this horrific turf war is over and that we have an agreement in place that will prove hugely beneficial to GMP, the people of Manchester and also, I'm hopeful, police forces beyond our streets. Further, for your information, sir, DS Greene will pull through and I plan to visit him this evening at the earliest opportunity to do so.'

Sir James stroked his beard thoughtfully and through his impressive whiskers a magnificent set of white teeth showed in a slight smile. 'That is good news on the DS and what seems like a case of "all's well that ends well", as a certain Mr Shakespeare might say!' he said and locked his eyes on Ferguson's flinty gaze.

It was at this point that ACC Trautmann's brooked dissent from his left: 'But Sir James, if I may, as we discussed previously, that is not quite the whole case and I would very much like to hear the DCI's thoughts on the firearms that sit before us…' she said, unwinding a contemptuous hand towards the guns in the middle of the table.

Sir James took another sip of coffee, then replaced his cup back on its saucer. 'Indeed, the ACC makes a valid point, DCI Ferguson. On Saturday I gave a press conference at which I unveiled a guns haul that you led me to believe comprised of military-grade firearms... but that is not the case. I'm now told they are decommissioned and no more capable of a lethal discharge than a pop gun. I await your explanation with interest, DCI Ferguson,' said Sir James, taking on a grim countenance.

Ferguson knew he had reached his now-or-never moment.

A cruel smile broke across ACC Trautmann's face, while Molly Malone pushed her chair back, folded her arms and skewered Ferguson with a stare that dripped pure malice as she anticipated the Boss's impending mea culpa.

'No problemo!' said Ferguson, slipping back into his usual, more relaxed mode of parlance. He pushed his own chair back and leaned across the desk, reaching out with his huge right paw and gripping one of the Tokarev TT-33 combat pistols.

'Now the first thing I must ask, Sir James, is what evidence do you have that these weapons are decommissioned, and what reliability do you put in that information and whoever provided it? I believe that there has not been time to check?' he asked as he pulled the eight-shot magazine from the Soviet World War II pistol.

'What do you mean, Ferguson... this is most... irregular,' stammered Sir James, clearly disconcerted by this unforeseen turn in events.

But Ferguson had centre stage and he was determined to make his act work. 'Excellent! The magazine is chambered with eight 7.62 by 25 millimetre rounds,' he said, slamming it back into the handle.

He held the Tokarev up theatrically, then slowly rotated it, examining the gun against the sunshine that was percolating through the blinds of the conference room. 'Note the black plastic grips with the raised star of the Soviet Union and the letters CCCP located around each point of the star. This, ladies and gentleman, was a 1942-manufactured firearm, as stamped, that played its part in the Great Patriotic War and now... well, we must prove that it is not obsolete but instead still capable of its deadly purpose!'

Ferguson stopped and pulled the hammer back with a flick of his right thumb. 'But one must be careful with the Soviet-made version of the Tokarev, for it has no safety and while we are... uncertain... if it is in fact decommissioned or not... care is very much needed,' he said, with extra emphasis on the last four words.

'But the great problem I have, right here, right now, is how I demonstrate if the Tokarev is... live and dangerous, and for that I need an assistant... DS Malone, are you happy to help?' he smiled as he lowered the Tokarev and trained it on the DS.

From the far end of the table, Trautmann almost exploded. 'Ferguson, you complete madman, what the hell do you think you're doing?' Then she pushed her chair back and got to her feet. 'Sir James, this is exactly why this maniac must be relieved of his command of the Flying Squad... he is absolutely out of control...'

Ferguson continued to loom large over Malone, the Tokarev remaining trained on her cranium; but before a clearly shocked Sir James could answer, the Boss beat him to the verbal punch: 'Please, bear with me, Sir James, there is indeed, I promise you, method to my madness. Now, sweet Molly, the big question is, are you prepared to stick or twist. It is you, is it not, who provided the information that claims these weapons are decommissioned and of no value and that because of that I have undermined the chief with my dishonesty? Yet how confident are you that your information is correct? Are you indeed certain enough to gamble… with your life, Detective Sergeant Malone?' asked Ferguson, desperately trying not to let the magnitude of the moment break his composure.

'I don't know what you mean, DCI Ferguson. You have obviously completely lost the plot,' replied DS Malone. Then she turned her head towards Trautmann. 'Ma'am, we need to call for assistance before this gets out of hand and someone is injured or worse by the DCI… the man is obviously completely unhinged.'

But from the other end of the table, Sir James had recovered his composure. 'I will decide if that is the case, DS Malone. Sit down, ACC Trautmann.' Then the chief constable steepled his hands and prepared to let the cards fall.

'Answer me, DS Malone. Where did you get the information that these guns were decommissioned and who provided it?' demanded Ferguson.

The Boss had turned the tables on her: Malone knew it and under severe pressure, she groped for a way out. 'I am not prepared to divulge the identity of a registered informant to a madman like you. I must protest, sir—' But she got no further, for Ferguson was already speaking.

'Then let me provide the answers to these two questions for you,' shouted Ferguson, his words drowning her protests out.

Then he pulled the Tokarev's trigger.

53

FERGUSON, his eyes pulsing, fired once... twice... thrice and kept on firing until all eight rounds had been discharged.

Behind her, the glass of the conference room window blew out, shattering into the sky outside. DS Molly Malone screamed wildly, then turned round and stared at what was left of the window. She gaped at the destruction, her mouth moving soundlessly.

Six feet away, Ferguson sensed his advantage. Replacing the Tokarev on the table, he said: 'Well, now we have established that the DS's information was incorrect, we must establish where she got it from. Further, if in fact she was indeed aware that she was peddling false information to the ACC in order to set up her direct senior officer, who occupied a position she has long coveted...' he said, shooting a contemptuous look in Trautmann's direction before returning his eyes to Sir James.

But before he could continue, the conference room's door flew open and Superintendent Johnson burst in. 'Is everything in order, sir?' he stammered.

'There is nothing for you to worry about, Johnson, just an impromptu live firing demonstration from the DCI, don't let us keep you,' said the chief, dismissing his batman.

As the door shut, Ferguson was determined to make sure there would be no reprieve for Malone and turning directly to Sir James he said: 'The reason that DS Malone was in possession of this information is that her informant is... or was... Emmanuel Summerbee.' Then he stopped for effect to let that revelation sink home.

Shock was written large on Sir James's brooding features, while Trautmann's visage had become ashen.

There was no doubt about it, the ACC Crime had not been aware of her DS's criminal liaison.

Ferguson rammed home his advantage. 'Indeed this was no normal cop/tout relationship… was it, DS Malone?' he snapped, clamping the palms of his hands on the table in front of him, his jaw jutting out in Malone's direction as he leaned forward menacingly over the conference table.

Molly was staring at Ferguson, her mouth still open. Seeing attention was on her, she closed it and gritted her teeth, attempting to regain her composure and retreat behind her best poker face.

'I don't know what you mean,' she straight-batted.

'Oh, I think you do, DS Malone. Let us look at the evidence. Firstly, there were the bungled turns at the Pepperhill pub and then Colina Amos' place, all driven by information you supplied from a vaunted informant of yours. Secondly, can you please tell me why you took so long to get to Alderley Edge and provide emergency help to ADC Thoroughgood when he and Lisa Crerand were being hunted like dogs by Summerbee's men and you were only minutes away? Also, for the record, can you explain, as first officer on the scene, why you failed to bag and tag vital items of evidence from that crime scene including a Škorpion semi-automatic machine pistol which mysteriously disappeared from the locus?'

From across the table, Malone was defiant. 'Garbage. You say the raids were bungled, but it was you who supplied the info behind the raid on Colina Amos's house and we both uncovered concealed firearms. Correct me if I'm wrong, but you have just demonstrated that these firearms are live… so you have just defeated your own argument… DCI Ferguson. This is ludicrous, it's complete fantasy!' sneered Malone and held her hands out, upturned, while she appealed silently to ACC Trautmann for help.

She got none.

But Ferguson had not finished: 'You miss my point, DS Malone. Tell us, please, just who could have informed you the guns were not active? The answer is the only person who could have furnished you with that gold-plated intel was… Manny One-Eye… your lover screwed you, sweet Molly!' said Ferguson, almost apologetically.

Across the table, confusion surfed across Molly's face.

The DCI turned towards Sir James. 'May I proceed, sir?' he asked, and received a curt nod in the affirmative.

'But what really hurts, Molly, is that you were prepared to betray your fellow officers and offer them up as sacrifices to your vaulting, naked, unbridled ambition… an ambition that you…' – and here Ferguson stopped and pointed towards Trautmann – 'were made a victim of… ma'am,' he rapped, smearing the last word with dripping contempt.

Then Ferguson returned his stare to Malone. 'It was you that betrayed the location of our meeting with the Crerands to One-Eye. You who tried so hard to undermine the whole deal before it was made, with your amateur dramatics and attempts to set us at each other's throats. You, DS Malone, who when you left made a call, a call to Emmanuel Summerbee telling him exactly where we were; and you did this because you knew he would see it as an opportunity that was too good to pass. Is that correct, DS Malone?' demanded the Boss.

'I have no idea what you are talking about,' said Molly dismissively.

'Oh, but I think you do, and now here is where it all gets really interesting. Your call to Summerbee wasn't the only one you made, DS Malone. My, my, you did have an interesting chat with DC Morgan didn't you?' smiled Ferguson.

Molly Malone's eyes met and held Ferguson's and for a moment the Boss thought there was resignation in them.

Turning to Sir James, the DCI smiled almost benignly. 'Sir, may I refer to contemporaneous notes I made recording a short statement made by DC Wally Morgan and signed by him in my GMP notebook?'

'You may,' said the chief constable, pushing his empty coffee cup away and settling back in his chair waiting for the coup de grâce to be delivered.

'I quote directly from DC Morgan's statement as follows: "I mean that by the end of the close of play tomorrow, DCI Ferguson's treachery will be exposed and he will be replaced as officer in charge of the Flying Squad by a new Acting Detective Inspector answering directly to ACC Trautmann and that new ADI will need an experienced and trustworthy DS at her side. I want that person to be you, Wally…"'

Then, Ferguson put his notebook down on the table and turned in triumph towards Trautmann. 'Now please tell us, ma'am – with respect, of course – who gave the soon-to-be-appointed Acting Detective Inspector permission to make that offer and of course promise her such a promotion, when the position mentioned was already filled. Filled by an officer who almost lost his life securing six million pounds worth of stolen cash from the biggest robbery in this fine city's history,' demanded Ferguson.

For a split second, Trautmann and Malone exchanged a glance, before the ACC cleared her throat. 'I… I gave DS Malone no such authority to make these claims…'

But Ferguson had done with the niceties of respect for rank. 'Maybe you did not, ACC Trautmann, but you certainly rewarded the good DS for the information she provided you with that the firearms were decommissioned… with the promise of my job. Because the truth is you have never wanted me in it from the day you were appointed ACC Crime… but there is one thing you did not take into account… ma'am…' said Ferguson, turning towards Sir James.

Through the lush folds of the chief constable's beard, a smile of full white teeth shone. 'DCI Ferguson was my appointment,' said Sir James staring down the other end of the table directly at Trautmann. 'It seems that DS Malone is not the only officer sat around this table whose naked ambition has clouded her judgement, for the truth… Michelle… is that you undoubtedly have the same desire for my job as your subordinate has for DCI Ferguson's,' said the chief vehemently.

Then he turned towards his intercom. He flicked the speaker switch and said: 'Johnson, your presence is required ASAP.'

A tense silence drew out before the conference room's door once again swung open and a bemused Johnson entered.

'DS Malone, you may leave us, but before you go anywhere you will hand over your warrant card to my chief of staff and you will make sure you are available at your home address for interview at the behest of our Professional Standards & Discipline department, at all times, if you value your freedom.' Then he turned to Johnson. 'Escort DS Malone from the building and make sure she is aware of exactly what is required of her,' ordered Sir James.

As Johnson took a step towards the DS, she turned in desperation towards Trautmann. 'Ma'am... this is... is not right... it is Ferguson who should be relieved of his warrant card...'

But her plea incurred the wrath of Sir James. 'Get her out of here, Johnson!' he snapped and thrust out a stilling hand as at the other end of the table Trautmann's lips started to move.

Malone shook off Johnson's grasp of her arm and stormed towards the door with the chief of staff in her wake. A moment later, silence reigned once again, as Sir James stared down the table at the ACC Crime and decided what to do with her.

His thoughts gathered, Sir James leant forward and steepled his hands, his face void of emotion. Almost Sphinx-like, he began: 'Let me give you a history lesson, Michelle. Back in the summer of 1981, before you had transferred from the Met Vice Squad, we in GMP endured a tortuous summer of rioting on Moss Side and on July 8, 1981, a date indelibly stamped on my brain, I was duty superintendent at Moss Side nick when a crowd of 1,000 youths besieged the station. All the windows were smashed out. Twelve police vehicles set on fire and we were placed under a state of siege. The riots went on for 48 hours with shops all the way down Princess Road, Claremont Road and the surrounding areas like Rusholme torched and left in charred ruins,' recounted the chief constable, stopping for a short pause.

From the other end of the table, Trautmann, who was desperately trying to figure out where this was going, played the game: 'I am very much aware of the Moss Side riots, sir, I transferred to GMP in the autumn of '81. But I was not aware you were the duty super there... it must have been hellish.'

For a moment Sir James played with a signet ring on a finger of his right hand, before continuing: 'It was indeed hellish. Chief

Constable Anderson, my predecessor, built up a mobile task force of some 560 officers in 50 Transit vans and Land Rovers and authorised the use of rapid dispersal tactics previously only used by the Royal Ulster Constabulary and the British Army over the water. Basically, he created snatch squads and an officer who led one of those squads from out of Moss Side nick was a section sergeant from Glasgow who had not long transferred to GMP, under something of a cloud, admittedly. His name was…' and Sir James let his words trail off.

Despite herself Trautmann, couldn't help the word 'Ferguson' from escaping her mouth, and as her gaze slipped towards Ferguson, she received a mischievous wink from the DCI.

Her jaw set as a bitter sinking feeling filled her.

But Sir James had not finished: 'I personally took charge of several of these raids and, in particular, on Claremont Road my squad became detached and surrounded and we had to put out an assistance call. The first help arriving on the scene was a Land Rover being driven by a giant ginger-haired Jock,' said Sir James, nodding in recognition towards Ferguson.

'We were completely surrounded when Fergie and his team arrived wielding cricket bats and all kinds of cudgels they had freed from the lost property section at Moss Side nick. I'll never forget the sight of them taking these bastards down like skittles. By God, Fergie, you were like a 1980s version of William Wallace, man!' said Sir James, smiling over at Ferguson as his mind replayed the scene on the silver screen inside his head.

But the chief soon returned to his point: 'Yet while we lived to fight another day and took back control of our streets, Sergeant Ferguson was himself injured in the line of duty, shot by a crossbow in his right leg.' Then the chief constable paused and opened a palm in Ferguson's direction. 'Would you mind showing us the scar you still bear to this day, Fergie?'

'I'd be delighted,' said Ferguson with a sunny smile and swinging his right leg onto the conference table, he pulled his trouser leg up and there, faded but still unmistakeable, was a three-inch scar.

'Thank you, DCI Ferguson. Now the point I am making, ACC Trautmann, is that I am always loyal to those who are loyal to me and have done me personal service, for I believe my elevation has been made with their help and I reward these officers accordingly, hence DCI Ferguson's appointment to officer in charge of the Flying Squad, which will shortly be upgraded with his promotion to detective superintendent,' concluded the chief.

From the other end of the table, Trautmann could not stifle a gasp, which was followed by one word of disbelief: 'What?'

Sir James had not quite delivered his pay-off shot. 'But you, ACC Trautmann, have singularly failed to show me loyalty. I promoted you, Michelle, despite your amorous approaches to ensnare me, on the basis of your sex, and you have repaid me with treachery. It was my mistake and now I must correct it. Your reward for that treachery is that you will be seconded to Cleveland Police Force acting as the independent police enquiry officer in charge of the child sex abuse scandal there and that will give you time to place an application for your transfer back to the Met. Do your job well, don't create a fuss and I may well even give you a glowing recommendation; fail to do so and I will take great delight in ruining you... once and for all.'

'You can't be serious... Sir James,' stammered Trautmann, pulling a hanky from the breast pocket of her tunic in a theatrical show of upset that left Ferguson's bushy eyebrows twitching with disbelief.

'Oh, but I am. All arrangements have been made. You start on Monday. Clear your desk over the weekend, ACC Trautmann. I would very much doubt that we will see you again in Manchester. You are dismissed,' he rapped, his voice rising almost to a shout such was the vehemence he delivered the last few words with.

Trautmann's show of emotion was fleeting and without a word she rammed her chair back, picked up her black attaché case and, fixing Ferguson with one final spiteful glance, left the room, almost taking the door off its hinges in the process.

'Jesus H. Christ,' said Marty Ferguson.

But from under the table, the chief had already produced two glasses and a bottle of Glenfiddich, and he poured them both a generous measure.

'Well, Fergie, I'd say we have at least three reasons to be cheerful! Everything went as planned – although I can't say I expected quite such a performance! I give you: to good riddance… Detective Superintendent Ferguson!'

Clinking the chief constable's glass, Ferguson said: 'By God, I'll drink to that, Jimmy!'

54

DS PADDY GREENE lay propped up on his hospital-bed pillows, looking around groggily. He had been lucky and he knew it; despite himself, every time he shut his eyes, Summerbee's ghoulish, one-eyed visage haunted him like some fiend from hell.

'Sweet Christ,' muttered Greene to himself and he again thanked his lucky stars that he had lived to fight another day.

'I'm afraid he was busy, so you'll just have to make do with plain old me and your boy, paddywhack!' laughed DCI Marty Ferguson from the doorway. 'Now here, have a grape!' he said, holding out one of his giant hands, in which a paper bag bulged with the fruit. He sat down in the chair on the right-hand side of Greene's bed.

Opposite him, Thoroughgood helped himself to a spare chair from the empty bed next to Greene's and took up residence.

'How are you, son?' asked Ferguson, his voice dropping an octave as his genuine concern for his old comrade surfaced.

'Sore, but alive. Been a bit out of it, Marty, but as you and the boy are both here you can tell me what the hell happened. Is Summerbee still—'

'With us?' finished Ferguson, ending his old friend's sentence as per usual, before snapping a grape from the bunch in the paper bag and tossing it into the air, letting it drop into his waiting mouth. 'Waste not want not, Paddy, son, as my dear old ma taught me! You sure you don't fancy one... seedless, of course?' he asked and received an amused but negative shake of the head for reply.

Ferguson placed the bag of grapes on top of the bedside locker next to the obligatory jug of water and, taking a breath, got down to business: 'So, where do I start? Okay… here is the nine o'clock news! Emmanuel Summerbee is no longer with us, you will be delighted to know, thanks to a bullet expertly discharged from the boy's Smith & Wesson that hit the bull right in his remaining eye; and as a result we have six million in cash back where it belongs, give or take a few notes. Peace has broken out with the Crerands, who are, as you would surely expect, old friend, going to spend most of the next few days helping us with our enquiries over a number of matters in return for immunity. So, at last it's all quiet on the western front, but fuck me it was a close-run thing, son, and we owe the wean here a big thanks for his marksmanship all right. So well done, Angus Bloody Thoroughgood… you'll do for me, boy!' smiled Ferguson, letting his eyes rest on the young detective and a broad smile break out across his ruddy chops.

'It… was my pleasure, Boss!' replied Thoroughgood, uncomfortable at receiving such blunt and unexpected praise.

From the bed, Greene, a little croaky, warbled again: 'What about Molly Malone and Mad Myra?'

'Yeah, what happened on Floor 11?' Thoroughgood chimed in. 'You never said a word on the way up and the suspense is killing me! I take it you're still in a job, Boss?'

'Patience, dear boy. As you know, I had other priorities when I left Floor 11, like getting these bloody grapes for our dear colleague here!' And with a wink he helped himself to another.

For the next ten minutes, Ferguson regaled them with a highly dramatic – and fully amateur – recount of the events that had unfolded in Force HQ Command's conference room, only interrupted by a verbal warning from the night-shift sister.

'Christ, I wish I'd been there, Marty! You're a mad man, though, Malone was right: unloading that Tokarev all around her and blowing out the windows... bloody hell, you've got balls, Marty, I'll give you that,' said Greene, managing half a smile.

Ferguson replied with a triumphant wink, but before he could add further embellishment, Thoroughgood spoke up: 'There is just one thing that bothers me, Boss. How did a hoard of decommissioned firearms become reactivated in less than 24 hours... or was there just one miracle of reactivation that occurred within the production room last night?'

Ferguson gave a chuckle, before revealing the source of the miracle: 'The care of productions is something I have always placed great importance on and it's imperative that the right officer is in charge of them. Fortunately, and of course completely coincidentally, the current production officer, Mick Jones, is an old comrade from my time at Moss Side nick and one who deserved a more deskbound job to ease him towards his retirement. With a little help from Mr Black and Mr Decker, the 1942 Soviet-manufactured Tokarev pistol, so helpfully marked with the letters of the CCCP around a black star on the handle, was brought back to its full and lethal glory... within four minutes, I believe!'

Opposite him, Thoroughgood shook his head while Greene smiled knowingly. 'Aye, yer something else, Marty Ferguson... by God, Trautmann must have been sick. The Cleveland Child Sex Enquiry – good enough for her! So, what of Molly Malone... will she end up being sent down?' he asked, fascinated despite the obvious pain he was in.

For once Ferguson was serious. 'I don't know. Sir James will have the final call and he may want to avoid the scandal of all this dirty washing being done in public. For my part I hope they throw away the key, but I have to give her this: she played her part perfectly and my money was on Wally Morgan being our rat. Anyway, we have more important things to discuss, like can you make it to Old Trafford on Saturday to help us celebrate my promotion to detective superintendent?'

From his bed, Greene almost choked on the water he was trying to sip. 'I'll do my best, Marty, you can bet on it, pal!'

'You've done well, boy, very bloody well by any standards; but before you go winging it off back up the road, I have a proposition for you,' Ferguson said as they made their way out through the imposing stone and brick façade of the exit.

'I'm all ears, Boss,' replied Thoroughgood, his hands shoved deep in his Harrington's pockets.

'It may or may not be news to you, but before Paddy arrived, he had already put in a request for a transfer to GMP. It's something we had discussed last year when we were on holiday with our missuses in Magaluf. His wife's folks live down this neck of the woods and her father is in a home at St Anne's, so a change of scenery makes sense for them. I know he was made an offer with a post in your gaffer's unit back in Glasgow but the big difference with his move to Mancland is it will come with a promotion to DI and a position in the Flying Squad sanctioned by the chief constable himself. An ace beats a king every time, boy... as you know!' concluded Ferguson with a wolfish grin.

Thoroughgood made no attempt to conceal his surprise: 'Jeez! But will he be able to cope with leaving Parkhead behind?'

'Obviously! Now, with the way things have panned out, there is going to have to be a change in our team and Wally Morgan will be moving up to DS, which is probably long overdue, and I will be looking for a new DC to come in. You've impressed me, Thoroughgood, and I would be more than happy, lad, if you signed on the dotted line with us on a free transfer that will also come with the substantive rank of detective constable with immediate effect,' winked Ferguson roguishly.

Thoroughgood did a double take. 'Really?' was the best he could do by way of a reply.

Ferguson smiled and placed a reassuring paw on his shoulder. 'Really! Look, I know it's a lot to take in and I will have to clear it with your gaffer and his chain of command, but I wanted to put it out there and see how you feel about it because I think there is a big future for you down here in Manchester. Plus, take your pick: United, City, even bloody Oldham – it all beats going to Firhill don't it, Gus?' concluded Ferguson, calling him Gus for almost the first time the young ADC could recall.

Standing opposite Thoroughgood, even in the flickering street light, Ferguson could see the consternation and indecision his offer had caused in his young colleague. He laughed. 'Look, take it easy and sleep on it; and don't worry, you won't have to keep staying in Sedgley House! We'll get you set up no bother with your own pad. But I will need to know by the end of the week and certainly before we join the Crerands for hospitality at Old Trafford on Saturday. You've earned a couple of days downtime, although we have a few things to tie up but by the end of the week – one way or another, I will need the Ts crossed and the Is dotted by then. Is that reasonable… Detective?' asked Ferguson, playing his ace by formally referring to Thoroughgood with his presumptive new rank.

It was an obvious ruse that nonetheless made Thoroughgood smile; but before he could answer, the sound of a car horn grabbed their attention. Looking across Oxford Road towards the Whitworth Gallery, he saw that Lisa's XJS had just drawn to a halt.

Once again Ferguson laughed. 'Aye, well I can see sleep may be the last thing you have on your mind tonight, boy! But seriously, it's a bloody good offer and in many ways Manchester ain't too different to Glasgow. You also have the chance of a fresh start here, which from my soundings may be good for you. Plus I can think of one young lady who might be very happy to hear about what I have just offered you!' And with a wink and a slap on the back the Boss headed off down Oxford Road.

55

THOROUGHGOOD soon found himself aboard Lisa's XJS. 'So where are you taking me for a pint and some decent pub grub?' he asked, smiling, before they exchanged a kiss of greeting that soon developed into something far more intense.

A little while later, Lisa was guiding the XJS through the city's neon-bathed streets. 'We are heading to the Old Welly, just off Exchange Square, which is – not surprisingly, given the name – the oldest pub in Manchester, having been established in 1552. That suit you, Detective?'

'The Old Welly… that's some name for a boozer! Honestly, I don't care just as long as we can hear the conversation we are having… because there is a lot to talk about,' said Thoroughgood, smiling unconvincingly.

Lisa slid him a sideways glance. 'Actually, the pub's full name is The Old Wellington. A lot to talk about? Is that a good thing or a bad thing, Gus?'

Thoroughgood gave her a sidelong glance and regaled her with what had happened. When he'd finished, Lisa let out a long breath.

'DS Malone was Summerbee's grass…' She whistled. 'Maybe she did come across as a bitch… but I would never have thought she was capable of… that. It makes you wonder, though, her telling him we were all at Reds… who else could have provided that info? Like I said, what a bitch!' Lisa concluded, telling it like it was.

By the time they had sat down under The Old Wellington's timber-sparred roof and Thoroughgood had slaked his thirst on a lager, he was at last ready to relay Ferguson's invitation to join the Squad. Taking a deep breath, he went for it: 'Okay, here we go! The Boss has just made me an offer... and maybe it's one I can't refuse!'

Lisa punched him in the arm. 'Come on, Gus, don't tease me!'

'He's offered me a position with the Flying Squad here in Manchester as a fully-fledged DC... and I just wondered how you might feel about that?' Thoroughgood asked, his eyes locked on Lisa as he waited for her reaction.

She slowly finished taking a sip of her Pernod, blackcurrant and lemonade, while all the time her eyes held his; and the thought occurred to Thoroughgood that she was studying him to see just how happy he was about the prospect of moving to Manchester.

'It would make me very happy, Gus, but that would only be the case if...' She let her words trail off.

It was the elephant in the room that Thoroughgood knew would have to be addressed... sooner rather than later.

Playing the straight bat, he turned her delivery back to Lisa: 'Which "if" is that?'

She held his gaze once again with those olive-brown eyes that had been giving him sleepless nights ever since he had first met her – concealed in a motorbike helmet and pointing an Uzi his way. 'Can you forgive me my past... is that something in you to do?'

She had said it and it seemed by the way she caught a breath that her words, delivered slightly in a rush, had surprised Lisa herself.

Despite the fact he had been waiting for Lisa's 'past' to become an item of debate for some time, Thoroughgood still struggled to find grace under pressure and reached for his pint pot in his attempt for a way out.

All the time he remained acutely aware he was under Lisa's intense surveillance.

At last he put the glass down and braced his back against his chair. 'Look, I know all about your past. I know that the turf war you and your father have just come through was a case of them or us, and having been on the end of Manny Summerbee's madness, I don't blame you for any of that... nor do I judge you for it.'

As he stopped for another sip, Lisa's hand reached out and her slender fingers wrapped around his wrist and squeezed.

'For the record, I also knew from day one it was you that was pointing that Uzi my way. Christ, I even found out the perfume you were wearing, which drove me demented through the visor of your helmet, was Chanel No. bloody 5 à la Marilyn Monroe! While I'm at it, I just wanted to let you know I could pick your eyes out at 20 yards in an ID parade. Christ, I can't get to sleep at night for them!'

Across the table Lisa smiled cautiously. 'I hope that is meant as a compliment?'

'You know it is!' But his smile soon started to fade, and it was not lost on Lisa.

'So, what's the "but", Gus?' she asked

'The "but" is, well, I believe you murdered Paulie Gallacher in cold blood. I think you had him waterboarded until he would give you what you wanted and when he didn't, I think you, or someone acting on your orders, took a knife and drew it across his throat and let him bleed out...' he concluded almost in a whisper.

Lisa's fingers recoiled from his wrist as if she'd had boiling water poured on them, but Thoroughgood had not finished, and he leant forward to try and make sure their conversation was not being overheard, even though the nearest of The Old Wellington's patrons was a couple of tables away.

'You see, I studied the post-mortem, Lisa, and it was all too clear from the amount of water that had filled Paulie Gallacher's lungs that whosoever was his torturer had very little luck getting what they wanted out of him. I think that what they wanted, besides the location of the arms cache, may have been a deal. To put it simply, Lisa, I think you tried to divide and conquer... and The Midget had none of it... so you made him pay.' The adrenaline pumping through him, Thoroughgood couldn't help himself and before he knew he'd done it, he had drawn his right forefinger across his throat for theatrical effect.

Almost before he had completed the gesture, Lisa's right hand was delivered open palm with a biting sting.

'You have it all figured out... Detective. Paulie Gallacher was the scum of the earth, Paulie Gallacher tried to have my mother abducted and Paulie Gallacher deserved everything he got. I don't know why I have wasted a minute on you,' she spat and slammed her chair back.

But the blow brought Thoroughgood's temper to the boil. 'Maybe because I saved your life on two occasions? The problem, Lisa, if I may be so bold – and now that we are talking frankly – is that there is a darkness in you, a darkness that anyone who is lucky enough to fall for you will find himself lost in—' But before he could finish his sentence, Lisa had reached for his pint pot and emptied the remainder all over Thoroughgood.

'This time you can sort your own dry cleaning!' she spat and turned on her heel and headed for the door, as the patrons of the Old Welly sat in stunned silence at the drama that had just unfolded before their disbelieving eyes.

Standing up and reaching for a napkin to begin his mopping-up exercise, Thoroughgood swept the customers of the Old Welly with a seething stare.

'That's all, folks!' was the best he could come up with.

56

'NICE TO SEE you've made a bloody effort, Wally!' laughed Ferguson as the longstanding DC entered the DCI's office. 'Christ, anyone would think we are a going to a bloody funeral not a football match!' said the Boss, before dissolving into a peal of laughter at the sight of his perennially shabby minion resplendent in a natty black single-breasted suit, white shirt and matching black tie.

'What you talking about, Boss? I just bought this down at Ralphie Slaters, thought I'd make an effort, like,' replied Morgan.

'Aye, well credit where credit's due, it's better than your usual excuse for a sports jacket. Anyway, you might want to have a look at the paperwork on my desk… it may be of interest to you, Acting Detective Sergeant Morgan!' winked Ferguson just as Thoroughgood walked through the door.

'Aah, Mother Mary, not you as well!' groaned the Boss.

At a complete loss to comprehend where the DCI was coming from, Thoroughgood stammered: 'S-Sorry…?'

But thankfully Morgan came to his rescue: 'Look, Boss, the kid needed someone to help him out with best bib and tucker, and at £50 old Ralphie has done him proud,' he said, unfolding a hand as if showcasing Thoroughgood's two-piece navy double-breaster.

But Ferguson's eyes narrowed. 'Wait a minute, what the hell is that excuse for a tie?' he asked, pointing incredulously at the garish yellow, black and amber silk number around Thoroughgood's neck.

'Er… well… it's my Partick Thistle club tie,' stuttered the young detective.

'Stone the bleedin' crows! We ain't going to a chimps' tea party, boy, this is the big time: an executive hospitality box date at Old Trafford for a derby with City. Old Crerand has really offered the hand of friendship here and we need to give it a damn good shake and make sure we have everything cemented for the brave new world ahead.' He sighed. 'Anyway, too late to worry about it now, but I warn you, boy, I will be giving that monstrosity some extra attention and probably before we get to our starters!' laughed Ferguson, clearly in ebullient spirits as he half filled three whisky tumblers with Glenfiddich.

Then, Ferguson stuck his head out of his lair and bellowed a 'get in here you lot' to the rest of the Squad who were at their desks, before turning back to Morgan and Thoroughgood. 'You two have a nice little jaunt of less than half a mile ahead of you, but before we start…' – he paused for effect – 'may I propose a toast to Acting Detective Sergeant Wally Morgan, who will be made substantive at the next promotion parade. To DS Morgan and his long overdue promotion!'

His toast, chorused by all and sundry, had caught Thoroughgood by surprise; and although he was slow to join the celebration, he was delighted to do so.

Initially he had found Morgan anything but his cup of tea; but the new Detective Sergeant's unswerving loyalty to Ferguson and his unfussy yet efficient way of doing things had grown on Thoroughgood. And when Morgan had offered to take the rookie detective on a shopping trip to Slaters to kit him out for their big day out, he had found, as a Partick Thistle supporter, he had a lot in common with the closet Oldham Athletic fan.

Glasses drained, the rest of the Squad exchanged backslaps and congratulations with Morgan; but when the DCI's room

353

had been cleared of the masses, the new DS cleared his throat awkwardly.

Ferguson, who knew his bagman almost as well as he knew himself, once again let his eyes narrow. 'Yes?'

'I've got an admission to make, Boss… I… I went to see Molly the other day,' he said, then quickly added: 'Just to make sure she was okay, like.' He stole a furtive glance towards Ferguson.

'You did what?' asked the disbelieving Ferguson.

'Look, I know she knifed you in the back, I know what she did was wrong but… it was me who gave her up… and I've worked with her almost every day for the last three years and known her for near enough eight. Her career is in tatters and she still doesn't know how far the chief is going to take this… Christ, Marty, she could end up behind bars at the drop of the chief's hat and you know what that will mean for her…' Morgan shrugged like a naughty schoolboy just come clean.

Ferguson, his eyes pulsing and a vein throbbing in his neck as if he was about to turn into a human volcano, had already poured himself another generous measure of malt, while from the other side of the table Thoroughgood didn't know where to look.

But Morgan had not finished: 'Look, Boss, I am 100 per cent loyal to you, as I have demonstrated, but at the same time I am a human being and I can't just turn off my feelings for someone…' Then as he realised the implications of what he had just said, his words trailed off into silence.

Ferguson's eyes saucered as Morgan's admission turned into a major revelation. 'Jesus H. Christ, this just gets better and better… you're telling me you've been carrying a torch for her… all this time?' he asked, shooting his left hand up to the fringe of his ginger mullet.

'I guess I am, but you needn't worry, Boss, for Molly never worked that one out, and now I guess I know why. But I just wanted to be straight with you, Boss… as always,' shrugged Morgan.

From his fly-on-the-wall position, Thoroughgood couldn't work out if it was the hint of regret and unrequited love tinging Morgan's voice that diffused the mounting anger that had started to work on Ferguson's craggy features, but in complete contradiction to his previous rage, Ferguson now shot out a conciliatory paw and patted Morgan on the shoulder in an act of unexpected, heartfelt empathy.

'That's bloody women for you, Wally. Look, I understand, I guess all of this shit about her must have hit you hard too? Anyway, son, I appreciate your honesty now I know where you are coming from. The good news is that I could never have invited her along to Old Trafford for a seat in a United hospitality box anyway when her blood probably runs pale blue!' He smiled sympathetically.

'Aye, she had a laugh when I told her where I was headed today,' admitted Morgan as the Boss refilled their glasses.

'Anyway, how about your love life, young Thoroughgood? I hope that has nothing to do with the fact that you've been stalling on an answer to my kind offer?' asked Ferguson, raising a bushy eyebrow in sync with his whisky glass and nodding slyly to Morgan, who clearly knew exactly what he was alluding to.

From the side of his desk, Thoroughgood shifted awkwardly on his stool. 'I just need a couple more hours to finalise a few things, Boss,' he stalled.

But Ferguson had had enough. He drained his glass and slammed it down onto his desk. 'I will need your decision by the end of today, boy. Now, Wally, why don't you speak some sense into the daft bugger on your walk to Old Trafford?' he asked.

With that Ferguson pulled open the top left-hand drawer of his desk and produced two Smith & Wesson. 38 snubnose revolvers. He pushed them over the table at his two detectives.

'You not joining us, Boss?' asked the new ADS, his eyebrows rising.

'Nope!' said Ferguson smiling mischievously before checking his watch. 'In around five minutes my lift will be picking me up, gents. You see, as poor old Paddy wasn't match fit, I had to arrange a sub… and Sir James Henderson was delighted to get the call off the bench!'

With that he looked down at the handguns and then back at his subordinates, flicking them a trademark wink as he pushed the firearms their way.

For a moment there was a stunned silence before they all erupted into raucous laughter.

Gordon Crerand sat immaculately clad in a black Armani suit and shirt that emphasised the red of his Manchester United club tie, while Lisa cut an eye-catching figure in a classic black Chanel lambskin tweed two-piece suit with a red polo neck ornately studded with pearls.

The Crerands were out to impress and as he surveyed Old Trafford's hallowed turf through the gleaming glass window of his executive box, Crerand smiled thinly in anticipation at what was about to come.

Turning to face his daughter, he wrapped a fatherly arm around her and whispered: 'I always thank God for you because of his grace given you in Christ Jesus. Never forget that, Lisa.'

'I know, Dad, I know,' she replied as he drew her close.

'May I ask what is happening between you and Detective Thoroughgood? You've been quiet all week, since your date with him on Monday… tell me, Lisa, is romance still in the air or not? This is a big day for us and with Sir James Henderson joining us I don't want any awkwardness spoiling things,' he said, turning to his daughter so that he could look her in the eye.

'There will be no awkwardness, Father, I promise you. I think Detective Thoroughgood and I both realise that we are… not right for each other,' ended Lisa lamely; and realising how unconvincing her words had just sounded, she cleared her throat ready to explain, only for a light rap at the door to interrupt her.

Into the executive box walked an immaculately dressed waitress in a club hospitality staff black and white uniform and bearing a bottle of champagne in an ice bucket.

'I am so sorry for interrupting you, sir, miss, but we have had to get in extra champagne to meet the increased demand of derby-day hospitality,' she smiled modestly, courteously dipping into what was almost a bow.

'There is no problem, young lady,' said Crerand, taking a seat at the head of his table before adding: 'Correct me, but do I detect a – how would I describe it? – Glaswegian twang in your accent?' he asked, noting the attractive blue-green fleck in her eyes.

Once again, she produced that self-deprecating smile, which to a man of Crerand's vintage was highly alluring. 'Not quite, sir, I'm from a village called Carluke, not far away in Lanarkshire.'

The scene made Lisa feel both uncomfortable and sad. For the truth was her dad was lonely and had been more or less ever since her mum had passed; yet here he was almost flirting with a waitress not much older than herself.

But there was something else, something she couldn't quite put her finger on. The waitress felt… off.

Taking a step forward, she flashed a brusque smile her way and dismissed her: 'My father and I thank you for your service, and if you can make sure our guests are well taken care of, I promise you will be well tipped. Now…' – she made a big show of checking her 18-carat pink gold Cartier ladies' Tank Anglaise watch, in a gesture designed to put the overly friendly waitress firmly in her place – 'it is two minutes to 12 and our guests, including the chief constable, are joining us at noon, so if you wouldn't mind…' And she inclined her head to the door.

'Of course, miss,' said the waitress, but before she backed away, much to Lisa's annoyance, she sent a particularly sunny smile Gordon Crerand's way, and he reciprocated warmly.

As Sir James and Acting Detective Superintendent Ferguson made their way along the hospitality box corridor, the chief constable was keen to conclude his pre-match briefing: 'I am delighted the Crerands have been so helpful and true to their word, Marty, but let's cut to the chase: what can we expect in this hospitality box? Has the man got any chat? I can make small talk as well as the next man, but kick-off is the best part of three hours away… so let's just hope there is no skimping on the champers, Marty!' he concluded, just as an attractive young waitress making her way along the corridor smiled his way, which instantly brought a full flash of gleaming teeth through his beard.

'Well, with waitress service like that I'm sure we will make it through to the other side, Jimmy, and in any case Lisa Crerand is… well… err… bloody ravishing!' said Ferguson, finally managing to coordinate his mind with his mouth.

As they reached the door of Executive Box No. 5, Ferguson ground to a halt and turning to Sir James he grinned. 'As Gordon Crerand might well say: "For what we are about to receive, may the good Lord make us thoroughly grateful"… or words to that effect!' And administering the classic police seven-rap knock, he swung the door open.

The Old Trafford hospitality set-up was so busy that Thorough-good and Morgan had been forced to take the stair to reach Executive Box No. 5 and by the time they trod the deep pile of the ruby-red carpet in the corridor, the latter was out of breath and the former frantically loosening his Thistle club tie.

'Have you met the chief before, Wally? I never thought to ask, but to be honest after my disastrous night out with Lisa at The Old Wellington, the thought of facing her old man and her is bad enough without sitting in a 12 by 12 box with a knight of the realm!' said Thoroughgood, rolling his eyes.

'The chief ain't so bad, kid. Look, no one is expecting you to be bessies with him, are they? Just try and make sure you don't let what happened between you and Lisa cause a problem, because if the chief thinks there is an issue there then you could have a problem with your free transfer! Which reminds me, ain't it about time you made a call on that? After all, you could come and join me at Boundary Park, cheering on the Lattics instead of all this prawn sandwiches, corporate fat-cat crap!' And they both laughed out loud.

As Thoroughgood's eyes returned front and he began to count down the hospitality box doors to number five, a waitress a few feet away on Morgan's side opened a service door. The noise drew Thoroughgood's gaze just as the waitress made her way through the doorway.

Even though he only caught just a glimpse of her side profile, it brought Thoroughgood to a shuddering halt.

'What's wrong, cock? You look like you've just seen a ghost!' said Morgan.

57

AS THE DOOR to Executive Box No. 5 opened, Morgan sent Thoroughgood a quizzical look that, followed by a warning lift of his eyebrows and without the benefit of words, more than got the message over that he needed to pull himself together.

Waiting for them was Lisa Crerand, smiling brilliantly. 'Thank goodness, you have arrived at last, gentlemen. I thought we were going to have to keep the champagne on ice forever.' She bid them entry into the box, where they saw Gordon Crerand was seated at the head of the table, his back turned to the pitch, framed in perfect technicolour through the box window, while Sir James sat opposite him.

Ferguson sat to the chief constable's left, and Thoroughgood immediately recognised the Crerands' bald security chief Yul at the far end; he spotted two spaces for Morgan and himself, and one at Crerand's right-hand side, presumably for Lisa. There was one more space, sporting a thin-lipped, suited individual whom he did not recognise; but he would have put money on him being a brief.

As he passed Lisa, Thoroughgood's eyes met and held hers, and her refined features tightened slightly.

"Beam me up, Scotty!" said the voice in his head helpfully.

But before long they had taken their seats. Lisa did the honours and with their champagne glasses full, it was Gordon Crerand who took centre stage. 'Gentlemen, I am delighted you could join me at our table. May I introduce my QC, Henry Brooks.'

And with that the suit nodded his head towards the assembled company and offered a 'Pleased to meet you, gentlemen' of his own to the new arrivals.

Courtesies and introductions were subsequently completed and with that Crerand was keen to move things on. Pushing his chair back, he stood up. 'On what is the most important day of our season, I ask you to charge your glasses and rejoice in what we have all come through in the last few days and to a future of mutual understanding!'

The box was subsequently filled with the scrapings of chairs and the toast, lame as it was, taken up; but such were the tortured workings of Thoroughgood's mind that he forgot to join the salute until Morgan's elbow found its way into his ribs. His brain was working at a furious pace and the direction of its travel was becoming increasingly troublesome.

"Could that really have been Emma in the corridor?" asked the voice in his head.

Part of him wanted to dismiss what he had seen and put it down to an error. After all, he had only caught part of her profile from the side, just before she had disappeared down through the service door.

Such was the internal strife going on inside his head that Thoroughgood failed to hear Sir James addressing him. 'Well ADC Thoroughgood, I am sure we are all, particularly Mr Crerand and his lovely daughter Lisa here, grateful to your interventions up on Alderley Edge and your expertise with a Smith & Wesson .38… but what I want to know, young man, is have you agreed to sign on the dotted line and join Detective Superintendent Ferguson's squad?'

The mention of his name triggered recognition and combined with a helpful dunt from Morgan's elbow, Thoroughgood's head snapped up and met six pairs of watching eyes all trained on him intently.

Opposite him, Ferguson barked a laugh. 'By God, boy, what's the matter, are you still torturing yourself over this bloody move? What's so difficult about it? You either want to join GMP or you hold your hands up and get the first train back to Glasgow because you cannae cope with the homesickness! Either way, son, we're bloody grateful, all of us sat around this table, for what you've done… but the chief needs an answer… and now would seem to be the right time to give it!' prodded the Boss, keeping his eyes on Thoroughgood to underline the fact he wanted his answer right here, right now.

But before Thoroughgood could get the words out, another voice spoke: 'Yes, Detective, we are all hanging on your every word, please, the suspense is… killing us!' said Lisa, emphasising the last two words, her eyes widening with their intensity.

Thoroughgood cleared his throat and let his gaze slide from Lisa to Ferguson and then onto Sir James. 'Forgive me, sir, if you don't mind I must excuse myself, there is something I must do before I can answer you properly and respectfully.' And with that he shoved his chair back and, sending a last glance Lisa's way, got the hell out of the box… fast.

The silence behind him was deafening; but right now, Thoroughgood didn't care, for what mattered most was that he found his ghost and the answer behind her appearance, because the evidence of his own eyes just didn't add up.

Making his way along the hospitality corridor, he opened the service door. He was met with the florid features of a waist-coated, overly plump, middle-aged waitress. 'What the hell do you think you're doing?' she snapped, desperately trying to keep a service trolley filled with chrome-encased dishes from skewing onto the carpet.

Thoroughgood smiled benignly and apologised profusely before flashing his warrant card, producing his usual introduction and asking: 'I'm looking for a member of your staff, Emma McCabe. Can you help me? This is urgent police business.'

A look of utter confusion engulfed the waitress's weary features and Thoroughgood decided to up the ante: 'Look, I'm afraid a member of her family has passed and I need to get the news to her as a matter of urgency. Who can best help me in this regard?' he asked from behind an increasingly grave mien.

'Oh love, why didn't you say? If you head down the service corridor you'll find Dick French, our service manager, and he'll be able to help, pet.' But before she had completed her sentence, Thoroughgood was already on his way.

The service corridor led to an open-plan kitchen, where a severe looking individual, fully dressed up in official United garb, was running everything with military precision from his clipboard.

The almost constant chimes of a service bell punctuated the air and the door at the side revolved with chefs delivering food to waitress staff who chuckled and chatted as they passed each other, swopping ribald stories about the clientele who filled the executive boxes and the rest of the hospitality tables.

His eyes devouring the scene before him, Thoroughgood was quickly able to establish that none of them were Emma McCabe. But as he finished doing so, he found himself challenged by French: 'You appear to have taken a wrong turn, sir. Let me redirect you to your box,' said the hospitality manager firmly.

Almost before the words had left the man's mouth, Thoroughgood's warrant card was in his face. The cop quickly produced a verbal description of Emma to accompany her name and combine with his tragic tale of manufactured woe.

French immediately worked his way down his staffing list with his red pen. 'Mmm, we do have a temp on with us, a Miss Celine Lynott, she definitely had a Scottish accent and fits your description... but the name...'

'Sweet Christ! That's her, never mind the name. Where is she now?' demanded Thoroughgood. French opened his mouth to chastise him for his rudeness, but the wild look in his eyes and the fact he had taken a step forward and was right in his face warned him that would be a mistake.

French checked his service list. 'In main hospitality, helping out the bar staff...' But Thoroughgood had already turned his back on him.

He sprinted his way back up the corridor, slaloming between frantic waitresses as he went, and in turn being met with a volley of curses and bugger-offs. When he reached the service door, he almost ripped it off its hinges.

As he stepped back into the executive box hospitality corridor, Thoroughgood found himself face-to-face with Wally Morgan. 'For fuck's sake, cock, what the hell have you gone and done? You need to get your arse back to Executive Box No. 5; I'm afraid you're about to have your balls busted and your return ticket back to Glasgow stamped with your teeth, courtesy of Acting Detective Superintendent Ferguson. I'm sorry, Gus, but your transfer to GMP is officially about to be shoved up your arse...' said Morgan apologetically with a shrug of his shoulders.

'Forget about that, Wally... you gotta get back along the corridor and get everyone out of that bloody hospitality box before they all end up full of lead!' screeched Thoroughgood, realising too late that his words had been overheard by a passing waitress, who stopped in shock.

'What?' stammered an incredulous Morgan.

Lowering his voice to a conspiratorial whisper, Thoroughgood continued apace: 'Listen to me, Wally, it's really important. I believe the waitress I thought I recognised is part of a hit team that have been sent here to take the Crerands out. She is here under a false identity masquerading as someone I know from Glasgow. The Crerands are about to be iced and whoever else is in the box will almost certainly buy it as collateral damage. You might not know it, mate, but you set the whole fuckin' thing up!' spat Thoroughgood.

'What shite are you spewing now, cock?' fired Morgan.

'Who did you visit midweek and share the details of your big day out with… Wally? Come on, son, she fucked us once and now she has absolutely nothing to lose and a whole lot more revenge to take. This is her one and only time to take it on everyone who has screwed her from the Crerands to the Boss… and then the icing on the cake that she doesn't even know about is the bloody chief constable is at the table as well…' said Thoroughgood breathlessly.

'Jesus…' Morgan groaned.

'Get them out the box, Wally, and pray you aren't too late. I'll alert Match Control pronto… somewhere in Old Trafford we've gotta hit team about to unleash mayhem and we haven't got a bloody clue where they are.'

58

CLAD IN MATCHING PARKAS and a couple of natty yellow woollen hats, their eyes hidden behind wraparound shades, the two ITV Sport Outside Broadcast personnel climbed up the steel steps to the up-and-over metallic corridor that led to their positions.

As they passed the exit onto the South Stand roof, they paused for a second and exchanged a knowing look.

'Un plan B, mon ami?' asked the hawk-featured, clean-shaven one.

'C'est une possibilité!' replied his colleague.

They continued their meander along the corridor and out onto the gantry, where they nodded and smiled nonchalantly to other broadcasters and the media staff from the two Manchester clubs about to do battle.

'C'est un jeu d'enfant!' said the bigger of the two men from behind an inky dark beard.

His colleague flashed a smile back at him. 'Child's play indeed, which we are about to be very well paid for, mon ami!' said McGrain, exhaling a plume of smoke from a drag of his Gaulois Bleu and luxuriating in the rich taste of the mixture of Syrian and Turkish tobacco.

It had only been three days since the Irishman had alerted them to this exceptionally lucrative job that was also going to supply the cause with some much needed extra firepower – but so far it had indeed gone without a hitch.

The binding and gagging of the two ITV staff broadcasters who were now sitting very tight in the back of their van in an Old Trafford car park had been laughably easy. The ITV lanyards that now swung from around McGrain and Spider's necks provided them with instant unobstructed access; and at last they were walking along the steel access ladder that would take them to the ledge where the broadcast cameras – and the best vantagepoint in the whole stadium – lay.

What was even better was that in the equipment bags that normally carried heavy-duty electrical equipment for their broadcast, they had the perfect transportation to conceal their own deadly arsenal: the weapons they needed to ensure that the Crerands were taken care of once and for all.

Emma's radio confirmation that they were in Executive Box No. 5 lodged in his mind, McGrain walked along the gantry, enjoying the slight sting of the gentle late-February breeze against his face. He hefted his bag, reassured by the weight of his beloved Fusil à Répétition modèle F2 concealed in it. McGrain smiled. He was confident he would have the perfect view to make the hit successfully: everything was going according to plan.

To his satisfaction, he saw that the position designated for ITV Broadcast personnel was at the far end of the gantry. As he took his seat, he was able to partially obscure himself from view by adjusting the positioning of the broadcast camera to obstruct the sight of unwanted eyes.

McGrain stealthily unzipped the tripod carrier, slipped the APX L806 sight from the F2 and scanned the hospitality boxes on the other side of the ground, counting up as he did so: 'Un, deux, trois, quatre, cinq… voilà!'

Standing behind his leader, Spider lit a Gaulois and waited for his gaffer to produce his reconnaissance report.

'Très bien, this is a room avec vue magnifique!' And with that McGrain signalled to his lieutenant to hunker down and look through the rifle sight.

'Indeed, mon frère, I see a man who matches Crerand's description and that… oh yes, that has to be his daughter, Lisa… what I could do with her, mon ami…' chuckled Spider.

His comments prompted McGrain to relieve him of the sight. 'There is way too much riding on this for you to be distracted… as you know, Spider.' But as McGrain took back the sight and retrained it on Executive Box 5, he could see that the picture, from the looks on the faces of Gordon and Lisa Crerand, had become altogether different.

Within a minute of leaving Morgan, Thoroughgood had found a uniform officer and flashing his warrant card in the wooden-top's face, he frantically delivered his warning, complete with descriptions of Emma, Spider and McGrain, for onward transmission to the match commander.

For now, he had no doubt that was who he was hunting.

As the cop scurried away, Thoroughgood's mind began to work frantically. The only way to make the hit was by sniper rifle and McGrain had proven deadly with his F2. What he needed to make the most of his accuracy was a vantage point, one that would provide him with a clear sight of his targets inside their hospitality box.

Thoroughgood emerged from a vomitory about halfway up the North Stand, which at an hour before kick-off was starting to fill up and was producing a growing hum of expectancy.

Looking across the Theatre of Dreams, he scanned the South Stand directly opposite. His eyes roamed to the top of the building, and he looked along the roof for anything out of the ordinary.

There was nothing that stuck out, but that very fact was the clue Thoroughgood needed. For McGrain's OP would be hidden in plain sight, and the realisation caused the detective to retrain his eyes just below the roof.

He turned round and peered up at the hospitality section, then back at the other side. Directly opposite, at just the right height, was the broadcast gantry.

"It's a no-brainer, mate," chimed the voice in his head and he immediately started to make his way down the steps, praying that Morgan had delivered his warning and that he would get to the broadcast gantry before McGrain unleashed his deadly fire.

Wally Morgan had arrived at Executive Box No. 5, but he did not know what to do.

Could he believe Thoroughgood? Could he afford not to? And Thoroughgood was right, the last time Molly Malone had information about a meeting involving the Crerands, she had not hesitated to set them up.

Now she had even more reason to repeat the tactic: she had been handed a unique opportunity to avenge Summerbee and one of those that had ended her career; and all because of his loose lips.

'Shit,' groaned Morgan, for the evidence was compelling: he had no option but to share his news with Ferguson. 'Better safe than sorry, mate,' he muttered to himself as he opened the door.

He was met by five faces filled with a variety of emotions, none of them welcoming.

Morgan immediately made his way to Ferguson and shot from the lip: 'Boss, I need a word, urgent like. Thoroughgood has just made me aware of new intelligence. He believes that Mr Crerand and his daughter are in danger of being iced right here and now and that we have a hit team somewhere in Old Trafford assuming positions ready to take them out.'

Ferguson's rugged features contorted in barely concealed rage; but before he could say anything, the chief constable jumped in: 'What rubbish is this you're speaking, man?'

'I'm sorry, sir, the only detail Detective Thoroughgood was able to provide me with was that a waitress he saw is part of the team and is here under a false identity. He recognised her from his time up the road, and he has begged me to get the box cleared while he alerts match command and gets all appropriate steps taken.'

Next to the chief constable, Gordon Crerand almost choked on his champagne. 'This is ridiculous, I thought all the loose ends had been taken care of: Summerbee is dead, so is Gallacher, and most of their minions are likewise in the wind or, according to you, Sir James, under lock and key... how can this be? Who the hell is left to coordinate a hit?'

To Morgan's left, Lisa Crerand started to articulate her doubt: 'Detective Thoroughgood can be... a trifle excitable...' She stopped in mid-sentence as realisation dawned and she said three words: 'That waitress... Dad!'

The words had no sooner left her mouth than the window of Executive Box No. 5 was shattered by a 7.62x51mm projectile.

The first bullet took Gordon Crerand out with a shot that entered the back of his head and exited through his right eye.

The second round exploded into Henry Reid's chest and threw him onto the hospitality table. The room was sprayed rouge with his vitals and the intricate glass table settings shattered, glass exploding into the air.

Engulfed by shock, Lisa started to scream 'Daaad…' just as Yul threw himself at her, wrapping his giant forearms around her and pulling her to the ground. Ferguson and Sir James threw themselves to the floor, but Morgan, who had been directly behind Lisa and partially unsighted by the initial impact of the bullets, was last to react.

That hesitation was to prove deadly. The remaining glazing in the hospitality box shattered again, and the third round exploded into his chest, pinioning him against the box door.

Cowering under the window ledge, Ferguson drew his Smith & Wesson and sneaked a peak, only for the frame to erupt into a spray of flying wood.

'Jesus H. Christ!' muttered the shell-shocked Boss.

59

'MERDE!' spat McGrain as he withdrew the F2. 'I got the father but not the daughter, and now we need to get the hell out of here.' He slipped the APX L806 sight from the rifle and adroitly removed the custom-made sound suppressor, then handed the F2 to Spider, who immediately slotted it in the bag.

His hawklike gaze swept the rest of the gantry and he saw that the other broadcast personnel on this exposed top tier of the stand were now enthralled by the mayhem he had unleashed in Executive Box No. 5.

The fans who had taken their seats below had realised something had happened, and the sound of shrill screams of women and children alike filled the air of the half-filled stadium.

It was then that a new sound joined their horrified calls: the stadium's alarm signal started to penetrate the four corners of the ground.

Exchanging quick glances, McGrain and Spider knew that there was no time to spare if they were to make good their escape. Both men got to their feet and started to make their way along the gantry almost unnoticed by the shocked members of the fourth estate who could not believe what had just happened at the other side of the stadium.

Smiling at McGrain, Spider laughed. 'They won't even know we've been here, mon frère!'

With a supreme effort, Thoroughgood had reached the media box below the broadcast gantry. Breathing hard, he pulled out his warrant card for yet another club blazer. 'DC Thorough-good. I have reason to believe that an incident which has just taken place in the executive boxes in the North Stand was caused by persons currently on the broadcast gantry…' But as he gulped in more breath, he was shocked to hear his words being treated with a mixture of disbelief and contempt.

'Don't know what you're talking about, Detective, everything is quiet over here, no problems… It's the North Stand you want, that's where the commotion is,' said the heavyset male, adjusting his club tie self-importantly.

'Listen to me, pal, just get the nearest cop to bring as many of his buddies up to the broadcast gantry as quickly as you can… because if you don't, you'll have innocent people's blood on your hands… understood?' rapped Thoroughgood. When the official hesitated, he took a step forward and grabbed him by the lapels of his blazer, then shouted 'Just do it!' at the top of his voice. Pushing the male away, he made his way towards the steel access staircase that would take him onto the gantry.

Making his way up the steel struts, Thoroughgood slipped his right hand inside his suit pocket and sought the reassuring grip of the Smith & Wesson. He thanked his lucky stars that Ferguson had made the call, due to the chief constable's presence, that he and Morgan would be tooled up for the trip to Old Trafford.

Thoroughgood removed his gun and proceeded with his weapon out, following the steps into a steel encased up-and-over corridor.

There was no way he was going to be taken by surprise this time – the recollection of the vicious press of the Spider's janbiya dagger on his skin from last time they met made his heart hammer.

But this time it was different: for this time they did not know he was coming.

As he continued to prowl along the corridor, an opening to his left provided him with a view onto the South Stand's roof, and the warning sign 'Do Not Walk On The Roof' brought a wry smile to his face.

He kept on walking, each step sending a fresh vibration through the metallic mesh. Fifty feet away, he could see daylight coming from the end of the corridor.

The gantry was in sight.

'Come on, you bastards; come and get it,' he spat.

As McGrain led the way along the red steel floor, he made a concerted effort not to meet the eye of any other of the gantry's inhabitants. It was not difficult, because their eyes were locked on events unfolding at the other side of the stadium.

They filed past a couple of microphoned-up former United stars who had previously been sharing a yarn as they necked hot coffee from polystyrene United crested cups, but now stood transfixed by what was going on in the North Stand – no one spared them a second glance.

Behind his wraparound shades, McGrain's eyes lit large in recognition. 'Well, well, Sammy McIlroy and big Gordy McQueen. Ah lads, that '79 final with the Arsenal must still be giving you nightmares! I nearly cried into my pint when that perm-haired bastard Sunderland got the winner!' he quipped.

The former United aces' features creased in a mixture of bemusement and surprise, but with a rueful shake of the head from McGrain and a grunt of laughter from Spider, the two former French Foreign Legionnaires left the former players in their wake.

Reaching the turn onto the dozen steps that would take them to the up-and-over metal access corridor, McGrain turned to his number two. 'After you, old friend,' he said and smiled as Spider took the steps whistling 'La Marseillaise' jauntily.

That was a mistake.

Thoroughgood heard the distinctive whistle before the yellow woollen ITV Outside Broadcast hat enveloping Spider's head rose above the height of the steps he climbed.

His senses already operating at a heightened level in anticipation of what was to come, Thoroughgood immediately made the connection between the French anthem and his prey. He dropped to a knee and trained the snubnose on the end of the up-and-over.

For a second, there was a moment of suspended silence.

Then Thoroughgood spoke: 'Bonjour Monsieur Spider!' he quipped and pulled the trigger.

60

THE SPEED with which Thoroughgood had been forced to get his shot off had made accuracy a challenge.

The sparking of the snubnose's bullet as it struck the corrugated side of the corridor to Spider's left flank confirmed a miss.

It was a close shave that saw Spider's initial surprise replaced by primal rage. From inside his parka he drew his own firearm, and to his horror Thoroughgood saw that it was a Škorpion sub-machine gun.

The dread realisation filled him with a desperate urgency to take the man-monster out before he could bring his vastly superior firepower to bear.

While his first shot whistled harmlessly past Spider, the second thudded home with lethal accuracy straight into his chest and the impact stopped him in his tracks. He folded onto the mesh below.

From behind his comrade, McGrain could see that Thoroughgood's accuracy had been deadly. 'Fils de pute!' he spat.

For a moment Thoroughgood permitted himself a smile, for that son of a bitch had just drawn first blood.

Then he backed off fast: he knew that the reality had not changed and that he was still hopelessly outgunned. His only hope of survival was a sharp exit onto the South Stand's roof.

Although he checked the body of his friend for life, McGrain knew already from the entry point of Thoroughgood's shot that any hope was forlorn. Cradling Spider's head in his arms, he saw that his old comrade's eyes had rolled and he had already breathed his last.

Closing Spider's unseeing eyes, through gritted teeth he whispered the immortal words of the Legion's iconic refrain, 'J'avais un Camarade'.

Then laying his brother to rest on the mesh, McGrain gripped his Škorpion and rose to his feet. 'You're mine, Thoroughgood,' he spat and advanced, his weapon trained and ready to spew death.

Thoroughgood had made his way out towards the roof as fast as possible and was now lying in wait. His back against cold metal, the voice in his head asked: "So where the hell did the bastards get a Škorpion from? Summerbee?" But as he glanced out onto the roof, a sinking feeling enveloped him.

There was nowhere to run to.

From the corridor, the sound of footsteps crunching off the mesh flooring stopped and the harsh intonation of that voice he had hoped to never hear again came to life: 'Magnifique, c'est notre vieil ami!' goaded McGrain's gravel-dashed Glaswegian tones.

The 'old friend' taunt made Thoroughgood's blood boil and he sprang round the corner, desperate to unload lead.

But McGrain's barb had been delivered to achieve that exact result and waiting on a knee, The Widowmaker poured rounds of .32 ACP back down the corridor almost before Thoroughgood got his single shot off.

Only just making it back to cover, Thoroughgood confronted his reality. His only hope was in reinforcements arriving… fast.

But the sound of footfall again clanking on the corridor's mesh floor meant death was coming his way.

'You run away like the coward I know you are, bitch,' taunted McGrain, once again looking to tempt his adversary into a rash mistake.

But this time McGrain got nothing and realising that time was not on his side, he marched on.

After a short pause, McGrain turned the corner into the roof corridor. 'I'm gonna enjoy gutting you, Thoroughgood!' he said, before making his way along the short egress route, preparing to climb out onto the roof. 'It's time to make you ma chienne!' he bellowed.

Clinging onto the metallic framing that crested the South Stand's huge roof, Thoroughgood's inner voice did the translation: 'my bitch'. A chill that had nothing to do with the February breeze or the altitude went down his spine.

Checking his snubnose, he saw the chamber had two bullets left in it.

"That ain't gonna be nearly enough, mate," said the voice in his head.

He glanced out over the roof. The top of the South Stand resembled a scene from a Meccano advert thanks to the metallic casing clamped onto the top of the structure. Any hope that he could elude The Widowmaker long enough for help to arrive was now all but gone – there just wasn't enough cover.

It was time to gamble. Thoroughgood knew he only had seconds to make his move. He ran across the roof, taking hold of one metal stanchion and then grabbing the next: he had to get behind the door and if possible above it.

He was too late.

'You and I… we have old business to finish, mon chéri!' taunted McGrain as he appeared on the roof and sent a salvo of lead the detective's way.

Forced to execute a dive in mid-run, Thoroughgood's right foot slid off a metal spar. As he hit the deck, the Smith & Wesson fell from his fingers, and he watched in horrified disbelief as it slid across the South Stand's roof and came to rest a few feet from the door.

"You're fucked now, mate," groaned his inner voice.

It was soon joined by that taunting delivery that he knew would haunt him from here to eternity. 'What a pity, Monsieur Policeman!' said The Widowmaker. Then, to Thoroughgood's astonishment, he discarded his Škorpion, almost contemptuously: for McGrain wanted to take special delight in settling this score and avenge Spider in a way the big man would have found fitting.

He loomed above Thoroughgood and a malevolent smile lit his face. 'I'm gonna gut you, pig!' he spat and the glinting Damascus steel of his janbiya hissed through the air towards Thoroughgood's belly.

But Thoroughgood had already rolled clear and the impact of steel on metal sent sparks flying.

It was now that the detective played his joker. As McGrain struck, he whipped out the old caving hammer he had grown attached to since it had helped save his life up on Alderley Edge from his belt.

Switching it round so that its vicious hook was facing forward, he brought it down with all his might on McGrain's hand, which was still extended from his own spent blow.

The Widowmaker let out a banshee scream of pain as the hammer ripped through his hand, sending the janbiya loose. It slid down the gentle incline towards the almighty drop to the pitch below.

Thoroughgood immediately scrabbled across the roof, desperately trying to get his own hands on the deadly weapon, his hammer stuck in his nemesis's hand.

His fingers reached its ornate ivory handle, and he gratefully gripped it as he heard McGrain's voice just behind him.

'You wee bastard… I'm gonna launch you off the fuckin' roof!' spat The Widowmaker, nodding towards the inner edge of their platform, which was getting closer and closer.

His heart hammering, Thoroughgood dived clear and put another set of metal stanchions between him and the vengeance-crazed McGrain, whose eyes now sparkling with homicidal intent.

The Widowmaker clamped the fingers of his left hand around the caving hammer that still impaled his right paw and finally ripped it free from his flesh, giving off the pain-wracked roar of a grizzly bear.

The only thing that could save Thoroughgood now was the Smith & Wesson, for in a hand-to-hand fight, even with McGrain wounded, the lethal expertise of the former legionnaire meant there was only going to be one winner.

But the gun was well out of reach. He had to keep moving, had to keep playing for time.

McGrain, wounded, dripping with blood and a vision of malevolent hell, was coming for him again.

Thoroughgood threw his last roll of the dice and launched the blade at his attacker; but this time his luck was out, and the janbiya cannoned into a metallic upright and clunked onto the floor.

'You're mine, piggy wiggy!' taunted The Widowmaker. Holding up the old caving hammer in his left hand, he spat triumphantly: 'I'm gonna crush your fuckin' skull like a nut!' And with that he closed in for the kill.

Weaponless, defenceless and hopeless, Thoroughgood gritted his teeth and prepared for his final fight. He backed off further and further, so he was almost at the edge of the roof, hoping he could at least bring McGrain with him. If he could just unbalance him, the fall would take both of them to their death on the hallowed turf of Old Trafford.

He focussed on McGrain's steps, trying to choose the perfect moment to strike, all the while carefully keeping his distance. But as he retreated, his eyes never leaving McGrain, with horror Thoroughgood felt himself slip and in a moment he was on all fours, grasping desperately for one of the Meccano-like stanchions. He held firm… just.

McGrain smiled wickedly. But as he came closer, a new sound ripped through the air.

Suddenly the grin of visceral anticipation on McGrain's face was replaced with surprise and then shock as his body was enfiladed by a withering burst of fire that sent his being into a jerking dance of death.

The high-velocity lead continuing to thud into his body, he was propelled past Thoroughgood. For a moment their eyes met and held, The Widowmaker seemingly suspended in the air.

'Au revoir, mon chéri!' taunted Thoroughgood and watched wide-eyed as McGrain toppled off the South Stand, then fell helplessly into the sky until he disappeared from view.

Looking up, Thoroughgood saw a familiar face waiting up by the vomitory.

'I owed you that one, boy!' winked the Boss, resting McGrain's discarded Škorpion on his shoulder.

61

SHOCKED and still disbelieving, wracked by huge sobs, Lisa held her head in her hands and stared blankly at the floor of Executive Box No. 2.

In the surreal aftermath of the triple shooting that had killed Gordon Crerand and his QC, and left Wally Morgan's life hanging by a thread, Sir James, after making a heartfelt apology to her, had been whisked away by uniform officers.

Uniform had quickly taken control of the bloody scene and in order to allow the locus to be preserved for Scenes of Crime she had been gently moved on to Executive Box No. 2, where she had been given this brief interlude to come to grips with what had just happened. Yul stood guard outside the box entrance.

'How could it have come to this, Dad?' she asked herself out loud, tears cascading down the sides of her face.

The day had promised so much and now her life was in ruins. Her father had brought her up, had always been there for her and had been the rock of certainty her life had been built on. Her father, who now lay cold, a dead piece of meat.

Lisa tried to stifle another sob as a sudden thud outside the door caught her attention. The door handle turned and then opened. She looked up, ready to chastise Yul for ruining her moments of private grief.

Yet it was not the reassuring figure of her hulking security chief that filled the portal but instead the champagne waitress.

Lisa jumped to her feet. 'What the hell are you doing in—'

But before she could finish her question, she found it had already been answered: in the form of the Glock 17 that the waitress was pointing at her head.

'I'm here to finish the job,' said the waitress.

'Who are you? Why… why are you doing this to us? What reason can you have…' But again Lisa was unable to complete her sentence.

The smile from behind the Glock was cruel and pitiless and as Lisa looked into the female's eyes, they seemed to pulse with a disconcerting energy. 'None of that matters now, no one can save you: not the bodyguard lying dead outside the door, not daddy and certainly not your new boyfriend,' she said, coating the last two words with a venomous sarcasm, before adding: 'Now get away from the window,' her voice rising an octave as her emotions started to broil.

Lisa did as she was bid while trying to make sense of the waitress's words. 'How do you know about us?' she asked, her voice paling away into silence at the terrible realisation there was in fact no 'us', no Crerand family any more.

'I'm told it didn't take long for Gus Thoroughgood to forget about me and get very cosy with you. That's a great pity for you, Miss Crerand. For not only have we been employed to help finish this job, but now it's not just business… you, you poor stupid bitch, have made it personal and you didn't even know it!'

As Lisa's mind started to whirr into action, the pieces of the jigsaw fell into place. 'You… must be Emma McCabe, the cop who was with Gus at The Blood Acre… but how the hell did you end up here? What has happened to you… Emma?' asked Lisa, uncomprehending.

'I am here because I found somebody who wanted me for what I am, not some version of what I used to be or what he

383

thought I was. I am here because my life was empty and mean-ingless and because someone filled all the emptiness – empti-ness I was drowning in. I am here to kill you, Lisa Crerand. But before I do so, let me tell you one thing: you will never have Gus's heart, because that belongs to someone else. You may think he is yours, but you will never have all of him while she still lives,' said Emma, her eyes opaque, her finger starting to flicker around the Glock's trigger.

'This is nuts. Can't you see, Emma, this… this just isn't right… you need help… let me…' But as she took a step forward towards the waitress, Emma snapped: 'Get back!'

Lisa immediately did as she was bid; but her words continued to spill out: 'The "someone else" you talk of is, I think, Celine Lynott? Is that what this is all about, Emma? But we can still get you out of this… you don't need to be a bunny boiler,' said Lisa. But as the words escaped her mouth, she knew she had made a mistake.

Emma stepped forward and backhanded Lisa with the Glock.

'You call me a bunny boiler and think that's going to save you? It's not me that needs help, Lisa Crerand, but your boyfriend. The bastard who turned his back on me when my mother fell ill and my life fell to pieces. But none of that matters. No, what does is that you get what you deserve, for now you know how I feel… Miss Lisa… for you to have nothing worth living for except your treacherous boyfriend!' spat Emma.

62

LEAVING TWO UNIFORMED cops to preserve the carnage at the top of the South Stand and its broadcast gantry, Ferguson had given Thoroughgood news of Gordon Crerand's death and the chief constable's near miss as they made their way down through the stand. Walking out pitchside, they were confronted by McGrain's inert, bloodied mass already flanked by cops.

Yet it was the news that Lisa had survived that Thoroughgood realised was all that really mattered to him. As they began their breathless climb up through the North Stand, he hurriedly brought the Boss up to speed with his fears over Emma in her new guise as a waitress.

Turning into the hospitality corridor and nodding at the cop standing guard outside the door of Executive Box No. 5, Ferguson couldn't hide his disbelief. 'Come on, boy, that's taking things a bit too far – she would have to be stark raving mad to have hooked up with McGrain and that dead grizzly lying on the broadcast gantry floor. Anyway, the place is crawling with cops. Miss Lisa may be heartbroken at what has happened to her father, but she will be ready for her knight in shining armour to come to the rescue again and then whatever has driven a wedge between you can be forgotten. Please sweet Mother Mary, then... finally... we can put this whole bloody feud behind us and you can sign on the dotted line,' concluded Ferguson, before coming up for air.

Thoroughgood couldn't help but ask the obvious: 'What about Molly Malone? She has got to be behind all this, Wally told me he'd visited her midweek and let slip we were taking hospitality with the Crerands…'

'I know, Wally has spilled. That's all taken care of… uniform are already on their way,' winked Ferguson; but as he turned the corner and his gaze reached the door to Executive Box No. 2, he bellowed: 'Ah shit…' For there, in a crimson puddle of his own vitals, lay the body of Lisa's security chief Yul.

The words had barely left his mouth before Thoroughgood had sprinted to the door and ripped it open.

As Thoroughgood entered, his eyes saucered wide in disbelief, but processing the evidence he said: 'Emma… it's over.'

She smiled unconvincingly but her eyes welled with tears. 'What's over… Gus? You and me? No, we were over a long time ago, despite your lies. You told me you loved me at St Serf's. It was a lie and you knew it; I could see it in your eyes, and I knew then that you still loved her and always would. But now… there is someone else, someone new. It is a pity she has to die!'

Behind him, Thoroughgood could feel Ferguson's presence and prayed that the Boss would let him play it out his way. 'McGrain is dead, Em; there is no point to this… we can get you help… it'll be all right,' he said, unable to stop his eyes slipping towards Lisa.

Spotting the change in his attentions, Emma caught a slight breath. As Thoroughgood's gaze returned to her, he noticed the Glock was starting to shake as the emotion spiralling through her confirmed what he had long suspected… she had fallen for McGrain.

Taking a step forward, he held out his right hand. 'Come on, Em. Please give me the gun and then we can talk this through.'

'No, Gus, it… it's too late for that,' she said and with her left hand she reached up to her eyes and wiped away a tear.

Then she pulled the trigger.

THE END